GIVING UP ELYSIUM

Also by

W.B. Clark

A Thousand Short Lives

There Are Stranger Stars

So You Want to Be a Witch?

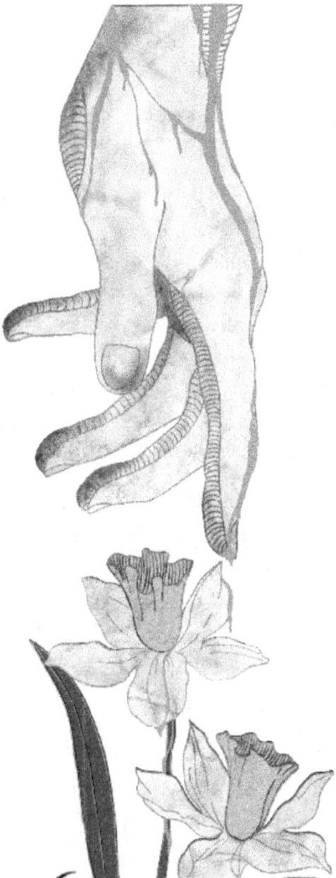

GIVING UP ELYSIUM

W.B. CLARK

Discovery Door Publishing

ISBN: 979-8-9865649-4-4

Warning

Be advised, throughout this novel there are scenes of graphic violence and gore. There are also discussions of self-harm, and suicide. In **chapter XI** there is rape, though in this specific case, it's implied not graphically depicted. In **chapter XIII** there is attempted sexual assault.

Dedication

For those who stumble along
the blurred edge of light & dark.
Know this, you are loved.

EHVARA
Vorna
Essenzos
Colos
West Window
The Holy City
Havmand Bay
Avanfa
Southern Region
Nasarr
Aethiopian Sea
Thyellodic Ocean
Castle Notos

The Blood Isles
Apotmos
Scylla's Passage
Wildwood Of the Wraiths
Anyalay
Manthros
Skliros
East Window
Kanthar
Amenian Sea
The High Forest
Thyellodic Ocean
N
W
E
S

Gods & Beasts of Miracle

A Lesson from the Moirai

Stories never truly have endings, just lulls and divergences. The same can be said of games, there is merely an intermission after the win, then—the game begins anew.

And what is a game, if not a long story?

Life is a game.

Life is a game.

Life is a game,

where all gods play,

and the score is immeasurable.

It

Has

No

End.

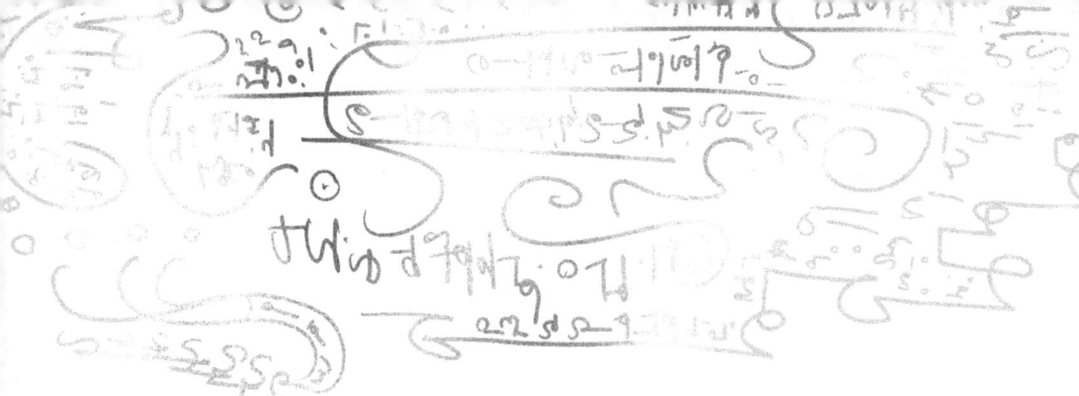

PROLOUGE

Time Unknown

Heracles

Hands painted crimson, the once slick blood has long dried, filling the crevices of my palms. Under the early morning twilight, I place a burial cloth over what remains of my children. One of my kind crept to this world while I wasn't looking and slaughtered them. No inhabiting species could've done this; my sons were of a stronger stock—they were half me.

A scream gets stuck at the bottom of my throat. My boys… Therim just started growing his beard, Deicoon's soon to follow, and gentle Creon was a lad of only five years. Hatred storms inside my chest. The butcher was slow and messy with their killing. My children suffered. Whoever did this flung my sons' pieces across the pebbled beach in a deluge of gore. Fingers, toes, a separated jawbone—I found each one under the moon's luminance. The jarring sounds of night carried on through my misery; caterwauling beasts served as a band of jesters while I sorted my blood legacy. But it was bound to happen. It's our way of things. I was expecting it when I hid my family here but had hopes it wouldn't. This remote planet was forgotten after my kin, and I nearly destroyed it a millennium ago. Just a reminder that nowhere is safe.

I stare out at the lake, my breathing slow. A fog glides across its flat waters, ensnaring the surrounding reeds. Maybe I should burn it at least—the simple dwelling of wood and clay at my back. It's where the three of them lived, along with their mother. Megara was given to me and did well enough, but the bitch found a way to hang herself inside. My eyes go to the pyre I built on the beach. Where was she when our sons were dying? I decide to leave her to rot instead. She should've died with them. Let her bloat until she falls.

I light my sons' pyre and watch black smoke build toward the sky until the fire completely devours their young flesh. For a brief time in my long infinity, I wish it didn't have to be this way. I'm so very tired of games. But the moment passes, burning out like an old star and a frustrated sigh leaves my weary lungs. Now I have a score to settle. Just another to add to the many with my kin.

It's a MAD World

Gods & Beasts of Miracle

West & East Windows of Ehvara

Ehvara was the first of many worlds created by the gods. The planet was used as a battleground during a ten-year war, known as the Titanomachy, between the Titans and Olympians. The Olympians prevailed, but Zeus, King of Gods, saw the destruction his kind had wrought on the fragile world. Ehvara was nearly destroyed, its people faced with the challenge of rebuilding. Zeus vowed then to never let Ehvara fall into great peril ever again. To keep sentry, he created two portals in fixed locations that serve as viewpoints into the world. The West & East Windows are now colossal tears in Ehvara's sky and are connected by a constellation of light that encircles all of Ehvara called the Lunetas Bridge. This light is most concentrated near the West Window.

But just like a window, there are two sides to these portals. Those who live in the Western and Eastern lands of Ehvara can see into the Gods' Realm from their side of the portal. Mount Olympus, decorated with its gold and marble palaces, is seen within Ehvara's West Window, and Mount Ida resides within the East Window. Due to this phenomenon,

Ehvara gains an additional sun and moon from the Gods' Realm. An invitation from a god is needed to pass through either portal. Without it, one cannot enter, even if they fly on a winged beast.

Part 1

A Shaded Genesis

"I'm fashioned into delicate glass,

with a thousand fissures set to shatter.

But if I could go back in time,

I would choose the same."

—Eimear

CHAPTER I

400 years after the deaths of Theirm, Deicoon, & Creon

5th Week of Winter

Eimear

Villagers who are either too young or already paired, stand at a distance against a tree line made of dark-red cypress sprinkled with snow. Their thrilled chatter for the coming ceremony echoes across the frozen glade. I turn my back to the crowd; somewhere amongst the masses are Mana and my brother. I can't bear to see my family's eager faces right now. I'm not exactly ready for what our goddess has in store for me.

Oh! Where is he? My eyes scan the youthful faces I'm corralled with. There are thirty-five of us waiting to be paired—an uneven number—a bad omen. I chew on my lower lip. It's almost time to begin, and my childhood friend is nowhere in sight.

A bout of hushed giggles and eager whispers has spread through my peers like a dandelion in spring. My throat tightens. I don't partake in their shared enthusiasm. What if Gareth doesn't show? What if I'm paired with someone else? The freezing wind picks up, blowing my fine, golden-brown hair around my face. I attempt to untangle it, but a new gust mocks my efforts.

"Wonderful," I mutter. Not only am I going to be paired with someone I don't want, but I'll be a complete mess when I stand before the priestess as well.

I pull my wool himation even tighter around my small frame and attempt to blow warm air onto my numb fingers. The nervousness wriggling in my belly does nothing to help stave off the cold. Neither does the close press of Paidia's[1] other unpaired, their proximity is only a tiny boon for my frozen bones. While I wait for the ceremony to begin, I examine a boy on my right—Cairo.

Victorious is the meaning of his name. Our goddess must favor Cairo to name him so. He has a head full of glossy black curls, umber skin, and is dressed in the same crimson and roseate layers as I—colors for love, the shades of companionship. We both recently came of age for the pairing, it's our fourteenth year, although I'm only eligible by mere days. Cairo catches my stare and his face breaks into a wide smile, showcasing dimples that could grab hold of any heart. Except mine.

I scowl in return and watch his happiness turn to confusion before he finally glances away with a touch of awkwardness. That's right, I'm not meant for you. At least . . . I hope not. Our goddess may

---

[1] A small fishing village off the shore of the Amenian Sea.

have other plans in mind. I almost feel guilty for my rudeness toward the potential mate; nothing is wrong with Cairo. The boy is nice enough, but he's no Gareth.

What will I do if he chooses not to come? The rising panic in my chest spurs me to look skyward for support. A section of the firmament is pulled back like a thick curtain, revealing an iridescent film over an eye shaped slit amongst the clouds. Behind the glasslike sheen stands Mount Ida and the Gods' full moon, a brother to Ehvara's own Sister Moon. For once, the Window inspires no answers in me. I close my eyes and pray to Metis[2]: Please, let Gareth show, and have the two of us paired. I've never loved anyone else; I would do anything!

When my eyes open once more, a spell of fresh snow swirls through the air, but Gareth is still nowhere in sight. My nose starts to feel runny. Soon, Sister Moon will fully transition from behind the Window, and then it will be too late.

The sky has already started to turn from its dark shade of blue to gentle hues of magenta and jade. Only once per year does the Lunetas Bridge[3] fully change from its constellation of white light to an

---

[2]Goddess of Wisdom and first wife to Zeus, Metis is revered only in Paidia as the Queen of Gods. The rest of Ehvara believes the goddess is dead, for she was swallowed by her husband.

[3] The gods' divinity concentrated and formed into a bridge that expands over all of Ehvara both day and night. It is said the light contains its own realm, but little is known or recorded about the Lunetas Bridge.

abundance of color while under a full Sister and Brother Moon. I breathe out slowly, trying to calm my erratic heart. Never in my life have I been terrified of Ehvara's miracle. I usually adore the event and celebrate the Twin Moon Festival like any other. In years past, I'd admire the sky while Mana danced around a bonfire with my brother on her shoulders, the rest of the villagers already drunk into an oblivion.

"But this time, it just feels ominous," I say softly to no one.

A comely girl beside me takes my hand, and I stiffen in surprise. "It's fine to be nervous. I am too," she says. Amara is one year my senior and has curves my body may never possess. I'm all bone in comparison. She's also much taller than me, but so is everyone else. I think I'm stuck this way for good.

I stare at our joined hands for a second too long, and it's as if she reads my mind. Her full lips form into a playful smile. "What if we're paired together?"

"I don't know. What if we are?" I'm embarrassed for parroting her question. It's as if I'm speaking to hear my own voice, or to justify my being here with everyone else. The others are prepared for a chanced mate. But me? I'm the worst type of person, wishing against the goddess' will.

Amara winks. "I, for one, wouldn't mind it."

Self-conscious, I observe the delicate features of her face and imagine running my fingers through her unbound hair—the sandy tresses are similar to Gareth's. If I were paired with Amara, would I always think of her as a replacement? Could I grow to love her?

"What made you wait a year? You're fifteen, aren't you?" I ask, sidestepping her attempt at flirtation. Gareth delayed his pairing too. He could've found a mate twice now.

At the last two ceremonies, my heart played like a terracotta disc as I watched him from afar. Just like the child's toy, my bundle of emotions would move down and up with the night's string of events. Gareth would arrive at the ceremony grounds with the other unpaired, only to not enter the priestess' circle at the last moment when the sky reached its peak radiance. I've been delighted all this time that he's chosen not to participate, but now, circumstances have changed.

Amara takes the hint and drops my hand, leaving my palm stinging from the loss of her warmth. I groan internally. I shouldn't have said anything. She was at least a balm to the cold.

The girl shrugs. "I didn't feel ready. It's…a serious thing we're about to do."

Has Gareth felt this way as well? What if he doesn't want a life-mate? I never considered the idea before, but it does happen. A handful of villagers are still unpaired by the time they reach their twenty-first year. A few are left without a mate by Metis' refusal, but for some, it's a choice.

Would being alone make him happy? I chew on the inside of my cheek. Oh! Why did we never talk about such things? I press my icy fingertips to my temples in frustration. Because I'm a coward. That's why.

Amara squeals beside me and taps my shoulder quickly in her excitement. "It's time! Look!"

With dread, I do. Overhead, Sister Moon fully emerges from behind the Gods' Window. Inside the window, her brother's twin light is just as radiant over Mount Ida and spills out onto us. I take a deep breath of moonlight and hold it in my lungs. It's as if my entire village joins me because a pregnant silence follows. Three heartbeats pass, then everything changes as the Lunetas Bridge flares in a medley of bright color. I can't help myself and gasp in wonder. The dark night has gone and been replaced by vivid, jeweled tones across the sky.

I'm jarred from my reverie when Chrysanthe's wise voice sounds over the crowd. "Should Metis choose it, on this bright night, each of you will be joined with the one who will make you shine in every way—"

I try to find the priestess through the crowd of unpaired, but even on my toes, I can't see over their heads. My lungs seem to petrify with every passing word; each syllable a divine nail to permanently close the door on mine and Gareth's future.

"—For the rest of your days together, your mate will help you to weather Zeus' storms, sail Poseidon's waves, and avoid Hades' dark shadow. Your mate will become your confidant, your light, and your heart. This is a great gift Metis shares with you, and Paidia shall prosper for it. Now come forth young ones and take this chance to be blessed."

My ears ring from the cheers of the other unpaired, my heart quickening double time with the clamor. They start forward, pushing me with them towards the ceremony. The time is nigh for Chrysanthe to channel Metis' will, and I search frantically from one familiar face to another in the throng, but Gareth is not among them.

What if I'm paired with someone disgraceful? I recall Burr's leery eyes when he chased me and some of the other girls last summer with a stick, he tried to raise our skirts with it. The deviant was shamed properly for the act, but still, I don't want someone like him. Or worse yet—what if it's Nishant I'm destined for? The boy has entered the circle five times and still hasn't paired, a sure sign he's been abandoned by the gods.

My lip quivers. "No . . . I don't want anyone else."

Panic blooms anew when I realize I'm at the boundary of the ceremony circle. It reminds me of a spider's early morning web, better to be admired and left alone. Large boulders surround the site and are artfully wrapped with metallic gold twine, their white streamers fluttering with the wind. At the center of our sacred space, a rotunda houses the marble statue of our Goddess decorated with garlands of gold winter flowers. Expertly carved, her peplos hangs from her hips and appears lifelike with all its folds. A battle helm rests on Metis' head, her long hair free flowing underneath to cover her breasts. My goddess' face is serene, her arms outstretched, palms open to the sky as if beckoning me forward.

"No," I say again, and my cothurnus become foot weights in the snow, stopping the procession behind me. My peers walk around my stoic form and give me wary glances as they pass the threshold. Soon, I'm the only one left on the outside, watching their backs.

He doesn't want me. Any scrap of warmth I had leaves my body and my lungs begin to freeze from the rejection. Tears cascade down my cheeks, the droplets cool as they reach the crevice of my lips. I try to save face and inhale slow tremored breaths while wiping at my eyes. There's always next time. I can learn to love another. The lie is like a spear through the chest.

I turn to go, and immediately collide with a solid surface. Dumbfounded, my gaze slowly travels up a torso cloaked in ceremonial red until I recognize a strong jaw, thin lips, hooked nose, and a concerned pair of green eyes. "You're…you're here!" I say to Gareth. But my excitement is immediately peppered with fear. He came… but did he come for me? Uncertain, I press my face into his chest.

Our breath mingles silently with the frigid air. At my back, the priestess starts to chant in the gods' language. A tongue so old, all ears have forgotten but for the golden ones themselves. Not even Chrysanthe knows what she speaks of. She says the sound is passed on from person to person as a feeling that bursts from the lips.

I gain a moment of courage and peer into Gareth's face, a kind face that I've known my entire life, a face that I love dearly. Does he see me as more than his childhood playmate? More than the temperamental daughter of his mentor? Even so, unless Metis gives her blessing, none of it matters.

In seconds, I make the boldest decision of my life and mouth the words, "I want it to be you." Regardless of the outcome, I'll take this chance to face the three Fates[4] if it means I could be paired with him.

He gives me a long look, one filled with determination. Gareth then takes my hand in an iron-strong grip and I'm speechless as he pulls me into the ceremony circle. He walks with confidence toward Chrysanthe, who still sings her incantations. She's facing the crowd of unpaired, Metis' statue is behind her, as if guiding her every word. The crone's dark eyes train on us as we continue to approach.

I stare at Gareth's back. What's he doing? Shouldn't we each wait for our turn like the others? A new fear takes root in my belly. Will our impudence anger the gods?

Sooner than I intended, the two of us stand with our fingers laced before the priestess. I've not been this close to her since I was a child on my Name Day. My throat feels too tight in her presence. Chrysanthe is a powerful conduit of the goddess. She helped name us, name all the children of Paidia through Metis' consecration. Her skin is still supple despite her age, her expression reverent. For a second, my gaze drops to my toes as shame settles over me. I follow the long train of Chrysanthe's bright robes; it's become a golden river of cloth in the snow. Scared, I raise my eyes to her shoulder, not ready to meet her scrutiny.

------

[4]Also known as the Moirai. There are three: Clotho, Lachesis, and Atropos who preside over the destinies of mortals. They know a person's life story before it's even a thought.

At our disturbance, the unpaired begin to whisper behind me. The villagers beyond have gone silent. I feel the hot rage of certain Elders burning holes into my back. Their imagined glares promise a hearty punishment for the disrespect we've shown. Goosebumps rise under the fabric of my winter chiton. What if Chrysanthe turns us away? No one has ever made such a demand before. Gareth, on the other hand, appears unfazed and squares himself.

The priestess ends her hymn with a sharp lilt, and her dark eyes harden at our insolence. Roughly, she grabs our hands, separating the two of us. In an instant, all my hopes for the future plummet with the falling snowflakes. We're not meant for one another. It's as if my breast is being torn open, my pumping heart and misery laid bare for all of Paidia to see. The moment is humiliating.

Gareth tenses, rebellion twitching in the muscles of his face, disobedience ready to roll off his tongue. What will the Elders do to him if he makes a scene? Time seems to suspend as I tilt my head toward the Gods' Window and focus on the bright medley of color mixed with the snow's flurries. I pray: Metis, please! Let us have just this one thing.

Gareth's voice is a low growl. "We don't have to—" but the crone holds up a finger, silencing him.

The hardness of Chrysanthe's gaze dispels as her irises turn a vivid gold. Her lips slowly pull into a knowing smile while her body relaxes into a serene bliss that only she can understand. I hold my breath as the priestess lifts mine and Gareth's wrists to her mouth and bestows a kiss onto each of us. She then joins our hands together, palm to palm.

"Eimear of Rhone—" her voice rings out with absolute authority. "—and Gareth of Aquil, you've been granted Metis' blessing. May your union last until the end of your days."

CHAPTER II

5th Week of Winter

Eimear

I'm deafened by the sudden shouts of joy from the unpaired around me and those beyond the ceremony circle. What just happened? I search Gareth's face for answers, his smile stretches from ear to ear, causing my stomach to summersault. We're truly paired then?

The old crone silently withdraws moonflower from the leather satchel around her neck and tosses the petals over our heads, ending our pairing rite. She nods to each of us and my face heats when I realize my palm is still pressed against Gareth's. Now that we're paired, per custom, we'll need to be more conscientious about our proximity to each other. Until adulthood, our focus should be on the purpose our names give us instead of one another. Every name has a distinct meaning and determines one's status in Paidia, thus, our children go nameless until their 7th year. Until the naming ceremony, young boys are affectionately referred to as Buma and girls are referred to as Pana. When of age, Metis judges a child's character and gives the blessing of a name, which foretells what role they'll take in the village. Since our naming, both Gareth and I have been diligent in learning our duties. We have important roles to fulfill and can't allow time for distractions.

I pull away, but Gareth quickly slips his fingers around mine and gives my hand a reassuring squeeze, his smile playful. I can't help but return it in full, the butterflies in my stomach still a flutter. Maybe just for tonight, we can enjoy in this simple indulgence?

"Eh hmm," Chrysanthe clears her throat, eyes a blazing gold and trained on us in a look that demands we behave.

"Excuse us," I mouth apologetically and provide the expected distance between us. Gareth gives her a disrespectful snort and turns on his heel to go. I hurry after him and pray to the gods that no reprisals will fall upon us after the festivities have died down. The Elders can be cruel when they wish to be. I've had my hands swatted with a switch often enough to know it. But why is he acting this way? Gareth has never been so blatant about his opinions in front of an Elder before.

We reach the edge of the circle and position ourselves to watch the rest of the procession. Despite my mate's attitude toward the priestess, there's a shy giddiness between the two of us. I eye him timidly. "I can't believe—"

"Desma!" I jump as the priestess calls out the name of an unpaired.

I make a face. There's really not much time in between the pairings, now is there? Etiquette demands that my attention be on the ceremony. With great effort, I drag my focus from my new life-mate and to the next pairing rite. Desma smiles nervously and leaves the others to join the priestess. Her footprints weave with the ones Gareth and I left behind.

"Begin!" Chrysanthe cries, her eyes are golden as she presses two fingers into the center of Desma's palm. Beyond the circle, someone drums a slow cadence on a tympanum and many villagers join in by clapping their hands, some rattle seistrons to the beat.

While everyone's attention is focused on the ceremony, Gareth leans into me, surpassing the distance of what's considered appropriate. I'm startled by the quick, soft press of his lips against my forehead. A most forbidden act until the Elders deem us ready. It's frigid and loud in this sacred space, but all the discomforts fall away because the skin where he touched me sings with fire. I wish he'd do it again.

We've had years of running games in the woods and building castles on the rocky beach together, but never *this*. Gareth quickly settles in his place next to me as if the sneaked kiss didn't occur. He surprises me again when he hooks the smallest of his fingers with mine, the act discrete because of the cover of our cloaks. I'm overcome by happiness and can't believe he's really mine.

I squeeze my eyes shut and mouth silently, "Thank you, Metis for this blessing."

Gareth whispers teasingly under the beat of the drums, "I was sweating there for a second. I thought the old hag was going to say no."

"Shhh!" I hiss and jab him with my elbow. "What if someone overhears you and tattles to another Elder?"

"Styx[5]," he winces. They'd probably make me read that damn book of Elder Marcus' until I go blind."

I imagine our teacher, his beard twisted to match his scowl, slamming his old tome of *Gods & Beasts of Miracle*[6] in front of Gareth, and I hide a smirk with my free hand.

A few heartbeats pass between us before I give him a sideways stare. I should be watching the ceremony, but I'm too curious. "Why were you late? I know our pairing wasn't certain, but I had hope. When I didn't see you outside the circle, I started to panic. You caught me leaving."

Gareth takes a deep breath before returning my gaze. "You had hope. I wanted assurance. I waited, so I—"

––––––––––––––––––––

[5]In reference to the River of Styx that serves as a boundary between Ehvara and the Underworld. The term is often used as a curse because one would have to be dead or in a most unfortunate predicament to grace those waters. The River of Styx is also sometimes less eloquently notated as the 'under river'.

[6] A magical text created by the God Kleio. The indestructible *Gods & Beasts of Miracle* is an account of every god, demi-god, their undertakings, and all wonderous creatures ever created. As new gods and beasts come into existence, the book grows larger with additional pages. Only nine copies exist in all the worlds. The ageless texts are fickle in nature and disappear and materialize into libraries as they see fit— the same is said for the stories they tell.

Someone from behind shushes him and our conversations dies. We'll be lucky if we get away with just a swatting from an Elder after this. Even still, I'm excited from Gareth's partial declaration. When did he start seeing me as a woman and not just a childhood playmate? I do my best to tuck my heart away and watch the procession.

The drumming tempo picks up as each unpaired takes their turn touching the priestess' open palm to confirm if Metis wills a pairing for Desma. The girl's brow pinches with unease every time Chrysanthe shakes her head no at a potential mate. *Bum, bum, bum, bum, bum, bum, bum, bum.* By the tenth attempt for a match, the tempo of the drum and the rattle of seistrons are nonstop. I begin to worry for her. It's embarrassing when Metis doesn't grant a life-mate. My fear is unfounded though, because as soon as Cairo makes contact with the priestess, she shouts, "you are bound!"

The drums and seistrons cease and both Desma's and Cairo's wrists are kissed by Chrysanthe. When moonflower petals are blown over the pair, I whistle and clap enthusiastically along with everyone else. In my joy, I glance at Gareth and note how his mouth is set in a grim line. What's gotten into him? The cheers at my back, however, distract me from worry, and the remainder of the ceremony passes by in a blur.

Afterward, under the bejeweled sky, I walk arm in arm with Gareth toward the bonfire at the center of the snowy glade; the distance we're supposed to keep as a new pair forgotten. Mixed with the sound of crackling flames, is a lighthearted tune played on a pan pipe and lyre, the melody sprinkled with intoxicated laughter. I scent mulled wine on nearly everyone as we pass through the crowd; I've always enjoyed the aroma of cinnamon.

Delighted by all the festivities, I shake Gareth's arm and say, "Isn't Metis grand? She paired everyone this time! Even Nishant, which hasn't happened in *years*. I've been really worried for—" But my words trail off at his uneasy expression.

Gareth glances toward some of the Elders congregated around the fire and whispers, "Does it not bother you? The lack of choice?"

"What do you mean—?"

"—My sweet girl!" The breathy song of my mother's voice interrupts. "Gareth! Congratulations! I cannot tell you enough how happy I am to have you as a son. I had a hunch you two would eventually pair." She envelopes me in a tight hug.

"Thank you, Mana," I say. The cloying scent of fruit from her mouth tells me that she too, has been partaking in the drunken festivities. My mother pulls away and grins at the two of us, her cheeks rosy and azurite eyes shining with mirth.

Mana is stunning and I've often wished to be her replica as some children are of their parents. However, our only similarity is the golden-brown shade of our hair. The rest of me, is well, *lacking*. Her perfect curls seem to taunt me as I try to will some life into the flat mop on my head.

"Now, Gareth," she tuts. "Enjoy the celebration till the suns' rise, but I expect you to be sharp tomorrow. We may have a baby to deliver; Cora is stretched to burst."

Mana says this, but I wonder if Cora knows that her new baby is going to be greeted by the hands of a drunk. My mother is already well into her cups, early-morning's bite will surely sting her.

Gareth sighs. "There's always someone to see." He isn't wrong. Mana was the only physician until she took him as an apprentice. All my life, she's been on the go from one island to the next caring for others.

My mother turns her full attention to me, placing her hands on my shoulders. "I'm so happy for you. Your father would be, too." She then crushes me with another hug.

My throat constricts at the thought of Papa and his absence tonight. Still, I manage to croak out a "Thank you" before we separate.

Gareth gives me a weak smile as he caresses the top of my head. "You have me now, and you'll have me always."

I'm comforted by his touch and attempt to lighten the mood. "Well, I'm blessed by the gods to have you both, and Buma too. Speaking of which, where's the little hellion at?"

Mana turns her head left and right searching. "You know, that's a good question. Last time I saw your brother, he was playing with Orion's nephew. Buma's a little young to understand the importance of tonight." She gives Gareth a wink. "He thinks you're still just playmates."

For once, Gareth appears sheepish and quickly looks away.

It must be all the excitement to make me act against village decorum, because I reach for Gareth's hand, and lace my fingers with his. If Mana disapproves, she'll tell us immediately. Or maybe, just this once, she'll let it slide. She's always been softer about rules than most.

He winks at me and turns to her. "If it's all right with you, I'd like to find my parents. They'll want to see us."

My mother waves us away, and I'm relieved that she doesn't seem to care about the distance we're supposed to have. "Of course, of course! I'm sure Aquil and—"

"No touching!" A voice filled with gravel chafes from behind, then my hand is pulled from Gareth's.

Miffed, I bite my lip and come face to face with Elder Solon, whose head is held up by a pillar of wrinkles, his glare withering. "You think I didn't also notice the nonsense you pulled earlier?"

He must've seen the kiss Gareth gave me. Now, I know we're in trouble.

"That rule is ridiculous and old-fashioned," Gareth counters. "We've always held hands, we're *friends*. This shouldn't change just because of the pairing."

Mana's face is stoic as she stares at the old man. She's never liked Elder Solon, they've had countless quarrels regarding village matters since I was a child.

He leans against his walking stick; the knobbed rod is intricately carved with silhouettes of the goddess and of our suns and moons. "Not anymore, you don't! Not until at least—and I say *at least*—her twenty first year, young man, when she's a proper adult. The Council of Elders waited two decades for Metis to name a new member, we cannot let this opportunity be squandered. Eimear's education is vital to the success of Paidia."

He points a veined finger at Gareth's chest. "And *you*, you're a Gifted one. What do you think will happen if you continue to run around, chasing after what's under her skirts instead of learning your art as the gods intended."

Mana gasps in outrage, and Gareth pushes Solon's finger away. "There's no reason to be a crude bastard about it."

I'm old enough to understand what he's saying. My mother, never shy when imparting words of wisdom on my behalf, told me what pairs do when they reach adulthood. The act is to be enjoyed, how children are made should we want them. Or, if we choose, we can share our child rearing responsibilities with another pair who can't have children. Anger grows hot and fast in my chest, the heat reaching my neck. What will eventually occur between Gareth, and I will be a beautiful thing. Elder Solon makes it sound dirty.

His eyes narrow to slits as he addresses Gareth. "No reason you say? You dishonor Metis and the blessings she's laid at your feet. Did you forget the meaning behind the pairing ceremony?" His crusty voice raises to a near shout. "It's so Paidia's young can focus on learning their trades instead of rutting about, spawning fools you've no business yet caring for! It's a grand gift from Metis to know your intended, to be alleviated from the worry of finding a suitable mate while you become your namesake."

My anger dissipates, replaced by a deep shame where there was none before. If I hadn't reached for Gareth's hand, if I'd kept my desires to myself, this wouldn't have happened. I owe everything to our goddess and I've all but spit in her face with my greed. My name means "All Knowing," the highest blessing a child could receive from Metis. It marks me as a god chosen Elder, not one elected by mankind. My thoughts should be centered on becoming more knowledgeable so I can be a proper council member for Paidia and a better mate for Gareth.

My life-mate scowls. "You and I both know this is just a show of power. A silly way to manipulate us so the council can have clout over—"

"We'll be mindful of our distance," I quickly say and take a few steps away from Gareth. It wouldn't do to further upset Elder Solon. The council could put us in the stocks. Or, petition Metis to strip us of our apprenticeships under the pretense that we don't merit the names given to us. If this came to pass, we'd be cast out into Poseidon's deep waters. Though, both outcomes are unlikely, at least for Gareth anyway—he was born under such an important star, his skills invaluable to Paidia. He knows this, which is why he can afford to be so brazen. As for me, well, others can be born and marked for their wisdom given enough time. The Elders can also hold an election for another council member if needed.

My intended glares at Elder Solon, then shakes his head before turning on his heel and charging off toward the crowded bonfire. My chest aches with each parting step. He'll be all right; compliance is best for this situation.

"A stubborn apprentice you have there, Althaia. It'd be best to keep a watch on him and your daughter. And *you* Eimear, you need to keep your skirts down." Elder Solon's wrinkles shake with each clipped word.

I'm too mortified to reply. Instead, I shiver against the cold wishing I wasn't here and stare longingly at the fire where Gareth has already disappeared amongst the villagers.

Mana, who stands behind me, clasps me by both shoulders. She says firmly, "Your input, *Elder*, is crass and uncalled for. My daughter has a fine head on her shoulders. Metis wouldn't have named her as a wise-one if she didn't, but of course you already know that. Eimear will do what's best for everyone." She kisses my head and says against my hair, "Sweet girl, you should go find Gareth's parents now. They're more than eager to congratulate you, and I need to set the Elder here straight on how he's allowed to speak to us."

"Now see here, Althaia! I'll not be sassed by the likes you." Elder Solon cracks the end of his walking stick against the frozen earth in outrage.

I wince as Mana's hands tighten on me. I don't have to turn around to know that the warmth in my mother's eyes has gone cold. Her relationships with some of the council have been hostile ever since Papa died, as if they blame her for his shipwreck. Which is absurd, she's not Gifted and can't control the weather like Zeus or the great seas like Poseidon. But sometimes, people just want a scapegoat for their anger.

Mana sucks in a breath as she attempts to compose herself before she lashes out with her fiery temper. My mother has never been afraid of the Elders like I am. As a healer, her position gives her a bit more leverage to say and do as she pleases. Still, one can never be too cautious.

"Mana, are you sure—"

"Run along now, it's your night and you should enjoy it. I'll find you shortly." She pushes me gently in Gareth's wake. Her voice holds no room for discussion.

I sigh as I trudge away, my shoulders sagging. She doesn't realize how the Elders take their anger out on me after she fights with them. I'll have to be even more diligent in my studies now. By namesake alone, it's always been a bit hard, they're stricter with me than the rest. The other youths don't get called on like I do. My private lessons are even more brutal as the Elders try to mold me into a somewhat respectable leader, a better version of *them*. Soon, the raised voices of Mana and Elder Solon fade behind me, and I've no doubt they'll be trading insults for a time. I cringe thinking about my next language lesson with the timeworn bastard.

I come closer to the fire and my thoughts drift once more as I overhear the drunken chatter of the villagers. Their all-too-familiar faces remind me that I'm forever trapped on Paidia's dull isle. Taking a moment for myself, I look up and search for solace from the Gods' Window within the chromatic sky. The twin moons beam like a smile. I confide to Metis: Goddess, if I could just run away, I think I'd be happy.

Gods & Beasts of Miracle

Metis

I am first wife to Zeus,

but I am much more than who I take to bed.

I am called wisdom,

I am called cunning,

but truly, I am the deepest of thoughts.

I whispered into my husband's ear between copulated sheets,

"Our son will be greater than you."

Like any mortal king, Zeus clutched his crown.

He swallowed me then, my barren womb a threat.

I sit behind his eyes now, my smile coy.

For I am Queen of Gods.

Long live my reign.

CHAPTER III

3rd Week of Spring

Nikko

The terrace double doors are open, and their silk curtains waft gently from a rare breeze. From my royal quarters, I have an impeccable view of the West Window and Holy City[7]. The marble palace, with all its cascading shrines, Doric columns, and higher to lower courts, was built by my ancestors on top of the tallest limestone hill in Ellanios. Below, in the city, there are thousands of dwellings. Each made with sun-dried bricks and roofed with tiles that have been painted in shades of purple—

---

[7]Established after the War of Gods by Zeus himself. Ellanios is the largest kingdom in all of Ehvara. The capital of this land is referred to as the "Holy City." Those who harbor ill will toward Zeus' beloved jewel are physically repelled, unable to breach its walls by any means or even enter through the front gate. Zeus' protection, however, does not extend to its lands beyond.

the God of God's own color. The salted waterways that snake expertly around the homes and businesses throughout the city, were designed by some of the greatest architects in Ehvarian history. But for all its beauty and canals, the capital of Ellanios is as dry as a brothel-maid's overused cunny. Meaning, nothing grows well here. Absolutely nothing. Flora is a sparse and coveted commodity. Only at the palace are there envious amounts of red pines, cypresses, and shrubs.

Night has nearly fallen over the metropolis, but only an Ellanion would think so. Those not locally born, or passing visitors, often complain how bright it is when it's time to put their heads to rest. The divine light from the Lunetas Bridge shines best over the Holy City, bathing it in a soft, ever-present glow, so it's never truly dark. Oil lamps and candles are relics in these parts, they're used only aesthetically or in ceremonies now.

For most, the city is a glorious place. There's lots of fun trouble to be had, so many taverns to sample from, mouthwatering dishes, and art that makes the toughest man weep. But honest to gods, I tire of it all, because the city itself is the only sight I ever see. A marble stone wall at least 400 meters high, surrounds the entire capital. Zeus' shield glistens like the most beautiful pearl but blocks the view of anything worthwhile, especially the ocean and the rest of our lands. The protection does keep the Holy City safe by repelling anyone with ill intent who draws near it. But I find the wall to be stifling, as a bird must when put in an elaborate enclosure. No matter how glorious the container may be, it's still a fucking cage.

A citizen or transient merchant can come and go as they please, as long as they harbor no ill will toward Zeus' jewel. But born as the only Prince and heir to the throne, my leash has been fashioned much too short. To be fair though, I've not let any of the royal burdens keep me from my jollies. For example, spanning the left side wall of my luxurious room is a floor-to-ceiling bookcase filled to the brim with leather-bounds. A passerby would think I'm well-versed in the written word, but if they were to peep within the pages, they'd blush, for my bookcase houses only erotica.

"Very unprincely of you, Nikko," I recall Mother's remark when she once pulled a book from my collection. "A worthless offshoot from a king's loins," would be Father's reaction if he were ever to discover the leather-bounds. He expects my focus to be on learning how to rule a kingdom, not on tricks to please whomever I take to the sheets. Even so, I have my indulgences and will continue to devour the sultry pages.

"Blessed storms, finally," I mutter while staring out the terrace doors. In the West Window, the gods' moon has made its appearance over Mount Olympus, marking the time for my nightly departure. Moon aside, the sky is a deep indigo within the Window, the only dark night I've ever known. It's a juxtaposition next to the Holy City's bright one, the bridge really does affect things here compared to the rest of the world.

I take a seat in the parlor arrangement at the center of my room, which consists of two chairs and a klinē with pillows. I'm busy fastening the multiple straps to my leather sandal when my twin enters from the main entrance unannounced. She's barefoot and wears her bedclothes. Jada's dark hair is braided expertly and pinned to her scalp; her midnight complexion and silver[8] monolid eyes are a mirror to my own.

As much as I love my sister, she can be a real nuisance, like now. "Ever heard of knocking?" I ask before tightening a strap. "One of these days you're going to walk in on me and a lover. It's going to burn your virgin eyes."

Jada rests her forearms against the back of the klinē and crinkles her nose in disgust, the tip of her tongue caught in between a set of straight teeth. "Don't make me lose my supper. And who're you calling a virgin?"

Her question makes me uncomfortable enough to leave my sandals well enough alone. Who in the Under has been tossing with my sister? Is it her pretty boy archery instructor? I did notice last week that he was leaning in a little too close, his hand lingered on her shoulder after he'd repositioned her arm.

My face must be a vision of murder because my twin laughs. "Father is right, you know—you're so easy to rile."

Immediately, the archery instructor is forgotten, but my scowl remains. I recall King Zephyr's reprimand from early this afternoon. My

---

[8]True born Ellanions are known for their dark skin, but foremost, for their bright silver eyes. The unique color is a direct mutation from the Lunetas Bridge's light shining heavily over Ellanios for centuries. Silver eyes have become a sign of Zeus' chosen people to the rest of Ehvara. The trait, once introduced into a bloodline, cannot be undone.

father's voice was cutting as he told me to sit down and know my place after I threatened Heracles' emissary, Erebos. What the emissary proposed for a truce was utterly absurd. I wanted to kill him.

"Easy to rile?" I say to my sister. "Only when it's worth getting angry about. Would you honestly go through with this charade of a marriage proposal between you and that fraud usurper Heracles, if Father asked you to do it? It's preposterous. He really thinks he's the legendary son of Zeus; the brute *must* be mad. That aside, no one's even laid eyes on the lunatic. Heracles has never been seen in the trenches fighting alongside his men, the only reports we have on him are rumors."

Jada straightens, expression turning somber. "Of course. I'll do it gladly if it means Ellanios and those I love are safe. Heracles has already taken half of the Southern Region, and our people rarely return from battle. Avanta nearly exhausted all their men and resources keeping Heracles' army at bay at the trenches. Their kingdom can no longer trade with us, fractured as they are. We can't keep sending Ellanios' sons to Avanta and gain nothing in return. If the fighting doesn't cease soon, we'll be cornered into a position as horrific as the War of Merchants[9]."

---

[9]During the Wrath of Ellanios, also known as the Early Wars, King Maarku wished to concur all of Ehvara. He sent soldiers across the Colossus Desert and Havmand Bay to wage war with the other continents. Little did he know that it is much easier to go to war than it is to cultivate land, especially when your god's protection is over-

I chew the inside of my cheek, frustrated. What good is Zeus' protection if, at any time, we can be starved inside our own walls? The Holy City is naught but a giant tomb for Ellanions every time a threat decides to lay siege. "If we abandon Avanta now, it will be just like Anyalay. My conscience can't sit with that."

Her silver eyes harden, and I know Jada is thinking about the slaughter of our grandkin, aunt, and cousins. It's been seven years since Anyalay fell to Heracles, but time doesn't ease the hurt of loss. My mother still has nightmares of the horrors her family suffered; their heads shoved onto pikes and displayed outside the wall of her childhood home. Her younger sister's head was sent to her by envoy, courtesy of Heracles.

"But Nikko, that's exactly why we should consider this truce. We can negotiate terms that include Avanta's safety, which would also put them forever in our debt. Come summer, it will be five years of constant fighting on behalf of others. Ellanios simply cannot sustain the

———————————

extended. In the end, King Maarku recalled his troops and hung himself out of shame. In retaliation, Kanthar, Anyalay, Apotmós, and the Southern Region withheld trade from Ellanios. This drought of trade lasted 100 years and is forever known as the War of Merchants. Farmland and crops had to be protected by soldiers from attackers who attempted to starve those inside the Holy City. As a result of the skirmishes and lack of commerce, Ellanios' economy declined, and the citizens suffered severely. To end the War of Merchants, King Udom of Ellanios proposed an alliance, where Ellanios would provide soldiers for a period of time to the continents, or a royal for marriage, in exchange for the shipment of goods.

losses. Our people won't stand for it, there's already unrest within these sacred walls." She gives the back of the chair a soft punch, brow furrowing. "It's not as if who I marry has ever been a matter of my choosing anyway. If a union with this monster will put an end to the constant war in Ehvara, then so be it."

I shake my head. "It doesn't make sense; he hasn't proposed a truce with any other country. Why doesn't Heracles try his chances with Ellanios on the battlefield first, like he did with Avanta? Why not fight us, until we're trapped behind Zeus' shield?" Heracles isn't a man to avoid bloodshed. He's already plucked three territories to call his own, like ripe plums from their tired branches.

Nonchalant, Jada shrugs. "Coin and sand of the hourglass, what else? The War of Merchants lasted a century. And even if we barricade ourselves within the Holy City and our bodies wither to bone and dust, Heracles still wouldn't be able to open the gates. Fighting in Ellanios is futile. No one wins."

But if you marry him, neither do you. What will happen to you? I try to block out the worst of my imaginings. Regrettable as it is, my sister speaks as a leader should, her stance methodical, unlike myself. The air in the room suddenly becomes all too suffocating, and I wish to end the heavy chatter of politics and the ever-present thoughts of losing the person closest to me. She'll be whisked away one day, a mere game piece on the playboard of kings, and I'll have to watch it happen.

"Well, I don't like it, and I don't mind telling Father so. But, if you go through with this marriage, poor Heracles will have his hands full. I'm sure he'll be begging the king to take you back a week after the wedding," I say, trying to breathe some lightness into the space between us.

Jada picks up a feather-pillow and tosses it at my head. I duck.

She scoffs, "You're insufferable! A week? That man won't last a day with me!"

We stare at each other for a heartbeat before bursting into laughter, and the rage that has been bubbling up within me settles just slightly. The two of us have always danced this way, steadying each other when one has misstepped. I'm not sure where I'll be once the music stops. Lost, most likely.

Pushing down the depression that swells from that thought, I remove the thong that holds my braids in place. My hair falls to my shoulders, covering the royal crest shaved into the sides of my scalp, which is Zeus' bolt between two bars. It means: The house that holds lightning. I usually wear my braids up, but discretion is necessary for tonight's adventure.

I walk toward the weapons rack ornately built into the same wall as my bed. It's the only feature of my room the queen approves of; the ability to defend oneself is a top priority of hers. I pray she never discovers the real reason I keep weapons. It's not purely for self-defense.

I take a moment to choose from the assortment of blades before I grab the decorated hilt of a short sword. I fasten it to my baldric which is expertly strapped over my black chiton. The steel is a necessary precaution in these dark times.

Jada eyes me, her disapproval as plain as Hera's must be when one of Zeus' flirtations results in another bastard born. "Up to no good I see. You know, if you're caught, Father will be forced to punish you publicly."

"Actually, I'm only up to good . . . *and* I need to channel my anger somewhere. There's nothing like beating the shit out of flea mongrels who prey on women in alleyways to set my world straight." I give her my most winning smile. "I'll be honest, they're usually grateful, and I find other rewards in those ill-lit alleys."

She isn't amused and crosses her arms over her chest. "Ellanios has well-trained soldiers who police the streets. Your vigilante antics aren't needed, and you put yourself at undo risk. You're a prince for storm's sake. Stop acting like a ruffian."

I wriggle my eyebrows at her. "Then why do you always cover for me when my absence is noticed?"

Her mouth opens, exasperated. "Because that's what sisters do."

I walk over to Jada and peer down at her cross face. At some point, I grew a head taller than her. Time flies. "Keep doing that for me, please?"

She moves to object, but I swing my arm around her shoulder and grind my knuckles against the top of her head with my free hand, messing up her braids. For once, I've gotten the jump on her. She's more upset about this marriage proposal than she's letting on.

"You're such a brute! I hope they catch you this time!" she yells, and I chuckle, though it isn't heartfelt.

My twin attempts to fix her mussed hair while I make my way outside and disappear off the terrace. Anyone else would break their neck scaling the slick side of the palace, but over the years I've turned it into an art form. Also, the sets of rope that I've expertly dyed to match the dark amaranthine tiles of the roof and the lustrous marble walls, help me avoid plummeting to my death.

Once I reach the ground, I bound over large limestone rocks pressed close to one another until I reach a narrow path that leads to the Holy City's agora. My sullen mood lifts as I stroll the streets of the bustling city. I admire the buildings, the numerous bridges and the canals that zigzag. This is the only time I'm ever truly at ease.

The tall stonework with its Doric columns is in excellent condition, the prior cracks repaired thanks to my expert supervision. Three years ago, the king, for my sixteenth birth celebration, tasked me with the responsibility of repairing and restoring the older edifices. At first, I was reluctant to take up any such duty, but I learned not to mind and came to enjoy it. However, Ellanios is vast and ancient, so I still have my work cut out for me, especially in the oldest sections of the metropolis.

Thinking of princely responsibilities, my thoughts drift to the schedule Father has set in place for me upon the morn. I'm quickly weighed down by burden again. There's not a moment of respite between all his advisors and the other matters of Ellanios I'm to learn.

It's always one damn thing or another that needs my attention. Well, to the Under with that! Suddenly thirsty, I head for the nearest taverna.

I glance at the sign, *Ambrosia of Anchiale*[10]. It features a goddess resting her heavy bosom on an overflowing chalice. I decide that if my head is going to ache come tomorrow, then by gods, I better make this bright night count for something.

Four rounds of nectar later and I'm laughing with a bearded fellow whose name I don't know—in fact, I never *asked*—when suddenly the gold liquid in my goblet turns to muddy worms. My goblet soon overflows with them, and their writhing forms spill out onto the table. Before I can explain, my companion's eyes go wide, and he stumbles away from my company in disgusted fright. A moment later, the sounds of his retching are lost in the noise of *Ambrosia of Anchiale's* guests.

My eyes narrow. "Ah! For fuck's sake, Jakab! Enough with your tricks. Turn it back and let me drink in peace!" I whirl around on the bench. A bit tipsy, I catch myself on its edge and lock eyes with my childhood friend, whose dreads have been dyed a seafoam green.

"Nah, I want to see you drink it. But you know it's still nectar. Appearances can be deceiving and all." He dumps himself into the seat beside me and gives a smug smile before taking a long swig from the goblet the bearded man left behind.

---

[10]Goddess of warming the heat of fire.

"You're full of yourself, thinking I won't." I only hesitate for a moment, eyeing the larva in my cup before I bring the brim to my lips and knock its contents back into my throat. Sweet burning liquid fills my gullet, and once I finish, I slam the goblet down onto the wooden table with a satisfied sigh. I burp in my comrade's face for good measure. "See there. Don't underestimate me."

Jakab waves my sour breath away. "By Zeus' wayward cock! I think Jada got all the good looks and human decency in your mother's womb and left not a scrap for you. I'll say it till the day I die—you came out a mongrel."

I shrug my shoulders and wave down a tavern maid, tossing her a coin with a wink and raising my goblet for a refill. "You're just sore because your illusions don't work on me, friend."

"That was just a parlor trick. You know better."

That I do. Jakab can conjure illusions on a grand scale. He's one of the few Ellanions who've been Gifted with a god's ichor. Somewhere along his family line, a god tossed their nethers about with a relative of his. The god's blood can be sporadic when it's been diluted over the years, in that it shows up rarely, skipping entire generations before showing itself as some miraculous ability. In my great-grandparent's era, there used to be more Gifted people, but since then, they've all but dwindled out of sight.

I sigh and lean against my friend. "Fuck all! I'm going to miss you! Why'd you have to come here and show your ugly face? I thought we said our goodbyes already."

Jakab sets his cup down gently. "Seven years will come and go in no time. And I couldn't *not* pay my respects to the Prince of Ellanios, seeing him outside the palace on such a fine eve where he shouldn't be."

I elbow him. "Why don't you just say it a little louder, like a hollering banshee, for the rest of Ehvara to hear you?"

Jakab's smile flashes and he clinks his goblet against mine.

"When I was born," I begin, "and my father was taking his pick of the babes who would be my future advisors, his hand stilled over your squalling form, and he said—" I pause and deepen my voice to match the king's, for effect— "We'll choose this one. He's the loudest git and should bequeath my son the worst headaches with his constant squealing."

"Ah yes, and I remember the long nights we shared a crib. You soiled yourself and stole all the blankets. The rest of us were left to shiver in our clean linen and think, what a handful of unlucky bastards we must be to serve a bed-shitter the rest of our lives."

As Jakab and I snort, we bang the table with our fists and tears form at the creases of our eyes. "No more! No more! My belly hurts from laughing so hard." I heave between gasps.

"See, there you go again, a bed-shitter and always bellyaching. Brontes, Dareios, and I have our work cut out for us."

His teasing sets me off again, but then, as the mirth fades, I think about the other two I was raised with and how they'll all set off in the morning on their long sabbaticals. For the next seven years, my crib-brothers will travel separately to different regions of Ehvara and gain status in the army before they return home and claim their titles of Advisory to the Crown—to *my* crown. The advisor sabbatical is a long-standing tradition in Ellanios legislation. Meanwhile, I'll be left behind to toil through the bitching and moaning of the public and my father's own brotherhood of advisors.

I pinch one of my braids between a finger and twist it, a nervous gesture. "I need the three of you to be careful. *You* have the upper hand in stealth with your illusions, but the other two? What will happen if they come upon some danger? Ehvara has grown dark since this imposter Heracles decided to go and be an utter prick."

Jakab waves a hand dismissively. "Your fears are like the feeble cries of an old crone beseeching her kin to eat proper. The boys trained alongside Jada in the sparring ring. Brontes and Dareios are both as skilled as you in weapons. Whoever crosses their path are the ones who should be wary."

At the mention of my sister, the muscles in my face tighten. I should tell him before he sets off. "Heracles has asked to wed her. I thought you should know. The king is considering it." My voice is barely a whisper, but Jakab hears.

It's quick, the slight pinch of his face before he regains composure. "None of my business," he says and drinks deeply.

Oh, but you wish it were. Of all the men who secretly yearn for my sister's affection, Jakab is the only one whose face I don't want to pummel. His interest was doomed from the start since the king would never allow it. Jada's hand is a potential alliance with another territory, her crown a shackle that buys Ellanios better goods and textiles—a fact that grates on me. If I didn't have a sibling, I would be in the same position as her, but because it's my sister's duty to make the sacrifice, I don't have to. The choice of who I marry is my only liberty. Although this freedom is really just a well-designed political maneuver to keep the commoners happy. For what common father or mother wouldn't be happy to marry off their daughter to become royalty? I join my friend in a round of joyless drinking. We all have our parts to play, as Father would say.

Our second goodbye is more tearful than the last, with the nectar burning inside our bellies. The other patrons throw olives at our backs and shout profanities because our blubbering is the stuff for women. But eventually, we part. It may not feel long for Jakab, because he'll be on an adventure of sorts, but the years are going to be a slow crawl for me. I'm really going to miss him.

Walking alone in the bright night, my insides begin to hollow without him by my side. The vigor in my step is gone as I roam the shadier streets of Ellanios for what I originally set out to do. My head is abuzz as my fingers toy with the strap to my sword. I've never killed anyone, but that doesn't mean I'm not formidable with a blade.

My eye catches fresh graffiti on the fractured stone wall of an alleyway, and I stop short. The message, "All hail the son of Zeus, true King of Ellanios"—drips in bright red paint. Below the oozing letters, is a crude drawing of my father and me hanging from the gallows. Apprehension creeps over my bones as I continue to stare. I'm a descendent of Zeus[11], but how well do my father and I stack up against a seed pretender who covets the throne?

I spit on the treasonous sketch. "They really believe that bastard is an immortal." Even though he hasn't been seen since the Early Wars[12], or Zeus, for that matter since the founding of Ellanios. "Fucking religious imbeciles. All of 'em," I slur and proceed to urinate on the dirty stone, aiming for the unskillfully drawn depiction of myself. "They could've at least done a better job. My face looks terrible."

"Get off me you loathsome brute! I said let go!" Comes the protests of a very agitated woman. "Ah. There it is." I finish pissing and head toward the direction of the dispute. It's not long before I find what I've been searching for: a surly drunk harassing a defenseless yet attractive enough tavern maid. A busty brunette, whose peplos hugs every curve and has my imagination wandering toward satin sheets and breathy sighs. I smile before burying my fist into the side of her

---

[11]King Vadim was the first ruler of Ellanios when Zeus began protecting the Holy City. However, the King of Gods wanted only the blood of his blood to rule over his prized jewel. Thus, Zeus forbade King Vadim from ever lying with his wife Agafya, again. The God gave his seed to Agafya, who then bore a son of Zeus'. As a half-god, Eanraig could command the winds and the storms, but he was not all powerful like his father. He died middle-aged after his horse kicked him in the chest, crushing his heart.

[12]During the Wrath of Ellanios, King Maarku made a plea to the gods for help in his endeavor for war. Zeus heard his descendent and commanded that Heracles aid Ellanios in overtaking the Southern Region. The Ellanion soldiers praised the immortal after witnessing his great feats on the battlefield. After the very last knee bent in Nasarr, Heracles left Ehvara with Zeus' permission.

attacker's face. A couple of hours and several drinks later, my cock finds itself buried in her.

CHAPTER IV

5th Week of Summer

Eimear

Were his shoulders always this broad? The day is just starting, but Sister Sun already burns hot. Gareth has gone a few paces ahead of me with some of the children as we race through the woods surrounding the village. Hushed giggles, the snap of a branch, and red leaves scattering—our sandals, decorated with amber beads, pound against the rock-strewn dirt. We are no more quiet than a band of drunk minstrels with a ready audience. This game of Kryfto we're playing helps to teach the young ones stealth, but they're slow to learn.

My breath comes in quick, uneven gasps, not helping matters. Styx! How much farther should we go? And what's the point if we can be found so easily? I can't help but roll my eyes at our silly brigade, but then my sights land on Gareth again. His presence takes up the entirety of my attention, the ache in my side forgotten. His summer chiton, dyed a deep green by his mother's own hands, is tied loosely to one side and reveals the sun-kissed skin of his back. When did he get so . . . muscular? He was but long limbs and bones this past winter.

A high-pitched squeal from an unnamed Pana comes from somewhere behind, and my jaw clenches in annoyance. For the love of Metis! I wish we could be alone again for once, like when we were children. Well . . . maybe not exactly like when we were children. Regardless, I've made this request to the goddess at least a thousand times since the Twin Moon festival, but it's gone unanswered. I'm as greedy as ever with my prayers. I've been hard at work with my studies, learning more about crops as well as perfecting my Ellanion dialect under the Elders' critical gaze. I think I've earned a bit of grace for my mind to wander here and there.

My preoccupied thoughts cost me though, as there's an abrupt tug at my scalp, followed by a painful sting. I forgot to duck down to avoid the overgrown branches known for ripping sleeves and tangling hair. I've left behind at least a strand or three and know Mana will scold me later when she has to pick the rosebud leaves from my hair.

Lungs ready to burst, I stop, doubling over, and curse between heavy breaths. The back of my head still stings, and I massage it as four or five children run past in search of hiding spaces in the woods. Good riddance.

"You know we're too old for this."

I look up in surprise and find myself disarmed by Gareth's handsome grin. It's the kind that causes your heart to do funny things, open and caring, making one feel special. His halo of wavy locks curls around his ears and drips with sweat, though his breathing is easy, as if we haven't been running around all morning.

In contrast, my breath is still uneven. I'm spent and can't muster a stride faster than a fool donkey. It wouldn't surprise me if my mouth was frothing like one as well. I like to blame my lack of athleticism on my stature. When the gods saw me screaming from my mother's womb, they tossed their shell[13] and it landed in favor of me being small. I don't think I'll ever grow an inch more. Despite this, and Gareth being older, I'm usually able to keep up with him during games. But ever since this growth spurt of his, it's now nearly impossible.

I give his brawny form a quick once over, powerful legs cut in all the right places, and decide that I'm perfectly fine with our reversed situation, the gods' shell be damned. "Well . . . don't slow down on my behalf," I say while trying not to die. The game *is* childish, but we both play for my brother's sake.

Gareth laughs at me. "You remind me of a backward yearling." He then shakes his head, "But don't let Buma catch you, we'll never hear the end of it."

Styx! He's thinking I'm like a damned donkey too! Is it my face? Just the notion is mortifying, and I wipe my cheek against my shoulder just in case. A quiet settles around us but for my drumming heart, and I realize we're alone. I silently thank Metis: Goddess you're too kind.

---

[13]When faced with the difficulty of choosing, it is custom to paint one side of a seashell black and the other white. A quick toss decides all.

I try to stand taller and place a hand at my hip to appear more feminine. Unfortunately, my fingers disappear into the folds of my yellow chiton. It falls just past my knees, but it might as well be an ocean of cloth over my tiny frame, hugging not one bit. I must appear as a boy, sweaty and shapeless as I am. I've no tits, no hips, and gods' forbid to bless me with a plump ass. Mana tries to remind me that I'm still young and that my curves will come with time, and to that I say, Kronos[14] hurry the Under up!

Despite my shortcomings, *literally*, I attempt a bit of sass in my tone that I imagine is flirtatious. "I should say the same. You know how he loves to trick." Upon hearing it though, and the topic being my own brother, I wish the gods would strike me down. Metis. Just end me. Don't let me toil further.

"Well, I'm not falling for any of his scams today. Best to find your place soon, he could be nearby." Gareth gives me a parting wink before darting off on his own.

I'm disappointed as his back fades amongst the burgundy copses. We're far enough away from the Elders' watchful eyes and not once did it cross his mind for us to run off in secret, or at the least, steal a chaste kiss.

---

[14]King of Titans and father to the first Olympians, but also, the ancient ruler of time.

"He must still think me a child," I mutter. What can I do to change that? I glance down, taking stock of the flesh I was given, and feel my insides wilt. "Not much."

Unhappy, I focus my thoughts on the game and begin to hunt for my own refuge. It isn't long until my eyes land on a large, twisted tree. Alive still, but likely split by a storm. Its base is hollow and big enough for me to hide in. At last, my size gives me the upper hand. I'm careful to tuck my body into the cave-like space so Buma won't find me. It's my brother's day of birth and to honor him, we made him the chaser for this game of Kryfto. Now that he's reached his seventh year, Buma will be blessed with a name at tonight's ceremony. I smile thinking about it. But even if it is a special day, I won't make it easy for him to find me. I sit and wait.

While hunkered in the cramped space, a cloying scent tickles my nose. The culprit is a damp, bright cerulean moss lining the ebony bark. Birds trill undisturbed from upper branches, their chorus of chirps and song echo amongst the brush. In the distance, there's a faint thump of unrestrained footfalls heading in my direction. I strain to listen. I'm surprised my hellion of a brother could catch up to me so quickly. But heavy panting followed by a thud, reveals a Pana with dark skin and tight curls, who has fallen near my tree. Unhurt, she giggles and picks herself up. I recognize her as Anson's daughter.

Silly thing. She'll be found if she doesn't learn to be quiet. I click my teeth loud enough to catch her attention and partially emerge from the hollow with a finger raised to my lips. The Pana, who could be no more than five, sees my warning. She blows me a kiss with her plump hand and offers a wet smile before taking off once again. The crunch of snapping twigs follows her fading footsteps. I shake my head and resume my hidden position, a smile tugging at my lips as I recall my brother's youngest years. Buma was cute when he was her age, but more so when he was a babe.

Hours after his birth, I was led into my mother's room by an Elder who volunteered to watch me. Mana sat in a rocking chair with Buma's squirming body in her arms. The light shone on her hair through the window, turning the beautiful brown tresses into gold. She gazed lovingly down at my brother and her lips stretched into a crescent when he cooed and wrapped a fist around her finger. As I joined them, adoration struck me at the first sight of his round face. Buma's eyes, the same as hers, were an endless blue. He reached for me with tiny fingers and touched the tip of my nose—an action so minor yet profound. Skin to skin, I made the decision to always keep him safe.

"And this is exactly what a good sister does. Playing a game meant for babes," I quietly moan. The backs of my thighs burn from holding my crouched position for so long. My mood turns prickly. He should've found someone by now.

I try to distract myself and observe what I can see from my hiding place. Leaves bright with color fill the limb of every tree, turning my surroundings into a pink and red prison. The veins of nature's webbing are made visible by the suns' light. Minutes tick by, stretching like an eternity. "What in the Under is taking Buma so long?"

More time passes, and I find a patch of dirt sparse of indigo grass. I begin to write with my finger, practicing the Voranian[15] alphabet. For me, it's better amusement than this monotonous game of chase. Though the symbols are crude, it's one of the most difficult written languages to master. Sometimes I wonder if the dragon people made it contrary on purpose. I think Elder Solon would agree; he told me their history is filled with backstabbing and scheming amongst themselves. Maybe they also use their language to deceive one another? It sounds nothing like my mother tongue, Padi, which has a much slower cadence, or the common tongue[16]—a bland language to my ear if I compare it to the other rich languages I know. I understand the common tongue's usefulness, but I wish more thought had been put into its creation.

───────────────

[15]Vorna is a smaller country known for its rocky landscape, harsh climate, and harsher people who are splintered into separate warrior tribes. Voranians are large in stature and while their males carry the gene, it's the females who possess the dragon shapeshifting ability. If the tribes were ever to come together as a united force, they'd have the ability to take the entirety of Ehvara by storm. As is, they fight amongst themselves and start skirmishes at Ellanios's borders to gain more land.

[16]Three hundred years ago, trade amongst the continents was established, but transactions were difficult due to Ehvara's phonological melting pot. A guild of merchants hired the best linguists to create a simple language that could be easily learned to make exchanges go smoothly. They named it Aplolexi. Over time, the argot evolved and became the common tongue. It's now used by many for its practicality.

A soft, crunch of leaves warns that someone is nearby. Most likely the hellion himself, judging by his footsteps. I stop my scribbling. Our game of Kryfto is coming to a head. If Buma walks just a few more paces, I'm finished.

My tired legs start to quiver, and I suck in a breath to hold myself steady. I'm appalled though when his footsteps begin to sound farther away. Styx, he's terrible at this. It's going to take him forever to catch someone. Too bad for him. I've decided that as soon as he's gone, so am I.

But at the sound of hushed sniffling, I pause all thoughts of escape. He must be upset because he hasn't found anyone yet.

My calves burn while I hover on the balls of my feet. At the same time, I'm struck by guilt. Buma's sulking continues until it reaches an outright cry, disrupting the peacefulness of the forest. The birds go silent.

Shit . . . I nibble at my lower lip. I've never been able to bear my brother's suffering. But he won't learn anything if I always coddle him. My legs tremble from the effort it takes to remain hidden and a muscle twitches painfully in the right cheek of my arse. Unable to hold my stance any longer, I come to my knees and crawl forward, peering just outside the base of the tree. I'll just check on him, that's all.

My brother stands a few yards away with his back to me. His chiton, cut from the same linen as mine, is spotted with dirt. His shoulders are hunched and his raven hair, worn free, moves with the light breeze.

"They're too hard to fiiiinnd!" He cries in a drawn-out whine before kicking up the forest's debris in a miniature tantrum.

Gazing upward, I face the twin suns, their light against the canopy brings colored dots to my vision. Defeated, I heave a long sigh. I'm much too soft. I rap my knuckles against the tree, creating overexaggerated noise, bits of crumbling bark dust my skin.

My brother whips around, his ocean eyes lighting up as they lock onto my hazel ones. He laughs with conviction and points a finger before crowing, "Ha! I *found* you! I win and *you* lose."

I give him the best performance of my life. "May Zeus himself strike me down. I'm so embarrassed, I've been caught by a nameless babe. I'll never be able to show my face again."

"I'm gonna tell *everyone*," he says a touch too smugly.

After a moment, I manage to get the rest of my body out of the hollow and stretch, spine cracking. Gods, I'm happy that's over with. Buma skips over to me with a dimpled smile. His face has begun to thin out, losing the roundness of youth. I wish he would stay little for just a while longer.

The stare he gives me is quizzical, head just slightly raised, and my breath catches. He'll come to resemble our father more and more as he ages. A flash of when Papa returned home after one of his long voyages, comes and goes.

"Are you feeling sick? My brother grabs hold of my chiton, his lips forming a pout that has become his staple expression.

It makes me sad that Papa never had the chance to see it. My father's ship capsized before Buma's birth and my naming. Ever since, I haven't been able to tolerate the depthless waters of the Amenian Sea[17], fearful that I'll receive the same fate. I'm a pathetic excuse for an explorer's daughter. What's the point of being adept in foreign languages if I'll just be stuck here forever? I can't even set foot on a boat to help the others with fishing, let alone see nearby isles. The council thinks I'll grow out of it eventually, but what if I don't? What if I can't provide for my people like my father could? A frustrated urge to cry comes up that I immediately suppress. I need to get it together now. It's a special day for Buma and I'm acting like it's a funeral.

"Yeah, yeah," I say and ruffle his hair. "Stop worrying about me and be happy the Goddess will finally name you this eve."

An impish grin settles on his face. "Maybe she'll call me Lord of Shadows after Hades himself." He lifts his arms overhead and wiggles his fingers in an ominous gesture.

Shit! I glance around to make sure there are no others nearby to overhear or see. It's sacrilegious to say such a thing, and to mention the God of the Under no less. Does he want to be known for a devil? I make

---

[17]Governed by Amphitrite, wife to Poseidon. Amphitrite is gentle in nature, her calmness is shown by the way her waters are rarely tempestuous which offers perfect conditions for fishing. Only when she argues with her husband can inclement storms be seen across the Amenian's glittering blue.

my voice stern. "The Naming Ceremony isn't a jest. If you behave poorly, Metis is going to peer into your soul and name you after a fool."

His olive skin pales a shade, and he sputters, "She wouldn't do that . . . would she? I mean, the goddess gave *you* a good name, and you're scared of everything."

"I am *not* scared of everything. You're just too little to understand." I pinch my mouth with my forefinger and thumb, brows furrowed. I'm astonished he's so lackadaisical about the ceremony. I was a wreck on my own Name Day. I mean, it's the most important day of a person's life. It would make anyone nervous.

My cheeks were salted with dry tears, throat raw from excessive crying, I was scared and had thrown a fit. If Mana hadn't put drops of firewater on my tongue to calm me, I wouldn't have made it before the priestess. When my fingers made contact with Chrysanthe's, her eyes glowed with flecks of bright amber, and her golden robes swelled as if a gust of wind were present. It lasted only a moment, but I was overwhelmed by Metis' divinity as her immense power ripped through my being. She named me—throughout my body, her mellifluous voice rang my name like a thousand chimes swaying in a gentle breeze. After she withdrew, I was left whole yet empty, wishing she'd return.

She named me well and even blessed mine and Gareth's pairing, despite our forcing it. I have the deepest respect for the Goddess and can't let my brother's insult to her pass.

My hand moves to my hip, and I pitch my tone hot enough to scald. "Yes, Metis bestowed me with a name that means *all knowing*. I haven't fully grown into it just yet, but Mana, when she was a girl, was given *Althaia*. Her name symbolizes *healing*. She grew to eventually become Paidia's physician. Despite my faults, you would do well to listen to me by namesake alone. I am after all, in line to become one of the next Elders." I look my brother up and down for good measure. "What will Metis name you after your mockery towards her? What do you think will become of you for it?"

My brother's eyes go wide, lowering his gaze in shame. His lip trembles as if he's about to cry. At the sight, my insides cave, making me feel like I'm the worst human to exist in all the gods' worlds.

No more guilt, he needs tough instruction to grow into a proper adult. Stiffening my back, I harden my heart against him and offer no comfort. "Play time's over. Let's go, son of Rhone, we've schooling to attend and shouldn't be late." I raise my fingers to my lips and whistle, signaling to the others that our game of Kyfto has ended.

CHAPTER V

5th Week of Summer

Eimear

Everyone in Paidia must attend lessons until they've mastered their prospective trade. Most lessons are private and tailored to one's namesake, but others cover a broad range of topics that both named and nameless attend. Today, our class is held at the ceremony grounds, where sixteen of us sit on the boulders surrounding Metis' rotunda. We're about halfway through the lecture when I catch my brother, who is perched on a boulder at the opposite side of the circle, glaring at me. His blue eyes have taken on a demonic quality that would make Hades proud. Maybe Metis *should* name him after the dark one after all. He's probably thinking of all the ways he can spurn me. My brow furrows as I mouth to him, "*Pay attention.*"

The little brat sticks his finger up his nose and wags his tongue, eyes rolling around in their sockets. I can't believe him! What a—

"Son of Rhone! You'd do well to pay attention. Don't think because it's your Name Day that you can slack in your studies. I'll make you voice an essay on Charybdis[18] if you keep it up," Elder Marcus barks at him from the rotunda. Metis' open arms are at his back, her statue less festive without all the garlands from the Twin Moon festival. The entire class stares at my brother in annoyance.

He sits up straight, his face morphing into a child of innocence. "Yes, Elder Marcus."

The old man dips his head in acknowledgment and strokes his winter white beard. "Now, where was I?"

Buma's eyes find mine again, my smile is smug as I mouth, "*Serves you right*." He forms a small fist, and I turn away from him, making a point of looking at our instructor.

Elder Marcus paces in front of the Goddess, his overly patched robes whirl with every turn. He carries the ancient text, *Gods & Beasts of Miracle* with him, the large tome a revered relic in our village. Marcus is a bit eccentric, but I adore him because his excitement is contagious, which makes his lessons much more fun than the other Elders'. He also doesn't harp on me like Elder Solon or swat my hands when I get an answer wrong. I settle into the warm timbre of his voice as he continues his lecture.

---

[18]A giant vortex of water on the northeastern side of the Thyellódic. Ships that stray too close are quickly devoured by the maelstrom. Little is known about what lies on the other side of the giant whirlpool.

"Of all the worlds the gods created, Ehvara is their pride and joy," he says while stepping down from the rotunda. His skinny arm makes a wide arc, up toward the Gods' Window where Mount Ida resides. "Ehvara was the first world crafted by the gods and used as a model for the rest—"

"Not this again, we've heard it so many times," Gareth groans under his breath. He fidgets next to me on the boulder.

I give him an elbow to the ribcage. "Shhh, this is my favorite part."

"—the humans made immortal, blessed to become World Walkers[19], have seen the gods' other creations. From their own tongues it was told that no other compares to Ehvara."

I wish I could be the judge of that. The mere thought of traveling, not only Ehvara but the gods' other designs, makes my heart ache with a mixture of excitement and jealousy. It's painful to dream of such things when leaving Paidia's small blotch of earth is next to impossible for me. Still, I often catch my thoughts conjuring images of what these fantastical lands are like.

Marcus walks between two boulders where a pair of Pana twins are seated. He heads toward a lone shrub and breaks off a small branch with rubicund needles before returning to his position under the rotunda.

---

[19]Handpicked by the God of Gods, these chosen few are entrusted with the task of emissary for Zeus and visit all worlds. They are known and referred to as his eyes and ears.

With his book under one arm, the Elder extends the branch towards the sky.

"Brother Sun from the Gods' Realm distorts the rays of our Sister Sun, making the foliage of Ehvara different from other planets." He lowers the branch and gives it a quick shake. "For example, in some worlds, this would be green."

The children who haven't heard this lesson before, chatter amongst themselves in disbelief while the older ones try to stifle their groans. Amara sits two boulders away from my brother, gazing at the sky, her expression blank with boredom.

Well, I guess he has told this story more than a couple of times. Elder Marcus has become forgetful lately.

"Styx, who cares?" Gareth laments.

A realm full of green would be a marvel to see in my opinion. Excited by the topic, my hand shoots skyward. "Elder Marcus, and what of Earth? Could you tell us about it?"

Gareth whips his head to face me, a pained expression written on his face. He whispers, "Why would you *do* that?"

"What can I say? I love history." I grin mischievously, and he turns the other way aggravated.

The Elder perks up at my interest. "Ah, yes, my dear! Earth is the other great world of the Gods, the second to be created in fact. During their war with the Titans, Ehvara wasn't the only battlefield. Earth saw its share of fighting as well—" Marcus stops for a moment to chuckle into his fist, "although, there weren't many humans left alive at the time.

Zeus had destroyed those on Earth and on some other planets too, for not honoring him properly many years before the Titanomachy. Unlike them, we Ehvarians know our place."

"And what happened after?" One of the twins asks.

I elbow Gareth again. "See, I'm not the only one interested in a good lesson."

He returns the gesture but with a wink.

Marcus continues, "Well, the Olympic gods won the war, and Zeus decreed over Ellanios, "As long as you sing for me, I will shine my light on thee. With a single thunderclap, light spread around the world and that, my students, is how the Windows and the Lunetas Bridge were created."

Ugh, we already know that. I want to hear more about the other worlds. I raise my hand again. "Yes, but what about the ancient city Aeolia?"

"Yes, yes, I was getting to that part. The universe seemed empty to Zeus when the only humans to worship him were on Ehvara. With a snap of his fingers, humans, known to us as the Greeks, sprang from the clay of Aeolia on Earth and on other planets as well."

My brother's hand raises next, an astonishing act. Could it be a sign of maturity?

He asks, "But how else is Ehvara different from these worlds? Do we have the same things?"

Our instructor wags an age-spotted finger. "Good question. On Earth, the Greeks know of Ehvara, much like how we know of them. As mere myths and legends. Though we are each, so much more." Marcus taps the same finger against his giant book. "These Greeks attempted to make Earth similar to Ehvara, but each world is different and makes its own advancements with time."

Gareth leans into me and whispers, "In other words, he has no idea and is being vague on purpose."

Disappointed with the Elder's lack of explanation, I eye the black leatherbound held in the crook of his arm. If only I could glimpse those pages. It's rumored amongst the villagers that the book appeared miraculously before Marcus as a child. He's hoarded its contents ever since, not letting anyone else near it. I take a moment to study his aging figure, the Elder's body is hunched from its numerous years. Maybe once he passes on to Elysium, Metis will bless me with a chance to read the great book.

When we're dismissed, Gareth waits for me as I gather my belongings. I pick up my leather satchel and wipe the stray blades of indigo grass from its surface. His bag is already slung over his shoulder.

Buma bounds up to the two of us. "Can we go home now?"

"No not yet, Mana asked for us to gather herbs after the lesson. She's low in supply," I say.

"I don't want to work!" he whines and tilts his head back dramatically.

Gareth ruffles his hair. "We'll make a game of it and be done in no time. You can race me to see who can find the most if you'd like."

My brother's eyes brighten at the prospect of a challenge. "You'll never beat me!" He laughs before darting off, zigzagging between the trees.

"Make sure you stay in sight!" I call out before shaking my head. "That child."

"I'd be lying if I said he wasn't a handful." Gareth offers a charming grin. My heart quickens in response.

Time flows easily while the tree limbs creak overhead with the breeze. There's a comfortable silence between us as we search the forest floor for Mana's requested herbs and mushrooms. But then—an age-old argument resurfaces.

"You know, Marcus assumes we're the gods' favorite just because of some floating mountain in the sky," Gareth says a bit aggressively while searching a large nagalia bush[20] for its orange berries.

"It's floating *mountains*," I correct him. "Remember, there are two Windows." Sometimes it's easy to forget there's another in the West. Though, it's unlikely that either of us will ever see it, which is maddening because it's considered to be the Window with a better view. Olympus and all its palaces reside within it. I'd give anything to see it just once.

---

[20]When eaten regularly, the berries of a nagalia bush help to improve one's mood.

Gareth grunts as he stretches to reach the berries at the back of the bush. "You can spare me the lesson. Elder Marcus talked enough to make me want to shove knives into my ears. *And*—" Gareth retreats from the nagalia and pops a berry into his mouth before packing the rest of his findings away. "—how *heroic* of Zeus to create not just one, but *two*, giant peepholes that block a large portion of *our* beautiful sky. If he really cared about Ehvara, he would've left us alone after nearly destroying everything. I mean, honestly. How perverse must he be to watch us constantly? I bet he's no better than a dirty old man up there. Something's not right about it."

It's scandalous he would refer to the King of Gods with such derision, though I'm not surprised. Gareth has always been this way when it comes to the gods. Still, a bit of fright would do him some good. "You aren't worried Zeus is going to strike you dead for speaking like that?" I say evenly and place a yellow mushroom into my satchel. This one is good for indigestion.

Uncertainty flashes in his green eyes while he peeks up at the Window, as if to make sure Zeus isn't there watching, ready to fry him. His reaction makes me feel the teensiest bit smug.

"No, still alive and standing," he says placing a hand over his heart, grin wicked.

I want to be mad at him, I really do. But that smile of his can make me overlook anything. I'm fourteen, I count to myself. Just seven . . . more . . . to go. I hope the years bringing me to adulthood will pass quickly. Though each second seems to feel like an eternity. The time will be a test of patience.

Despite my feelings, I pitch my voice to sass. Because if I don't, there'll be no end to this kind of talk. "Zeus created the Windows to stand guard and protect us, not to spy on us. The universe is large, with an infinite number of planets he could look at. According to Elder Marcus, no other world has anything similar to our Windows. Therefore, Zeus must favor Ehvara the most."

"But even if that were true, you've heard the stories; it's not our world that's Zeus' prized possession, but the Holy City within it. The light from the Bridge doesn't shine as brightly anywhere else but there. He's not trying to protect Ehvara at all, he's probably stashed something away in the City and just doesn't want anyone else to find it."

Gareth speaks of Ellanios. Other than during the Twin Moon festival, the Lunetas Bridge is considerably dimmer over the rest of Ehvara than it is in Ellanios' capital. I'm envious of the Holy City. It's considered the heart of Ehvara; Zeus named the jewel his chosen kingdom after the Titanomachy. I've been told the light from the bridge shines directly onto the city, illuminating the metropolis even at nightfall. The godly light is what makes the Holy City prosperous and will forever grant Ellanios Zeus' protection. Not only that, but the Holy City is the closest city to the West Window. It really does have everything.

My desire to wander the world reemerges with the turn of the conversation to Ellanios, and I can't help but be disgusted with my fears that keep me rooted in this place. Even in my dreams, I've no refuge to explore, for the waves always claim me just like my father. I pray to Metis nightly that I'll grow out of it by the time Gareth, and I are old enough to wed. His talents should be shared with the world and there is wisdom to be found in traveling. Paidia would only benefit from it. We just need a ship and a cure for my fear. But both will be hard to come by. Wonderful.

"You're wrong about Zeus," I finally tell him. I know my response is lacking, but I can't think of anything else to say. This discussion is beginning to wear on me.

Gareth rolls his eyes. "You take all these myths too seriously. You should focus on something else."

My temper flares. What is it with these boys today? Why do I have to be the one to set everyone straight? "Myth? Was Metis a myth when she named you?" He winces. At the very least he's ashamed of his insult toward the Goddess. Everyone named in Paidia has felt her powerful touch during their naming ceremony.

His voice is hushed. "I just don't think you should let the gods rule every aspect of your life, is all I'm trying to say."

I'm conflicted; I don't want there to be trouble between us, but his lack of respect toward the gods is beginning to grate on me. I let out a sigh and glance at the herbs in my satchel. We're not even half-way finished yet. "Let's just drop the topic for now. We're both stubborn and at this rate, Mana will skin both of us if we don't gather everything she's asked for."

"You've a point there." Gareth tugs on a strand of my hair as if to tease, but his eyes are lowered. "You're always thinking ahead and know what to do, I like that about you Eimear."

He turns away from me, and I watch his back as he searches for more herbs amongst the woods. Clutching my satchel to my chest, my pulse thrums beneath the leather. We were so physically close just now, my mind can't help but wander to where it shouldn't. Goddess help me.

CHAPTER VI

5th Week of Summer

Eimear

Hours later, arguments have been long forgotten under the intense heat of the Sister Sun. She sits high in the sky, her glaring rays making my skin sizzle. I slip a packet of eldaflora into my satchel and wipe sweat from my brow. The little white flower is known for its antibacterial properties and grows best at the forest's edge, which offers very little shade.

Gareth shoulders his own bag, his green chiton soaked through with sweat. He looks off into the trees briefly and then back to me. "Should we go for a swim? We've gathered enough I think."

I chew on my bottom lip, mulling it over. It's a trek back home from here and I don't want to be pressed for time.

Off to the side, my brother groans. He's sprawled against a tree stump, fanning himself. His cheeks are flushed a bright pink, forehead framed by wet curls. The game between he and Gareth ended long ago when the hellion first began to tire. He really should cool off before we go. I nod to Gareth, no more convincing is needed. "Sure, I think we've earned it."

At the very mention of work ending, Buma perks up and grins. "Finally! I thought we'd be here forever."

I don't comment on how he has mostly rested while we toiled. He's still a child after all. We head toward a freshwater spring that's a mere fifty yards deep into the woods. The water is crystalline, with dusty pink sand and indigo grass at the bottom. When we arrive, Sister Sun reflects against the surface, making it sparkle.

I avert my eyes, but not due to the water's glare. I'm suddenly very conscious of Gareth as he drops his satchel and begins to strip down to his perizoma. I had no shyness before our pairing, but the simple act feels different now. He discards his chiton onto a nearby branch and, as I debate sneaking a peak or two, he and Buma run past me. They laugh as they jump into the spring together.

Damn it all. A missed opportunity. But . . . he'll need to get out of the water, eventually.

I follow them, the water a pleasant shock to my senses as I sink below the surface. When I swim to the top, I turn over onto my back and the rosy forest greets me from above. Unlike the other two, I'm required to keep my clothes on for modesty's sake, and parts of my chiton billow around me with trapped air. I inhale deep and I'm met with the crisp scent of pine mixed with floral tones from the water. It's moments like this, when everything peacefully comes together, that make me feel grateful for the life I have. "Thank you, Metis, for the many blessings," I whisper.

My eyes wander beyond the forest's covering to watch the Lunetas Bridge and the East Window. The twinkling light of the bridge is just barely visible during the day and even from my viewpoint, Mount Ida is impressively large on the other side of the window. The mountain is covered in red trees and our Brother sun currently casts his golden light upon them. As I continue to admire the East Window, I wonder what the gods think of us. Do they praise our works and forgive our blunders from up there? If I asked Gareth for his opinion, he'd probably say: "Does it matter?" So, I keep my thoughts to myself.

I turn my head to find him suspended in the water not far from me. A mixture of light and shadows from the trees skitters across his handsome face. His eyes are locked onto my chest where my dark blue strophium shows through my soaked chiton. His expression morphs into one of embarrassment when I catch him staring, and he quickly turns his gaze toward the sky.

Well, well. Who looks like a backward yearling now? I find the attention flattering though, and can't help but be giddy.

As if Buma senses my happiness, he quickly comes to ruin it. A shout pierces the solitude of the forest and there's no time to move before he cannons into the spring. The young hellion barely misses me and sends a wave of water directly up my nose. I cough as I swim myself upright, but even then, there's no relief. The little pest continues his assault while laughing demonically and splashes water straight into my face with no sign of stopping.

He must be sore from my reprimand earlier and is taking his sweet revenge. Little shit. I grab hold of his shoulders and settle my full weight on top of him, sending him under. He kicks and squirms beneath me, churning water. Only when I'm satisfied that he fears Hades and the Under, do I let him up for air.

Buma tries to catch his breath and whines, "You're bigger than me! That's not fair."

My sneer could cut glass. "Then don't start a fight you know you can't win."

"It's always a constant scrap with you two," Gareth says sounding annoyed, and dunks both of us.

My arms thrash wildly as I swallow more water and wonder if my life-mate even loves me at all. These boys are animals. With a final elbow, I resurface with my lungs on fire and shove water Gareth's way, making sure to get him in the face. He awards me with a playful smile, hair dripping. I scowl in return.

"You scratched me, Eimear!" Buma says with a pout and protectively reaches for the side of his neck.

Gareth focuses on the hellion who started it all. "Here, let me take a look at that."

I strain to see while treading water, but under his small fingers, there are three bleeding marks, barely an inch long, but deep enough to sting. I got him good. The trail of blood is quickly washed away by the spring, and Gareth's face brightens with excitement. I already know what he's thinking and don't like it.

"Now's as good a time to practice as any," he says.

My stomach constricts with nervousness. "You know you're not supposed to without Mana around. She forbids it."

My brother flips onto his back and kicks gently away from the two of us. He mocks me, "You always do what everyone says. Mana isn't even here, no one would know but us."

I grit my teeth at his ridicule, the flash of embarrassment all too real. Even before I was named, I was this way. It's as if I was born with a box around myself, never stepping past its edges. I have an innate need to please my mother and the Elders, to not cause trouble, and to follow the rules set in place. The other children have taunted me many times when we've played games together: *Eimear the prim, Eimear the old maid, Eimear the slag[21]*. The rigidness that possesses me, mixed with my fear of the ocean, has made me an oddity for my age.

I chew on my lower lip as I stare at the East Window and self-loathing moles its way into my chest. I wish I could change myself.

"What's it gonna be Eimear?" Gareth asks.

---

[21]A poisonous, prickly, violet-colored slug that burrows itself into the ground and emerges after rainfall only to fuss and whine at an unpleasant pitch. It's an insult to be called a slag, for they are considered nettlesome.

It's true that Mana would never find out. A trickle of rebellion spreads through me like a spring freed from drought. I put on a less-than-confident smile. "It wouldn't hurt, I guess."

"That's my girl!" he exclaims. Buma whoops along with him and my diffidence lessens a fraction at their praise.

We make our way toward the water's edge, and Gareth grabs onto a tree root before hoisting himself up and out of the water, the muscle of his back on display. This time, I'm more thoughtful and take in an eyeful while I can.

Good gods, Metis just keeps on giving.

Gareth crouches to take Buma's hand, but before he can help him up, the brat takes the opportunity to send water into his face with a triumphant, "Ha! Take that, you siren[22] lover!"

Gareth glances at me, chin dripping, eyes wide with surprise—a reaction that mirrors my own—my brother hangs onto his arm and snickers. Buma's too young to know that I'm the one he insulted. In other lands, Siren Houses are common, but they don't exist here in the village. It would be a sacrilegious profession. When we pair, it's a sacred act, not something to be shared with just anyone or paid for.

"You know what, you little Dolos[23]?" Gareth says, while pulling my brother up who screams in false fear, "I've had just about enough of

---

[22]A creature that lures fishermen and sailors to their deaths from the depths of the ocean. The term, however, when uttered on land, also refers to women and men who labor as prostitutes.
[23]Dolos is a spirt of trickery and wiles.

you." He reaches for a discarded chiton and shoves it over Buma's head, winding it round and round, before sending him blind into the woods. Naturally, the hellion mistakes it for a new game and wanders off on his own, giggling as he bumps into things.

Gareth helps me out of the water next, his grip strong. I shake my head in disbelief once I'm on land. "I don't know where he heard that kind of talk. It certainly wasn't from Mana or me."

Gareth's brows pinch, his nose crinkling upward. "I think he may have picked it up from Orion's nephew. He's been sitting by that lout during most of their lessons together."

I try to recall the boy's name whose ceremony was just last year, but my hand is still intertwined with Gareth's, and thoughts of Buma's foul language disappear. Gareth, too, glances at our hands and a scolding heat rises up my neck when our eyes lock.

He stammers awkwardly, "You know I could never think of you like that, as a siren."

I open my mouth to blurt something foolish, but Gareth beats me to it. "Well, I'm not saying that you couldn't be. You're beautiful and usually beautiful women are sirens, and someday I would like to—" he puts a fist to his mouth, and mumbles, "—I'm just going to stop talking."

The blood in my ears pounds from the meaning behind his unuttered words.

Clinging to the rebellion I felt earlier as if it were a lifeline, my feet close the distance between us until my chest meets his bare torso.

With our fingers still laced together, I squeeze his hand. In truth, my mind has fantasized a multitude of scenarios that would make even the gods blush. It's indecent for us to be having a moment like this, and yet, my body yearns to do more. I should be embarrassed, but I find no shame in what we're doing. I think the comfort comes from knowing him my entire life. Like a storm with its clouds or the stars with a moon, we just go together naturally.

Admiring Gareth's shoulders, my fingers trail across his damp skin. My imagination wonders what it would be like to place a kiss there—a thrill runs through me, all the way down to my toes, much like the night we were paired. Gareth's eyes contain a heat that makes my stomach dance, and any prior thoughts of chasteness are entirely ignored. He leans in closer, taking the plunge, his lips hover just above mine and my heart races for what comes next. I close my eyes—

"Styx!"

What? My lashes flutter open as Gareth recoils in pain. For a moment, a thought crosses that Metis has put a curse upon my mouth for our transgression. But when he reaches for the back of his head, and I see Buma holding a handful of pebbles behind him, I know there's no divine intervention at play. The nuisance of my existence wears nothing but a savage expression and his perizoma.

"Hands off my sister or the next one is going where it hurts." He tosses a pebble up in the air and catches it with his free hand for good measure.

My first real kiss thwarted by a brat who doesn't even have a name yet. I bite the inside of my cheek, furious. Mana explained to him what a pairing is and has given my brother the duty of chaperone for today, as well as any other time Gareth and I might be alone. A position he has taken all too seriously.

Gareth puts his hands up in mock surrender while giving me a wink and slowly backs away. "Let's get your neck looked at," he says to my brother. "That good enough?"

Buma shrugs. "Sure, but don't do it again or else." He makes a grand show of staring intently at Gareth while stowing two stones in the folds of his perizoma before dropping the rest. He lifts his chin in the air and sticks out his chest for good measure.

I hide the slip of a smile with a hand. The situation *is* annoying, but funny at the same time.

Gareth waves him off. "All right, all right. I got the message." He retrieves his chiton, ties it in place, and we find our way out of the woods and into a glade of wild weed, grass, and rock-strewn earth. The light wind turns the clearing into a rippling blue sea. After the three of us sit, I take a moment to admire my surroundings, ever impressed with the natural beauty of my small world. My attention shifts only when Buma tilts his head to the side, exposing his neck so Gareth can examine the minor wound I gave him.

Mana took Gareth as an apprentice two years ago when he started showing signs of possessing a healing Gift. There currently aren't any other gifted people in Paidia and his parents thought he could learn best from her. Even without the blood of a god, she's an exceptional physician. Now, instead of fishing alongside his mother or working in his father's leather shoppe, Gareth tends to patients with Mana and is learning the way of herbs. We suspect he's a descendent of the God of Medicine, Apollo—though there's no way of proving our theory unless the god himself visits in the flesh to claim him.

My life-mate's eyes are strained with concentration as his hands move over Buma's neck. Sweat begins to form on Gareth's brow, and his hair, still damp from the spring, sticks to his face. The scratches aren't terribly deep—I don't have talons—but Gareth hasn't practiced on many humans, mainly small animals. Mana doesn't allow it just yet because if he does it for too long, the healing makes him sick. She says Gareth depletes his own life force when he uses his Gift, and *the Return* will begin if he goes too far.

Nothing happens for a few tense, quiet minutes, but then the skin on my brother's neck begins to repair itself as if time is flowing backward. The dried blood pulls itself back into his body, and the skin slowly knits itself up over each mark. I'm struck with pride at the miracle, and silently give thanks to Metis for blessing me with Gareth. I imagine all the good he'll be able to do once he's fully practiced and trained. The maladies he could cure are endless.

Finished, Gareth lets out a shaky breath along with an amused chuckle as he sits back to admire my brother's unblemished skin.

I reach out to Gareth and touch his arm. "Are you feeling unwell?" His skin has taken on a waxy pallor.

He studies his hands for a moment, turning them over. "There's no trace of Decay, I didn't work long enough for the Return to start," he pauses taking a breath. "I'll be fine, I just need to rest," Gareth finishes, his voice weak.

I grow further alarmed, imagining his fingers rotting away. The possibility of it hadn't occurred to me, the wound being so minor. It's a blessing to be Gifted with a god's blood, but it comes with great risk, a curse really. To *Return*, means for the Gift to go back to the god it came from. The Decay, once it starts, is reversible if one is careful with the appendage. But it spreads quickly, and if not stopped in time, fatal.

I wince, realizing what Gareth just risked. Mana has cautioned against the return many times. I knew we shouldn't have gone along with this; it was foolish.

My brother, in his own world, doesn't notice Gareth's fatigue—he's too busy searching the ground while rubbing at his freshly healed skin.

"Eimear, where's something sharp so you can cut me?"

I raise an eyebrow at him. "Why the Under would you want me to cut you?"

"I want to see my skin go back together. Can you nick my arm real good this time?"

"Not a chance."

Buma lets out an exaggerated huff, clearly not satisfied, and falls onto his back. I don't understand how Mana shows so much patience with him when he's like this. I turn away from my brother and check on

Gareth. He appears lost in thought, even puzzled, his skin still a shade too pale.

"Are you sure you're all right?" I ask.

His eyes meet mine. "You shouldn't worry so much. It's not healthy."

I snort. "Says the person who can literally rot alive."

"I'm not worried about that, I'm careful. But . . . it was strange. I could actually *feel* his emotions while I was healing him. It's not something I've experienced before."

Tension pools in my belly. "Was it a bad feeling? Did it hurt you?"

Gareth's smile is gentle. "No, he was just happy. And again, I'm *fine*."

Reassured, I check on the hellion who has since got up and started to poke holes in the ground with a stick, moping because I won't inflict any more wounds on him. I roll my eyes. "You know, it's not normal to ask people to harm you."

He scowls. "That's not what I meant, don't act so smart if you're not." He turns his back, giving me the silent treatment, and resumes mass destruction on the glade.

I shrug and Gareth's lips curl slightly as he leans back into the indigo grass. I hope he's amused by our bickering at least. I'd hate it if he stopped spending time with us. Choosing to ignore my brother's antics, I join Gareth. The Sister Sun starts to dry my damp, dirt-stained chiton, but I know it's useless. I don't need a visit from the Fates to foresee a strong reprimand from Mana in my near future. She paid a good amount of coin for the yellow dye.

Gareth's hand bumps against mine, distracting me from thoughts of my impending doom. Very quickly, a happy warmth spreads in my breast as our fingers interlace, my worries forgotten. We watch the clouds and point out their shapes. What appears as a bird to me, is a rabbit for Gareth. He's obviously blind. The white fluff has formed around the Gods' Window, and gives the divine portal an even more mystical appearance.

I whisper half-jokingly to Gareth, "You know, for someone who's been Gifted by Apollo and named by Metis herself, you seem to enjoy dismissing the gods and their blessings. You're fortunate they love you so much. Maybe you should try showing some gratitude before they rescind their affection?"

He immediately props himself up on his elbow and looks down at me, expression serious. "I don't feel lucky. I want to live my life unbothered. Everything we do in our village is based on what the gods want, even who we marry. But why? We've never even seen one of their kind."

"Well, that's—"

Sheepishly, Gareth averts his gaze and interrupts me. "For years, I was terrified I wouldn't be paired with you and waited until I could try to force our bond. Even with how things turned out, I think it was just a fluke. I won't be grateful for that. Why should the gods determine who I spend the rest of my life with?"

Whatever point I was trying to make is forgotten because I think Gareth just confessed his love for me. The excitement has me dumb. I want to say something in return, but the words seem to be caught in my throat, my mind blank. I think he understands my silence because he gives me a shy smile and gently squeezes my hand before lying back down in the grass. The sky is bright overhead, and a light breeze scatters tiny rose-tinted leaves that tickle my skin. Lying here in the glade with our fingers intertwined, I think about how I want this moment to last forever.

Gods & Beasts of Miracle

Chimeras

What a dreadful fright the chimera, a creature composed of various beasts like a morbid collage. Apollo sculpted a pair of chimeras from marble as a gift to impress his lover Hecate, a goddess and witch combined. Thrilled by their figures, she conjured life into the beasts from the magic of her womb. Wild and untrainable, they singed her chambers with their fire breath. In her rage, Hecate cast the chimeras out into the world. The pair flew to the rolling hills of Ehvara where they multiplied and devoured nearby humans. Over time, their generations of offspring bred with lower beasts and their kind lost the ability to ignite the flame within their throats.

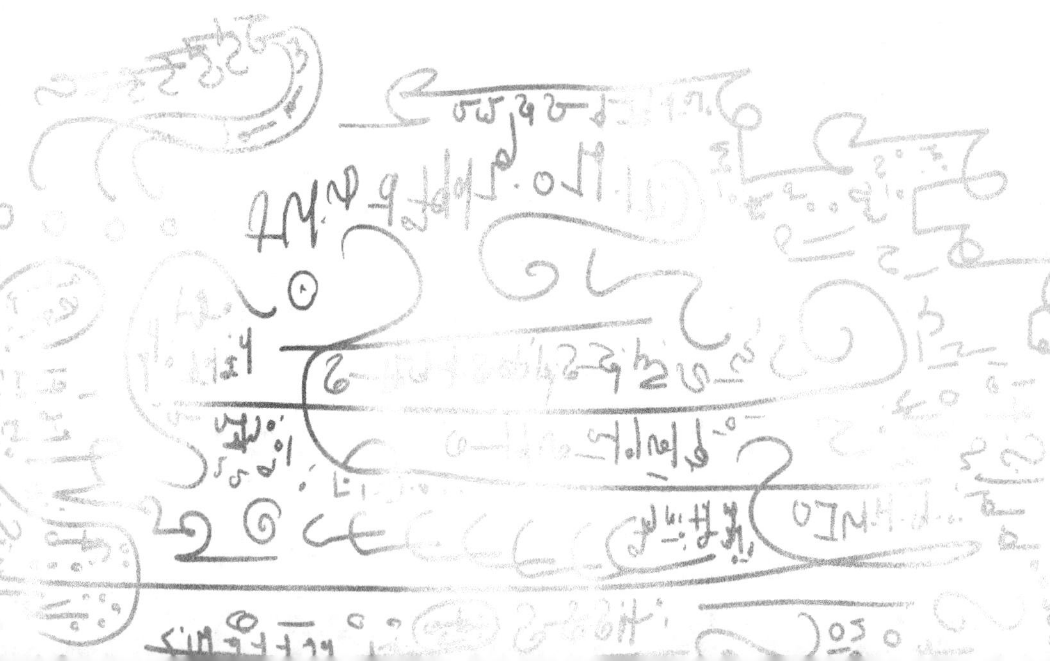

CHAPTER VII

5th Week of Summer

Nikko

I feint left and pivot before I slam the hilt of my practice sword into my sparring partner's kidneys. He grunts and both of his knees hit the dirt. The tip of my blade leaves a trail of sharp kisses up his sweaty spine before it presses firmly into the back of his neck.

"Do you yield?"

The soldier, a few years my senior, nods his head as he struggles for breath. "I do."

We've stripped down to our sandals and perizoma to spar, a custom usually practiced in the nude. But ever since my mother was crowned, she's insisted on keeping up with the martial art of Anyalay, her motherland, and trains alongside the soldiers. Thus, the king had our sparring attire—or lack thereof—changed for her modesty's sake.

I extend a hand to my partner and help him to his feet. "You're weak on your left side. Watch for that, or the enemy will gut you for it."

He bows his head in respect. "Yes, your highness. I'll add more drills to my routine."

"See that you do. You're dismissed." I watch his back in envy as he exits the training ring, and a fellow soldier claps him on the shoulder. The two make their way to the barracks beyond, and I'm left alone to fester. I'll never fight in the trenches or any real battle for that matter.

As the only son of the king, I'm not expendable. Not that Ellanios has seen battle in my time or my father's. Other than minor skirmishes at our borders, the land has been at peace for centuries. All our men's fighting is done elsewhere, their blood spilled on some other king's or queen's land, all so Ellanios' soft citizens can remain indulged.

I want to be prepared though, just in case. The blade twirls in my hand before I stab a mock attacker. When I've killed ten imagined men or more, I wipe the sweat from my brow and return the sword to its rack at the edge of the ring. Light footsteps approach from behind.

"Who pissed in your morning meal? That scowl of yours is horrific. Maybe I should teach you a lesson and give you a real reason to pout."

I turn to Jada, her hair is braided into an intricate hive on the top of her head, and she's dressed in sparring attire that mother approved: a long-sleeved gray-blue robe with white trim, tied off at the waist, and a matching white belt. The skirt reaches her ankles but is slit at both sides, revealing her deerskin boots and dark blue trousers.

I'm sweating more just by looking at her. For the life of me, I'll never understand this tradition of dress. I have the ultimate freedom of movement, whereas my sister is constricted by an abundance of fabric. She's clothed more now than in the standard peplos most women wear in Ellanios. Modesty must be the curse of women.

"Big words," I say, "for someone who spends more time on her hair in the mornings than in the training ring." Which is a lie, since my sister drills harder than anyone I know, but I like to tease her.

Her lips curl into a feral smile, she reminds me of a mountain cat, and I know I'm in for trouble. Pain flares upside my face as she successfully lands a kick to my jaw that sends me sprawling backward. I always forget how fast she is. What Jada lacks in stature, she makes up for in speed.

My palm lands on the ground and at the same time, I kick my leg out. She sees it coming though and jumps, dodging my attack with ease. While I grew up practicing the blade, my sister favored hand-to-hand combat like our mother, who was considered an expert in Anyalay during her golden years.

I'm steady on my feet again and charge at my sister, throwing a punch, but Jada pivots past and uses my own momentum to send me to the ground. She pins my wrist at an awkward angle, and I have to lean forward so none of my bones break.

"Yield! I yield!" I howl at her, but Jada tightens her hold.

"Nope, not until you take the comment back about my hair first."

My tendons feel as if they're being ripped apart. "Fine! Fine Your hair is shit! Doesn't look like you tried at all!"

"Hmmm . . . I don't think you mean it though. How about, Jada is the greatest sister of all time, and I have nothing but piss for brains."

"I'd rather die," I manage to spit out. Jada puts more pressure on my wrist, though, and I can't tolerate it any longer. "Fucking Styx!" I glare at her, repeating "I have piss for brains, and you're the greatest!"

The laughter from my twin is loud in my ears as the tension on my wrist is released. I flip onto my back and scoot away from her as quickly as possible.

Her grin is cocky. "I don't know why you're always training with steel like a barbarian, it would do you some good to learn another form of fighting, especially since you're going to be a king someday."

I stand and recapture the braids that have fallen loose from their leather thong at the top of my head. "That's yours and the Queen's expertise, and it's called a sword thank you very much."

She rolls her eyes. "Maybe I wouldn't kick your arse if you did. And what if you're put in a position where you can't draw a blade?"

I walk past her, and whisper for the sake of taunting, "Relax. I only let you win." Knowing her answer, I raise my arm just in time to block her punch. Jada aims a knee for my manhood, and I jump away swiftly to protect my prized jewels.

"And anyway, I don't want the crown. Never have. So, when the priest lays it on my pretty head, what if I say, 'fuck all' and pass the piece of metal to you as my first and final decree? You'd be queen then.

It's never been done, but that doesn't mean it can't be. It would give you incentive not to marry this so-called son of Zeus, or anyone at all for that matter, if that's your wish." I'm not surprised by how serious I am. In truth, all I've ever wanted is to fuck around.

Jada stills, and I see hope light her eyes before it quickly dims. "The people would never accept it. Not in Ellanios. Zeus is male and King of Gods. They want the same for Ellanios."

"They'll get over it, other cultures and countries across Ehvara have accepted women in power. Kanthar[24] is a prime example. Ellanions would adapt."

Jada shakes her head before charging and throwing another punch. I avoid her fist with success, but only because it lacked spirit behind the drive.

Her voice is colored with defeat when she speaks. "You know, our people see the women of Kanthar as outcasts, worshippers of goddesses who've defied Zeus. Evil women. Also, Kanthar was the first to fall to Heracles' might. Our citizens blame the country's demise on their monarch's sex, saying she wasn't strong enough because she was a woman."

---

[24]The only country in the history of Ehvara to be ruled entirely by women. They worshiped only goddesses and had temples throughout the country, paying homage to their deities. The temples also served as safe havens for those in need. It is suspected to be a land full of witches.

The way history is told versus the truth is a nasty thing indeed. Kanthar was ambushed, and Father reneged on his treaty with them. He refused to send Kanthar additional soldiers when their queen pleaded for aid. Our men stationed in her lands were slaughtered because of his callousness and greed. My sister and I were only eleven at the time, but both of us were present in the throne room when Father made his ruthless decision.

I send a kick to Jada's chest; she catches my heel, but I remain balanced. "The sheep in these walls may believe the late queen is solely to blame for Kanthar's ruin, but we know the truth—" I pin her with a dagger-like stare. "It wouldn't be the same for you, Jada. You're beloved by our people. You really could be queen if you let me make it so. Are you afraid to become one?"

My sister shoves my heel and charges once more. This time, her punches hold the anger of her inner demons and are bloody relentless as they find their home on my body. In a final attack, she extends her fingers and spears me under my rib cage. I cough from the blow and take a knee, yielding with my hand raised.

"Brother, what you're proposing cannot be done, not in this lifetime. It's foolish."

I wheeze and attempt to argue. "But—"

She presses on. "You cannot change so abruptly what has always been, it has to be done slowly. The people already chatter about Heracles coming to lay claim on what is rightfully his. They believe he's Zeus' holy son. If you renounce your crown and name me as queen, Ellanios would not survive the civil unrest."

I feel thoroughly beaten. She's always had more wit than me. I'm never going to make a great king. I won't even know where to start when the time comes.

"Wipe that expression from your face now," Jada says as she extends her hand to me. I take it, letting her help me up. She then grasps my shoulder. "You'll do just fine as a ruler, I know it. And your plan would never work anyway. Your coronation is decades away, and Heracles is a threat now. As much as you want to, you cannot keep me from the wedding march."

I shrug. "Father hasn't confirmed the alliance yet, and if you accepted my proposal, I would've figured something out."

She sighs but then it turns into a chuckle. "You're really something else you know that? Trying to *give away* your crown!" Her eyes brighten with excitement. "*But* if you *really* want to create change when you're king, you could pick a girl child instead of a boy for one of your son's advisors and start from there. And then, maybe someday, Ellanios could have a queen as ruler. You could do that."

"Maybe so."

I look at my sister then, the half of my father's seed that was made for greatness, and wish that she was born male, and I, not at all.

My eyes are as dry as my father's humor. I've been studying the layout in front of me for hours now, the new construction designs for the ancient sector are troublesome. Mathematical notations are marked across the papyrus, and my vision blurs from the strain of it all. It's not coming together how I'd like it to. My ink-stained fingers drum at the edge of the desk as I chew the end of my reed pen.

I jump at the knock on my chamber door, almost spilling the inkwell.

"Nikko," Queen Himari calls out and enters without permission. My mother, originally from the eastern lands of Anyalay, recently turned forty, though you would never know it. Her beauty is still fresh like a young woman's, her ivory complexion stands out against her long, glossy black tresses. The only quality Jada and I inherited from our mother is the narrow shape of her eyes.

She harrumphs. "You've ink on your cheek."

I go to wipe it away but think better of it, not wanting it to spread.

The queen's nose crinkles further with distaste when her dark eyes glimpse the papyrus on my desk. "Your father gave the project of building restoration to you as a boy to help you step into your true role as a prince. You're nineteen now for gods' sake, it's time you put your toys away and pass it to someone whose station is befitting. Kings don't dirty their own hands."

I become distraught. The thought of giving up the very thing that makes me feel worthwhile is agonizing, but I quickly mask my pain as I've been trained to do. Kings don't show weakness. It's difficult, but I will my face to go blank as I crumple up the designs and toss them in the basket beside my desk. "Of course, my Queen. Now, to what do I owe this pleasant visit?"

Her lips quirk upward, showing the dimple of her right cheek. A smile I haven't received since I grew old enough to stop playing at her feet. "No fiery temper? No rude remarks? My dear boy, you may have grown into a man right before my eyes."

What? I'm stunned by her rare praise. My mouth opens and closes, searching. "Thank you," I finally say with hesitancy.

With a flourish, my mother pulls a rhipis from the folds of her lilac peplos and begins to fan herself. With the exception of sparring apparel, even she dropped Anyalay's traditional attire. The summer heat in the capital is brutal. She paces my room briefly before her gaze lands on my leatherbound books. Shaking her head she opens the terrace doors in silence and steps out onto the balcony. I follow her.

"I have a request of you," she says as she stares out into the Holy City.

"Pardon?" The Queen never asks me anything. She demands.

"During tonight's symposium, Ellanios needs you to dance with Andromyda, the young Princess of Apotmos."

At her phrasing, my insides coil. I fear where this conversation is going. "And why does Ellanios need such a dance?"

With a flick of her wrist, the Queen snaps her rhipis shut and leans against the balcony railing. "King Narcyz is old, and her mother dead. The girl's brother and sisters passed from the same plague. As of now, Princess Andromyda is his last living heir and next in line for the throne."

"And? We have a treaty with Apotmos, it's valid for another decade."

My mother closes her eyes, annoyed, and breathes in deeply. "My son, you lack the mind to think ahead and at all possibilities. If only Jada were a man."

The insult stings even if it's true.

"This war with Heracles has cost Ellanios deeply. We've lost our trade with Kanthar, with An—Anyalay."

The queen briefly stumbles over the name of her motherland, and we both pretend not to notice.

"—and half the Southern Region." She lowers her tone, eyes hard. "Avanta will be next if your sister doesn't wed this madman."

I clear my throat. "What does this have to do with a country we're already cozy with?"

"Stupid boy. What if that little chit decides not to honor our treaty when her father dies? What if she spreads her legs for an Earl of

Manthros[25] or worse, a Voranian king? What then? Another war, that's what, and one easily avoidable if she's enamored with you instead."

The indifference I achieved earlier begins to unravel, I close my eyes trying to keep my composure before opening them again. "You're asking me to give up my one luxury as Father's heir. It's my right to choose whose hand I take. And she's still a child, barely ten, if I recall correctly."

"Luxury? Boy, there are no luxuries in war. Look at your sister. She'll be given to a lunatic, and you're concerned with your own marital choices? How selfish."

My mother's face is flushed in her anger, possibly thinking of her past. She was married off like chattel as my sister is soon to be, but unlike her, there's no way of insuring Jada's safety in the union. Should the marriage turn sour, Ellanios can't afford to go to war on her behalf as Anyalay would have done for my mother.

My father became besotted with her when he traveled to renew Ellanios' treaty with Anyalay. He amended the trade agreement, not only exchanging goods for soldiers during the visit, but buying a queen as well. Royal custom gave the object of his affection no recourse. At

––––––––––––––––––––

[25]A country of seafaring people and mercenaries who worship Aries, the God of War. The strongest of Manthros, the Maketae, sail throughout Ehvara to pirate and raid, bringing honor to Aries. Prior to Heracles' rise, Manthros was one of the few countries that partook in the slave trade.

least they loved each other for a time during their marriage. Guilt's knife twists sharply in my gut. If Jada can marry for Ellanios, then so can I.

"Fine. I'll do as you ask. But ultimately, it's the young princess' choice; she may not have me."

My mother visibly relaxes at my surrender and a coy smile rises to her lips as she walks toward me. She places her folded rhipis under my chin and lifts my face upward. "There may still be hope for you." Her head tilts sideways in thought. "Wear indigo tonight. It'll bring out the gray of your eyes." She winks. "It's also her favorite color. Or so I've heard."

CHAPTER VIII

5th Week of Summer

Eimear

It's late in the afternoon. The vanity mirror in my mother's bedroom reflects her displeasure. She attempts to comb the tangles from my long hair, her mouth set in a line. A stray red leaf becomes unstuck, floating to the ground. All the while, my stomach flutters with excitement. I'm fantasizing about the kiss I almost shared with Gareth just hours ago.

A heartbeat more and we would've— Styx! I'm brought back to reality, the teeth of Mana's comb bite at my scalp, snagging on an unruly knot.

She picks out another leaf and purses her lips. "I don't know why you're smiling, missy. It's Buma's Name Day. The *one* day I need you presentable, and you come back looking like some wild thing from the thicket."

I will my expression to be neutral, Gareth aside, it's difficult to do while Mana continues to curse under her breath as she works. She doesn't notice how alive she appears, but I do. It's the same when she's brewing a difficult medicine and the brew isn't turning out as it should—tapping her wooden spoon against the kettle and cursing as if her anger will change things. Buma and I usually laugh from the stairs at her expense. I'm trying not to laugh now.

Speaking of brews. A peculiar aroma begins to drift into the room. The kettle downstairs must contain one of Mana's medicinal draughts. An extraordinarily pungent one at that.

My attention shifts to my hazel eyes reflected in the mirror—the same color as my father's eyes and the only indicator I was ever his kin. Rhone was a big man, with a personality to match. Mana was the only one who could temper him. He'd go quiet just at the sight of her. He was so in love.

After my father was lost to the Thyellodic[26], Mana arranged for an empty funeral pyre to honor him. Her bright eyes had gone cold and flat as she caressed her barely swollen belly. Papa never knew my true name, or his son, at all. I wonder if he'll know me when I join him in

---

[26]The largest body of water in all of Ehvara, governed by the Sea God Poseidon. The Thyellódic Ocean is temperamental, just like the god, and home to an assortment of beasts. Voyages across its waters can be deadly. One must have years of salt under their belt on the surrounding seas before attempting a journey.

Elysium? The heavenly plane is where the gods put all good souls, I've no doubt that's where my father is now.

A tug on my hair rustles me from melancholy thoughts, and I'm drawn to my reflection once more. Intricately woven braids are tied at the base of my neck with white ribbons. The rest of my hair falls in waves down my back, something I could never accomplish with my own fingers. Mana is a kind of sorceress that way.

Through the mirror, her scowl has been replaced with a look of satisfaction. "That should do it! It was difficult, but I like the result." She stands with a hand on her hip, admiring me. "Hopefully your pretty face doesn't get you into trouble later."

I stick my tongue out at her, "I'll never be as beautiful as you."

Mana winks. "No need to be modest. Aphrodite has blessed you."

I gaze upon my image and see a small, boring girl that always does what she's told, seated in front of a fiery woman who's never backed down, or burned out, even in her most sorrowful moments. I long to grow into my skin the way Mana has. Everyone has high hopes for me as one of the next Elders. I just pray I can live up to them.

My mother gently places her hands on my shoulders and leans down. "I know you've already done so much for me today; I was nearly out of those herb packets you and Gareth foraged."

I grow suspicious. From her tone of voice, there's a new task coming my way. "Yes?"

"Well, I have a brew over the fire for Galen, and I can't leave it just yet."

I turn toward her exasperated. "Does he have foot rot *again*? This is the third time now."

Mana shrugs. "You know how he is; the old man never takes care of himself and his wounds sour for it. But—"

"*But?*"

She laces her fingers together and winces, "I've been so busy that I forgot to buy Buma a gift for his ceremony. Can you go to market and fetch him something he'll like?"

My eyes widen a little at that. My brother's a hellion through and through, but it is custom for every attendee to present the newly named with a gift after their ceremony. It would be shameful if his own mother were to come up to him empty handed.

I raise a finger, "Only *if*, we can say that it's from the two of us."

"You forgot too!" Mana swats my arm playfully.

I smile at that. Turns out, we have more in common than I thought.

The marketplace at the center of Paidia is only a short walk through the woods. Buma's ceremony isn't until two hours after nightfall, and Sister Sun has just begun to sink from the sky, her brother dipping behind Mount Ida within the Gods' Window. I have plenty enough time to shop.

Even so, I try to walk quickly but find that my dress gets in the way. My ceremony peplos goes past my ankles with sleeves that billow at the shoulders and a neckline so high it could be considered choking. Whatever miracle curves I do possess are swallowed by all the fabric. I look like a gods' damned child. Annoyed, I pick up the extra length, exposing my knees, and proceed to stomp through the wood in an unladylike fashion.

Soon, the liveliness of the market permeates the silence of the forest. A musician from somewhere beyond the gate blows a spirited tune on a double reeded aulos, and I can't help the grin that tugs at the corners of my lips. Some may already be a bit drunk. The day's celebrations are all for my brother's sake, even though he is too young to understand the why of it.

For most, it's just an excuse for merrymaking, but every time a child makes it to their Name Day, it's a sign of our village's prosperity. The name Metis bestows upon them will determine what kind of place they take amongst our people. I wonder who the little hellion will become once he's named? Whatever his calling may be, I hope he won't have to wait as long as I will. It will be many years before I become an Elder.

And what happens between now and when I turn thirty-five? I'll be considered an adult when I reach twenty-one, but it will be two additional cycles before I'm permitted to join the council of Elders. And then, even more time before I can take a place of seniority. What am I supposed to do with all this time besides learn? I can't board a boat to fish, or travel like Papa. I'm not particularly skilled in any craft besides languages. I grimace as the uneven design of my last loom work comes to mind and the Elder's scolding along with it. Weaving is certainly out of the question.

But as the petite stone fence that marks the boundary of the market comes into view, I set my shortcomings aside and let the fabric of my peplos fall to cover my ankles. The enclosure is laughable because it can keep nothing out nor in—chickens escape all the time. I break from the tree line and a light breeze immediately cools my skin. The scent of flowers and sea salt is strong in the air. Upon entering the gate, there is an assortment of tiled roofs and undersized multicolored clay houses lined with blue budded shrubs. Hydria, the village potter waves at me from her stoop as she pulls a sheet from a suspended line.

No. No. No. No. Not today! People often want a remedy for some minor ache or woe and I'm the perfect messenger to send back to Mana for it. I return the gesture but don't stop for conversation and instead, walk faster. She makes a face, but I don't bother myself with caring as I leave her behind. I'll apologize to her later, after the ceremony.

Towards the agora, the atmosphere is energetic with music while my fellow villagers mill about. Today of all days is special, but more often than not, around this time they like to gather—not to buy anything, no, but to share gossip. I usually have to stop myself from rolling my eyes when I overhear bits and pieces of their dull chatter, and today is no different. Passing under the large, wooden arch erected at the market's entrance, I sigh as a villager's obnoxious voice grates on my nerves.

Sal, a skilled fisherman, speaks with one of my mother's customers who I've seen on several occasions. "Yeah, the lad was caught with his pants down, doing something indecent to Orion's pig at the back of the—"

"Oh, *gods*," I hiss and cover my ears, embarrassed enough for the two of us. Sal's voice is *loud*, and he isn't even trying to be discreet with a topic I'd rather not hear about nor would most decent people. How disgusting. It must be that boy again, Orion's nephew. He lives three dwellings over from the fisherman. My brow lifts high with indignation, and I make a mental note to lecture Buma on his choice of friends. He should stay away from that child after their lessons. My tongue clicks against my teeth. Sometimes it's like the people of Paidia are an extension of bad family I can't escape.

Oh, what is that? I give a quick sniff and note the enticing aroma of roasting meat. I hurry to the booths where I forgo the venison and instead, trade my coin for a cheese pie.

"Thank you, Artos. Yours are the best," I say to the baker and bite in, the crust buttery on my tongue.

The nearly bald man winks in return. "Any time. But tell that brother of yours to stop nicking sweets when he thinks I'm not looking, or else I'll put him to work."

The little shit strikes again. I put another drachma on his table. "For your troubles, but tell him yourself tonight. Or, better yet, *thief* painted onto his forehead in red will look real nice, don't yuh think?" Considering my brother's age, this would be the Elder's punishment for Buma if Artos were to report the theft.

The baker grins and sends me off with a wave. "Nah, I won't do that to him. See you later."

Damnit, I should've kept my coin. He was just teasing me. Slightly bitter, I return his wave and continue eating my pie as I peruse the wares of nearby merchants. The market is made up of several stalls and tables with bright curtains that separate them.

Past the stalls at the market's end, there's a dock where fishermen tie their boats. The small vessels currently knock against one another as the waves push them alongside the salt-weathered structure. It's not much, but Paidia does well for itself. We're surrounded by the Amenian Sea, making it easy to trade with our isle neighbors who paddle in on their own crafts. And fishing is abundant.

I often complain, but Papa would boast how there's freedom in being small and secluded from the rest. Our people don't bend a knee to kings or queens because we're simply not part of any region or fiefdom. We're much too far away for all of that. Paidia is at least a few weeks journey past the Amenian Sea and through the Thyellodic to reach the nearest continent. No one would trouble themselves with sailing here. It'd be nice if they did, though. I'd at least have someone to practice my language skills with.

I study the familiar faces around me, and my throat becomes tight. I feel like I'm suffocating from the sameness of my life. Some nod or wave at my passing, but friendly as they are, I just want something more, something different. What would it be like to go on an adventure? Like a hero's journey told in stories? I snort at the thought and wipe away any remaining flakes of cheese pie near my chin. "That'll never happen for me."

Papa was fortunate, he could escape the mundane as he pleased. Being the merchant with the only ship that could survive the crossing, he was in high demand. He'd be gone for months at a time making trade and supply runs for Paidia and the nearby isles. Papa would bring back trinkets, books, and maps from the lands he traveled. My love for languages came from him. Some of my happiest memories are the ones where he told me stories about different continents in another tongue.

Maybe that's why I'm stir-crazy. There hasn't been extravagant trade or, for that matter, any real news of the outside world since pieces of his ship washed ashore years ago, wrecked beyond repair. And it's not like we have the resources right now to build another ship of that scale. My eyes do a quick sweep of the entire market. It's just been us all this time, and the occasional isle visitor with similar supply problems. I've known the same people my entire life—their retold stories etched into my being as if they're my own. Sometimes when you love something, you want to experience it over and over again, but in this case, everything has gone stale, like old bread.

As if the gods wish to prove my point, a seagull shits on a nearby fisherman aboard his boat, mending a net. He curses in return, fist raised. Even the bird knows it's no good here and the same can be said for all this rubbish. My fingers toy lazily with the remaining drachma in my dress pocket while I walk past each stall of carvings, pottery, and woven tapestries I've seen time and time again. There's nothing new, and Buma won't like any of this.

For a moment, I stop my wandering to glare at the sea that keeps me confined on this small blot of soil. But as I watch the waves swell and fall, I squint, puzzled. It appears as if something is bobbing in the distance. When I blink though, it's gone.

"Oy, Eimear!"

I turn towards the shout, to find Beryl, a robust woman, waving in earnest from her stall. My mother visits her often—she gave birth to a precious daughter some weeks ago. I can't afford to be rude like I was with Hydria.

With reluctance, I walk over to her. "How are you and the baby?"

"My heavens, girl! Your mum is a blessing, I tell you. My little Pana just wouldn't stop crying. She was colicky as can be, but your mum whipped something right up and now she just sleeps right on through the night. I can finally rest myself."

"Well, that's good to hear," I say cheerfully and start to back away from the stall. All mothers love to speak of their children and I don't want to be stuck in a conversation about her newborn for too long.

Beryl stands with her hands on her hips. "I saw you shopping, are you looking for anything particular?"

"Just something for my brother—" I give her an embarrassed smile— "I know it's close to time, but I forgot with all the running around I do."

"Ah! For his Name Day gift, I take it. Listen here, once you have a baby it doesn't get any better. My memory is utter shit now. So, you have that to look forward to once you're old enough." She taps a meaty finger on her table. "Well, have a good look here. I just cleaned some new ones this morning. I'm excited to see what Metis has planned for your brother."

Beryl deals in jewelry and gems, but times have been tough on her business since my father's ship wrecked. Most of the stones are ones she found washed up on shore, polished sea glass, or when she and her life-mate dare the dangerous by scavenging nearby caves. Still though, her wares are often too expensive.

But Mana will hear of it if I'm not polite. So, I inspect them, knowing there isn't enough coin in my pocket to purchase anything.

She notices my hesitation with keen eyes and smiles. "You know what? I've been sleeping so well because of your mum, I'll give you anything from over here, it's on me." Beryl sweeps her hand over a dozen or so gemstones at the end of the table.

"Are you sure?" I ask surprised.

"Yes, yes!" She waves at me. "Consider it further repayment for your mum's help."

Examining the section of stones she gestured to, one immediately catches my eye, and I point to it. "Can I take this one?" It's the smallest out of the lot at least, so it shouldn't hurt her purse too much. I hope.

"Of course! I think he'll like it. I found that one on the beach just yesterday. You've a good eye as well."

I reach for the azurite; its edges are rough, and the color is a similar blue to my brother's eyes. I have to pinch it carefully between my forefinger and thumb so as not to drop it. When my skin makes contact though, a tickling sensation works its way up my arm and then toward my heart. *How odd.*

Ignoring the peculiarity, I slip the gemstone into my dress pocket and as the feeling fades, give Beryl a gracious smile. "Thank you so much, it's perfect."

Humming to myself, I take the final bite of a honey cake I purchased. Off to the side, I spy sandy hair and broad shoulders draped in ceremonial white. Gareth bends over in front of a stall, lifting a crate full of tools at the instruction of his father. Aquil's green eyes, lined with crow's feet, crinkle at the corners when I raise a hand in greeting.

Most days, the older man fishes with his wife, but sometimes he sets up shop in the market to fix worn down shoes and to sell his leather goods. I skip over to his stall and lift a torn boot from a nearby crate. "Business is good, I see."

"It is. Anything I can fix for my future daughter-in-law?" he asks. Aquil is like an older version of Gareth, his hair speckled with gray. He glances around and behind me for a moment before adding, "I don't see your brother with you, he must be preparing for tonight."

I realize I'm alone for once and that a rare opportunity has presented itself. I quickly weigh the cost if I'm caught by the Elders or my mother. The imagined confrontation fills me with anxiety, but another glance at Gareth makes my fears fall away. I give him a wink that his father doesn't see and place the boot back inside the crate with care. "He's very excited for it. Nothing I have needs repair, but can I borrow your son? Mana has a remedy she wants help with back home and asked that I fetch her talented apprentice."

Aquil raises a brow and glances up at the sky. "Really? At this hour?"

"Yes, it's for Galen. Mana and Gareth were working on it earlier together but didn't finish." The lie comes out casually, but my racing heart tells a different story. For a moment, I don't think he's going to believe me, but then Gareth interjects.

"Pa, it'll be fine. I can meet you and mother at the ceremony with Eimear's family."

Aquil strokes his stubbled beard. "Well, if Althaia needs you, I guess it's fine—"

"Thanks!" Gareth takes my hand, and before I know it, we're running through the market pretending not to hear his father call after us. We dodge the people who get in our way, their stares full of disapproval, but we're laughing and nearly out of breath by the time we reach the cobbled street of the village. The prying eyes of the bustling market are left far behind.

"Your mother needs help at dusk, aye?" he asks in between pants.

"What can I say? I had to get creative. Excuses to get you alone are hard to come by."

His answering grin is cocky. "Oh, is that all you wanted? I guess I better leave then."

Joking aside, my hand instinctively reaches for his wrist, stopping him. I want to say something clever, but Gareth's green eyes are alight. When I look into their depths, anxiousness spreads through my belly and any words I was about to muster go dry in my mouth. I'm frustrated by my inability to speak and as my gaze lowers, our clasped hands become a focal point. A taboo.

We really shouldn't be alone together. An image of the boring girl from the mirror comes to mind as if to mock me, and I come to a decision: I don't want to be her anymore. I pull Gareth into a gap between the two dwellings nearest us, out of view from any strolling passersby. Whatever happens is for none but the two of us to know.

The sky is a mix of dark orange and blue from the setting suns, and the alley is shaded from the roofs above. Stray weeds brush against my ankles as I rise to the tips of my toes and, softly, press my lips against Gareth's. His astonishment at my boldness is worth the chance of being caught. There's no hesitation from him when he kisses me in return, his fingertips gentle on my cheek.

I've always wondered what kissing would be like—I didn't expect the heat it would bring or realize that I've been starving without it. Hungry for more, my body prods me, and my tongue slips past the barrier of his lips. With his face so close to mine, I can smell the leather from his father's shop and an underlying earthy scent. My heart pounds beneath my rib cage as our connection deepens until I think it may burst. He breaks the kiss first and traces my lower lip with his thumb; the skin there still tingling from our embrace.

"I've pictured doing that hundreds of times," Gareth says. His voice has taken on a throaty tone.

The inside of my head is a jumbled mess, but I manage the words, "Me too."

Gareth takes a step back and coils an escaped strand of my hair around his finger. "You look pretty; I've never seen you wear your hair like this."

"You look pretty too," I blurt out unexpectedly and then immediately want to disappear into a dark hole where no one will ever find me again. What's *wrong* with me? We've been alone a million times before this. Not so much since we were paired together, but now of all times I say the most moronic things.

I try to save myself. "That's not what I—" but Gareth covers my mouth with his and backs me into the clay wall. My feet almost trip over the weed-bed, but my hands grab onto his arms to steady myself.

My verbal blunder is forgotten as my tongue explores the softness of Gareth's lips and the taste of honey behind them. I'm caught between a sense of awkwardness and wonder at how my body knows what to do. We're chest to chest now, and my hands lower to his hips. When he moans, it makes me feel powerful and encourages me to be bolder. My fingers slip under the fabric of his chiton and the muscles of his stomach contract at my touch.

Gareth's hands are shaking as they graze the fabric over my breasts and a wicked part of me wishes he would drop them lower. Obeying my body's demands, I grab his wrist impatiently and see confusion in his eyes as he mistakes my action as a sign to stop. Hiking up my skirt, I kiss his captured fingers and guide them to where I'm burning the most, taking pleasure when his breath hitches. He devours my mouth anew.

My thoughts become incoherent, and my thighs quiver as he explores the slickness between them. But the creak of tired hinges comes abruptly from my left, startling me. Gareth removes his hand and quickly pulls on the hem of my peplos to cover me.

"Don't stop on my account!" Otis, a man who is missing a few teeth, leans out of his window and leers at the two of us. His window shutter continues to creak as it sways with the breeze.

Before mortification has time to register, Gareth grasps my elbow while giving our peeper a rude gesture and leads me back out to the street. "Dirty bastard," he spits in Otis's direction, face thunderous.

I have to stifle a laugh with my hand. I'm riding a high I've never felt before, and the thrill of being caught has me ready for more. "It's all right," I tell him. "I've a better idea."

Gareth holds my hand the entire way to the ceremony grounds. Night has fallen and crescent Sister and Brother moons have emerged. The route is lined with burning lanterns that hang from lower tree branches, giving the forest a pleasant glow and lighting our way. I know that Mana is going to be furious with me for not returning home immediately. But as our footsteps blend with the sounds of crickets and croaking toads, thoughts of roving hands overpower common sense. I push the worry of my mother's anger aside.

We come into view of Metis and the rotunda. Her celestial form is illuminated by the surrounding lanterns, making her appear even more divine. I've felt a connection to the Goddess ever since she blessed me with a name that carries the same meaning as her totem. At the sight, foreboding pricks at my skin. I know what I'm doing isn't very wise, a slight to the Goddess as her namesake.

Maybe I should just go home? But Gareth places a trail of kisses down my neck, exchanging my unease with desire. Forgetting the Goddess, my family, and all the rest—I turn and press my lips against his, enjoying the weight of his body as we sink down into the indigo grass.

CHAPTER IX

5th Week of Summer

Nikko

The palace ballroom is overly decadent. Its high ceilings and cream walls, laced with patterns of gold, house the tallest windows in Ellanios. Originally structured to showcase the brightly lit night, they're draped in imperial purple. The floor is a mixture of pearl and gold etchings with a singular amethyst embedded in each tile. When my ancestors built the palace in reverence to Zeus, they lacked no expense but created a structure as gaudy as a madam in a siren house. It's a damn eyesore. My eyes scan the throng of nobles below, dressed in their regalia, and I can't say the lords and ladies fare any better. Their necks, arms, and fingers are adorned with every jewel from their treasure troves, it's a wonder they aren't embarrassed at their efforts to appear important.

Once a month, my father invites the nobles of Ellanios to wine and dine with us. Our allies are extended the same invitation, though the kings and queens may choose not to attend and will send an emissary in their stead. Brooding, I stare at the crowd as I lean against the balustrade atop the grand staircase, chalice in hand. This will probably be the last time for such pleasantries till we have this usurper business sorted. I tip its contents into my mouth, and the thick red wine coats the back of my throat.

I discreetly cough into my fist before setting the empty chalice on the tray of a passing servant. The woman smiles shyly as I take another and give her a wink in thanks. I watch her sashaying hips as she retreats, thinking about all the comments my crib-brothers would likely share about her wonderous backside if they were here. Ordinarily, I'd be with Jakab, Brontes, and Dareios, cutting up and scouting for whoever I'll take to bed at the end of the festivities. But on this eve, I'm alone.

I miss those bastards already; these halls feel cold without them. The collective voices and lyre from the skolia are entirely too loud for my liking, and the singers' droning on about the virtues of Zeus makes me want to shove nails into my eardrums. I'm not drunk enough for this madness. All around me, our guests dance and drink, their cheerful faces oblivious to the fact they're consuming the palace's last stores of alcohol. Avanta hasn't sent a shipment in months, as their vineyards are on Heracles' side of the trenches.

"To the Under with it," I say and down my drink before replacing it with another. I sway and glare at King Zephyr sitting on his throne, his face impassive, which means he's enjoying himself. A circlet of gold leaves rests on his braided hair and he wears an ankle length chiton of deepest purple. The Queen sits next to him, on his left. Of course, he isn't worried. Jada will solve all of Ellanios' problems for him.

Father's gray eyes are alert as he nods at something the wrinkled man on his right has said. King Narcyz of Apotmos has seen better days; his fair skin appears sallow. I take a deep drink. Mother was right; he's on his deathbed.

From my left, Jada appears and takes the chalice from me. "Yia mas," she says with a wink before she drinks all my wine.

"I wasn't going to drink that at all," I tell her.

My sister sighs with contentment and returns the emptied chalice to me. "You know, you have a reputation to uphold. Shouldn't you be on the prowl for one of the noblemen's treasured daughters or perhaps—" her eyebrows do a merry dance— "an adventurous son?" My twin sweeps her arm in a grand arc over the crowd. "I mean, just look at all the doe-eyed subjects below who are besotted with you, hoping for a chance to toss with a prince of Ellanios." Jada props her elbow on the railing and rests her chin on her fist. "But instead, you're standing here, scowling as if someone left a steaming shit in your bed."

I steal another chalice from a servant and their passing tray. I am in a mood from dodging mother's request to dance with Princess Andromyda all eve. I roll my eyes playfully. "How uncanny of you to concern yourself with my conquests."

The princess of Ellanios shrugs her shoulders. "At least one of us is getting fucked."

I nearly snort the wine I just sipped. "Gods! You are going to be the death of me." I don't want to think of my sister that way.

Her grin is mischievous as she pulls on my arm. "Enough with your dreariness. Let's go dance and show these foreigners how it's done, brother."

The dimple Jada inherited from the queen shows on her cheek, and I can't help but give in. She leads me down the stairs and onto the ballroom floor where, with a clap of her hands, the crowd parts for us. She nods to the musicians with a grin. They replace their lyres with reed pipes and tympanums, positioning their hands to play. The nobles' chatter begins anew but with a touch more excitement. I arch a brow at Jada as she positions herself across from me and calls for wine.

"The Dionysiac?" I ask, impressed. If I *had* to worship a god, Dionysus would be my pick of the deities. Out of their lot, he seems to be the one with the shortest stick up his arse.

She lowers her voice so only I can hear. "Might as well, if it's going to be our last eve of the god's great nectar for a time."

A servant approaches and hands us each an oversized gold pitcher filled to the brim. I mouth to my sister, *'Good choice.'* With another nod of her head, the musicians begin. They drum a steady beat on the tympanums and blow a buoyant tune on their reed pipes. The crowds on either side of us clap as I tip the pitcher into Jada's mouth. When it's my turn, she pours too much and I end up coughing, the red wine staining my indigo chiton in the process.

She giggles. "Oops."

I wipe my mouth and spit. "She-devil."

Jada simply winks at the insult and begins the dance. I mirror her movements. We glide to the rhythm of the tune, our right feet kicking out with each turn as we lift the pitchers high above our heads before bringing them to chest-level. Upon finishing the movement, we each fill a spectator's chalice, and they join us at the center of the crowd before sharing their own wine with another. When our pitchers are half empty, and the center is sprinkled with fellow dancers carrying their chalices of wine, both Jada and I place our pitchers atop our left shoulders. We each balance them with a left hand and carefully extend our right arms out in a graceful arc with every new turn.

My sister laughs and I glance in her direction, my eyes catching hers.

She yells, "See? You're happy now!"

I bellow back, "Only because I'm drunk!" By this point, I know Jada has to be feeling the effects of the wine as well.

After we fill the last chalice of a waiting guest, we tip our heads back and guzzle the remaining wine from our pitchers. The crowd around us cheers, and I yell out in triumph when I finish first. But as I wipe away the dribble of wine spilling from my mouth, the ballroom becomes uncomfortably hot, and everyone nearest to me spins even though my portion of the dance has finished.

Shit. The gold pitcher falls to my side, the world endlessly turning as my vision crosses. I stumble from the fray of dancers, leaving my sister behind before I fall like a jackass, right in front of the nobles. Blessed Lady Tyche, Goddess of Fortune, is with me because I manage to reach a nearby wall and lean on it in relief. Though I have to press a fist against my puckered mouth to keep the rising vomit at bay. "Styx, I'm gonna be ill for the rest of the night." Curse her for wanting to dance the drunken steps.

"You're a lively prince, aren't you?"

I squint, searching for the source of the voice when my gaze lowers, and I'm met by a small girl child swathed in powder-pink. "And you are?"

Her blue eyes turn icy, and she flips her coiled, blond hair over her shoulder. "You don't recognize the heir to Apotmos' throne?"

Fuck me, this is Princess Andromyda. "My apologies. It's been . . . a while since we last saw one another." Right now, searching for proper words in my wine-impaired brain is like a green boy's fingers fumbling for his first lover's sweet spot. "You were this big the last time, I think." I hiccup and gesture dumbly with my hands.

"I was most certainly bigger than that," she says hotly. She sticks up her nose. "I'll forgive it this once since you're out of sorts."

I wince as my mother's request demands attention, the Queen always gets what she wants. Better get this over with. "Would you . . . fancy a dance with me?"

"Even if you were the last living male in Ehvara, I would not. But thank you for the kind offer."

She's grown up to be a little bitch. "Well . . ." I say awkwardly into the space between us. I don't know how to respond to her with a finesse befitting her status. And a spot near my temple has just started to throb.

"Don't fear, prince. I'll tell Queen Himari you were a delight."

Surprised, my head whips back in her direction which makes the wine in my stomach inch ever upward. Sudden movements are bad. Very bad.

The princess raises her chin. "I know of her plans for a marriage arrangement between us." Her gaze goes to the crowd of dancers. "But know this, Prince of Ellanios. Anyone who dares to point their balls and cock toward me will have their appendages swiftly removed and shoved in their mouth like a stuffed pig."

I clench every muscle to keep myself from laughing. "You're quite bold—for a girl of ten years. Don't misunderstand, I had no intentions with you beyond a dance. I'm not ready to be married off myself."

Andromyda inspects her manicured nails as if bored but then leans closer to me and whispers, "I do not look it, but I'm twelve, actually."

I almost lose my composure and snort, but something about her calculated eyes warns me not to make jests. Instead, I say, "You have my deepest apologies again, my lady. How can I make it up to you?"

A slow smile spreads on her face. "In truth, I don't want to dance with you, but I do have a matter of discussion if you will listen."

I bow, ignoring the building discomfort in my belly. "My ear is all yours."

The princess' face turns somber. "I do not wish to marry. *Ever*."

Poor girl, you're royalty. No one will ever care for your desires. Even still, I pretend to consider her statement with great seriousness. "I see. That may be difficult to accomplish. Your father and your people will wish it on you."

"Soon father will be dead, and then it will not matter what he wants. I come to you because I will need allies when I take my throne as queen."

And here I thought Jada was a demon incarnate. I'm shocked by the girl-child's callousness toward her kin but hide it from my face. "Ellanios is already an ally of Apotmos. What worries you?"

"Throughout history, female rulers have not been welcome. My advisors will expect me to marry, and the surrounding countries will think me weak without a king. I'll need strong backing from Ellanios to make my claim as a sovereign queen legitimate."

I chuckle. "Child, you are only twelve. You may change your mind about marriage in the future."

Andromyda's voice is a low hiss. "Do not patronize me. I did not sell my soul so that I could be undermined by the likes of you."

I recall that her mother and siblings passed by a sudden plague. Wait. Does that mean she—

The small princess sees my understanding and eyes glittering like the brightest of gems, she silently mouths the word "poison."

This time, I cannot muster coherent speech, and I peer around to see if anyone heard her confession. However, the festivities are still in full swing and no one pays us any mind.

She continues, "I'll create the world and life I want. No one will change that or stand in my way. Unless they want to be crushed, that is."

I stare at the tiny fist she presents to me and sputter, "Why would you tell me any of this?"

Her shoulders relax as she leans against the wall. "Because I've heard you are a lover of women. You are different than most of your sex. You treat your sister as your equal. I had hoped you would see me the same."

Maybe she's misunderstood my activities for something else. I would laugh if I weren't so disturbed by her admission. However, my mind drifts back to the sparring ring this morning and Jada's suggestions for the future. Change is a difficult task to accomplish. At least this girl is trying. Albeit she may be evil at her core, eliminating her family to sit on a throne.

"I can sympathize with wanting to be in control of your future, but I don't condone your methods. I prioritize my family above all else."

With a pointed glare, Andromyda steps away from the wall. I know she's readying to flee, and I hold up a hand to stop her. "Despite your transgressions, when the time comes, you'll have my full support.

It's an unfair world we live in, and I'd like to see it changed for a brighter future for all."

The girl's lips curl upward into a predator's smile. A snake who has found a bird's nest full of eggs and the mother gone. It gives me a chill.

"You are full of surprises," she says. "I shall never forget your generosity, Prince. Should you ever need aid, send word. I will extend a helping hand." She dips in a low curtsy, her eyes mockingly innocent. "My thanks for the riveting conversation. I look forward to our friendship."

Princess Andromyda skips away to dance amongst the nobles' children of similar age who have gathered together. She blends in with the small ones, a jubilant child like any other. The surrounding guests are ignorant of the monster who graces their presence, just as I was mere moments ago. She waves at her father who beams at her and raises a hand in return. Queen Himari notices our interaction and nods in my direction.

I wink, confirming my success. If they only knew.

Gods & Beasts of Miracle

Heracles

Hero.

Lover.

Father.

Murderer.

I was born for misery.

Yes, I have the strength of a hundred men,

but what is the strength of a hundred,

when the divine are my enemy?

400 years it took to find Pride,

to convince Zeus of my love.

And now,

the gods will watch,

as I desecrate their worshipers,

and will them from existence.

If I am to be known by blood,

then let the sky rain crimson.

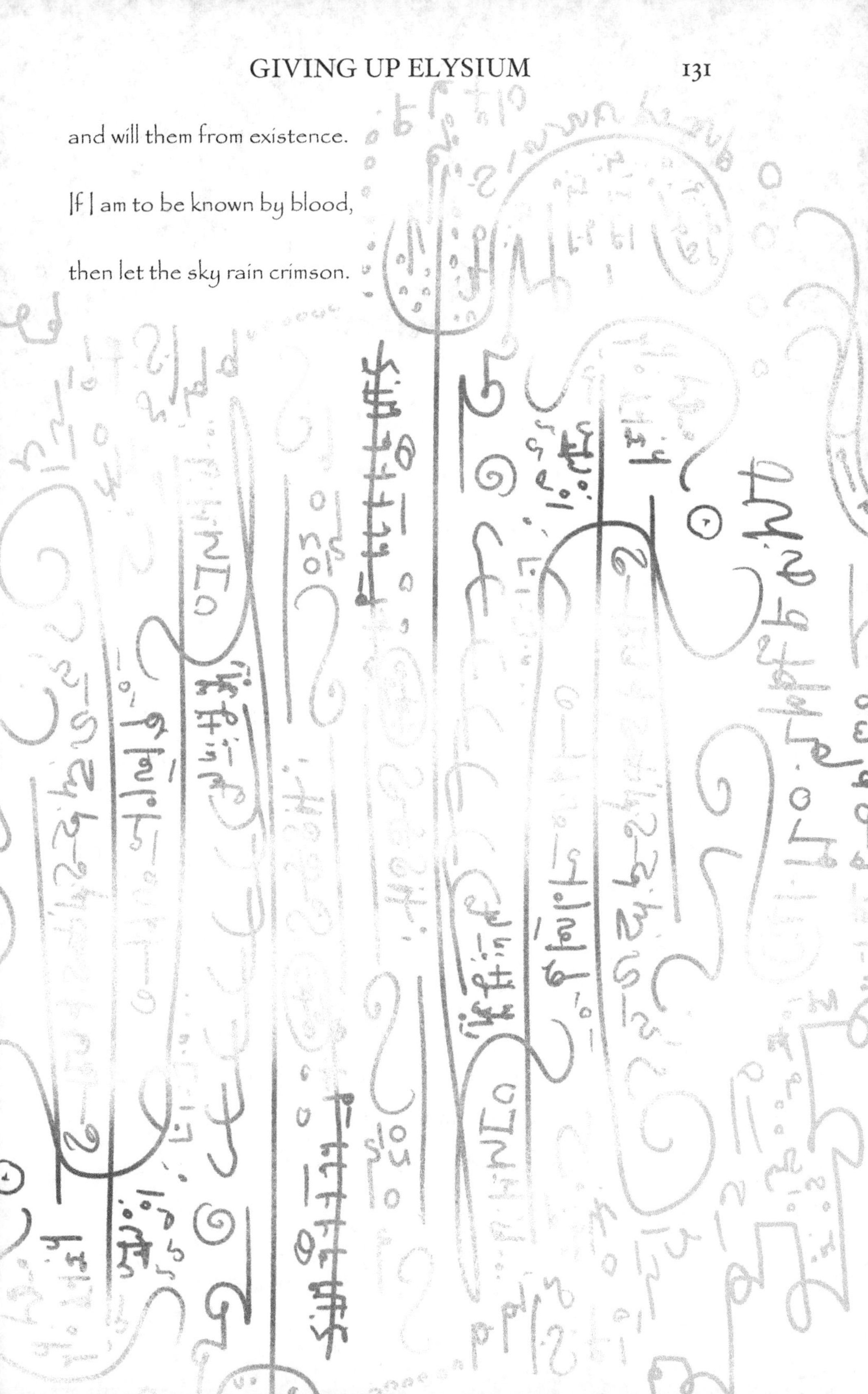

CHAPTER X

5th Week of Summer

Eimear

I'm nestled close to Gareth's side in a bed of grass, my fingers spin circles over the planes of his chest. He kisses my temple and says to me, "I am the luckiest man in all the worlds to be paired with you."

My fingers stop their dance, and I grin as my eyes find his. "And why is that?"

"Because—" he rolls until his body is positioned over mine "—you are the most wonderful person I've ever known."

I open my mouth to disagree, but something about the way his hair falls and how he looks at me as if our souls have known each other longer than this lifetime, makes me fall silent.

Gareth toys with a strand of my hair, "You are extraordinarily loving, and smart, and brave."

This time, I snort. "You had me until you said brave. We both know that's not true."

"Not many people can stitch a wound without losing their morning meal like you can."

He doesn't mention how my stitches are usually crooked, leaving terrible scars for my victims. Which is why Mana only lets me assist if she's in dire straits.

Gareth places his forehead against mine, "I wish you could see you the way I see you. Then you'd know what I'm talking about."

Tears prick at the corner of my eyes as deep emotions well up inside me.

Love.

Acceptance.

Everything I've craved and thought I'd been lacking—Gareth has made real. I kiss him gently, placing my hands on either side of his face. When I pull away, my heart makes the words tumble past my lips, "I love—"

Gareth tenses against me and interjects, "Do you smell smoke?"

My feelings of affection are quickly replaced with apprehension. I sniff the air and catch a hint of fire on the wind. "I think so."

We help each other up, and I notice a faint glow of orange spreading across the sky beyond the trees. It's coming from the village. Panic sets in. "Is that—is there a fire you think?"

"It is, but the bonfire for Buma shouldn't be lit yet."

"And it should be here. Not over there," I say slowly.

We share a look before taking off at a sprint, following the trail back toward the village. It doesn't take long before Gareth is farther and farther ahead of me. I try to make my legs go faster, but my breath comes in gasps, my lungs unable to keep up with the pace. He stops and waits when he notices me lagging behind.

When I reach him, wheezing and desperate for air, I set him straight. "Go! I'll catch up to you."

Gareth's eyes dart between me and the smoky sky, his indecision at leaving me apparent.

He shakes his head. "I can't. We don't know what's happening. It might be dangerous to separate, I need to know you're safe. We'll go together."

There's no time for this. I give him a kiss on the cheek and step away. "Whatever is happening, you'll be more useful than me. I'll be fine. Go." When Gareth remains motionless, I reach for his shoulders and turn him toward the village. "You have to. What if someone's injured?" I shove him forward.

Frustrated, he tousles the hair at the back of his head. "I'll meet up later with you then," he says reluctantly.

"I'll find you. Now go! We're wasting time."

I know Gareth wants to argue but he gives in to logic. My breathing still labored; I watch the blue grass kick up at his heels as he runs faster than before. Soon, he is out of sight, blending in with the woods and I curse, wishing I could keep up.

By the time I reach the village gate, I'm sweating profusely, a painful stitch jabbing at my side like a thorn. At the sight of the broken fence, my heart leaps to my throat, and I try hard to swallow back the rising bile.

Oh, goddess. No. No. No.

The bushels of flowers are no more and the dwellings are encased in flame. A roof tile falls to the ground with a heavy clatter. The pounding in my ears does nothing to drown out the blazing inferno nor the screaming villagers. I cough, choking on thick air. The salty smell of the Amenian Sea has been replaced by a cloying scent of smoke and burning debris. My eyes unsure of where to linger, search frantically and find Hydria, the potter, lying spread-eagled in the street, encased in a puddle of her own blood. My limbs become paralyzed, I can't look away from the clothesline wound tightly around her neck, or the axe that protrudes from her chest.

I ignored her earlier . . . that was the last time I'll ever— A nearby scream rouses me from my guilt. I know I can't just stand here, I have to do something. My legs shake, taking uncertain steps forward, following the shrieks from the marketplace.

Did Gareth go to the agora? Where is he? Before I can pass the gate, an unfamiliar man appears from between two burning homes. He's dressed in clothes I've never seen the like of, black leather stitched into a tunic, and trousers decorated with an assortment of knives and . . . *bones*. Skeleton fingers as well as an old jawbone hang on a long necklace like a badge of honor. Other remains and dark feathers are weaved throughout his long hair. This strange way of dress is terrifying, but truly, it's his half-mask fashioned into the face of a vulture that makes fear swell inside me. The blood-red wrinkled flesh has eye slits that are rimmed black, and a long, bone-white beak covers the warrior's nose.

Amidst the crackling flames, the giant drags a longsword behind him; the blade scrapes the cobbled stones with each predatory step. He lifts his weapon and darts to the opposite side of the street, disappearing into an alleyway where a brief cry is cut silent.

Gods! Oh gods!

Petrified, I dart off the path and cower behind a tree in the forest, my hands tremble as they cup my gaping mouth. A high-pitched noise whines in my ears, silencing the cacophony from the village. What's happening? I ask myself the same question over and over. I lose track of how long I stay this way, my mind refusing to understand the burning scene behind me or the horror wearing a vulture's mask.

Garbled voices approach, and new terror takes hold of my muscles, straining them with tension. The intruders speak in a foreign tongue, their syllables ending with a hiss, reminding me of snakes. I know I've heard it before, but my fear overrides any semblance of understanding.

What if they find me? Hydria's broken form comes to mind, and I hold my breath to keep from hyperventilating. It feels like an eternity before the men pass far enough away for their slithering language to recede into the night.

Rising slowly from my hiding place, I take hushed steps away from the village and deeper into the woods toward home. Anxious thoughts regarding Mana and Buma fill my mind. I need to know they're all right. When I'm at a safe enough distance from the bedlam, I take the trail at a sprint, my prayers frantic: Please, Metis! Let everyone be safe! It seems like seconds until I'm at the tree-line near the bottom of the ridge that faces the pride and joy my Papa built.

I stare open mouthed, my heart slowly breaking. The home where I took my first steps is ablaze. Flames burst out from broken windows, the welcoming doors to my safe haven knocked down as if someone kicked them in.

What if Mana and Buma are in there? What if they're burning? I scream for the two, until my throat is raw, hoping they're not inside. When neither appears, I become desperate and head toward the smashed doors.

The air near my home is unbearably hot and black smoke billows from the damaged openings, making me cough. I call out to Mana, my lungs struggling. Heavy moments pass, and I almost convince myself that my family has gone elsewhere when a faint cry comes from within. I gape at the burning doorframe, my fear making me hesitate.

Should I find Gareth first for help? The masked giant with the sword and an image of my life-mate's gutted body invades my mind. No, No. He's safe. He has to be. A loud crash from within forces me to focus. There's no time, I have to go in by myself.

The flames bite at my skin as I pass the threshold. My father's hand carved table is overturned, the chairs splintered. Torn cushions, fragments of glass, and broken pottery litter the floor. My chest hitches with grief at the sight of Papa's singed maps and ripped book pages behind the vestiges of Mana's rocking chair.

However, as I evade scattered glass, droplets of blood on the ground grab my attention. One of them must be hurt. I double check, but neither my brother nor Mana are on the first floor. Newfound urgency seizes me, and I move quickly toward the stairs. My eyes water from the heat and smoke, blinding me to a stray shard that goes through my sandal, embedding itself into my foot. I suck in from the pain and inhale more black air.

Dizzy, I pause to steady myself. At this rate, I'll suffocate before I find anyone. Searching frantically, I stumble to Mana's work table and grab a cloth amongst the uprooted plants before submerging it in a bucket of water. I bring the wet fabric to my mouth and nose—I should be able to buy my lungs more time with this.

Parts of the staircase are on fire, but I ignore the fear telling my feet to stop as I make my way up. The intense heat scorches, and I release a pain-filled moan into the damp cloth clutched tightly in my hands. Skipping the last step with a jump, I notice the doorway at the end of the hall belonging to Mana's room is a wall of flame and my stomach drops to the floor. Goddess, please don't let her be in there! The flames climb higher, and I'm unable to move, standing dumbly at the edge of the stairs—fear has finally caught up and won't let me go.

What am I supposed to do? I'm so tired . . .

"Mana! Eimear! It's hot, help me!" Buma's wails snap my drooping eyes open just as my body pitches forward. More alert, I right myself and proceed to Buma's bedroom. I discover it's untouched by fire, but empty. Styx. Where is he?

"Help! Someone! Help me!"

My room! Racing to my bedroom, I find that fire has claimed one side of the small space. I start to panic but then realize Buma's shouts come from within the wardrobe at the opposite corner. I wrench the doors open and find him curled into a ball, wrapped in my fallen clothing.

"Eimear!" he cries, reaching for me with his small hand, his face red and blotchy from heat and tears.

I meet his outstretched fingers and pull him close to me. "It's all right, you've been found. I found you." In truth, though, I'm not sure if the comforting words are for him or myself.

Buma hiccups and says, "They broke in, and Mana told me to hide, but she never came back!"

I falter, the hair-raising sound of a sword dragged against the bloody street makes me think the worst. No, no, I tell myself. She just went to get help, that's all. I ignore the fact that my mother never returned for her only son. I grab the woven blanket from my bed, moments away from being eaten by flame. We need to leave now.

I drape the cover over his shoulders before handing him the wet cloth I'd been using for myself. "Keep this against your mouth and climb onto my back." My brother glances worriedly at the growing flame behind me but does as I ask.

He isn't heavy, but my legs shake from the adrenaline high, my limbs protesting his added weight. Still, I try to keep low to the ground to avoid the thickened smoke. My lips form into a snarl, bearing the pain—*don't give up.*

We return to the hall, and my brother whimpers when he sees the stairs engulfed in flame. I do my best not to show my own despair. Readjusting his weight on my back, I warn him, "Hold on tight and keep your head buried," before pulling the blanket to cover both of us as much as possible.

Goddess, please be with us! I pray and run blindly through the flames. Pain envelops my legs and air doesn't reach my lungs. It's only by Metis' miracle that my body doesn't give out before reaching the ground floor and making it through the broken door frame to open air. I collapse in a coughing fit onto the grass and Buma rolls off me quickly, discarding the cover that is now on fire. He stands with haste and stomps on the fabric, putting out the small flame.

My mind reels as our family home burns steadily in the background, years of fond memories dying with it. Processing what Buma and I just survived is difficult. My hands shake as I examine the burns on my legs. There may be some scarring, but nothing too serious. Gareth can heal—my train of thought halts abruptly, interrupted by a brutal image. I push him from my mind, not wanting to consider the possibility that my life-mate may be gone.

Instead, I check on Buma who is brushing soot from his clothes—he's frightened but appears whole and well. My own dress, once white, is now completely covered in black, the hem destroyed. "Do you know where Mana is?" My voice is hoarse, weariness settling into my bones.

His eyes are big and full of tears. "No, we were waiting for you to come home, but then Mana saw someone strange coming from the woods. She told me to go upstairs and to not come down no matter what." He looks down at his sandals and wails, "I heard her scream, but I don't know what happened or where she is!"

Guilt rises from the pit of my stomach. If I hadn't run off with Gareth, I would've been here to help. I swallow hard and try to think of what to do. Mana always kept extra supplies out back in the storehouse, and there's only one place where anyone in the village would gather if they survived—the ceremony grounds.

"Stay right here while I get some things."

My brother appears horrified at the idea of being left alone; what little color he has, completely drains from his face. "But what if they come back?"

"I'm just going to the storehouse. I don't know if someone dangerous is hiding there. If I scream, you run. Understand?"

His bottom lip quivers, but he nods. I stand up with a grimace and grab the blanket. It's charred black but still sufficient for carrying supplies.

I give my burning home a wide berth as I make my way to the backyard. Each step sends pain up my right leg, and I begin to limp. Now that the adrenaline has left my body, I feel the glass in my foot, which continues to cut while I walk. This won't do. I stop for a moment and brace myself against a tree.

The shard is planted firmly into my sandal, I can't remove it from the bottom. I grit my teeth and my fingers hold tight onto the tree's trunk, bark sliding beneath my nails. With a deep inhale, I pull the sandal from my foot in one quick motion.

Styx! I bite down on my lip as the glass slides out of my skin. Blood seeps from the wound and I continue cursing because the shard can't be removed from my sandal without slicing my fingers. I make the decision to toss my shoes and hope the forest floor will be kind to my feet.

Okay now, supplies, and then we'll find Mana and Gareth. I attempt to rally myself and slap my cheeks to chase away the fatigue. Breathing out, I continue my journey. When the yard behind the house comes into full view, my world tilts until it falls, shifting to become a new reality. My insides give a violent twist, my heart tears. A scream builds deep from my belly, working its way up through my sternum, and into my open jaw.

"MANAAAA!" I shove my fist inside my mouth to keep the shrieks muffled. In front of me, my mother's broken body is illuminated by our burning home. The red trees are a backdrop to her ruined flesh. She lays over a fallen log, her white ceremony gown now crimson and in disarray. Her chestnut hair that once shone, is darkened by a wound at her temple—the unbound tresses swept to the side reveal Mana's cold upturned face and vacant eyes.

"Mmmmhhhhhhmmm." My teeth press down harder against my hand, piercing the skin. Tears come fast like a broken dam. Unable to look away from her cut throat and the blood spilled on the ground, I crawl into myself where memories descend in a rush.

Mana laughing when she danced with my brother by the fireplace one winter, her smile dazzling and warm. Mana's honeyed voice as she sang while grinding herbs at the table. The way her patients would perk up when she walked through their doors. Her body comforting as she held my brother and me close on sleepless nights. Mana's gentle hands braiding my hair. Her arms strong as she held me close as we cried together at the news of Papa's passing. The person who once told me she hurt when I did, who shared all my pain. A glittering light in my life snuffed out and gone.

"MANAAAA," escapes from my spasming throat. The sight of her lifelessness sends a wave of nausea through me, and I throw up. Small rocks dig into my knees, but I hover frozen over my mess. This isn't real, I'm not here. It's not happening to me, it's not happening—

"Eimear, are you all right?" Buma's not-so-far-away voice brings me back.

He can't see her like this. "Everything's fine—" I manage to croak out. "Stay where you are." Rising slowly from the ground, numbness spreads through me like a disease as I continue to stare at

Mana. There's vomit on the edge of my lip, and I wipe it off against my dirty shoulder before picking up the charred blanket. My steps are heavy and sluggish as I make my way toward my mother. Small cuts on her arms and legs, where the assailant must have attacked her, become more apparent when I draw closer. Bile rises at the back of my throat.

With tender hands, I tug on Mana's arm, but her weight is too much for me. I only succeed in rolling her off the log and onto her back. My fingers feel separate from my body as I fix her dress and close her eyelids. One question runs endlessly through my mind: *Why?*

I caress Mana's hair and whisper, "Thank you for loving me the way you did. Thank you for raising me and being strong when I couldn't be. I'll mourn your absence for all of my days, until the gods themselves close my eyes." I place my lips against Mana's forehead before laying the blanket over her.

Buma's unnerved voice calls for me yet again. "Eimear! You're taking too long!"

Not wanting to leave, I gaze at my mother's covered figure a moment longer. Her pyre will come later. I need to get him to safety first. I stand, every fiber of me trembling. I place my right hand over my heart and give thanks for the life she blessed me with. "May you find peace in Elysium, Mana." My voice is barely a whisper on the smoky wind. Behind me, the flames cackle with a snap.

CHAPTER XI

5th Week of Summer

Eimear

Buma eyes my empty hands. "Where are the supplies?"

"Gone," I say gruffly.

"Oh. What about Mana? Where do you think she is?"

My body freezes. "I don't know." I force the lie out through gritted teeth before walking past him and into the woods. It's dark out, but the fire from the village lights up the night sky, giving some visibility.

Buma follows behind. "Where are we going? What happened?" He murmurs to my back.

I'm taking him to the ceremony grounds where it should be safest, but I don't answer him. My movements are mindless, one foot in front of the other. The underbrush cuts my bare skin, but I don't care or react. I lose track of how long we travel through the woods. I can only think of Mana's broken body, I can't unsee it. Only when I feel faint do I stop and reach out to steady myself on the nearest tree.

My brother tugs on my dress. "Eimear, are you sick?"

I plaster an imitation of a smile on my face before turning to him. "I'm fine, let's keep going." I can't tell him about Mana just yet. Safety is the priority. I put more effort into my footing and walk as quietly as possible. Screams still echo across the woods from the direction of the village, making my stomach churn. Buma hears them too and puts his hands over his ears. After a while, he sinks to the ground, tears falling from his ashen cheeks.

"We have to keep going," I say and try to pull him up.

He resists me. "No! It's scary! Let's wait for Mana to find us."

Mana . . . She would know what to do now. I want to curl into a ball and cry on the forest floor. Instead, I look at my brother who is falling to pieces. He's only seven, I need to be strong for him like Mana was for me. I take a deep breath and let the air out slowly, attempting to regain a sense of calm. My arms hang loose at my sides when my hand grazes the pocket of my dress. The stone!

My fingers dig and pull out the gem Beryl gave me. I'm surprised it didn't fall out. A whisper stirs in my ears when I close my fist around the stone, but I can't make out the words. Rubbing my eye with my free palm, I try to wipe away the exhaustion. I must be hearing things.

I kneel beside Buma. "I have something for you," I say as brightly as I can muster. He looks at me with watery eyes, but his interest is piqued. "I got this special just for you, and I know it's dark out, but it's the color of your eyes. Wait, no—it's the color of Mana's eyes." I choke out the last words but open my fist to show him the azurite gemstone.

My brother squints, but makes a decision nonetheless. "It *is* the same color," he whispers in the dark.

"Keep this with you, it has special powers to make you strong." He stares at me dubiously and opens his mouth to argue, but heat radiates where the stone touches my skin, and I know exactly what to say next to calm him. "It's true. How else would I have been able to get us out of all that fire unscathed? It's because the stone is magic."

His eyes go wide as he scrutinizes the gem in my palm. "Are you sure I can have it?"

My fingers smooth down his wild hair before dropping the stone into his shirt pocket. "Keep it safe for me okay? Don't you feel stronger already?"

Buma's expression turns serious, and he nods his head. "I do."

"Good. Let's keep going then," I say and help him to his feet.

Deeper into the wood, the screams from the village become faint, and by the time we get to the ceremony site, they can't be heard at all. I take one brief moment to feel anguish for my fellow islanders, then steel my mind. Survival is everything, the only thing that matters right now.

But my dreams of rescue vanish when I survey the grounds. They're empty, no one else is here.

I clamp my teeth together as I breathe. Our sacred place has been desecrated. The grass is scorched, remnants of the fire still glowing, and our Goddess has been beheaded under the pavilion.

"Why would they do that to her?" My brother stammers and rubs the top of his cheek drowsily. "Do you think Mana came here? Where do you think she—"

"I don't know," I snap, silencing him to avoid further questions and the sorrow their answers would bring. When I start toward the grounds in hopes of making the Goddess whole again, Buma follows behind, his pace at a shuffle.

Metis' head is face down behind her monument. I gawk at the fractured shrine. I'm filled with anger and resentment; the storm within me reaches its thunderous apex. You did nothing! You didn't protect Mana or the village!

I scream and shove the head with my heel, tilting Metis' face so that she watches me with one eye. "I hate you," I hiss and spit upon her. The saliva trails slowly down her cracked face. Unnerved by the sight, I turn my back on the Goddess.

Buma has taken a seat on the blackened earth, legs drawn into himself, his expression blank. Worry quickly douses my anger. I step forward to offer him comfort, but as my foot makes contact with the sacred earth, I'm hit with a wave of apprehension—a sense of dread and an urgency to act, so powerful, that I'm overwhelmed and fall to my knees.

What's this feeling? My brother yells for me, but his voice becomes an echo, moving farther away. Anxiety presses heavy on my person before everything around me goes black.

Did I die? I'm disoriented and blink in confusion. It's so dark here, or . . . is it? I see my hands in front of me as if I were in daylight. I slowly observe my surroundings—or lack of them— and find that I've been transported to a black void that has no end. What is this place?

I attempt to take a step, but my equilibrium is thrown off and I fall forward. I throw my hands out to catch myself, though there is nothing below to hold onto—only darkness. Even so, my palms slap against the solid black and my heart hitches, mouth going dry as terror builds within me. I hear nothing, not even my own breathing. The horrific scent of smoke that hounded me all night is gone. The emptiness of it all has my mind racing. Gods, where am I?

I close my eyes and count to thirty in hopes that I'm hallucinating. Yet, when my lashes flutter open, the black void is still very present. What the Under? I try to move, but my mind doesn't send the command to my leg. Fear has its hold on me.

"Buma? Are you there?" I call out to the void.

Silence. My stomach sinks to my toes, my brother is nowhere to be found. He's all I have left. What if something happened to him? What if he dies like Mana?

Flashes of her corpse push me over the edge. "No, No, No," I plead to the black, pulling at my disheveled braid. The tears I've been holding finally come, and I sob until my throat goes raw. I'm lost to the pain of it all, and only when I have the sensation of someone watching me, do I turn from my despair. I search my left and right but there's nothing.

Suddenly, I'm surrounded by light, the warmth floods my back, like an afternoon sun. It sends a calming sensation throughout my body. Curious, I look up to find that a Gods' Window has appeared against the black. For the first time, the iridescent barrier is fully open. But instead of Mount Ida on the other side, Metis' colossal eye fixes me with an unearthly stare. My fear dissolves in her presence, and I stand transfixed in awe. How beautiful.

The Goddess' iris is rimmed with bright gold and when I reach for her, she begins to cry. Her golden tears fall from the heavens and drench me in a salty flood. There's pressure on the front-most part of my brain and then a tingling sensation. A girlish voice invades my mind.

//Can you hear us now?//

//Who's this?// I ask. The voice sounds drowsy, like she just woke from a deep sleep. In contrast, the very cells of my skin are invigorated as if they're bursting with new life—I take a step back, the sensation overwhelming.

//*Metis Gifted you with her essence, which has woken us briefly.*// The girl yawns. //*We can't stay awake long, being as we are now. When it's time, trust our intuition.*//

I'm spellbound by this voice inside my head, but then a gut feeling registers and my throat tightens. Something terrible is about to pass. But what?

I stare at the Goddess' golden iris in wonder, not comprehending why she would grant me such knowledge. I open my mouth to speak, but Metis blinks and the solidness below my feet disappears. Unfazed, I find myself falling backward into the abyss. My stomach moves to my chest and my hair whips around me. Even so, I'm transfixed by the Goddess' bright gaze as I descend.

She blinks again, and phantom images fly past. Some are vivid, others too fast to see. I know they are events in my life that haven't happened yet and may never. An aroma of cloves permeates my nostrils, and the flash of a gold hoop catches my eye. I want to grab hold of it, but I can't stop falling. The scent of cloves dissipates, and a handsome face, seemingly carved from midnight, emerges.

"Nikko?" The name springs from my lips and I'm certain it belongs to the handsome face, even though we've never met. I blink and his face is replaced by flames that caress a familiar tree line, the stars long devoured by a golden blaze. My feelings of wonder are replaced with horror as I watch myself in the ghostly mirage.

It's as if the smoke is already burning my lungs when I inhale too quickly. My nails split as my fingers dig at the pebbled ground, shredding blades of indigo grass. Fresh sweat drips onto my face. "Goddess, please no! I don't want to see it!" I scream. Pressure builds on my spine. "Metis stop! Don't make me feel it anymore!" In the mirage, my brother cries alone in the dark. Images of sorrow, of agony, take their hold. Phantom fingers claw and claim. I know the drama playing out before me will occur within the next few hours if I allow it.

But what if I choose differently?

The scene changes, and this time my brother screams for mercy. The light leaves his eyes as a dirty hand slits his throat with a dagger of carved bone. His blood cools the burnt grass, while my phantom self cowers in hiding—guilty, but unscathed. I'm disgusted by the sight, angry tears flow as I remember Mana rocking a newborn Buma in her arms. "Damn you, Metis, for being cruel! I regret all the years I've spent loving you," I hiss to the golden eye above me.

Fraught with despair, I search for something to anchor myself. As if summoned, a gold thread appears within reach, and I grab hold. Everything slows until I'm left suspended in the black abyss. The thread in my clenched fist pulses, matching the rhythm of my heartbeat. I realize I'm connected to it somehow. But how and why? My thread of life begins to slow as does my heart and I'm convinced I'll die soon if I stay much longer in this eerie place.

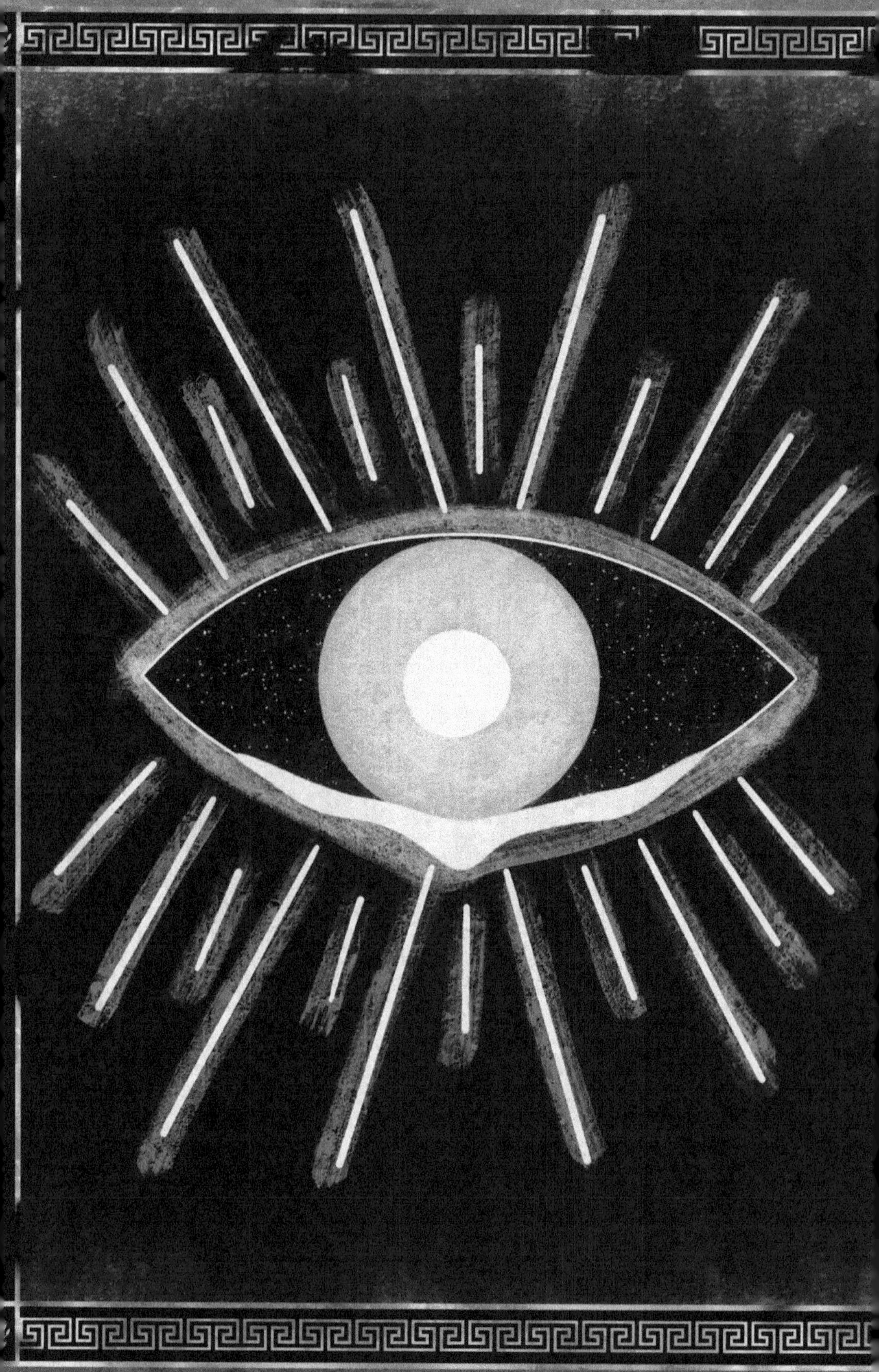

"Make your choice, little daughter," the voice of a thousand chimes rings out.

The golden thread in my hand dims, its pulse slowing to a dull thump. The girl inside me knows my choice before I can form the words to tell Metis.

//*We have a long trek ahead of us,*// she says. Her voice is a whisper without sound.

Metis understands my decision and invades my senses, she's everything within me. I feel myself being torn apart from the inside when she speaks.

"Little daughter, know I regret all the pain you will endure on your journey."

Fury runs rampant inside my heart. "You deceitful witch! I want nothing more than your destruction for letting everything on this night come to pass."

"There is much you do not understand, and you may seek my demise later if you wish it. But for now, good luck my champion." Metis' eye pierces me with a sorrowful gaze before blinking, and I'm thrown from the void.

I gasp as air fills my lungs, and the panicked shouts of a terrified child call my name. Small fists pound at my right shoulder. It's as if I'm waking from a trance. I glance to the side and see my brother's tear-streaked face.

"You were here but you weren't here!" he yells at me.

The fluttering sensation in my belly returns, and when the voice inside me speaks, it offers knowledge only a priestess should have. Looking past my brother at the base of the Goddess' statue, determination settles into my bones. I grab Buma by the wrist and drag him toward Metis' figure.

"You're scaring me!" he cries.

I ignore his pleas and use my knee to press the bottom of the marble mount. A spring underneath clicks and gives way, and the trap door swings open. Inside, there's a hole large enough to fit a child and nothing more. Whatever did Chrysanthe use this for? I shake my head. It doesn't matter, not anymore.

Drawing Buma closer to the door, I kneel down in front of him and place my hand on his chest. My brother's heart thumps like a freshly caught hare, and the voice takes over. We speak in unison:

//Son of Rhone and Althaia.//

"Son of Rhone and Althaia."

//By the power of the Goddess Metis,//

"By the power of the Goddess Metis,"

//We name you Zadok.//

"We name you Zadok."

//Your namesake is Justice.//

"Your namesake is Justice."

Zadok stares at me in confusion before I shove him inside.

He screams and presses himself farther into the hole. "Eimear! Your eyes . . . they've turned gold."

I raise a finger to my lips. "You've been named for justice, do what you can to live up to it." Zadok opens his mouth, but I stop him from talking. "We don't have much time. I'm about to be taken far away." He starts to cry but I shush him and stroke his hair gently before resuming my warning. "Whatever you hear, whatever happens, you mustn't make a sound, or you'll die. Do you understand this?"

Zadok silently mouths the word, "Yes." Fresh tears stain his cheeks as he stares at me.

"Stay hidden. Don't come out for two whole days."

"But why—"

"Just do as I say!"

He whimpers, but this is not the time for coddling. Those days are over now.

"Many years will pass, but I'll find you, and we'll see each other again. I promise."

"Years! What do you—?"

I put my hand over his mouth to quiet him and then sense something else—the azurite lying in wait, inside his pocket. My eyes narrow as I discover its seductive pull. Tricky thing. It'll keep him alive at the least. "Use that stone wisely. Don't let it use you," I tell him.

Zadok's eyes widen in surprise, and my chin jerks upward at the sound of bawdy voices. They're here. I'm out of time. Sudden exhaustion hits me in a colossal swell, all remaining energy within me is depleted. This must be what Mana would define as the Return.

On the verge of collapsing, something wet dribbles from my nose and touches my lips, tasting metallic. I quickly wipe the blood away, smearing it across my face, and gaze at my brother one last time. He wears an expression of horror, his mouth quivering.

"I love you so much," I tell him, and gently close the door, leaving it slightly ajar for air. As long as he stays inside, he'll be safe. My lungs are on fire, and I use my last reserves of energy to crawl in front of Metis' statue and prop myself up—I can't make it any farther to hide.

//Eimear . . .// The voice calls faintly. *//You won't hear us for some time, but know that we're together, through all of it. Trust what you feel—//*

I don't hear her anymore, the shell of my body unable to contain the girl any longer.

Two men emerge from the woods adorned in bones and leather. Like Hydria's killer, they wear vulture masks. Their strides are confident, and their clothes are stained with the blood of my people. The one whose teeth have been sharpened to points, gives a low whistle. "Well, what do we have here?" He looks to his companion, "Armon, I was right to check this location. I knew prey would come."

I'm weighed down by exhaustion, but not fear. This time, I understand their snaking tongue well enough. They must hail from Manthros.

Armon speaks to me directly, there's a star-like birthmark on his bobbing chin. "You aren't here all by yourself, are you?" His ice blue eyes behind the red mask are hateful.

I do my best to stare straight ahead and pretend not to understand. I don't want to give Zadok's location away.

The one with the sharpened teeth whistles again. "Well, I think she could use some company." The warrior gives me a wink as he draws closer. "You're quite a beauty underneath all that soot."

I flinch as he wipes ash from my face with a calloused finger.

Armon glances uncertainly at the man, "I don't know if we should, Jud. The captain will be out of sorts if we damage the goods."

His companion licks his lips. "Nothing wrong with a little taste now is there?"

Pig. I hate the gleam in his eye, but I'm so weak that I can't raise my arms to strike him. I spit on him instead, the saliva lands on his beak.

Jud swings back his hand and cracks me across the face hard enough that my head hits the ground. I don't make a sound as he reaches for my dress with his thick hands and raises it above my thighs. Instead of watching him, I stare at the soft patch of grass where Gareth and I laid together mere hours before. Through it all, the sculpted head of Metis watches me with her uncovered eye.

The wrongness of it lodges a seed of unrelenting hate deep inside my heart, tainting me. I cannot forgive the death of my mother nor the brutality I endure. A piece of my soul breaks off—a fragment I'll never reclaim, my light forever dimmed.

On this eve, I'm fashioned into delicate glass, with a thousand fissures set to shatter. But if I could go back in time, I would choose the same.

Part II

Discovering Darkness

"If death is what you want, then you

should pray louder to Hades."

—Steilos

CHAPTER XII

5th Week of Summer

Eimear

Little things register first. Birdsong, the wind rustling trees, shaking their leaves. I've been in and out of consciousness through the long hours and have a sense of vertigo. I open my eyes. Mana's braids have shaken loose, the ribbons torn, creating an entangled curtain that spills past my downturned face. Rocks skitter in the wake of black boots and I realize I'm slung over my captor's shoulder like a sack of grain. My lips twist into a snarl. Beast.

Dawn has broken across the sky; the morning rays highlight wet dew on the grass, but it's still night for me—the scented memory of sweat and smoke sticks to my nostrils. Time is suspended as I relive the violation of my body and soul. I wish I were dead. I imagine my captor's bone blade sliding across my throat, the lethal blessing putting me out of my misery. Despite the morbid fantasy, my pulse jumps under the skin of my neck, reminding me that I've a whole lifetime to suffer.

Jud's heavy-footed steps jostle my injured body, sending sparks of pain throughout my pelvis. I clamp down on a rising whimper. Meanwhile, Armon whistles a jubilant tune as he strolls ahead of us. They're both bastards. My mind conjures the worst for them, and I desperately hope it comes true. They shouldn't be allowed to live after what they've done. But they aren't the only ones to blame. Metis shares the same blood on her hands. She abandoned me…abandoned everyone.

My only consolation is that we've put enough distance between us and the ceremony grounds. Zadok should be safe enough. I would cry for him, but I've no more tears left. For a moment, I let myself make believe I'm the girl I was when waking yesterday. That the past day never happened, and I'm breaking fast with Mana and Zadok at our table. She laughed and smiled so much then, celebrating the fact that her son was to finally be named. Now Zadok will remain forever nameless to both his parents. The thought fills me with rage. I bite my tongue to keep from screaming, resulting in a garbled sound that makes my captor pause. He slaps my backside, *hard*, and gives my body a shake.

"Shut it!" he growls before resuming his stride.

I go quiet and try to envision Metis' golden eye. The divine meeting is like a dream now. The harder I try to remember specifics, the more the memory eludes me. My jaw clenches as I try to speak to the girl inside me: //Rid me of these two barbarians!//

Silence is her response. Defeated, my head sways with the cadence of Jud's steps.

When I'm brought to the market, it's unrecognizable—my village utterly destroyed. Low flames smolder what remains of the buildings and the homes beyond. What once smelled of sea breeze and flowers has been replaced by burning flesh and smoke. The blood-slick streets are littered with the bodies of my slaughtered people. Stalls have been overturned atop the dead, leaving splintered fragments in their bruised flesh. The shock of it all steals the breath from my already aching chest. How did I ever think any of them a bother? A new panic grips me. What if Gareth is here? I search for his body amidst the familiar forms but don't find my life-mate.

What if he went home?

Did they hurt him there?

What of his family?

Are any of them alive?

The prospect of Gareth's green eyes turned to glass isn't something my fragile mind can handle right now. He has to be alive. Any other answer would be unacceptable. Though the thought of seeing him whole and well again is equally terrifying. What would he think of me now? I wear a coat of shame tight against my skin, the clinging grime stuck forever. I'll never be able to look at him without feeling it. I was supposed to be his. Metis blessed it. So why?

Jud's boot collides with a demolished stall. He catches himself, but my vision is forced sideways by the momentum and I see Beryl's face amongst the rubble—her mouth gapes wide. Mismatched gems have been shoved into her bleeding eye sockets, the stones glitter in the sun.

Something in me breaks.

A guttural scream that contains the loss of my mother, the village, and my innocence, rips from my throat—at the same instant, I wrap my thin arms around Jud's neck and sink my teeth into the skin just below his right ear. I thrash him with wild kicks.

"I'll kill you! I kill you both!" The threat is muffled in his bloody collar, and I taste sweaty, broken flesh between manic bites.

My captor swipes at my head with his fist in an attempt to fight me off. "ARRGGGH! You little bitch!"

Armon laughs, making me bite down harder in my rage.

"Fuck!" Jud barks and grabs a fist full of my hair.

He pries me from his body and throws me to the ground. I land in a rolling heap, the impact bone jarring. But the fire in me isn't done burning. I rise up on my hands and knees to face Jud, and spit his bloody flesh from my mouth. "You taste like shit," I hiss in my mother tongue.

Jud's mask has slipped upward, revealing a fat nose riddled with busted veins. He readjusts it, pressing a hand to the wound at his neck, and takes three menacing steps towards me. "Dumb cunt, that's gonna cost you."

Armon places himself between the two of us while pulling a rope from the satchel belted at his side. "We don't have time for this shit. We've played around enough. You can't beat a dog and expect it not to bite. I warned you. We should've trussed her up from the get-go. Now stop swinging your small dick around. We have to get back to the ship."

Ship? My fury is quickly doused by fear. Oh no. . .

Jud's eyes are hard behind his mask. He sniffs. "No need for insults Armon."

I'm shaking as they bind my wrists together.

"Up with you," Armon grunts and roughly pulls me to my feet.

I'm terrified as we walk toward the harbor, thoughts of being swallowed by the Thyellodic plaguing each step. My fear does me one kindness. It tells me I'm not ready to die just yet.

The three of us join a long line of invaders who carry their loot of goods with them. They're donned in vulture masks and similar worn-out black leathers that sport an assortment of bleached bones. Most of them are tall and stout, their physique much larger than anyone I've ever seen. Weapons are strapped to their backs and buckled to their thighs, marking them as skilled killers. Paidia never stood a chance. I'm sure the Elders would've come to the same conclusion and surrendered to spare lives if given the opportunity. But it wouldn't have mattered. I openly glare at the foreigners. Their goal wasn't to conquer but to annihilate.

A cart goes by, and I clench my fingers into a fist. I would recognize the contents anywhere—Sal's gold armlet and his life-mate's silver wristband with the sapphire chips in the leaves. Dyed tapestries, food, and spices, amongst other things, are pushed by an invader with blood smeared hands. I'm disgusted. The livelihood of my people sorted into piles to be sold or traded, their lives a mere inconvenience. My eyes follow where the line leads, and I stare dumbstruck at the massive transport.

Never in my life have I seen a ship this size. The vessel is painted to reflect the color of sea water, with translucent sails that billow in the wind. Only by a catch of light would one notice the vast sheet of material against the sky. The owner must have deep pockets—only Arachne[27] herself could've woven such fabric. Now I know how they came to Paidia unseen. The ship is camouflaged against the sky and sea. It would be too late for anyone by the time it's sighted.

At the end of the dock, a slim, elegant man stands apart from the rest. He's clad in black like the others, but his clothes—a long-sleeved tunic tucked into fitted trousers—are woven with fine cloth. The silver belt at his waist is more ornament than practical and his black hair tied back in a gentleman's fashion makes him appear as an oddity amongst the combat-hardened crew. I watch as he inspects the goods brought before him by an invader. The man takes note in a leather book he holds between long fingers and then motions for my people's belongings to be taken aboard the ship. It's not a long enough wait before it's Armon and Jud's turn.

---

[27]A skilled weaver condemned by the gods and turned into an immortal spider. Arachne resides in the highest cliffs of Apotmós and weaves her finest silks that repel fire in exchange for entertainment or the jewels of kings. Those seeking her work must take heed, for the climb to her tower is treacherous and a millennium of boredom has made her cruel.

My legs freeze. I've a sense that if I get on the ship, I'll never see my home again. No! I tilt my head to the Gods' Window cast in great colors of blue, orange, and pink from the suns' rise, and I plead for salvation.

"Metis, help me! Zeus! Anyone! Please!" But the gods turn a deaf ear to my cries.

Jud tugs on my rope. "Quit your yowling, girl! That tongue sounds like sorcery."

The pull feels like a death sentence. I resist. The rough wood of the dock digs into my blistered feet as I try to run. The attempt is futile and only makes Jud angrier; he swears at me and yanks all the harder. I'm whipped forward and land face first onto the salt etched dock.

Heartsick, I lift my busted chin and find myself in front of the potential aristocrat. He's striking, with high cheek bones and dark intelligent eyes. For a brief moment, I hold his gaze, and I'm chilled, feeling like a hound's prey. He's dangerous—more so than the others. In appearance, this man seems to be the embodiment of sophistication, but I sense something worse than malice from him.

I rise slowly from the ground.

He stares, sizing me up, and takes stock of my condition. There's a coldness behind the glower. The moment he notices blood on my dress, the monster within him shifts, ready to lash out. Thankfully, he doesn't address me.

"You damaged a prized good?" he says with a voice devoid of emotion.

Jud and Armon glance at one another, but Jud speaks first. "Now look here, Ker. We may have…played around with her, but we're just taking what's owed to us. We go from place to place and never get nothing! I'm tired of it."

Ker's expression remains blank. "You fucked her too then? Now that she's been used, we won't obtain the highest price for her. She's obviously young. You should've chosen someone older for your antics."

Armon points at Jud, "I told him not to, Sir."

It's uncanny, watching two warriors who've tortured me succumb to fear in front of a man much milder in appearance.

Jud turns on Armon, "Why you piece of—" His insult is cut off, replaced with a silent scream.

He rakes at himself with curled fingers, his vulture mask falling. It bounces off the dock and into the water. Before I can get a good look at Jud's face, his head begins to expand in size like the vocal sacs on a frog. What's happening to him? I'm mesmerized by the gruesome spectacle.

The skin of his cheeks and forehead stretch until they rip, blood gushes from the torn flesh. As his shrieks reach a crescendo, Jud's eyes bulge from their sockets. I don't comprehend the butchery at first and search for an answer, scanning the area around me. There! Ker has his hand slightly raised past his hips, fingers spread wide, the only indication that he's the one causing Jud's pain. He's Gifted with ichor. The realization that such a monster could be blessed by a god almost makes me wet myself.

Ker closes his fist, the action forcing Jud's swollen head to finally burst like one of my mother's failed pies. Bits of skin and gore spray in all directions, and I'm bathed in the blood and brain matter of my rapist. I'm frozen by astonishment. My mouth gapes wide as my breath comes in quick hitches and a deafening buzz fills my brain. Jud's decapitated body falls to the ground with a sickening thud at my feet, his blood warm beneath my toes.

Silence envelops the dock as every working man stills. Ker clears his throat and methodically takes out a lace handkerchief. With it, he wipes away a splash of crimson on the side of his mouth before stowing the cloth back inside his chest pocket. The demon slowly draws a cold gaze across the pier.

"Let this be a lesson!" His icy voice carries over the hushed men. "Damaging the Autokrator's property is punishable by death!"

Autokrator? Property? I've been reduced to merchandise? A piece of my foggy memory becomes clear. It's really happening. Metis showed me this scenario. The foresight, unfortunately, doesn't make it any easier to endure or less shocking.

As I survey Jud's truncated body, I experience a wild feeling, similar to thrilling satisfaction. You deserved this. My smile is manic. I take a grand kind of pleasure in his death—something I didn't know I was capable of. The girl I was yesterday has been replaced by a wretched ghoul. Did Metis answer my prayer for vengeance? My chin turns toward Ker, evil incarnate, and I have my doubts. No matter. I'll take what justice is given to me. I don't care who serves it.

In appearance, I'm a lunatic, bound in a tattered dress splotched with blood and I'm grinning with sick satisfaction. Armon notices the change in me and cautiously takes my rope before pushing my body toward his master. The monster touches my face with careful fingers that cool my sudden bloodlust—the act compels me to swallow. This close to him, my eyes register a thick silver chain peeking from under the collar of his tunic. The metal emits an ethereal glow.

Ker closes his eyes, sniffing the air. "Blood suits you," he whispers before forcing my mouth open to examine my teeth.

He's right. I set aside thoughts of the peculiar jewelry he wears and wonder at the creature I'm becoming instead. He pokes my body with his quill, and I wince when it prods a fresh bruise.

Seemingly satisfied with his inspection, Ker writes in his ledger, and speaks to Armon. "The other ship has already sailed ahead with the new inventory." He gestures toward the massive vessel before us, "this one is filled to the brim with slaves. Be grateful I'm accepting her at all."

Armon bows his head. "Yes, sir. My humblest apologies for the late delivery."

Ker makes a sound of disgust and tosses a bronze drachma to my captor.

I watch captivated as the coin summersaults through the air, light glinting off its edges. Time has slowed down, allowing me to permanently mark the transaction in every crevice of my brain. I'm worth one pathetic bronze piece. I chose this path, but still, I curse

Metis. I'm ill-prepared for my future as a slave; the Goddess didn't grace me with visons of what comes after.

The drachma lands in Armon's hand and he quickly shoves it into his pocket before tugging on my rope and pulling me onto the damnable ship. It's my first time on a floating craft since Pápa's death, and even after all these years, I'm still afraid of the water.

I take a final look at Paidia. Smoke wafts in the sky from the smoldering debris, the village gone. The bodies will be too much for Zadok to bury. They'll most likely be left to rot in the hot summer suns. At the very thought, I have to swallow the bile rising in my throat. A goodbye to the dead is on the tip of my tongue, but the words fall stale in my mouth as I'm jerked roughly below deck.

CHAPTER XIII

5th Week of Summer

Eimear

Piss, body odor, death—the stench crawls up my nose. My throat spasms with revulsion, the intense ammonia making my eyes water. It's dark, but the barest hint of sunlight breaks through the tight spaces in the planking above. What I can make out in the dim light is fouler than the overpowering smell. Hundreds of dirty bodies are pressed in close together, chained to the walls, floor, and supporting beams throughout the middle of the ship. Muck sloshes about over the floor to tease my ankles like waves from the sea. Gods, this must be people's—I stop the thought, not wanting to give name to what I'll soon be sitting in.

Armon peers around with narrowed eyes. He has his nose pinched under the vulture's beak of his mask in a futile attempt to ward off the stink. "I don't see space for you."

I'm flooded with sudden hope at the prospect of not staying below deck with the others, but my optimism is short-lived.

"Listen up, scum!" He switches from his slithering language and calls out in the common tongue, "Any of you dead yet?" Silence greets him, the air thick with doom. He bares his teeth. "I asked a question, don't make me ask again!"

A rattled cough breaks the quiet and the owner's voice croaks from a wall on the port side of the ship—their answer confirms my lodgings for the duration of the sail.

Armon grunts to himself and pulls me forward. We wade through the mass of bodies and filth infested floors while the captives avert their eyes from us. He stops to growl at me, "Your bronze coin isn't worth walking through all this shit."

A retort is on the edge of my lips, but it dies at the sight before me. Chained to the bottom of the wall is a small grotesque figure— bloated and discolored with signs of putrefaction. I can't judge if the person was male or female, and my stomach begins to heave, the stench too overwhelming.

Armon tugs hard on my restraints. "So help the gods, if you puke on me, I'll kill you here and now. Ker would never know. That dandy fuck is above wandering down here."

I lift my bound hands to cover my nose and somehow manage to keep the vomit at bay. I memorize the star-like birthmark on Armon's chin that looks like a splotch of misplaced paint. I may not know his face, but I swear by the unholiest of the Under, I'll recognize him one day and make him pay for what he's done to me.

The bastard pulls a key from his pocket and unlocks the manacle around the figure's rotten wrist. He shoves the body with his boot, and it hits the floor with a soft thud. The captive to the body's left makes a feeble attempt to distance himself, and on the right, a woman with vacant eyes sits slumped.

My horror spreads anew in a sweeping chill when he clamps the filthy manacle around my ankle. At the click of the turning key, I can't help myself—I whimper.

Armon pats the side of my cheek. "Happy travels."

"Fuck you," I hiss and slap his hand away.

He snarls, grabs me by the hair, and slams my head against the wall. The burst of pain reminds me to keep my mouth shut. Just before losing consciousness, I note the splash and scrape of the swollen corpse being dragged away.

I wake to slimy filth and darkness. The stomps and lewd curses from the barbarians above is raucous compared to the stillness of the captives around me. My nausea is made worse by the insistent rocking of the ship that creaks with every dip. I squeeze my eyes shut as the churning in my belly becomes too intense. I think I have a concussion.

Visions from the previous night cross my mind like a dream. An older couple dragging me from the water after my failed attempt at navigating a canoe across the sea. Bits and pieces of my life that could've been if I had chosen to hide behind the trap door instead of putting my brother there. A completely different story. It's something I can't make sense of, an alternate life with people I've never met.

I hope Zadok will find a stranger's kindness. My choice is one I'm content to live with, but what will become of him? The unknown terrifies me. I hug my knees to my chest and wince from the pain I find there. The cuts and burns are still fresh on my legs and now covered in filth. I force myself to breathe slowly in an attempt to calm my racing heart. As I stare at the muck around me, I know infection is unavoidable. I'll be lucky if I don't lose a limb.

In the quiet, guilt closes in on me like a shadow's cool caress. Even if I hadn't run off with Gareth, there's nothing I could've done to save Mana from those monsters. I know this, but still, living hurts.

And what of Gareth? Is he alive? Did he find safety or did those brutes put him on a ship as well? I clutch at my ruined dress and grab a fist full of it, right above my heart.

Why did any of this have to happen?

I fight the tears that beg to come as I inspect the massive hull where at least three hundred—maybe more of us—are chained and piled in together. To my left, a man sits slumped over, the points of his curved spine are sharp against the back of his chiton. He isn't dead, is he? I suck on my bottom lip and inspect my other side. I'm met with a mass of tangled brown hair and glassy eyes. She fixes her empty gaze on me and when she speaks it's plain that she's delirious.

"That was my daughter you know." Her voice cracks.

"I'm sorry," I whisper back to her. She must be referring to the person chained here before me.

She continues, "Naite passed four days ago . . . I begged them to give her to the sea, but no one would touch her. They left her here to rot." Her face contorts, and she begins to weep. My heart breaks for her.

I place my hand over hers. "May her rest be gentle in the Elysian Fields."

She dips her head in a soft nod, and a fat tear slides gently into the crevice of her mouth.

My palm warms where my skin touches hers and I gasp as I'm suddenly flooded with information I shouldn't know. She loves music. Was a singer…wait no…a storyteller for her people—a historian by song. How do I just know this? It's like I can almost see her in my mind with her tribe gathered around her.

I don't know what to make of it, but I do want to comfort her, if only to distract me from my own pain for a moment. A tune comes to mind, and I hum a melody Mana used to sing to calm my brother. It's soft and gentle, just as she was. My voice wavers at the sudden memory of her brutalized body, but I continue humming, tasting fresh salt on my lips. It's not long until the woman's eyes close in sleep.

Still humming to myself, I relive the destruction of my home. Mana's death, Zadok's frightened face, and the brutality I endured—

fury claims me. My rib cage feels as if it's going to burn up from all the anger inside. The tune I sing dies out as my throat constricts, and this time I can't continue. My hands clench hard enough that the woman pulls hers from my grasp with a sleepy moan. I survey the grave faces of those around me. Each one must have a story similar to mine. Whoever orchestrated this is evil.

Something begins to take shape—a resolve I've never possessed before. I will myself to be unbreakable, to become steel. I'll survive this. And I don't care what it takes, or how long, but I'll find out who's responsible, and send them to the Under.

I'm jolted awake by the touch of phantom hands, my body thrashes, and my chains clank against the sodden floor. Heart racing, I try to wet my lips, but my tongue is dry. After a few more panicked beats, I realize I'm not under attack. Still, it's hard to calm myself.

Frustrated, I move to stand. There's nowhere for me to go, bound as I am, but it's better than sitting in filth. I stare at the misery around me, there are no words to accurately describe such despair. The hull is thick with wracking coughs and sobs. It makes my skin crawl.

I stretch my arms overhead to shake off the feeling. By the way the light casts from the stairway, it seems the suns will be setting soon. What day is it? My stomach rumbles as I'm hit with an intense wave of hunger. With a groan, I slide back down to the floor. I can't remember the last time I ate. The woman next to me still sleeps, though her skin has turned chalky and sweat slowly drips from her brow. She must be ill. Even so, I envy her oblivion.

A low snicker comes from my left.

Following the sound, I shudder as brown eyes stare back from a grim, sunken face curtained by dark, shaggy hair. The man next to me, who I thought might be dead, is awake, and I have his full attention.

The fine hair on my arms stands on end and the fluttering sensation begins anew in my belly. There's something not right about him. I'm struck by sudden dizziness, and what little energy I have is depleted further. It takes a moment to get my bearings. I've felt this before.

He sizes me up, and I must pass inspection because, as my luck would have it, he opens his mouth. I note the decay of his bottom teeth.

"You're a peculiar one," he says and brings his head even closer to my face.

His breath is sour, only an inch separates us now. I scrunch my nose and turn away. "I don't know what you mean."

The man appears feeble, but his hand moves fast like a viper when he grabs my chin and forces me to face him. "It's your eyes, I've never seen anything like them. What a peculiar color—"

"Don't touch me!" I snarl and swat his hand away.

The lout leans his head back and lets out an empty chuckle. "Don't be angry. I haven't had this much excitement since entering this gods' forsaken shit hole."

I turn away in an effort to distance myself but can still feel his eyes bore into me.

My stomach sounds again, and I become more aggravated with hunger and the uncertainty of my situation. I'm pathetic. The internal declaration I made to myself to become stronger is almost forgotten, reduced by basic needs. I grind my teeth against one another, the man puts me on edge, but what can I do? We may be stuck together for a long time by the looks of it.

"Are we fed here?" I ask, not bothering to face him.

His reply is a slow drawl, "Evera' few days or so."

I pause and run my tongue along the roof of my mouth. "And water?"

"A ladle in the afternoon." The man's voice is dry and gruff, but he continues, "You were passed out when they came by earlier."

It takes a moment to digest this information, but I put together why the girl from earlier died. I turn to the man and look him in the eye. "How long have you been here?" I whisper.

He exhales a long breath. "It's hard to say, time passes slow down here with nothin' more than the dark and your demons hauntin' yuh. But, if I were to guess, I'd say almost three weeks, maybe longer." The man motions his head toward the woman beside me. "She and her daughter were here before me."

Three weeks . . . I clutch my chest, alarmed at the prospect of being held in these conditions for that length of time.

He eyes me. "I heard you talkin' to her earlier. She's originally from the High Forests[28] from what I gathered. She been wailin' in that tribal gibberish since her brat was thrown into the Under. Funny she chose to talk to you."

I recoil at his callousness. Did he ever have a family? Does he not know what it's like to lose someone he loved?

He strokes his unkempt beard. "It seems they're just snatchin' anyone nowadays, but especially lil' pretty things like you." The man gestures above deck. "They've been raidin' well-to-do villages along the coastlines for years. I didn't think it would be a problem for my humble home, but seems like I was wrong."

I force myself to relax just enough to appear friendly. Insensitive as he may be, I might learn something. "They hail from Manthros am I correct?"

"Fuckin' Maketae mercenaries! These sons of whores will do anythin' for a bit of coin." He coughs, his last words turning into a hacking fit. ". . . though they weren't always like this. They've lost their way."

---

[28] A rain forest known for its particularly tall trees reaching heights past 400 feet. The tribes residing in the wood are often warring with lethal beasts that stalk the underbrush. To adapt, the tribes build their homes amongst the upper branches of the forest, and use gliders and swings for transportation.

Maketae. I recognize the word. I think they're a special kind of warrior in the far eastern continent, and they worship Ares, the god of war. I know little else about them, although something nags at me. "Who's the Autokrator? Isn't it an old term for emperor? I heard it spoken before boarding the ship. I thought Ehvara had no such person."

He stares at me. "Are *you* daft, girly? How can you be so ignorant?"

My face flushes hot with embarrassment. My knowledge of the world is seriously outdated. I clear my throat. "It's just . . . different where I'm from. Remote compared to most other places." *Was* different. Paidia doesn't even exist anymore. I smother the feelings that come with the thought.

He scoffs. "Well, that's shit. It doesn't bode well to be stupid, especially for a girl your age."

What's wrong with him? I'm floored by his rudeness and don't bother this time with a response. Instead, I make myself interested in the dried blood on my dress, but then stop in disgust when I realize its Jud's. I wish I could be clean of him.

"Well don't get all sullen on me. I'll tell you what you need to know about the Autokrator, better that way for where you're goin'."

My skin breaks into gooseflesh. Where am I going?

"He took Kanthar first about eight years ago. Not long after, the fucker set his sights on Anyalay and nearly killed the entire fuckin' royal blood line. Ever since he got his foothold, he's been conquerin' nearby lands little by little with his army of Maketae. Fuckin' warmongers—"

He spits toward his feet before he continues. "The Autokrator must've made a pact with Ares for the God of War's worshippers to bend the knee so swiftly. The son of a bitch Autokrator goes by Heracles. The realms are at war now because of him, girly."

War?

Ares?

Heracles?

It all sounds like legend not life. I don't want to believe it, but then again, I did meet Metis herself. I scrunch my face in contemplation, vaguely remembering a lesson with Elder Marcus. He spun a daring tale about Heracles engaging his half-brother Ares in an epic battle, which Ares lost. In all the stories he told, the brothers hated each other. Why would they be working together now?

"You can't mean *the* legendary Heracles?" I ask, just to be sure.

The man scratches his head. "I've never laid eyes on the demigod myself, but rumor has it that Zeus sent him down from Olympus to punish Ehvara. My opinion though, is that he's just another miserable bastard out for blood and a good fuck."

Why would Zeus want to destroy his greatest creation? It doesn't make sense. But Metis didn't save her disciples either. There must be something larger at play for the gods to abandon us all. My resolve for revenge wavers at the thought of taking on an immortal such as Heracles. The task too large for someone like me. Despite our threadbare relationship, I send a quick prayer to Metis for help. I'm more than angry with her for what she's allowed to happen, but she did choose to spare me whatever her reasons may be.

I gesture to the others in the hull. "But what does Heracles need with all of us?"

The man shrugs his shoulders. "My guess is that openin' up a slave trade brings in a good amount of coin. Nothin' says to fall in line like slappin' shackles on people."

Despair snakes up my skin before it coils in a knot, making itself comfortable as if the feeling plans to stay for some time. "Is that what's to become of me then? To work until I die in some field . . . or citadel?" I wrap my arms around the curve of my grimy knees. "That's cruel."

The man sizes me up again, but this time, with a leer. "With a face like that, there's only thing you'll be good for. It's the siren's house for *you* girly."

I'm enraged. "I'll have you know that I'm proficient in several languages. Not only that, but my mother was a healer, and she taught me how to make medicine. I'm sure my talents won't go to waste."

"The Maketae must've addled your brains before throwin' you down in this shit hole." He guffaws. "Once they got hold of you, that was it! Your fate was set. In this world, you aren't anythin' but what you're sold to be. It's a kindness I'm warnin' you really. Now you can prepare yourself. The day your sullied feet touch land again, you'll be bought by the nearest brothel and fucked every which way until you can't anymore. Only then, will you be killed. And that, girly, be the hard truth of your life."

His words strike harder than any hand could, and a part of me wilts beneath them. However, the other part—my blackened heart—urges me to rise with its newly instilled cruelty.

I lean forward until we're almost nose to nose and whisper with venom, "I hope that wherever you go, there's no light in your life. I pray to the gods, that when you die, the gates of Elysium will deny you entry and cast your vile soul to the Under. May Hades rip the bones from your person again and again and feed them to his hound for all of eternity." I spit on him for good measure.

His eyes narrow to slits, riled by my curse. He's quick when he grabs me by the neck and begins to crawl on top of me. "You know what, you little chit? I'm goin' to teach you a lesson. I'll give you a taste of what's to come."

I'm flooded by remembrances of rough hands the night before.

"No!" I scream for help, but the woman beside me is comatose and the others nearby ignore my cries, shifting their gaze from the brutality. I seethe while the man fumbles with my dress, searching for my hip.

But this time is not like before.

No, the darkest part of my soul calls for vengeance, demanding bloodshed—like Jud's bursting carcass. I'm made of something different now.

You.

Will.

Die.

My body stills as I assess my opponent and draw from Metis' Gift. My stomach summersaults, sensing the man's weaknesses through his touch. His hold on me is feeble, lack of food has robbed him of full strength. I know exactly what to do.

With outstretched hands, I run my fingertips alongside his grime covered face. I pass his wiry beard, the sneer of his lips and the rise of his pocked cheeks, until, my thumbs make contact with his eyes.

I press my nails in full force.

He screams and attempts to escape backward, but I move with him until my body is on top of his. "Did you think you could hurt me? Did you think I'd let you?" I whisper.

The man's fists beat into the sides of my arms, but my hold is firm and can take the pummeling. Beneath my thumbs, his eyes are soft and slick. They give way with a squelch when I increase the pressure. It's like popping an overgrown cyst—something I watched Mana do many a time. The man begs, his voice rising to a shriek—but it's too late, the damage has been done.

You shouldn't have threatened me.

I acknowledge for the briefest of moments that I should stop, but then I realize I don't want to. I ignore the girl that worries for her soul, and instead, relish the blood that flows from his sockets onto my palms. I press my thumbs deeper.

When I'm satisfied, I let go and ease off him. Sufficiently blinded, he whimpers and claws at his face, searching for something that can never be again. As I survey the pathetic creature he's become, a flash of Jud and Armon taking turns makes me go still with rage.

It's not enough.

The chain sways from his wrist and I take its length in my hand before wrapping the iron around his neck. In the limited space, I press my elbow against his sternum and pull the chain as hard as I can to crush his windpipe. The lout's screams are garbled as his body thrashes. I observe his face turn purple with cold fascination.

Breathing heavy, I crawl off the man's fresh corpse and rest my back against the ship wall. His face stares at me with mutilated sockets. I kick his head the other way so I don't have to see the sin I gladly committed. The people closest to me avoid my fierce stare. Soon, it becomes apparent that the woman next to me has gone stiff. She died in her sleep.

Stunned by my blood lust, I stare transfixed at my hands until the slickness on my palms goes dry, making their creases more pronounced. I wait for a Maketae warrior to appear and pass judgment for my crime, but one never comes. As I sit, I come to a realization: I killed someone and don't even know their name. Emotions sift through me in the darkness until I'm strained raw.

He was going to hurt me.

But I didn't have to take it that far.

People with morals don't kill.

But it felt so good.

I liked it.

My body shudders, but not for the murder I committed.

It's the enjoyment that haunts me. I've discovered red is my favorite color.

Gods & Beasts of Miracle

Hades

I defeated the Titans,

alongside my brothers.

Poseidon was given the sea,

Zeus the sky,

and I, you ask?

I was left with mists and shadows.

My brothers smiled nervously,

thinking me unhappy with my lot.

Little do they know,

tranquility is found best,

in the dark.

CHAPTER XIV

8th Week of Summer

Nikko

Harsh morning light spills through the window, commanding me to wake like a cross lover who's discovered I haven't been faithful. The result, jarring and painful. Fuck. My head is pounding. I rub the sleep from my eyes as I lay in. . . another's bed? Where am I? White sheets decorated with red flowers are tangled around my waist. I grin. Definitely not mine.

Scrambled memories of last night's drunken debauchery appear through the fog in my brain. I stretch as the naked man beside me stirs in his sleep. My gaze trails upward from the hard plains of his abdomen to admire a sharp jaw line and the mussed brown hair that kisses his caramel skin. What was his name? I trace the curve of his hip with my fingertips, his flesh is soft as silk. The faint recollection of a tavern comes to mind, a dark corner, and the man's full lips pressed against my own, teasing and taking.

I sit up with a wince and the pulsing ache radiating from the base of my skull intensifies. Styx. That'll be the last time I partake in any bar's homebrew. Since trade has nearly stopped from Avanta, the taverns in the Holy City have taken matters into their own hands. With the growing threat of a siege upon us, spirits are in high demand and customers happily give their coin, even if their drink tastes of piss— myself included. I'm surprised father has let supplies dwindle this far, and that Jada isn't already shackled to Heracles. What's he waiting for? Does the king have a plan?

The handsome charmer beside me stirs, and his arm snakes around my waist, pulling himself closer to my hips. I instantly harden at the thought of another toss, but then close my eyes with a depressed sigh— duty calls, and I'm already late. Fuck all, where are my clothes?

I glance around the room and find last night's attire crumpled near the door. As someone who's used to sneaking around, I quietly remove myself from the bed and grab my clothes on the way out. I put them on as I head down the stairs of the two-story dwelling. At the bottom, I freeze when I come in contact with a child playing amongst toys in the center of the room. From their similarities, I know it's his father who slumbers upstairs. His Ellanion eyes widen at the sight of me.

Trying to appear friendly, I raise a finger to my lips with a wink and cross the room in a hurry to get my arse out as quickly as possible. I shut the front door behind me and lean against the frame with a relieved sigh. That explains the floral sheets. If he's wed, I've at least escaped the morning without an awkward confrontation with the missus.

Peering around, I find myself on a crowded street in the ancient sector. A pang of longing strikes as I think back to the new design left unfinished in my wastebasket. The block-like buildings here are in great need of repair. From a second story window across from me, an elderly woman empties her piss pot, and the contents nearly land on a man walking below. He waves a fist in outrage, and the two trade curses back and forth as the onlookers strolling past continue pulling their half-empty carts.

I shake my head. Of all places, I crawled into the damned slums last night. It's at least an hour's walk back to the palace. I groan, thinking of the lessons and meetings I've missed this morn, and the earful I'm bound to receive as a consequence from the king. Best be off then. As I amble through the throng of peddlers, I lift the shoulder of my chiton and give it a sniff. Taking in the scent of the other man's cologne along with hints of the tavern where we met, a grin pulls at the corners of my mouth. Whatever the punishment may be, last night was worth it.

"You smell like a siren's cunny!" My father roars in a rare form of rage and throws a vase of flowers at me that I expertly dodge. It shatters against the study door behind, showering me with water. The guards have been dismissed, but I'm surprised one hasn't burst into the room to check on their sovereign. Given his mood, they are undoubtedly staying away on pain of death. It's only the two of us, but the eyes of past great kings judge me from their portraits on the wall.

I pick a stray flower petal off my shoulder and watch it float to the ground with purposeful disinterest, if only to fuel the king's anger. I enjoy seeing his fury. It's a novelty compared to his usual stoicism, and—unlike the Queen who can easily box my ears—my father doesn't pose a physical threat. He's all bark with very little bite. To this day, it amazes me that she married him willingly, trade agreement or no.

"Of all the things, you missed your first council meeting as Prince of Ellanios! How do you expect to lead a country if you cannot show up for a simple meeting? Do you not care about the war we're up to our necks in?" The king bares his teeth at me. His everyday calm face has been replaced by a mask of ferocity; a vein bulges at his temple. *I've really gotten under his skin this time. I decide to push him further.*

"What do I know of war? I'm kept in the palace like a well-groomed dog. I can't fight alongside my people. I'm not Gifted. Everyone knows I'll be nothing more than a figurehead when the time comes for the crown to be passed to me. And it's your brotherhood of advisors who make the decisions. You just agree or disagree, *your majesty.* So honestly, what's the point?"

The fire in him quickly dies. and he sinks slowly into his chair. "Is that really what you think? I've failed as your father and king then."

I'm taken aback by the sudden honesty, and guilt twists my stomach. It's uncanny to see one's father, let alone a king, admit failure, and I'm at a loss for words. This war is taking more of a toll on him than I thought.

He rests his forearm on his desk and makes a fist beneath his beard before taking a deep breath. When the king speaks, his gray eyes pierce my soul. "There will come a day when the games of your youth will end, and you'll be forced to make hard decisions. Know this Nikko: You are more than a puppet, and your choices matter. The words you speak are heavier than you realize. It's high time you learned their weight."

A feeling akin to fear crawls up my spine, I may have mouthed off too much. I lower my voice and attempt to smooth over the situation. "I'm sorry for missing the council meeting, I was caught up with another matter. It won't happen again."

The king leans forward and waves a bejeweled finger at me. "No. It's too late for that. I can't have you continue to waltz about like the idiot you are. You're a grown man, and someday responsibility will weigh heavy on your shoulders. You are ill prepared for your future as king and a continuous nuisance in my backside. So, help me Zeus, you will learn your place as a Prince of Ellanios."

My mouth goes bone dry. I don't know the exact moment but, like my mother, there was a day when he stopped being a parent and became my sovereign instead. Once I left my swaddling, their caring arms were replaced with expectations and the constraints of a gold leaf crown. He speaks of the weight of words and truly, I've been burdened since I took my first steps.

"Guards!" he summons, and the doors open behind me.

A man of arms bows deeply. "Sir?"

"Fetch Erebos for me would you please."

I arch a brow at my father, confused. "Heracles' emissary? What does he have to do with this?"

My father plasters a false smile on his face. "Why, he arrived at the palace gates early just this morn, to check on the progress of our treaty with the Autokrator. As a Prince of Ellanios, you now have the honor of escorting our most esteemed guest through the Holy City. At the council meeting—that. You. Missed—he requested a viewing, and we are *all* too happy to oblige him."

My jaw drops. "Surely you jest! He's the enemy. How could you agree to such—?"

The king bangs his fist against the desk and hisses, "You'll obey me in this and will show our guest the highest respect. Whatever his fancy may be, indulge him. That's an order. Or would you prefer a prison cell for the next few weeks to ponder your ill life choices?"

As I face off with my father, I see the moment he regains his cold calm, and know I cannot win. "As you wish," I say bitterly.

"Remember your words with this man, Nikko, and learn the art of balancing their weight."

As if to taunt, recollections of my dalliance the night prior come to mind—the scent of marjoram at the nape of my lover's neck as I bit down on his skin before thrusting myself inside him. Was he worth it? My eyes stray to the high, domed ceiling, knowing that what lies ahead of me will be most unpleasant.

Fuck.

Well, this is incredibly uncomfortable for a multitude of reasons. I sneak glances at the man walking by my side in the bustling street. I'm baffled by Heracles' emissary as he gazes upon the Holy City's agora with a mixture of curiosity and contempt. He studies my people and their activities as one would inspect a newly discovered species. He sees no kinship despite our shared humanity.

Slightly taller than me, Erebos is slim but still possesses a muscular build. He has rich brown skin with eyes dark as coal and glossy hair to match, pulled back in a knot. Despite the heat, and in the fashion of the Southern Region, he wears an elegant full-sleeved tunic of black with a high collar. For the life of me, I can't guess his age; there's a timelessness about him. We've barely spoken a word since leaving the castle, but I watch, annoyed, as he peers down to adjust the red handkerchief at his chest pocket for the umpteenth time. For whatever reason, it doesn't stay in place. Unable to handle myself, I finally explode.

"Those are about as useless as a woman's undergarments. Even I know they're only used for formal occasions in the south. There's no reason for it in Ellanios. It makes you look like a prude. Just lose it."

Erebos stops abruptly, causing the person behind us to bump into him and curse before they walk around. He deadpans, "I cannot."

"And why is that? Do you hope to impress my father? I can tell you, he doesn't care about handkerchiefs."

"No." He says and continues forward, sniffing the air as he does. Strange man, this one.

I catch up to him. "Is there anything in particular you'd like to see in the city? Perhaps the grand temple of Zeus?" Anything to hurry up and get this over with.

He pauses in his stride to observe a man juggling balls that are afire. Beside the entertainer is a small dog with a basket strapped to its back to hold coins. I intend to drop a bronze piece to pay for a show, but after I consider my company and his disinterest, I change my mind. The wiry pup yaps at the two of us, as if upset by my rejection, before darting behind a stall to hide.

Staring after the dog, Erebos says without emotion, "I've no warmth for Zeus."

If I were to be honest with him, I'd say he has no warmth for just about anything. The emissary is lucky it's me he's speaking with; any other would take offense. Some diplomat he is.

"Well, how can this humble Prince be of service to you then?" I say strained.

He closes his eyes and sniffs the air once more. His long lashes open in a flash and he points. "What is that?"

"Huh?" My gaze follows his finger and I almost smirk. "Ah, you have a sweet tooth, I see. Well follow me, we can get you sorted."

He follows after me to a cart labeled, *Erotes' Delights*[29] where a woman with large, hooped earrings and painted purple lips stands with her hip cocked.

She purrs as she ogles the two of us, "My dears! I've never seen a sight ever so sweet as the two of yee. I could just eat both of you handsome men right up!"

Erebos appears unfazed by her flattery and single-mindedly points to a candy covered plum wrapped in silver tissue. "I wish to have that. Give it to me."

I'm incredulous, and say sternly, "Manners please. You are a *guest*, remember that."

He tilts his head sideways as if he doesn't understand my frustration. Unnerved by the black depthless pools of his stare, I break eye contact first. Unbelievable, this fellow.

The cart owner winks and wets her lower lip. "I don't mind. I appreciate a man who knows what he wants." She opens her rhipis with

---

[29]Erotes are little winged gods of love and sexual desire.

a flick of the wrist and says behind the folds, "That will be three drachmae."

This time the merchant is the one to offend and I gesture outward with my hand. "Don't you think that price is a bit steep for a single plum? Do you take us for fools?" I can afford it of course, but principle matters.

"I would never have that sort of thought for such two strapping men!" She flips her hair over her shoulder and shrugs. "With the war though, it's hard to come by good inventory. And this is no ordinary plum, I can assure you of that."

My oaf of a companion reaches out with his hand, as if to take the fruit without further consideration. Not thinking, I swat his wrist.

Erebos goes unnaturally still before turning those monstrous eyes on me. "Did you just hit me?

For the first time, I notice the abnormal length of his canines, but I ignore the oddity and him. I'm furious for a number of reasons—the war, babysitting a dimwit who lacks social graces, and being taken advantage of in my own city. I'm about to walk away from the two, but the cart owner realizes she's about to miss a sell.

"Wait, now don't be sour with me! I'll sweeten the deal for you. I'll throw another plum in," she says with reluctance.

My shoulders droop as my rage fizzles out at her desperation. I'm still a little hungover from last night and lack the gumption to care about anything anymore. I don't particularly like plums but concede to the merchant's price. She needs the money, everyone does. The vixen flashes me a smile that hints of carnal desires when I press five coins into her hand. "For hard times."

"Oh, you'll definitely be having a hard time, my kind sirs." She says this with another wink and looks between the two of us before handing us each a candied fruit.

I shake my head, she's a strange one too. "Good day, my lady."

We continue our stroll through the Holy City and Erebos takes a moment to study his prize before shoving the entire plum into his mouth. With his cheeks bulging, he attempts to chew.

I can't help but stare in wonder. Good gods! Where from the Under did Heracles drag this fellow from? He's not like any emissary I've ever met.

The bizarre man turns to me, eyes slightly wide. A dribble of honey leaks from the side of his lip and with his mouth still full, he gushes, "It's so good."

I'm stupefied. Erebos is a walking contradiction of lethal predator and child-like innocence, and I find it difficult that I'm unable to properly read an opponent. What do I do?

Unaware of my turmoil, Erebos stares at the uneaten plum in my hand with longing.

No. Fucking. Way.

Like a barbarian, I too shove the entire candy into the gaping hole of my face and take a moment to savor it. My tongue is met with an explosion of sweet flavor laced with an underlying herb. I watch in satisfaction as Erebos' eager expression turns to disappointment. This is delicious, but where have I tasted it before? I search my mind but can't find the answer. It doesn't matter.

"That was rude." Erebos says, voice clipped.

"*Excuse me?*"

"You hit me earlier."

"What?"

"You. Hit. Me. At the stall. Remember?"

"I barely tapped you! And may I remind you, that I did just treat you to the most expensive plum you'll ever find in Ellanios."

Erebos stares me down with that uncomfortable gaze of his.

I stammer, "Are you wanting vengeance for such a slight?" My father is going to be pissed. What if I just ruined any chance of peace for Ellanios?

"Whatever else in life is there but revenge? You have a sparring ring with weapons, yes? We'll settle it there." He turns his back on me and heads in the direction of the palace, bumping into patrons who don't move out of his way in time.

He's a lunatic. My hands clench at my sides. "Well, if he wants a fight, he's got one."

I swallow the lump in my throat. This feels different somehow. Like it's serious. Erebos and I each have a sword and stand opposite to one another. I've changed into formal sparring attire, which consists of a dark-purple chiton covered with a silver breast plate paired with matching greaves and a helmet with a tall crest. Erebos wears similar gear, though in the yellow and gold colors of Heracles. The thick, silver chain that rests above my opponent's collarbone seems out of place. He's more muscular than I thought. I'll have to be careful.

A small crowd of ten unarmed soldiers stand around the sparing ring, curious and waiting. Some clap and cheer for me.

"Give him a thrashing, Prince!"

"Show Heracles' mutt that Ellanions have nothin' tuh fear!"

I take note of those who offer no support. I'll remember their guarded faces, they may be part of the faction praying for my father's demise. I'll have to report it.

Refocusing, I point my sword at Erebos. "Let it be known to all, that you, Heracles' Emissary, requested this fight. That Ellanios has treated you kindly, and you spit on our hospitality. You are, by far, the worst diplomat in all the worlds." My father is going to throw me in a cell. I had one simple task, show the man around, and now we're crossing blades.

Erebos cocks his head like a dog, eyes on my weapon. "You're upset, Prince? I've been told a little conflict is healthy for relationships. It makes them grow stronger, so they don't become stale." He leans into a fighting stance, sword held high. "First to draw blood wins."

What. What?! Who tutored this man in diplomacy? But I don't have time to ponder Erebos' abnormalities because he lunges first and aims his sword at my right side where my breast plate doesn't cover. I quickly block his thrust, and my arms shake from the blow. "Are you trying to kill me?" I gasp as I try to push him back. I guess Zeus' protection only extends to the Holy City itself and not its citizens.

His eyes hold no emotion, just a black abyss of nothing. "If I were, you'd already be dead. Now tell me, Prince, what's it like to feel as you do? Your expression hides nothing. Scorn, outrage, joy, attributes any human should possess. How can I make those faces?"

Thanks for reminding me how I should control myself better. I'm the exact opposite of what a King of Ellanios should be. "You're insane," I say, sidestepping his question. I parry with a series of blows that force him to retreat. Erebos chose the wrong partner for this dance of swords.

He halts my attack with one of his own. "I'm not insane. I'm simply trying to learn. Why won't you listen?"

"Maybe because your people are killing my people in the trenches as we speak, and instead of being with them, I'm here playing chaperone with you," I say through clenched teeth and send a kick to his stomach.

Erebos recovers quickly and charges, swinging his sword with deadly grace over and over again. I can barely keep up. He's better than me, I realize with fear. He presses me backward, his face mere inches from mine. This close, I have a sense something is hiding beneath that blank stare of his.

"It seems we can't reach an understanding then. But you should know, I have no people," he whispers.

Erebos aims his sword at my face, preparing for a final strike when he suddenly freezes, dropping his weapon altogether. The blade rings with a clatter when it hits the ground and the soldiers at my back scream at me to finish him quickly. He groans, as he doubles over. "Something is wrong with my body, it's . . . it's . . . burning up."

Confused, I lower my sword. Then the fire he speaks of hits me too. The inferno courses through my body like an unstoppable force. My eyes widen when my manhood stiffens beneath my chiton.

You'll definitely be having a hard time, my kind sirs, the merchant had said.

Good gods, she thought we were lovers! I now recognize the taste of the herb known as the Silent Kiss. I was foolish enough to try it once and swore to never take it again.

"Is this what it's like to die?" Erebus moans as he attempts to stand up straight.

I note, both with satisfaction and concern, that his eyes have taken on a glassy sheen.

Even while lust pumps through my veins, I'm left dumbstruck by Heracles' emissary for what seems like the hundredth time today. "Have you never… I mean—surely *every* man has."

He takes to the ground with his knee. "Died? No! I think I would have known if I had."

Prick. He must be jesting with me.

By this time, the soldiers grumble amongst themselves that we're no longer fighting and begin to disperse, their free entertainment done for.

I can't help but laugh at the situation even though the linen rubbing against my skin has my body wanting to fly apart. "Some nose you have there. Of all the stalls and candied fruits, you had to pick the one laced with a strong aphrodisiac."

Erebos grabs himself and groans. "I am but a dog."

I cross my arms, blade still in hand, my mood turning serious at his insinuation. "While I have no doubts about that, you best conduct yourself respectfully these next few hours. I've sampled the Silent Kiss before, and there's little chance to be rid of the affects until it has run its course. I can take you to a brothel and leave you with a bit of coin if you'd like. But I won't have you terrorizing the unwilling."

"A brothel?" The emissary struggles over the word. The cord keeping his hair swept back came unfastened at some point, and now it falls loosely around his shoulders.

I hiss as another flash of heat assaults my groin. To the Under with this. I'm done. I need to find my own release and soon.

I pull the purse full of drachmae from behind my breast plate and toss it at his feet. "Brothel, or even your hand if you wish it. But the fucks I can give are certainly not for you, sir. Should I find that you ignored my suggestion, Heracles' diplomat or no, I'll have you strung up by your balls."

Erebos gives no response to my threat, his face a cloud of confusion as he suffers.

"Oh, and just because you deserve it," I take my sword and point it at his neck. "It was *first blood* you said, right?" I place the tip of the blade at his collarbone and cut upward, just enough to lift the chain he wears and draw blood. "There, I win," I say coldly and turn to go.

"You . . . were able to move it?" Erebos mutters behind my back, but I don't have the care to worry about his mumblings and leave him alone in the ring. My mind shifts to the bulge under my chiton. I've problems of my own.

CHAPTER XV

Time Unknown

Eimear

The constant rocking of the ship is hypnotic. During the sway, I mostly contemplate how I don't know who or what I am anymore. The brutal voyage and isolation have turned me into some unrecognizable creature—an observer that notes pain or numbness, and little else. Every now and then, a glimmer of the girl I used to be emerges, making me feel, making me think, and she is *unbearable*. I promptly smother the ghost when she appears.

Poseidon's Thyellodic is known for its monsters. Through the endless days and nights, the beasts stalk the vessel. I can hear them outside the walls, begging to be fed. I imagine long scaled bodies wrapping themselves around the flanks and crushing us to splinters. The destruction would be welcomed.

I no longer fear when a mercenary rushes down the steps and drags a screaming, boney victim back up with them. They only do this when the roar of the sea dragons becomes too intense, their skulls attacking the bottom of the ship like a relentless battering ram. I assume the Maketae pitch their captive overboard, because silence and frenzied splashing is followed by the person's departure. Should I volunteer next time? The death would be quick.

My belly makes a sound, it hasn't learned to stop hoping just yet. I inspect my ribs through the soiled material that used to be a dress. The first time a warrior threw pieces of a rancid, gray mass at my feet, I turned my nose up, preferring an empty stomach. However, as the gnawing of hunger became too agonizing after several days, I put my scrupulous behavior behind me and ate what they consider food. I couldn't keep it down, it tasted of curdled milk—but I found that when I vomit, it's like I get to eat twice.

I survive on spite alone.

Thirst is worse than the hunger. I whimper and beg with my mouth open when it's my turn to receive the ladle. The mercenary that feeds or waters me is different every time, at some point they removed their masks, though their faces are still a blur. It's a punishment for the Maketae to serve, and they're anything but kind. I'll receive a random kick or slap when they come and go, my skin is spotted with dark bruises and shit. I only become truly upset though, if they toss my water away.

"Hmmm…hmmm…hmmm…"

………….

"What makes…a dandelion a weed, death a foe, and a god, a god?" I ask the dark.

…………..

I pull at my hair.

"Hmmm…hmmm...What makes a dandelion a weed, death a foe, and a god, a god?"

I scream:

"WHAT!

Makes!

A

God!

A

GOD?"

…………..

…………..

…………..

"Perspective," I answer.

CHAPTER XVI

10th Week of Summer

Eimear

We've made land. A commotion of stomps, shouts, and cheerful curses comes from above deck as the mercenaries offload their stolen goods; they're happy to have survived another voyage on the Thyellodic. Hours have passed since the ship docked, and I grow anxious that I'll remain in this dark hull forever. A man chained to the beam across from me thrashes and mutters to himself—bubbles of spit swell at the corners of his mouth as he belts a wild laugh. His mind broke some weeks ago.

Or has it been months?

He isn't the only one. We've all been whittled down to bone, but there are some amongst us who bang their heads against the wall, patches of hair missing from their constant pulling. I'm nervous with excitement and worry about my own sanity. No sane person would happily begin life as a slave, but I'm desperate to get off this ship and into the light. I reach for the hair plastered to my head and my fingers get stuck in the tangles. At least my unruly mane is still intact.

A sudden coughing fit produces a sticky substance from my burning lungs, and I sink down into the space that has been my home for what seems like a lifetime.

What if I can't get up?

I place a hand over my distended belly. One of the mercenaries came by with fresh bread and dispersed it to the captives. I ate my portion greedily, like a savage dog, but I'm paying for it now. My stomach is accustomed to being empty. Mana would've cautioned me to chew slowly.

For once, the gods answer my prayers because my savior and demise arrive. A burly Maketae warrior enters the hull followed by a smaller one. They don't bother speaking but unlock our restraints one by one and shove us toward the stairs in a line. My legs slip from lack of use, but I press my hand into the boney back of the person in front of me as I right myself. The woman moans from my weight, but she's too weak to do anything about it, and I've grown callous enough that I don't care.

It's my turn to exit the hull and the kiss of the suns is both painful and euphoric. My eyes flutter to a close, blinded by the sweet, glorious light—the crisp scent of ocean water and the breeze that tickles my face has my knees buckling. Seagulls call overhead, their beautiful song moves me to tears. I forgot what it was like to feel something other than misery. Another slave's knee bumps into my spine, cutting the beautiful moment short. I'm grabbed roughly by the arm and pulled to my feet.

"Move it or I'll toss you into the Aethiopia![30]" The mercenary barks.

We've come this far?

I make my feet move, but a shuffle is all I can manage. My muscles are feeble. I lower my head and bring my hands up to shield my eyes. It's minutes before I'm able to see without the light burning my retinas. The ground is cobbled with alabaster stone, and my scrawny legs are covered in a thick layer of brown. I risk a peek sideways to find fresh blood splatter. It's a glaring contrast against all the white. A man lays on his side unmoving. From his clothes and stench, I know he's one of us. He must've tried to make a run for it. Shifting my gaze ahead, I'm amazed to see a small city with tall alabaster buildings and turquoise jeweled rooftops built into a slope of mountains full of blushing foliage—a magnificent sight. We must be in Nasarr[31].

The artisan town is abuzz with life, a musician plucks the strings of a lyre while children play in the streets. Patrons stop to examine exceptionally made trinkets displayed on market stands, and a man with

---

[30]In reference to the Aethiopia Sea, governed by Benthesikyme, Queen of Waves. Benthesikyme is the daughter of Poseidon and Amphitrite, her waters are known for their deep swells.
[31]A smaller province of the Southern Region recognized for their splendid rooftops and artisan jewelry.

painted skin juggles brightly colored orbs near a gushing, pearled fountain. Not far from them, a merchant sells honeyed apples to a girl dressed in flowing blue silks. The sight makes my mouth water.

I remember my father pointing to the province on one of his maps. He mentioned how Beryl would pester him to make a side stop for brooches before journeying farther north to Avanta. Beryl . . . my wonder for the city immediately ceases at the memory of her punctured eye sockets. I look back to the bloody corpse and note how those in the market sneak glances at him before averting their gaze—smiles plastered on their faces like painted masks, they resume their shopping.

What's going on here?

On the surface, Nasarr appears abundantly beautiful, but there's an underlying sickness, a wrongness at its heart. Is this Heracles' doing?

While we walk, I count roughly two hundred captives left alive in line, with me placed close to the middle. Four Maketae warriors are mounted on horseback, and trot alongside us with weapons at the hip. Their armaments gleam in the suns, They hold rags under their masks as if to ward off the stench of us. Armon isn't among them, and I can only hope that he was eaten by a beast during our voyage. The thought of his flesh being ripped apart by wild fangs brings a slight smirk to my face.

Before the dock completely disappears from view, my eyes land on a short plump man wearing a gold headpiece with a plum-colored feather. He fidgets uncomfortably, sweat sliding down his cheek as he speaks with a strained smile to Ker. From his expression, Jud's killer seems as if he'd like to do the same again and make the plump man's blood fall like rain over the dock. Instead, Ker pulls a small pouch of coin from the pocket of his long jacket and spins on his heel, tossing the pouch over his shoulder. He barks an inaudible command.

What is that ichor-blessed bastard up to? At the snap of a whip to cobblestone, I jump, leaving thoughts of Ker behind, and move faster to keep up with the others. The people of Nasarr ignore our stinking parade as we march through their city. They continue going about their daily business as if we aren't being treated like chattel. I want to scream at them. Don't you see us? What they've done to us?

For the smallest of moments, I'm startled that I can still be upset by another's cruelty, and by the fact that unkindness can be normalized. There's still a kernel of the girl I used to be within my heart. The notion terrifies me, because that girl is naïve and can be easily hurt. I curse her to go away and raise my head towards the East Window that hangs at a distance in the clear, blue sky—a reminder the gods are always watching.

Why did you abandon me?

The air is thick with humidity and rivulets of sweat pour down my face as I strain to walk up hill. I'm afraid of falling and not getting back up, so I force myself to keep going. As we climb higher, the bright stone walls of the city begin to fade into a dull gray, and I discover the epicenter of Nasarr's disease. The Maketae herd me and the other captives into narrow streets littered with debris and into zigzagging alleyways where all light seems to disappear. A purple smoke clings to the air, promising danger.

I pass a dark corner and watch, open mouthed, as two men sporting delta tattoos, swipe at each other with knives while gamblers with sharp faces cast their bets. Weathered taverns have their doors open to reveal drunkards and women with weary, kohl-lined eyes who serve them. This area of the city could be labeled seedy at best[32].

Our group is spat out single file into an open yard and we're shepherded to a gray pebbled wall at its border. I lean up against the slab for a moment and my body sags, thankful for the respite. I don't think I can walk for much longer.

A warrior dismounts and shouts in the common tongue, "Disrobe pissants!"

Undress? I inspect my soiled garment that has a horrific tale etched into every fiber. As much as I'd like to be rid of it, I'm mortified at the prospect of leaving myself bare in front of the others. But a sudden pop, followed by a cry of pain reminds me that I no longer make decisions for myself.

"This isn't a leisurely affair! Off with your clothes now!" The brute unfurls his whip once again and lashes out at a man towards the end of the line. The slave's forehead is cut swiftly by the popper.

Styx! My fingers shake as I disrobe.

What is *that?*

---

[32]Scylla's Passage is named after a nymph turned monster who devours unfortunate sailors with her long reaching demon heads on the waters of the Thyellódic. One must possess a large set of balls or guileful cunny to traverse these harrowed streets full of deceitful charm.

In my nudity, I notice a bright mark above my heart, mostly hidden by the grime coating my skin. I've never had a such a spot before. I don't have time to fully examine it, so I bring my mass of hair forward to cover it and cross my arms in an attempt to conceal my body. The others take on similar poses, and I avert my eyes in a useless attempt to give them privacy.

We're ordered to wash as buckets of water are carried over with bars of soap and scrubbing brushes. The bristles grate painfully across my skin but I'm able to remove most of the muck. Once uncovered, I hardly recognize my flesh. What was once sun-kissed, is now pale. I'm a walking specter. The thought makes me chuckle darkly. How fitting.

Afterward, I'm bound at the wrists with rope and herded naked with the others from the yard to behind the wall. I count roughly twenty uncovered cages that loom in the not so far distance, some are full of dreary eyed people and others remain empty. I whimper at the prospect of being locked up again and so soon, the dark hull of the ship ever pressing against me.

When I'm shoved inside one of the cages, I crouch down in a corner to hide myself. It's really happening. I'm going to be a slave. I think back to the nameless man I murdered and his heartless words. Despite her abandonment, I pray to Metis in hopes that he was a liar and that I won't be sold to a brothel. I won't survive it.

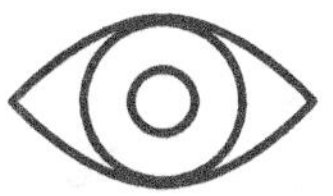

I've been in the cage for hours. It's now late afternoon and the angry suns beat down on me, unforgiving. My skin has turned red from their glare and my mouth aches for water. My shipmates, if you can call them that, have taken similar curled positions in the dirt and alongside the barred walls. I haven't spoken a word to any of them since the nameless man tried to hurt me. No camaraderie was built during our time together in the hull, any words between us now would be pointless.

A large crowd has gathered, some laugh and chew on dried meat as they wait for the sale to begin, others ogle me through the bars, assessing my worth. When I peer into their greedy eyes, I wonder which I'll be sold to. Will it be the portly man with the belly? Or the woman whose red nails have been sharpened to talons?

A warrior raps his sword against the bars of my pen. "Up with yuh all! It's time to go!"

And so, it begins.

Captives are brought out ten at a time and from what I can overhear past the rowdy crowd, they're sold to the highest bidder. My body tenses up, going cold despite the heat. I don't want this to happen. I want to go back home.

I weep uncontrollably. I want my mother, Zadok's chubby cheeks, and Gareth's gentle touch. I just want to be with my life-mate and hold his hand, to feel safe. I want to watch Zadok's big smile widen and hear his wild laughter when he's been mischievous. I want Mana to protect me from all the evil in this world, to heal the wounds inside my soul that haunt me in my sleep.

I try to imagine this is all an illusion. That I'll wake and see Mana's lovely hair shining in the sun as she sits and reads a book by the window. In my mind's eye, she looks up at me with her blue gaze and pulls me into a hug where I inhale the earthy scent that clings to her. In her arms, I'm home and nothing else matters.

My body is racked with sobs when a gruff mercenary comes and yanks me up by my bindings. "Fuck you! You pig-fucking bastard!" I scream at him with my dry throat. In defiance, I use my weight to sit back down.

"Get up!" He snarls and slaps me across the face.

When the pain registers, I'm brought back to reality. This is my fate, but a god could change it. Please, don't send me to a brothel! I pray to Metis.

I'm led out of the cage with nine others. We're brought up onto a large wooden platform and stand nude in front of the seedy crowd. The man with the gold headpiece and plum feather paces in front of me. He speaks quickly to his audience while gesturing to each of us, but I'm too numb to hear.

I'm overcome with humiliation as the mass of strangers look upon my nakedness with hunger. I squeeze my eyes shut. The word *"Sold!"* rings out with such clarity that it blocks all other noise for me.

I'm in a daze when I'm yanked off the platform and led through the mass of soulless people.

How could they do this to another person?

I'm led into another cage and notice that it's occupied mostly with women and young boys, none of whom I've ever seen before. They must be slaves offloaded from other ships. They're a mix of skin colors and body types, but their defining quality is that they're all striking in some way or another.

I address the person nearest me, a busty woman with long russet hair. "Where are we going?" I murmur.

Her exquisite face morphs into an expression of pity that sends a rush of fear through me. "A place where you're too young to be." Her reply is slow and the sympathy in her voice too much to bear. I take a step back.

Hopefully your pretty face doesn't get you into trouble later on. Mana's words then were innocent, but now they seem cruel.

I stare wide eyed at the Gods' Window and think how the divine ones must be mocking me from their high towers—my pain and debasement merely fodder for their own entertainment. Metis gave me a gift, brought me to her presence, warned me—but I don't care. It's not a fair trade. She's a goddess for fucks' sake, she could've saved everyone. The rage that follows is all consuming. "I hate you! I hate you all! You're worthless!" I curse the gods, saliva flying from my lips. I physically feel it when a barricade encloses around the chord of my soul, cutting me off from the almighty above. Good riddance.

I stand in the cage staring but not seeing. Time passes in a blur as my insides are eaten away by misery. I only become aware of my surroundings when those who share my fate begin to stir. Others have joined the cage since I entered, and we're now ushered out in single file by a Maketae warrior with a dark beard. I'm led past the crowded platform, toward an open-faced smithy where a man dressed in soot-stained apron stands beside a burning forge. His arms are meaty, and he warms three branding irons in the flames.

The warrior talks with the blacksmith briefly before grabbing a woman at the head of the line, he forces her to the ground in front of the forge. She struggles against him, begging in her native tongue, but her pleas fall on the ears of demons. The blacksmith takes a fist full of hair, holding her in place, and reaches for a branding iron, it's end bright like the twin suns. He presses the hot metal to the back of her calf, and I didn't know it, but human skin sizzles and pops like any other creature when met with fire. When he's finished, the blacksmith slathers the burn with animal fat and her cries blend with the collective recoil of those whose flesh is next. Some pray, some curse, and others wail a low song of peril. We're promptly told by our handler to shut the fuck up.

She's pulled to her feet and taken away, but the script *pornai* is seared into her skin, marking her a whore for all the world to do with her as they wish.

I'd rather die.

My thoughts are frantic as the blacksmith moves on to the next person. Escape isn't an option, but I won't resign myself to a life of endless rape. A reckless idea takes form as I wait for my own branding.

Am I capable of it?

Another slave ahead of me screams.

If it doesn't work, I'll take my own life. My eyes close as I try to prepare myself for the worst. Too soon, it's my turn. Not needing to be threatened or dragged, I walk steadily toward the blacksmith and sink to my knees. Behind the vulture mask, the Maketae warrior eyes me with suspicion, but he shrugs once the blacksmith sticks a used iron back into the fire. As he reaches for a fresh one, I spring into action and wrap my fingers around the hilt first. I've had everything stripped from me, what's one more thing?

The blacksmith is taken by surprise and stares dumbly for a second, while the warrior behind me shouts a curse that I can't make out over the rush of blood pounding in my ears. But they're too late, this time, I'll take something from *them*.

I press the hot glowing shaft of iron across my face, and oh gods, do I scream. The scent of burned flesh fills my nostrils as the skin from above my right brow and down to my left cheek hisses under the intense heat. With an agonized gasp, I release the scorching metal. The pain is unbearable, but nonetheless, the deed is done.

"Fuck!" The warrior yanks me up by my hair and glares as he takes in my ruined face.

"Should I continue?" The blacksmith asks, eyeing the two of us.

My handler curses under his breath. "No, the buyer won't accept her like this. I'll have to see if some other bastard will pay for her so I can get a portion of the coin back."

It actually worked. The thought of success brings a smile to my lips that stings my singed skin and earns me a kick to the ribs.

"You better wise up and not cause more trouble or I'll cut your worthless throat, the lost coin be damned." He whistles for a comrade nearby who takes his place in the proceedings.

I'm led from the stockades at an ungentle pace and taken down an alleyway that stinks of piss. The suns have begun to dip, and as the sky darkens, our shadows dance across the ground, adding to the sinisterness of Scylla's Passage. Off to the side, a man thrusts vigorously into a woman plastered against the stained alabaster and discarded rubbish. Her eyes are glazed, and she winks at my gawking while sucking on the rolled paper she holds between her fingers. The smoke from the blue lotus[33] sends my lungs into a spasming fit, which brings a

---

[33] Also known as *nymphea caerulea*, the petals can be used for medicinal purposes but when smoked or soaked in wine, the user is put into a euphoric state.

wave of fresh pain to my face. I'm reminded by the rattle in my chest, how ill I've become.

I may die just yet.

We stop in front of a noisy tavern, *Dionysus'*[34] *Cup* is written on a partially unhinged sign dangling next to the door. The warrior ties me to a post meant for horses.

"Stay here," he grunts before turning his back and going inside.

His idiocy gives me a spark of hope, and I quickly begin using my teeth to work on the knot around my wrists, ignoring the painful throbbing that has taken over my entire face. But my fingers are purple and swollen from being tied for so long and my teeth struggle with the knot. Shit. Shit. Shit! I'm not able to loosen it in the slightest. A keening sound of frustration leaves my throat.

Too exhausted to stand any longer, I slide to the ground, my bound hands are above my head. As though it's on fire, the pain in my face becomes increasingly worse. I can't begin to imagine what it looks like. At least I missed my eyes. Old habits die hard, and I almost send my gratitude to the gods, to Metis, but then think better of it. I got myself out of the siren's brand without any help from them. They don't deserve my thanks.

The suns have fully set, and the temperature drops considerably. Still naked, I shiver against the night. Drunks walk in and out of *Dionysus' Cup*; some stare, some spit, and others make rude remarks. I

---

[34]God of wine and pleasure.

pretend to not hear them and ignore the feeling of their saliva sliding down my skin. I close my eyes. My face hurts terribly, but I'm afraid to cry, afraid of what the tears would do to my wounded flesh. I stay this way for a while and go numb from the cold.

The door opens with a clatter, sign swinging before finally meeting its end and falling uselessly to the ground. Pain bursts at my hip when the warrior kicks me, his foot ready for another blow.

"Get up, you piece of shit. It's your lucky day because I—"He doesn't finish. A fist connects with his head, and he hits the cobbled ground with a hard thump and doesn't stir.

"Don't damage the merchandise."

This new voice is low, masculine, and dangerous. I struggle to raise my chin, but I'm able to see a large man in his mid-thirties—or maybe older, in a stark white tunic. His shoulders are broad, and he has a thick neck. His face is stubbled, and his hooked nose rests between unnaturally bright, amber eyes. In appearance alone, the man is a force to be reckoned with. However, it's the twin scimitar blades strapped to the sides of his dark breeches that catch my attention. By the way he carries himself, I'm sure they're not mere decoration.

I've fallen down into myself, and I'm weary in a way one does not easily recover from. It's taken everything I am to survive. And for what? So, I can endure more pain? Zadok would be better off never seeing my sorry self ever again. I can do nothing for him now anyway.

I study my presumed purchaser and expect him to be no different than the men I've met since leaving my tiny isle. I beg him, my voice hollow, "Please just kill me now. I can take no more."

"Kid, if death is what you want, then you should pray louder to Hades. It's pointless to pray to me." He inhales deeply on a long pipe and runs his fingers through messy brown hair that catches on a gold hoop in his right ear. He takes the pipe from his mouth and blows a cloud of smoke in my direction; the taste of cloves touches my tongue. I've smelled this scent before.

My eyes widen in shock.

"Fuck, you look like the Under spit you out from the depths of Tartarus[35]."

A bark of laughter escapes past my cracked lips, pulling at the wound on my disfigured face. I grimace and give him a hard stare. "Maybe it did."

The fluttering sensation returns, pulling low and fast in my abdomen. I'm transfixed by his amber stare, and the skin on my arms turns to goose flesh. He's not a good person. But, I sense that he means me no harm. I get a peculiar feeling that fate brought us together.

His name comes to mind and I break into a peal of mad laughter. Protector of children eh? The meaning of his name. The gods do have a sense of humor.

---

[35]A deep abyss below the Underworld used by the gods as a prison for their greatest enemies.

"The fuck?" Steilos says a bit unnerved.

My savior is a gambler and a killer to boot, not the wholesome figure I'd wish to run into nor would any other child for that matter. The information comes to me in an instant, a knowing I somehow just know.

I begin to feel pressure inside my head, as if someone is pressing their thumb against the front-most part of my brain, and then, a voice similar to my own, speaks inside my head. *//He can be important to us,//* she says.

Am I dreaming?

Steilos is speaking to me again, but I can barely make out the words. I've no energy left. I sag against my restraints, my eyes closing as I begin to lose consciousness. All the while, the voice inside my head speaks with persistence: *//Follow him. Follow, follow, follow, follow, follow...//*

Gods & Beasts of Miracle

A Lesson from the Moirai

To those who stumble along

the blurred edge of light & dark:

Be careful

of the voices

you listen to.

CHAPTER XVII

10th Week of Summer

Eimear

I wake disoriented to the sway and creak of wheels over uneven stone and the steady clop of horse hooves. My face is on fire from my self-inflicted butchery, the air frigid, and hard on my lungs. Opening one eye, I notice that a wool blanket has been draped over my naked frame.

Where am I?

I sit up slowly, managing to keep myself covered. Someone has tucked me into the back of a wagon crowded with crates and baskets. Stars flicker in the night sky, and from behind me comes the faint glow of a lantern. I turn toward the light and find Steilos sitting quietly with his back to me. He's smoking his pipe with one hand and holding the reins of a palomino horse in the other. I stare at the swords on the bench beside him.

"Don't even think about it. I could slice you up in a blink."

Gritting my teeth, I lay back down, and pull the blanket closer. It scratches my skin, but at least it's warm. Steilos draws from his pipe, and the smoke's clove scent wafts by.

"You're a quiet one," he mutters.

Perplexed, I say nothing. It's odd, this feeling. There's a sense of contentment where none should be. I'm in danger, but it's as though I'm not. I'm not scared at all.

//You can trust him…//

The fluttering in my stomach returns and I shake my head from side to side. This feeling is illogical.

//But trust yourself first.//

I freeze, unsure if I've truly gone mad. My mind previously rationalized that hearing someone speak to me in my head was due to stress. Am I talking to myself?

//Well yes . . . and no. We are we.// The voice is similar to my own, though she sounds a bit more spirited.

"Oh gods!" I sit up frightened.

//You'll startle Steilos if you keep that up.//

The wagon lurches to a stop as Steilos tuts to his horse, "Whoa Lady, whoa." He turns to me, brow raised. "I'd ask what's wrong, but I imagine you've been through the Under and back. You have the likeness of a skeleton, and half your face is charred meat. I don't want to be rude to a young lass."

//See, he has manners. We'll be just fine with him.//

I gape at Steilos. "There's . . . a voice in my head."

//Our voice.//

He appears just as confused as I am and speaks to Lady. "Maybe they beat her too hard." My vision darkens, and what little strength I have leaves altogether before I tumble sideways. Steilos catches me before I hit the side of the wagon.

//Eventually your body will get used to holding the both of us.//

I sit up with a start and realize two things: I've been asleep, and I feel no better than before. //Are you there?// I immediately ask the voice inside me.

Silence.

"You're awake!" Steilos calls from the other side of the wagon.

Slowly turning my head, I inspect my new surroundings. It's morning, and the wagon has stopped on the side of a hill. A breeze blows just enough to bend the tall indigo grass down the slope, and an assortment of rocks and rubicund shrubbery jut from the hillside. Leagues away, is a view of Nasarr. I'm so far from home. I clutch the woolen blanket more tightly. Zadok, I promise to find you again, no matter how long it takes.

Steilos approaches with a fresh plum in hand. "Here, catch," he says.

My reflexes are slow, and the fruit hits my shoulder before bouncing to the floor of the wagon. A primal hunger takes over as I watch the plum roll to a stop against a crate and I instinctively reach for it, forgetting the blanket as it falls away. A moan escapes my lips as my teeth bite into the plum's soft body and its juice sprays the inside of my mouth. I'm so hungry. Too soon the morsel is gone, and I'm left with nothing but the pit. I'd eat it too if I could. Instead, I lick the remainder of the juice off my fingers like an animal.

"Ahem." Steilos coughs.

I turn to see he has averted his eyes, and it takes a few seconds to put it together—I'm naked. I snatch the blanket and cover myself quickly. Fear overrides my intuition.

"Pervert," I hiss, remembering the two barbarians who harmed me. Steilos faces me then, his amber eyes have narrowed. The intensity of his glare is as sharp as the blades he wears. I swallow involuntarily.

"Kid, I don't know what sick fucks you've been handled by, but don't insult me. There's nothing about your flat self that I find appealing, and I've a woman with the biggest tits waiting for me back home." He gestures to his chest, emphasizing his point. "What are you, twelve? My appetites are not for children."

I'm baffled because Steilos's hands are still groping the imaginary breasts he has given himself. "I'm fourteen actually," I manage to say.

He shakes his head and leans over the side of the wagon, searching through the crates. The bulge of his muscles shows beneath his white tunic, and I'm reminded how easily he could snap my neck. He pulls string out of a basket and a folded cloth from another.

"Take this and tie it about yourself," he says gruffly before shoving the string into my hands.

Confused, I glance down at the twine, but then he turns his back giving me privacy and everything clicks. Ah. I wrap the wool blanket around myself and use the twine to secure it, managing to fashion it into a dress—though the blanket hangs poorly. But it's better than being nude. "I'm finished." I tell him.

Steilos cocks his brow with a sigh before handing me the folded cloth. My fingers open it to reveal a slice of cheese and bread inside. My mouth waters, and this time, I chew slowly to savor each bite.

He leaves me to my feast and busies himself with the mare, brushing Lady's white hair and golden coat. She becomes excited when her owner pulls a treat from his pocket and feeds her. "You really don't like to talk, huh kid."

I snap. "What do you want me to say? Thanks for buying me? Well fuck off." Pain and hunger have made me reckless.

Steilos throws his head back with a hearty laugh, one that's genuine and deep. I haven't heard that kind of sound in quite some time. Lady nickers beside him. "You still have some life in you; I like that."

I keep quiet, finding his lightheartedness insensitive.

"You can call me Steilos by the way."

I don't tell him I already know his name, but let a few moments pass before I grind out "Eimear" between bites of cheese.

He steps away from Lady and lights the pipe that never seems to be far from him. He takes a long draw. "I know you're Godmarked, kid. Your eyes gave it away first, but then I saw the mark when you were eating that plum like a savage."

I don't start at the term, "Godmarked," merely accept it. Revelations concerning gods have lost their surprise since I encountered Metis. Oh, and the fact that I now have a being inside my head that isn't me, but is me. Yeah, still trying to piece that one into a pattern that makes sense. What's one more for the list of unknowns?

Even so, I pause from my meal and reach for my left eye. Zadok and the man I murdered both mentioned a change in color, but it's not as if I've had a mirror on hand to give it much thought. When my fingers come into contact with the burn, it stings immensely, and I jerk away with a hiss.

Steilos notices, his expression full of pity turns my stomach.

"Sorry," he says. "I don't have any medicine to help you with that beastie . . . Not much can be done for it though, if I'm being honest."

I glare, not wanting his sympathy. "You mentioned a mark, what did you mean?"

He raises his chin toward me after exhaling from his pipe. "See for yourself. It's on your chest."

Oh! I did see something on my chest yesterday. I reach for my makeshift dress and peek under the top. Right above my heart rests a mark the color of gold and in the shape of a diamond. The silhouette is birdlike, similar to an owl—one of Metis' many symbols. My fingers trace the outline of the mark, finding it smooth to the touch, as if it's always been there.

//Hello voice that I somehow hear, do you know what this means?//

She remains silent. I sigh, irritated. She only speaks when she wants to. With reluctance, I ask Steilos, "What's it mean to be Godmarked?"

He takes another slow draw before replying. "You've been touched by a god, kid; that's the mark they left on you."

There's no awe in his voice, but there is pity, as if I've been cursed. "You don't sound thrilled for me."

He chuckles. "Anything to do with the gods stems from tragedy or ends with it. Looking at you, I'd guess yours is the former."

My back goes rigid, thinking of the night I was taken. I made a choice to save Zadok but did those events need to occur? The Goddess should've just saved us herself. Saved Paidia, my family, and destroyed the bastards who came for us. I want to deny it but know in my marrow what he says is true.

He strides toward me and rests his arm against the edge of the wagon before pulling up the sleeve of his tunic. On his inner bicep rests a dark red mark in the shape of a vulture, the symbol for Ares. I recoil immediately at the sight—the Maketaes' masks, burned into my memory forever.

Fuck. Fuck. Fuck! I scramble to get out of the wagon and have a leg straddled over the edge, but Steilos is much quicker and meets me at the other side. He catches my flying fists as if they're no more than mosquitos and pins me with his giant hands.

"Let go of me!"

"Whoa there!" Lady nays and stamps her feet in a show of distress.

I fight against him. "You're one of them! How could I think for a moment that I could trust you?"

Confusion crosses his face before it clears. "Oh. You think I'm . . . ?" He shakes his head. "Kid, you can't be more wrong, though I'll say it's in my blood. But you can't fault a bastard whelp for where he was born."

"So, you *are* from Manthros! You're one of those Maketae beasts." I try to rip free from his grip but only end up tiring myself out.

"You're going to hurt yourself if you keep moving like that! Just settle down! I'm not going to do anything to you."

I'm crouched in the wagon, teeth bared, but Steilos slowly lets go of my wrists and backs away with his hands raised.

"See? No threat. I've never been mistaken for one of the Maketae before, but I didn't think about the mark nor who I got you from. It's not something normal people can see, only those who've been

Godmarked themselves. I'm the only one alive with this particular ink, same goes for you."

What? Now I'm confused, but the fucks I have about the answers to my questions are zero. Despite my pain and exhaustion, I search the wagon for a weapon but don't find one.

"You're not going to find anything, and trust me, there's not a chance in this world that you can best me using the flour and wine in those baskets. So, for both our sakes, just take a moment and settle the Under down."

I watch him with wary eyes, searching for an opening to make a run for it, but I know that it would take a god's miracle for me to escape.

Steilos touches his chest. "Yes, I originally hail from Manthros, but not all people who are born there are warriors. My mother was a freewoman and chose to earn her living in a siren's house. My father? Not even the almighty Zeus himself would know—let alone Ares—how many patrons she fucked. So my sire is a mystery *but*, I was a runt as a child, and let's just say I didn't meet the qualifications to be a warrior."

I seriously doubt that. Every part of Steilos was sculpted for battle. "Your people . . . took everything from me."

The look of pity I hate so much reappears. "I know," he says. "I can see that as clear as the suns above. But I'm not them, I swear my life on it. And it's not an excuse, just a fact, that the Maketae haven't always been this way. When I was a lad, it would've been an honor to join their ranks. But those great warriors of the past are no longer, they're nothing more than sea-faring pirate scum now—" Steilos stares at the ground for a moment. "It may not mean much, but I'm sorry for whatever those evil bastards did to you."

Sincerity. It tugs on my gut like a lifeline. Maybe he's not so bad? I study his peculiar amber eyes that seem to hold the unspoken promise of protection. My gaze then travels down to his godmark, the predator that mars his skin. I must be a fool. But if I judge a person on the actions of others, then that would make me even a greater fool. And I was not named to be a fool.

I cross my arms over my chest. "You were marked by Ares then? The God of War? His bird sign is the vulture. It's fitting I guess, seeing as Manthros and their heathen warriors worship him."

Steilos grins, coming closer. "Kid, they are the only ones mad enough to idolize him."

They. So, not himself? Maybe we have more in common than we realize. I think back to his comment earlier about the gods. "Since you've been touched by one of them, will you tell me, are you the former or latter? Does your story start with tragedy or will it end with it?" I ask.

His smile disappears. "I pray you never find out." Steilos leans against the wagon, returning to his pipe. "It's time to go."

It's been over an hour since we began moving and Steilos hasn't spoken another word. I sit behind him, inside the wagon. For all my intuition, I don't feel comfortable sitting beside him at the front. But is he really just going to leave it at that? Brush our conversation aside? My patience has left me. "Is that all you're going to say about it then?" I ask and then mimic Steilos' deep voice: "'Godmarked means you've been marked by a god.' Well, no shit. And according to you, *I'm* the one who doesn't like to talk." I turn and look at his back expectantly.

He waves my comments away with a flick of the wrist. The sway of the wagon and the clop of Lady's hooves create a sense of familiarity. I feel Mana's embrace for a moment as my head begins to nod. I can see her standing over my baby brother's crib, rocking him gently as she stares out the window. Groggy, I stare up at the sky and wonder for the thousandth time: Why me?

//Because the gods need champions.//

I'm instantly awake at the sound of the mysterious voice and sit up straight while trying not to alert Steilos. //Who are you?//

//We've already told you, We're you.// It's an odd sensation, she has no body, but I know she's rolling her eyes at me.

//That doesn't make any sense,// I tell her.

//Not to you, but here we are.//

I hardly know how to respond. What does one say when they've gone mad?

//You're not mad. Whatever Metis shared with you that night has brought about an awakening. Think of us as you, but a different version. A sacred version.//

I scoff out loud at that, causing Steilos to offer me a worried glance, and I quickly pretend to be enthralled with a passing bush. After a few moments, I direct my thoughts to this 'sacred' version of myself. //If you've truly been with me all this time, why are you speaking to me now? Why were you quiet when I was stuck in that dreadful ship? I could've used a companion during those long weeks.//

//We've been with you, the entire time, through it all. We told you before it would be this way when we woke, and to trust yourself. Your body had to adjust to hearing our words. Although you've felt us many times.//

The fluttering sensation. I hadn't realized, but even now, it's happening. //So, you're an extension of myself?// I ask her.

She titters, *//You wish. It's more accurate to say that you're an extension of the "we."//*

//Well, aren't you just full of yourself.//

//Yes, we are! We love us.// I sense her beaming with joy, and I entertain the idea for a moment that I'm not going insane.

//If what you say is true, then all the premonitions and random knowledge I shouldn't know, that's all you? Like the man on the ship, or how I know I'm safe with Steilos?// I ask.

//It's us! We told you, We are we.//

//I'm having a hard time understanding all this.//

//It's fine. Right now, your human mind can only stretch so far.//

//Then . . . you know everything about everything?//

//We are not omnipotent.//

//You're confusing me.//

She sighs. *//We only know information that concerns us, and it changes all the time with the choices you make. There are infinite probabilities. You are an extension of the "we," but you also have free will. We can guide you, but you don't have to listen to our advice.//*

//Will you always tell me everything?//

//Life would be dull if you knew everything. It would also cloud your judgment and ergo, your free will. But when we say something, it's in your best interest to follow our advice.//

//Dull? Dull! I would welcome some dullness. Will you really not tell me?//

"Kid, is everything all good back there?" You're not dead are yuh? I haven't heard a peep since you started sassin'."

My body jerks at Steilos' voice. "I'm alive," I say while turning to him. Just going a little crazy over here.

//You're not crazy.//

Steilos snaps the reins lightly then turns to speak me. "Kid, are you sure you're all right? That burn is pretty gruesome."

I don't think I should say anything about her. He wouldn't believe me anyway . . . no one would. Styx, I don't even think I do.

I clear my throat, "I'm about as good as I can be, considering I have no idea where we're going or what all this business is with the markings and strange-colored eyes."

//We could tell you, but we'll just let him explain.//

Her flippancy brings out a certain kind of aggravation in me.

A flash of guilt passes across Steilos' face but then it's gone in a blink. "Whoa, Lady," he says, bringing up her reins and halting the wagon. "You're the only other person I've ever met with a god's mark." He pauses for a moment, as if searching for the right words. "You've probably already noticed this about yourself, but once you're marked, you're granted a Gift, like those born with a god's ichor."

//It's us. We're your Gift!//

//For the love of all gods, will you please shut up if you aren't going to be helpful? It's difficult focusing on two conversations at once. Especially when one of them is going on inside my head.//

//Well now, we'll just mind our own business then.//

With great difficulty, I bring my focus back to Steilos. "Do you know what the gods want? Why they marked us?"

He fishes for his pipe before answering. Once he locates it in his pocket, he lights the briar and the scent of cloves permeates the air. "All I know is that those who have it are supposed to be a champion of sorts for the god who chose them. Gods are fickle as they come, everything's a game to them. Fuck if I know what they're playing at, making us their pawns and such."

I bite my tongue; I sense a half-truth but I'm not in a position to make accusations without giving myself away. "What about the God of War?"

He chews on his pipe some before answering. "Ares doesn't speak to me. I've only met the bastard once."

"You mean he didn't tell you *anything* about what it is he wants?"

"Kid, I'm making an assumption here, but when your god appeared like magic before you, did the two of you become good pals and have a nice long chat that made sense? Or did they leave you feeling bereft and all kinds of confused?

Damn it. "Well . . . have you—how should I put it?—championed anything?"

"Far from it."

His most honest answer of the day.

An awkward silence follows, and just when I think Steilos has finished questioning me, he continues. "What's changed for you since you were marked?"

Everything. I almost snort. I could lie to him but decide to stick with a partial truth instead. "I somehow just know things . . . sometimes." I finish the last part lamely because it sounds absurd. But instead of ridicule, I'm met with excitement.

He almost drops his pipe. "What kinds of things do you know? Can you see the future?"

//Not quite, only in relation to yourself. As we told you before, it's constantly changing. Only some scenarios are certain. Everyone else's free will mucks it up a bit for us.//

I'm not sure how to explain it to him. "It doesn't work like you think." I pause, biting my lip. "It's more like heightened intuition I guess, and I become exhausted afterward." Even for the past few minutes, my energy has been draining a little at a time.

"A good skill to have. it'll keep you alive."

My sacred-self purrs agreeably.

"Hmmm…If I were to guess, a god of wisdom marked you," he says scratching his stubbled chin.

Steilos knows his gods well. "Goddess," I correct him. "It was Metis."

He gives me a wink. "I'm that good, kid."

I roll my eyes. "And you? What were you given?"

"Ha! I'm not telling you my secrets, but I'll say the fatigue goes away with practice."

"But I just told you everything!"

Steilos wags a finger at me. "A lesson—don't ever give anything away without payment first."

//He's right.//

I scoff, *//Well, you could have warned me. Isn't that your job?//*

//It's called free will, love.//

"Fine. Keep your secrets then," I say to both of them. I've a lot to think on, like how I could champion anything, let alone a goddess, in my situation. And why would I want to? She let my life fall apart. I hate her.

//Yes, she did. It's unforgivable.//

//I'm glad we agree on something.//

"Steilos, why did you buy me in the first place? And where are we going?" I edge my voice with venom. I haven't forgotten that I'm a slave still, even with all his pleasantries. He exhales one last time before he puts the pipe away.

//He's quite the chimney.//

At length, the man of mystery clears his throat. "Well, about that—"

A tremendous roar cracks the air like thunder, the sound making me feel like prey. Terrified, I hunker down inside the wagon and cover my ears.

I hear Steilos reach for his scimitars. "Gods' damn it! I was hoping for no trouble today."

CHAPTER XVIII

10th Week of Summer

Nikko

Why didn't they make this with a bit more cushion? I'm a prince of Zeus for gods' sake, this royal tush deserves it. As instructed, I sit on my throne, but whoever thought that solid gold would make a good chair was sorely mistaken. Heracles' emissary has paid us another visit and the Queen, Jada, and I have all been summoned to the throne room to play along with my father's ruse that we're a united family.

Erebos is dressed far too elegantly in the style of the Southern Region. It doesn't suit him now that I know his personality, or the lack of one. I'm not sure why, but at least the bastard didn't rat me out. My father asked how our excursion went, I didn't bother to mention the candied sex plums or the foolhardy duel. He only knows that our stroll around the Holy City played out in a very diplomatic fashion. And hopefully, it stays that way.

Erebos appears indifferent as he inspects the nails of his left hand, waiting for my father's permission to speak. Most would think him a harmless aristocrat, but his onyx eyes don't fool me; there's something else going on behind those black coals. He could've easily gutted me in the sparring ring but he didn't. I won't forget it.

His gaze finds mine and, for a moment, it's as if there's just the two of us in the throne room. Something ignites in his stare. Does he think we're friends after what happened? To the Under with that. He's my enemy. I give him a look of disdain. My father gives a slight nod of his head and Erebos steps forward. Finally, the posturing is over.

"King Zephyr, I've come to present Princess Jada with a betrothal gift on behalf of the Autokrator."

What an archaic title. Only a limp-dick man would call himself so. When the emissary speaks again, I imagine what it would feel like to run him through with my blade.

"A boy of ichor, a Gifted healer for the Princess. Should she ever fall ill, the Autokrator wishes to restore her to the best of health."

There's a slight intake of breath around the room. Gods' blood—ichor—has become a rarity not only in Ellanios but for the entirety of Ehvara. It's repulsive to exploit the descendent of a god, and it's considered sacrilegious as well. Erebos motions with his hand and, from the open throne room doors, a boy only slightly younger than myself is pulled into view by two of Heracles' men. His hands are bound by gold manacles with a collar around the neck to match. My anger spikes.

To the Under with this farce and my forefathers celebrated cold-calm. This is outrageous. I wear my emotions openly and without shame. I want the Emissary to know what I think of his gift, and speak out of turn. "You're aware that Ellanios doesn't partake in the slave trade. It's a disgusting business. The same goes for those who participate in it."

Erebos doesn't spare me a glance.

"Nikko. You will treat our guest with respect, or you will remove yourself." My father's Ellanion eyes are like the brightest of diamonds, sharp and cutting, set in a face cold as granite, which is how mine *should* be, but I can't seem to keep my damn temper in check. His deep voice doesn't raise in volume, but commands authority just the same, and assures me of what a fuck-up I am.

My fingers clench the arms of my throne as I stare at my father, who's never been fatherly in any sense of the word. How different we are. I sometimes wonder if my mother made him a cuckhold. I hate all this stoicism and the fact that nothing is as it seems. It's exhausting trying to figure out what he's thinking behind that solemn gaze.

And why has he prolonged his decision on the alliance? With the steady increase of market prices as well as reports of the tyrant making further progress in the Southern Region's trenches, tensions have been high in the Holy City as of late. Every morning there's a crowd at the palace gates demanding my father sign a treaty with Heracles, or as they call him: The True Son of Zeus. I was the first one to think that Father would make Jada into a sacrificial lamb, but he hasn't. The king has bided his time, stringing Erebos along. But why?

I plaster a smile on my face as fake as a woman's breathy sighs on her arranged wedding night, and dip my head in mock deference toward the diplomat. Though, the anger never leaves my eyes. "My apologies for the outburst."

"None is needed from you," Erebos replies quickly.

That's not the reaction I was expecting after what happened last time.

My father's voice is flat, "Emissary of Heracles, we accept your gift with gratitude."

Ugh. I have to keep myself from rolling my eyes and instead survey the boy below. He looks as if he's traveled to the Underworld and back, despite his fine white clothing. His cheeks are hollow, and his head is missing sandy patches of hair. He stands with his head bowed and hands clasped in front of him. I don't understand how we can continue with this farce.

Jada leans into the arm of her throne, her long braids grace her elbows, and her lips are pressed into a straight line. She's playing her role well, but I feel as if I can read her mind. She doesn't plan to keep the boy, much to my relief. Our mother's dark eyes are unreadable, her clenched hands in her lap are the only indication that she's upset at all. Heracles conquered her homeland and slayed my grandparents as well as her sister. Ever since, she hasn't been able to forgive my father because he didn't send additional reinforcements to Anyalay, even when she pled with him to do so.

My father is still busy being obsequious. "Please give Heracles our best regards."

"You mean the Autokrator," Erebos corrects the King and gives a sweeping bow, the silver chain he wears hangs just barely outside his tunic.

At the emissary's remark, even my father grits his teeth, and Jada hides a smirk behind her hand. "He's so strange," she mouths to me. The Queen shakes her head at the two of us, giving a silent warning to behave ourselves.

Really, he's the worst at diplomacy. It takes all my self-control to watch the King placate him.

Erebos straightens and addresses both my parents. "King Zephyr, Queen Himari, the Autokrator is optimistic that he'll have an answer from you shortly and has asked me to stay until you come to a decision."

My eyes nearly pop out of my skull. Styx! He's going to be sticking around? For how long? This is Heracles' way of pressuring us.

My father waves a hand, dismissing the emissary. "I'd expect no less. Odelia, will you find accommodations for our guest?"

The palace attendant, at her post by the door, bows then speaks directly to Erebos. "Sir, if you will, follow me please."

When the doors close behind them, the room erupts, and my mother's voice is the loudest with the brunt of her anger directed at my father.

"This is your fault!" She slaps the arm of her throne. "We wouldn't be housing that snake or allying with a tyrant if you'd taken care of Heracles when he was nothing more than a house cat. Now he's a lion, and we're at his mercy."

My father says nothing at her outburst, but a shade of regret lingers in the way he holds his shoulders. They've had this argument many times; enough that it has broken the love between them.

The meaning behind my mother's words finally registers. I glare at the King. "You're going through with it then? You'd marry your only daughter off to a lunatic?" I stand quickly, swept up in fury.

His gaze is like ice. "Sit down, boy. You're getting too old for tantrums." My father pinches the bridge of his nose. "You still think like a child. Start strategizing like a king or your head will never be worthy of a crown. Follow Jada's example; she knows her duties and puts Ellanios before her own desires."

The flames of my rage are quickly doused by shame, because he's right. My sister would make a far better king than me. If I could trade places with her, I would.

She watches the two of us with a half smirk before speaking up. "There's no need for anyone to be upset on my behalf and anyway, father hasn't fully decided yet. What I'd rather discuss, though, is this boy here that everyone is ignoring and treating so poorly."

We stop bickering and turn to look at Heracles' forgotten *gift*. Slavery is outlawed in Ellanios; the idea of keeping him is preposterous, but I'm not sure we can let him go either with him being a gift of war.

The boy remains with his head down. I'm not sure he understands what's happening.

My father addresses him. "Boy, what is your name?" When the slave doesn't answer, my father switches from Ellanion and repeats his question in the common tongue.

He understands this time and looks up, green eyes desolate. "Gareth, Your highness."

"And where do you hail from Gareth?"

The boy's mouth quivers for a moment before he answers. "I come from Paidia. It's a small fishing village. Or was, before it was sacked, sir. I mean, your highness."

Paidia? I've never heard of it or even seen it on a map, for that matter. It seems the usurper is leaving no stone unturned in his quest for domination over Ehvara.

My father has the decency to at least look troubled. "It's under unfortunate circumstances, Gareth, but welcome to Ellanios. You are now in my kingdom, and we don't accept slaves like some other countries do. However, you've been caught in a web of political negotiations, and I'm not able to let you go back to your homeland until these negotiations are over. Please stay at the palace as my guest until further notice."

Gareth's expression turns to shock, and he bows so deeply that the chains from the shackles on his wrists touch the floor. "You have my utmost gratitude, your highness. Thank you for your kindness."

The King leans forward with interest. "Is it true that you possess a god's blood? One that can heal?"

The newcomer fumbles for his words but manages to find them. "Yes, your highness, although I'm still learning. I'm not that skilled yet, if I'm being honest."

My father drums his fingers against the arm of his throne and nods his head in thought. "You have my permission to study as much as your heart desires during your visit as my guest. There are no known healers with your abilities in Ellanios, but we have an expansive library, and I'm sure there are books from years past on the subject."

"Thank you, sir. I'll make sure to take advantage of them while I'm here," the boy says with another deep bow.

The King claps his hands together, eyes searching for a servant. "Please see this young man's shackles removed and get him to new living quarters." Two attendants step forward and give Gareth tentative smiles as they take him by the hand and lead him out of the throne room.

"If you're smart," my father leans back in his throne, and turns to me, "you'll befriend that boy and hope he decides to make a life here in Ellanios." He taps his chin. "We could benefit from someone of his abilities. Heracles may be a violent usurper, and what he's done is appalling, but the boy is an opportunity we shouldn't waste."

I sour at the idea; I don't treat people as tools. "I'll think about it," is all I say, and the King rolls his eyes with displeasure.

"You've got to be fucking kidding me," I swear, hours later when I spy Erebos with his bow and arrow. He stands alongside my sister in one of the palace's long and narrow courtyards. Ivor, the archery instructor walks behind them both, adjusting their stance to his liking.

"Okay, now fire!"

The two let their arrows fly. Erebos hits the makeshift mark stationed at the far end of the yard and my sister misses. Her arrow veers too far left and lands in the pink shrubbery that encases the entire back wall.

"I thought you said you weren't skilled with a bow! You should be giving me lessons!" She exclaims and playfully shoves the emissary's shoulder.

What's she doing? He's the enemy.

Erebos stiffens at her touch and studies the princess's face longer than what's considered socially appropriate.

Ivor notices and his lip curls in a blatant show of jealousy.

Oblivious, Heracles' emissary finally speaks and gestures toward the target. "I don't consider this level to be skilled. The distance is not far between the mark and us."

Jada's face breaks into a bright smile, and she laughs. "You're too funny! If I had known, I would have dragged you to one of my lessons sooner—on one of your earlier visits. This instructor here is a bit dry for my taste." She winks at Ivor who isn't amused.

Does she even know that he's infatuated with her? I've a knack for picking up on these things. Ivor's hand has lingered more than once on her shoulder during their lessons, and I've caught him staring at her on a few occasions. But that's not the problem right now.

I can't help but ruin whatever it is they're up to and call out casually, "Shouldn't you be taking up say . . . weaving or pottery or, I don't know, maybe something a bit more girly?" The three turn and look in my direction. "I mean, poor Ivor's got his work cut out for him with that sorry shot of yours, Jada. And I don't think Heracles will find the skills of archery pleasing in a wife. If you're bored, you should try on wedding gowns instead of using archery to pass the time."

I walk out from under one of the archways lining the courtyard as if I'm unbothered, though I'm actually furious. How could she, of all people, be friendly with one of Heracles' men? I was forced to play nice with the bastard, but what's her excuse?

My sister considers me for a moment with her mouth slightly upturned and her eyes squinted in concentration. She reaches for an arrow and nocks it against the bow. I freeze mid-step and wish I hadn't spoken as she turns the weapon on me. With the aim Jada just displayed, I might lose an eye or worse—one of my precious jewels.

Blessed Ivor holds out a hand to stop her, "I don't think that's—"

"Would you like to say that to me again, my dear brother, whom I love not so very much right now?"

Ivor's mouth drops in shock. "Princess, you really shouldn't do that."

I hold up my palms in surrender. "Let's not be hasty, I was only jok—"

Jada releases the arrow, and it speeds past my face, nicking my left ear in the process.

I hiss and reach for the injury, my fingers become wet with blood. "You actually shot me!"

My twin shrugs and hands her bow to Ivor before bending in a slight curtsy toward Erebos. "Truly, it was a delight. We'll speak at length later."

She leaves him then, taking long strides across the courtyard to me. Jada leans in toward my bloody ear. "You should know by now, I only miss my target when I *want* to miss." She clasps me on the shoulder. "Best go to the infirmary." She winces. "Hopefully your ear won't scar."

I glare as I whisper, "You're consorting with the enemy. He brought a slave to Ellanios. A *slave* Jada."

"He is but a messenger, a puppet. Imagine, if you will, a kind of slave to Heracles. Much like I'll be soon. I prefer to get to know others before I judge them." She glances back at Erebos and winks before facing me again. "And I'm going to need friends when this is all said and done. Is it so wrong of me to choose one from our future allies, albeit an attractive one? Now if you'll excuse me, I have an appointment with the seamstress to browse swatches for my *wedding gown*." Her last words are uncharacteristically bitter, and I'm filled with shame for antagonizing her.

Jada leaves and I stand bleeding in the courtyard, feeling like a fool as Ivor clears away the archery gear. I'm wary when Erebos approaches me.

"Prince may I speak freely?"

I snort. "Don't you always?"

He reaches for the chain under his collar and rubs it between his thumb and forefinger. "I have excellent hearing."

My brows narrow. "Eavesdropping, now are you? Emissary, should I consider you a spy?"

Staring off in the direction where my sister went, he says with a straight face, "I think you are what most people would call *a jackass*, your highness."

I give him the moutza[36], extending my five fingers wide toward his face. "Fuck you, Erebos," I say and walk away. I really hate that man.

---

[36]A gesture of great insult that promises misfortune to the recipient.

CHAPTER XIX

10th Week of Summer

Eimear

In my lessons with Elder Marcus, I learned many things, but one can never be truly prepared for beastly monsters. I stare open mouthed, my panic quickly rising as the chimera slowly makes its way up the hill. Two jagged, spiked horns protrude from the beast's golden mane. Its lion's mouth, pulled back in a snarl, reveals snake fangs the size of a man's fist. At the shoulders, the lion's body ends and another creature begins. The large cat's front paws have been replaced with a vulture's talons and its hindquarters with cloven hooves. Its spine is lined with barbs and whipping back and forth at its rump, is a scaled tail with a serpent's head. I'd think the chimera stunning, if I wasn't so fucking terrified.

The monster stops its trek up the hillside and leans back on its haunches, preparing to strike. Surprisingly, Lady stamps at the ground and tosses her mane with a cheeky neigh as if warning the creature to stay back or there'll be the Under to pay. Steilos on the other hand, groans, like you would if shit were found on the bottom of your boot instead of finding a hungry chimera in the way and ready to pounce.

Twin swords in hand, he stands and gives me a backwards glance from the front of the wagon. "Since the war started, they've been migrating farther south. We're in luck though, this one doesn't have wings."

I'm frozen as my fingers grip the side of the wagon in fear. "You mean…they can *fly*?"

He smiles. "Sit tight; I'll be right back."

Dazed, I watch as he launches himself off the wagon to land gracefully on a nearby rock. Lured by the movement, the chimera follows him and Steilos raises his scimitars in a fighting stance. The beast growls, and its tail weaves back and forth. The snake head fixes its piss-yellow eyes on me, venom dripping from its open jaw. It lashes forward snapping its long teeth, and I scramble back against the far side of the wagon, fear getting the best of me. I was out of reach before, but a little more distance can't hurt.

My sacred-self pipes up, *//Ground yourself, Eimear. You can command it to go away if you wish. Some creatures will listen. But then again, some won't.//*

//Tell it to go away? I'm great with languages but do you really think I speak chimera!//

The snake weaves its head and lashes out again, biting air.

//*Spoken word is not the only way to give commands. Ground yourself and find out.*//

//I don't understand what you mean when you say that.//

//*You need to feel for it.*//

//Isn't that the same thing as winging it?// I swallow as I grapple for any sentience beyond myself, but my heart is pounding so gods damn hard. I can't concentrate. My vision darkens at the corners, my energy nearly drained.

"Come here, yuh big puss!" Steilos calls while tapping his blades together.

My heart leaps into my throat as the chimera gives a final threatening roar and launches its muscled body into the air, talons raised to shred my new companion. I know I'm next in line to be butchered if I stay here. I contemplate if I have the stamina to run when I see Steilos' mad grin, as if the chimera is a gift from the gods meant only for him.

He jumps from the rock, twisting his body before running his blades through the underside of the beast. It yowls and blood pours from the creature's gutted belly before it falls into a crumpled heap. Steilos lands gracefully with knees bent, twirling his blades and the chimera's gore spatters the ground.

It's dead. Just like that? It all happened so quickly, that my brain has difficulty processing it. I'm not knowledgeable about swordplay, but I recognize that his skill is beyond advanced even for someone mastered in the art of blades. This must be his Gift from Ares.

A spec of blood has marred the shoulder of his tunic. He scoffs, then tries to clean it but only manages to spread it, permanently staining the white fabric. He tsks. "Another ruined. My old lady is going to be sore with me."

On shaky legs, I stand up in the back of the wagon and stare at the dead chimera. Its corpse lays sideways, innards spilling out, blood mixing with the indigo grass, turning it black. The snake end twitches, eyes closed, taking its final breath.

The situation is surreal. All my life, I wanted to escape my small island and face monsters just like this one. But as the creature passes to the Underworld, sadness and regret plague my insides. Its glorious mane and glossy scales will shine no longer. Life will never thrum in its veins ever again. The chimera must've had reason to attack. We may have skirted too close to its nest or even traversed its hunting grounds. And now . . . it's dead.

Why am I getting emotional over this? It just tried to kill me. Perhaps, I feel a kinship because, like the chimera, I'm doing my best to survive in a world that keeps trying to destroy me. I gaze at its lifeless form and can't help but wonder when I'll meet the same fate.

Steilos sheaths his swords and stretches with a grunt. "Gods, I'm getting old. I could've handled that sooner in my younger years." He eyes me carefully. "What's the matter, kid? You look like someone who missed out on the last cheese pie."

"Where are you taking me?"

He rolls his shoulders. "We better hurry, or more will come. Chimeras like to eat their dead."

This arse just completely ignored my question. But I guess it's more important for now to keep moving.

As Steilos hoists himself back into his driver's seat and fiddles with his pipe, I kneel inside the wagon and pray for the first time in many weeks. But not to Metis who abandoned me, or to any other god on Olympus—no. For the first time ever, I pray to the God of the Under.

"Please be gentle with this soul if it passes through your gate. The beast was just following its nature." As soon as I finish the prayer, there's a stirring in my heart, that brings a sudden chill. I know without a doubt, Hades heard me.

"Can you *please* just tell me where we're going? Or even why you bought me?" I ask Steilos.

Pipe in his mouth, he eyes me but turns away to face the road. The heat of the day has me exuding sweat from every pore, putting me in the foulest of moods. We're moving at a quicker pace than before in case any other dangerous beasts are lurking about. The wagon jostles and bumps, making my face sting and my arse hurt. There is also the ever-persistent pounding in my head, as if Hephaestus[37] himself is taking to it with his great mallet.

Styx! I feel myself levitate as the wagon catches air and I'm brought right back down, landing on my tailbone. For fuck's sake, this is awful. Just on time, my chest heaves with a rattled cough to add an extra bit of misery.

"Well, kid, I need your help," Steilos finally says.

I look down, examining the skin and bones I've become. I cowered at the first sign of a chimera, and I'm crippled by nightmares of roving hands, the slimy feeling doesn't leave when I wake. He's mistaken. I'm useless. "You must be wading through the dark river if you're asking help from me—" I rub my chest. My lungs feel like they are full of fire. "I'm your slave now, aren't I? You could just order me."

"You're not a slave…well … not for me anyway," he says slowly.

Any hopes I had disappear. Not that I particularly care for Steilos, but he's the best person I've met so far in the storm of Underfire and shit that has become my life. I'm afraid to ask but do anyway. "Who owns me then?"

"To begin, you need to know that I'm a man of many ventures."

I eye him skeptically. "No, I need to know who owns me."

---

[37]God of blacksmiths, fire, and the forge.

Steilos clears his throat. "As I was saying, I'm a man of many ventures, one of which, is handling goods and other requests for one of the Autokrator's generals."

Heracles. "Is he *really* an immortal? The Autokrator, I mean." For the moment, gathering information about the person who's responsible for ruining my life is more important to me than where I'm going. The bastard needs to pay for what he's done. Who knows when I'll have another chance to learn about him? Besides, wherever Steilos is taking me, I don't plan on staying there. I'm going to run away at the first opportunity.

"I dunno," he says talking around the stem of his pipe.

"How can you not, if you work for a general of his?" I ask, incredulously. I'm not getting the sense that he's lying, but still, the utter lack of knowledge frustrates me.

"Kid, aren't you the one who just happens to *know things*," Steilos says. "I've struggled to survive since the day I came out of my mother, wet and screaming. It's not made a difference to me whose head wears a crown, swinging their dick about. And for the record, it's not as if I've laid eyes on the bastard. His generals are the wards of his territories."

My face must appear pathetic because he continues with a sigh. "Only one of his generals could confirm who and what Heracles is.

There *are* whispers, though, that the Autokrator never leaves his stronghold in the Blood Isles[38].

My mouth goes dry at the very mention of the cursed land. Located in the far northeast, it's usually only referenced in chilling tales around a hearth. Anyone who is said to have traveled to the Blood Isles has gone insane or never made it home alive. I groan. "It'll take a miracle to find someone to sail me there and they'd have to be half-mad already to even consider it."

"What? You wanting to have a good ole chat with the Autokrator? He's almost brought half of Ehvara to its knees and you want to go *see* him?" Steilos continues to laugh at me until he coughs.

I scowl as my insides melt with embarrassment. What a dumb slag I am. He's right; how could I ever claim revenge over someone so powerful?

//We'll play the long game.//

//But how am I going to do that? If you haven't noticed, I'm pathetic.//

//You have yet to rise. Trust yourself, and you can do anything. Have faith.//

//My faith, along with many other things, died on that ship.//

//No, we do not speak of gods or goddesses—//

---

[38]A cluster of islands with jutting formations made of augite. Little is known about the isles, other than they are cursed to weep blood and the rapid fog that descends is said to drive men with good hearts mad.

Pushing her aside, I return to my conversation with Steilos, who's more real than the chittering girl inside me. "Then who's this general I'm being carted off to?"

He removes his pipe from his mouth and fully turns to me, letting Lady steer. "Charos, General Charos."

His name means death. Who would name a child so? "Sounds like a serious fellow," I say with mock bravado.

Steilos is silent for a beat, all amusement gone from his face. "He's a cruel man. I don't take a child to Castle Notos[39] lightly. He was given stewardship over the lower half of the Southern Region when he and Heracles' men descended upon the land. It's why Nasarr is the way it is now, infested with malice and decay."

An icy fear settles into my marrow. Ares' champion just slayed a monstrous chimera without breaking a sweat, and he's worried about a man. What kind of person can General Charos be? "Then why take me there at all?" I ask quietly.

He slides a hand down the length of his face. "I'm a peddler of sorts to the General and make supply runs for the castle and any other

---

[39]Formerly known for its artistic brilliance, Castle Notos was built by the finest artisans from Avanta and Nasarr more than 600 years ago. For many generations, the castle was maintained by the Techni family, a noble family whose members were famously known for their skill in all art forms. When Charos claimed the castle as his own, he cut the tongues, eyes, and fingers from every living Techni and sent them to Avanta's King as a declaration of war on the Southern Region.

unique quota the damned fucker requests. Another set of hands this time, amongst other things, was on the list Saray gave me."

"Who's Sara—"

"When that mercenary waltzed into Dionysus' Cup bragging he had just what I needed at a fraction of the usual price, I thought it was my lucky eve, and I'd pocket the rest," Steilos says cutting me off. It's as if he's confessing his sins to the gods and not to a small girl who's seen better days. There's anguish in his eyes, but I've no pity for him.

He continues on, "But when I saw you, just a wisp of a thing, just a child, I realized I'd made a mistake. I was going to let you go, but then your blasted eyes gave you away as a Godmarked, and I knew our crossing was fated by the gods. You see, I've been searching for a rare item for a long time—nearly half my life—and I've never gotten close to it. Until now. I'm certain it's in the General's possession, but I'm not able to verify this information myself or if it's located in his castle. Such a feat requires stealth." Steilos points a finger at me. "But you, you're different. You can sniff it out with the help of your Gift, and no one would suspect a young girl of all people. The gods brought us together for a reason; I'm so confident of it that I'd gamble away my left sac."

Gross, my nose wrinkles at the imagery. He speaks the truth, but it doesn't make me happy in the least. The gods did bring us together, but I don't give a shit about what they desire anymore. "No. I won't do it," I tell him and turn away.

"No? You can't just say no!" He must pull at the reins, because Lady slows, and the cart comes to a lurching stop. "You're not in a position to."

I laugh. "You're right, I'm not, but I have a gut feeling because, you know, 'I just know things,' and it's telling me that you can't do shit about me saying no. You're just a big softy with pointy blades, and I'm not afraid of you."

Steilos draws himself up in a menacing posture and steps across the wagon's bench to stand in front of me. He palms the hilt of one of his blades. "You were saying?"

I'm nervous, but I'm also confident he won't hurt me. Pushing against the wagon for support, I rise to my feet and bring my hands to my hips. "I. Said. No." The air begins to feel thick as anger rolls off Steilos' body in waves. He's a man used to being obeyed, not defied.

"Fuck!" he grinds out between clenched teeth instead of making good on his threat. The large manchild turns and kicks a nearby crate before jumping from the wagon. He strides away, cursing as he goes.

Relief washes over me, and I sink back down until I'm sitting once again. I can't believe I did it. I said no. Standing next to a patch of flowers, Stelios stares up at the Gods' Window and the twin suns as if asking for answers. I hope he looks long enough to burn those bright eyes right out of his skull. I reach for my temple, the ache in my head is building and the rest of my face feels ready to melt with the heat. The burn wound is infected. I close my eyes, searching for relief.

"Kid, you look like shit."

I give him a withering look, "Well, I feel like shit you jackass."

For a moment, Steilos stares at the ground. "I'm sorry for making that request of you."

"I'd be a fool to help you," I say as lean against the wagon. "And there's nothing you've done to deserve my aid anyway."

He nods his head, as if he's made a decision. "It's about a day's travel back to Nasarr. I have some friends there that can take care of you until you're better. It won't put me behind schedule too badly. It's the least I can do. Though I caution you to head for Ellanios if you can find a boat. Avanta's the closest free kingdom, but it's impossible to reach by horse now. They're bound to lose their footing at the trenches anyway. Soon the entire Southern Region will be no place for a girl such as yourself."

Is it true? I'm free? That's it? I'm done? No more pain? I don't quite decipher all of what he says as I'm in a state of euphoric shock. Steilos climbs back up to the head of the wagon and my hopeful thoughts take off in a gallop. He guides Lady in a turn, heading her back the way we came, and I start to cry. When tears reach the burn on my face it stings anew, but I don't care because I'm *free*.

Minutes pass, my consciousness fading with the need to sleep, but something underlying prods me, like an itch I can't scratch, that inhibits me from sweet oblivion. I realize I'm grinding my teeth. I won't be able to rest until I find out why.

"Steilos, you mentioned that you were searching for something. What is it?"

He inhales from the tip of his pipe and then exhales the scent of cloves. "I suppose there's no harm in telling you. Ares tasked me to find and secure a gemstone of sorts, a very specific citrine. Sounds like such a small thing, but it must be some divinity shite the gods are playing at if he wants it."

For a second time, my world tilts sideways. I remember . . . A natural azurite, the color of Zadok's eyes, rough and fitting between my two fingers just so. Though I don't recall exactly what, something was off about it when I said my final goodbye to him. It must be my Gift acting up, because I know without a doubt, there's a connection with that azurite and Steilos' citrine.

//Will a stupid rock lead me back to my brother?// I ask my sacred-self.

//*You could go with him. It's your choice though. Your life*// she says.

//Are you telling me that if I go with Steilos, find this citrine, that I'll see Zadok again?//

//*You already know the answer to this. Trust yourself.*//

//But… Is there no other way?//

//*There are always other routes, different paths to roam. This one is presenting itself now.*//

//But what if another one doesn't appear? What if this is my only chance?//

//*You must learn to trust yourself. It's your life. Your choices. We can't make them for you.*//

This fork in my path makes me anxious. Which way should I take? What if I choose poorly? My heart doesn't want to go, but logic tells me that I'm in a foreign land with little resources. That I'm a spec of dust in the vast world and that finding Zadok is going to take a miracle. The ongoing war will also complicate matters further.

I scream into my palms trying to muffle the sound before glowering in the direction of the East Window. Why? Why me? Why do I have to decide these things? There's no answer, not from Metis or my sacred-self. Only a familiar, damning silence.

"Kid, are you all right?"

"Turn around," I manage to say.

"What?" Steilos says shocked.

"Take me to this General Charos. I'll find your citrine."

When he halts Lady once more, she whinnies in obvious irritation.

"Kid, are you sure? Charos is ruthless and will make any sack of shit mercenary you've dealt with look like child's play." His expression is stern. "The moment you're caught snooping, it's over. You're dead. He's been blessed with ichor and his hobby is extracting blood from others. Charos won't make allowances for a young girl, understand?"

I swallow, finding the task of stealing from a general who possesses a Gift, a little more than daunting. But no matter the difficulty, finding the gem will put me on the path back to my brother. "Do you want me to help you or not?"

Steilos appears uncomfortable, scratching at his chin, but he doesn't decline the offer.

I roll my eyes. "That's what I thought."

I reflect on what it's going to take to get back to Zadok. The road ahead will be long and filled with unknown dangers. As I am now, I'm not enough. Once again, I eye the man's scimitars. "I want something in return as payment for my trouble. Well, three things actually."

He nods. "Anything within reason. You've wised up. Never do anything for free."

"Well, I want my freedom, a home, and I want you to teach me the way of the blade," I say, counting with my fingers.

His eyes spark with something like surprise and a hint of mischief, but the smile he gives is sincere. "Now that, I can do."

A cough seizes my chest. Ugh. It's getting worse.

He notices and changes to all business. "While you're at Notos, try not to draw attention to yourself. Even if you feel like you're dying, push through and keep up with any task assigned. If you appear too weak, Charos or one of his guards may decide that you're not worth keeping and then we're both in trouble."

Cheeky bastard. I cough into my fist. "How very kind"—I cough—"of you to be concerned on my behalf."

Steilos eyes me again. "Kid, it's not too late to change your mind."

I shake my head as trepidation fills my heart. I can't believe I'm doing this. I *should* give up while I'm able instead of going on a treasure hunt in a mad man's castle. What new Under am I getting myself into? The fear is evident in my voice when I say, "What else can you tell me about him?"

Steilos shifts nervously in his seat. "I don't know much if I'm honest, but out of the five generals, Charos was the last to join their ranks. As for the kind of man he is, the scoundrel laid waste to nearly every village and city on the southern side of the trenches upon his arrival. He only left Nasarr untouched because it's a port city, and it's rumored that Castle Notos was saved because he fancies the artwork there. It was all done on Heracles' order, but Charos is the type that enjoys dealing pain. The man loves games, especially ones that involve blood."

"And you're *working* for such a monster?" I ask, horrified.

"Hey now, I told you, I'm a man of many ventures. I don't discriminate against gold."

I snap at the other girl inside me, //Why in the Under would you tell me to follow such a person? He's absolutely terrible!//

She doesn't respond.

Steilos continues on, "The stone is likely to be near or on the General's person. If you discover it, light a lantern and place it in the top north window of the castle. I'll have an eye on the window every eve and will come back for you when the lantern's lit."

My anxiety jumps to its peak and I begin to chew on the tip of my thumbnail. "I don't know how I'm going to steal from him though. Sounds like he'll kill me for sure."

His eyes go wide. "Kid, no! Charos will do worse than just kill you if you try thieving from him. I only want you to *locate* the stone, I'll figure out the rest."

Well, that's a relief. I almost start to relax when I quickly realize something. "But what if it's not there at all? You can't expect me to search endlessly," I say.

He holds up six fingers, for a moment it looks like twelve. I close my eyes and breathe out slowly, waiting for the nausea to pass. Another sign of infection. I need medicine soon.

"Six months. You just have to survive six months and give it your best. The sooner you locate the citrine, the quicker you leave. But if you can't find a trace of it within that time, I'll come back for you still."

I roll the rough cloth of the blanket I wear between my fingers as if it'll bring me some comfort. I'm not the trusting person I used to be. "You swear it? Even if I don't find this gem you're wanting so badly, you'll come back for me?"

"Kid, I swear it on my soul, may Hades have it if I abandon you. And let me tell you this, even if you don't find what I'm looking for, you'll still get what you want. I'll teach you how to master the blade and put a roof over your head for as long as you wish it, stone or no stone."

I feel hopeful for a heartbeat. This may just work out for me. I ask just to be certain, "Not as a slave though? As a free person?"

Steilos cocks an eyebrow. "You'll be a free person with a paid job. I don't accept free loaders."

I feel as though I'm getting the shitty end of this bargain, but I'll have somewhere to stay and be able to earn my own coin when this is all over. I'll also be one step closer to finding Zadok. If I survive that is.

I extend a hand to him, my skin damp with sweat.

"It's a deal," he says.

As we shake on it, the rightness of this new adventure sings to my bones. A sense of purpose settles over me. At least I have a direction now. It's a start.

Gods & Beasts of Miracle

Uranus

Ruler of heaven,

husband to earth,

father of titans,

and cruelest being,

after Cronus your youngest

rose and castrated your godliness

with his mother's scythe,

and threw your seeds to the sea,

where did you go?

Part III

Light in the Shadows

"Of all things first, I'm a healer.

I'll not let the cruelty of men,

nor the world for that matter,

change the good inside me."

—Gareth

CHAPTER XX

10th Week of Summer

Eimear

Lady snorts with exhaustion as the wagon rolls to a stop. I'm burning up with fever, my skin cold and clammy and dusted with grime from the road. Nausea rolls in my belly like the large swells in the Aethiopia Sea. The sickness could be from my burn, but I'm not ruling out the filth-infested water from the ship. Either way, the Under River is calling my name with a sweet song now, urging me to come take a swim. Was it all for nought? Am I to die in the back of a wagon? I think of the soil of my home. It would've been better to die there alongside my people, not in some foreign land.

Staring at the stars above, I wonder if Mana sees the same ones in Elysium. Maybe I'll join her soon? Or, will it be Hades welcoming me on his damnable river? My vision swims with dark spots as I fight to stay awake, and every inch of me thrums with pain after bouncing against the wagon's floor for hours on end. //Hey sacred-self, do you think this is it? Is this where we die?//

Silence.

There is a round of urgent chatter outside the wagon, a familiar baritone voice stands out. What's Steilos saying? Did we arrive at Castle Notos? He appears from the side, his jaw tense as he takes stock of my condition. Without a word, he scoops me into his arms and cradles me to his chest. For a brief time, I'm a child again, safe in the arms of my protector. It's dark, but under the faint glow of the Lunetas Bridge, I'm able to make out massive dark gray stone standing against a backdrop of rolling hills. Oh gods. The vomit I've kept at bay threatens to surface, and I press my face against Steilos to stop the vertigo.

He barks orders to a person I can't see. "Don't dawdle. Just unload it all you oaf! And where the fuck is Saray? I need to see her *now*."

The person mumbles an apology and something else, but the pounding in my head intensifies and I can't hear the rest. Steilos turns around, taking long strides that make my skull want to split in two. We go indoors and he takes me up a circular stairway where we pass numerous paintings along the stone walls. After a time, we finally come to a wood door along a dim hallway. Steilos kicks it open with such force that it clashes loudly against the stone on the other side. The sound makes me flinch.

"Master Steilos!" The woman's voice is filled with disapproval.

"Shove it, Saray, and clear the table. She's dying."

"*Oh!* Oh dear!"

There's a clatter as things I can't see hit the ground and, not a moment later, I'm laid atop a long table. Steilos keeps a comforting hand on my shoulder and from what I can gather, I'm in a messy sewing room of sorts. There are cloth and spools of yarn everywhere. Suddenly, an ample woman with a caramel complexion appears above me. This must be Saray. She wears a crisp apron over a sage green dress and looks at me with one concerned dark eye. The other is concealed by a leather eyepatch. She tosses a thick, black braid behind her shoulder and glares at Steilos.

"What's this you bring me? Look at her!"

It must be worse than I thought.

Saray places a gentle hand to my brow. "She's got quite the fever! How's she even breathing in this condition?"

Steilos shrugs. "I got her for half the price; General Charos likes to save his coin, you know that."

My body stiffens at his callousness, but his hand gives my shoulder a quick squeeze, reassuring me that it's an act.

"She's no good to us half dead, you brute!" Saray gives me a critical stare, "And she's damn near my daughter's age at that. You're lucky the General is away fighting at the trenches! It'll give her time to patch up, otherwise he'd nail your balls to the floor for wasting his coin."

"Well, the great lady Tyche, must be smiling upon me then," Steilos says, smooth as glass.

"At least the Goddess of Fortune finally shows her teeth to *someone* around here," she scoffs with a shake of her head. "Give me a moment, I'll go sweet talk Angus and see if he has something to break her fever."

When Saray shuts the door behind her, Steilos lets out a breath. He appears above me. "Kid, we are lucky that Charos isn't here. If the General saw you like this, he'd skin the both of us."

I swallow, sick to my stomach. "I don't feel . . . lucky at all."

He crouches down so that his head is next to mine. "You won't be here for long. I promise you that."

I suck in sharply as fresh pain sweeps over my body. "What makes this citrine so special that Ares wants it?"

Steilos averts his eyes from mine. "He didn't say, only that I'm supposed to retrieve it."

The lie gives my skin the sensation of something oily sliding down its surface and makes my stomach tighten. A compulsion to speak comes over me and the voice that comes out is mine, but not mine, *"Steilos, take heed or your lies will be your undoing. Do not cross us."*

A mix of shock and fear pools in his eyes, mirroring my own. Was that a divination? He stands, quickly backing away from me as I try to sit up but fail.

"Six months, I swear it. I'll be back for you in six months, unless you find it sooner," Steilos says firmly. "And don't you dare put a curse on me. I've got plenty enough of those already."

The door swings open and Saray enters.

"All right, missy, let's see if this'll get rid of that fever." She holds a vial in her hand and glances between the two of us. "Everything all right in here?"

Steilos smiles handsomely, as if nothing's awry, a trickster in every way. "Of course! But I must be off. I've other commitments." He offers her a dramatic bow with the sweep of his hand and then comes up with a wink. "Saray, give the General my best regards."

"Ha!" She snorts and shoots him a dirty look. A second later, he is out the door.

I begin to hyperventilate. The only person who has shown me kindness, no matter how little, just left me behind. I'm alone with yet another stranger in an unfamiliar place and must survive the next six months—if I survive the night.

"Are you having trouble breathing?" Saray asks with concern as she leans over me.

I shake my head no.

"Afraid then? Not of me surely! The gods know there is already enough of that around here." Her face is full of pity as she examines mine. "That burn is awful! You're lucky, though, seeing as the General is out and Angus was kind enough to whip up a draught for your fever."

There's that word again, *luck* . . . as if I have any. If I could, I would cloak myself in it and hide from the gods and all the mess I've gotten into. Saray uncorks the vial in her hand; the smell of its repulsive contents reminds me of one of my mother's foul concoctions. "Angus?" I ask her, while resisting the urge to cover my nose.

Saray is slightly hesitant before responding. "He's a cook down in the kitchens. Before his servitude to the General, he was a healer."

Servitude, well that's an overly pleasant way of putting it.

"What do I call you, dear?"

"Eimear."

"Well, Eimear, from now on, follow my directions and you'll be just fine. I delegate tasks for all the ladies here. Tis my duty, granted by the General himself. Now let's get you patched up before you go passing out on this table; you're as pale as marble!"

She eases me up into a seated position and has me drink the contents of the vial. The liquid is dark, thick, and tastes worse than the odor. I almost cough it up, but a stern look from Saray quails me to submission and I force the medicine down. Ugh, this must be made from gravinroot,[40] hopefully this Angus person prepared it right or I won't see morning after all.

"That should cut your fever and help with the infection," Saray says and stuffs the bottle into her apron. I open my mouth to give my

------

[40]An orange colored root found in the mud of stagnate ponds. When cooked precisely, its medicinal properties cures infections, however cooked incorrectly, it serves as a poison.

gratitude, but the words don't come. Instead, a blackness consumes my vision, and my body falls backward onto the table. My fingers twitch against the wood. The damned cook made it too strong.

When I wake on the table, I take note that my body still feels like shit but considerably better. The pounding in my head is at least gone. Saray appears above me, her thick braid grazes my shoulder.

"You've been out for the last few hours. I'm surprised you're awake at all in your condition," she tuts and disappears from view. I slowly turn my head to see her store a needle and thread in a basket on the floor. She then folds a sage green tunic and places it with the thread. "Can you walk? I'm not strong like Master Steilos and can't carry you."

Right, he's gone. My fingers graze my lips, what was that earlier? The words were mine, but they also weren't, and carried a weight to them. I prod my sacred-self for answers, but she remains dormant. Another mystery I'll have to ask her about if she decides to speak to me again. I take a deep breath before sliding off the table. When my legs touch the ground, they don't immediately buckle, which gives me some assurance. I take a moment to steady myself and nod to Saray. "I can make it. Am I allowed to ask where we're going?"

"For a bath, you reek. I can't have you sleeping in the servant's quarters smelling like that, you'll wake everyone. Now, follow me."

Motivated by the prospect of being clean again, I follow her out of the room. As we descend the stairs, the lit sconces cast our shadows along the way, making the paintings on the wall eerie. It's slow going as I have to brace myself against the stone banister while taking shaky steps. To my discomfort and surprise, Saray is patient with my slowness and doesn't seem bothered when I have to stop and gather myself. At the moment, it seems I'm not able to use my Gift of knowing, and I find her easygoing nature suspicious. From what Steilos told me, Castle Notos is a nightmare; I don't imagine that kind of ambiance breeds kindness. After stopping for a fifth time to rest, I finally snap at her, "Why are you bothering to help me?"

Saray's one eye regards me with sternness. "Other than it being my duty, I have a daughter somewhere out there in the world close to your age, and I hope that whoever she's with is decent and shows her some compassion."

My mouth opens and shuts, the snide retort I had prepared dies on my lips. I begin to feel awkward and regret thinking ill of her. Saray appears as if she wants to say something else but decides against it. Instead, we carry on in an uncomfortable silence. I only break it when a particular painting catches my attention. The brush strokes made so skillfully, that it almost appears real.

"What *is* that?"

I've never seen the like, a triangular structure, not made of stone but of iron. As if thousands of blades were melted down and molded by a sculptor's expert hands into a large intricate design. It's so tall that it reaches the sky. In the background, there's a sunny blue sky filled with bright clouds, but there's no window in it for the gods to look out from. My frown deepens. And why is the grass green?

Saray smiles. "There are many painted like that here, beautiful things you've probably never seen before. This one I've heard, is called the Eiffel Tower."

"*Eiffel Tower*," I repeat slowly. The words feel strange on my tongue.

Her grin slips just as fast. "But now, only the gods know what the artists had in mind. Castle Notos was passed down for generations to the Techni's, and General Charos killed the entire bloodline before seizing this place as his own. They were the stewards and secret keepers of all artifacts you'll soon see here. It's sad really . . . *but* life is more interesting with a bit of mystery to it."

She continues down the steps, and I follow behind lost in thought. Green grass? Where have I...? My eyes widen. So, our former teacher, Elder Marcus, wasn't full of mule dung when he spoke of other worlds! I wish I could tell Gareth— I stop there, the magic of the moment ruined. Mysteries of life don't really matter when you don't have a loved one to ponder them with.

It takes time, but we finally reach the ground floor where I must've entered with Steilos. The magnitude of the hall makes me

pause. Dark wood rafters fill a tall ceiling, and the stone room stretches on in an endless length with wide arches that are held up by solid pillars. Beyond each arch, a stained-glass window is beautifully embedded, the moonlight from outside making the glass refract a kaleidoscope of colors, turning the walls and floor into a hushed rainbow.

At the center of the hall are large double doors with a design I can't quite make out, etched into the surrounding frame. There's a man on each side of the entrance, and I assume the two are guards. They wear uniforms of dark cloth, seemingly light in weight—a sleeveless tunic tucked into matching pantaloons that end in leather boots. It's impossible to miss how each guard wears a coiled whip clipped to his belt and, on the other hip, a short sword. They aren't Maketae warriors by any means, but my wonder concerning the great hall instantly ceases at their presence.

The blond on the left looks past Saray to study me for a moment. His mouth turns up in a sneer. "Oy! You must be the ugliest cunt I ever saw." He snickers to his counterpart, "Rhys, you dolt, take a looksee. Doesn't her face make you want to spit up your evening meal?"

Rhys catches sight of me, his nose wrinkles in distaste, and he bends over pretending to retch. The blonde crosses his arms and leans back against the wall, his smirk full of childish pride.

My insides go cold. I think back to the ship, to the nameless man I murdered, how it felt to have his body go limp and sag against mine while my chain crushed his windpipe. I imagine a similar end for the two men in front of me. What would it feel like to hold a blade to their throats? To watch the steel slide across their skin like ripe fruit and have them bleed until their eyes shine like glass? My mood is deadly. If my jaw were clenching any tighter, my teeth would crack.

Saray takes my hand and dips her head toward the two. "If I may, good sirs, we have duties to attend."

The blonde appears annoyed but motions with his hand, granting us permission to leave. Saray pulls me to the left, ushering me down the hall, and it seems as if we walk forever. Other tapestries and peculiar artwork fill the walls, but I have no time to admire them because there are more guards in the corridor. I keep my eyes downcast—heeding Steilos' advice to be as inconspicuous as possible. Some of them briefly pause to stare as we walk by, and I sense their recoil at the sight of my face. For her part, Saray gives my hand a tight squeeze when they do, a small comfort.

By the time we come to a room that is a cellar of sorts, my nausea and headache have returned, my mood deadly. Miscellaneous household items are discarded against the walls, along with dried goods. And in the corner of the room are stone steps that lead down to darkness, giving the space an ominous presence. Can there really be a bath down there?

Saray grabs a lantern from a shelf and lights it before making her way down the steps. When I don't follow, she calls out to me. "Do you want to get cleaned up or no?"

The thought of washing the dried sweat and grime off makes me perk up a little, and I quickly follow her. The journey downward is long for a set of stairs, but to my surprise there are no signs of dust or cobwebs, assuring me the passage is used often. The farther we descend, the more cave-like the walls become and, at a certain point, it feels as if we've left the castle entirely. By the time we reach the bottom of the steps I'm bent over, out of breath, and shaking.

Saray stands with the lantern close to her face; the light casts an eerie shadow, making her appear sinister. She wears a kind smile but given the circumstances, it makes my skin crawl. I think of what my own face must look like and instantly feel ashamed of my thoughts. I, of all people, have no right to judge.

"Trust me, the climb is worse," Saray says. "I'd like to say it gets better with time, but that would make me a dishonest woman."

"I'll take your word for it," I manage to tell her.

She winks with her good eye and continues walking. When I stand upright, I notice three passageways carved into the limestone cave and groan at the prospect of additional stairways that could yet appear. We take the middle corridor, and to my relief it's not long before we reach an open cavern with a considerably large oval spring at its center.

How odd. I sniff the air. Instead of an earthy smell as one would expect for such a dark place, there's a heavy fragrance of mint to the cave.

Saray stands with her hip cocked. "Down here are the servants' quarters," she says, her voice lightly echoing off the cavern walls. "Let go of any shyness you may have because this is a shared bathing room. The lads bathe first after the evening meal each day and then the ladies.

Tonight is an exception to that rule. Don't try to trade your bath time for more sleep or it will earn you a lashing. The General doesn't like his help to stink."

On the verge of delirium, I manage a head nod. She gestures to help me out of my makeshift dress, and unties the twine wrapped around my waist. At this point I'm grateful for the help, and any modesty I used to have died when I stood naked at the auction in Nasarr. In the process of undressing, my hair is swept back from my shoulders, exposing Metis' golden mark; something I nearly forgot about. But I guess Steilos was right about it being invisible to others because Saray's gaze passes over the owl shape and instead, inspects my protruding rib cage and the wound at my ankle.

She appears disgusted. "I'll never understand it. No good are you to anyone half-starved and nearly dead. You can barely work in this condition; they might as well have killed you on the ship."

The rancor in her comment catches me off guard. Did she lead me all the way down here just to kill me? I have thoughts on how to kill her first when she takes me by the elbow and leads me toward the pool of water.

"Now go ahead and wash off; it's a bit cool but it's better than nothing. Soap's in the corner." Saray turns her back to me and walks toward the exit. I'm left standing on my own, naked and confused.

"Where are you going?" I ask her retreating form.

"I have other duties that were postponed at your arrival. I can't finish them if I'm down here babysitting you now can I? Just don't pass out and drown before I get back."

Gods . . . she really doesn't mean me any harm. And here I was plotting her demise.

It isn't until Saray is gone that for the first time in weeks, I'm truly alone. The cavern is dimly lit, giving it an uncanny appearance, but I've been in worse places and appreciate the rare solitude. I crouch down to study the spring water, which seems dark as night.

"Hmmm," I say to myself. "It must be reflecting the ceiling."

There are multiple eddies in the pool, each moved by an unseen force, and I have second thoughts about submerging myself. The chimera comes specifically to mind. What monster could be lurking under the surface?

Timidly, I cup water in my hands but then quickly let it go, shaking the black drops from my skin. Nope! That water is most certainly off color. "Ugh, why would anyone bathe in this?" I shake my head. "I don't think I can do it."

It starts with a twitch, but like before, my nose detects the fresh aroma of mint. I eye the black pool. Is it coming from this devil's spring? Curious, I dip my fingers in. The liquid is cool to the touch, but not unbearably so. I give my hand a quick sniff. "Ah, they must put some type of herb in the water, maybe that's why it's this color."

First mystery solved, but it doesn't change the fact that I'm in a cave, and this spring is about as spooky as one of Elder Marcus' ghoulish stories. I take a deep breath and debate whether cleanliness is worth the risk of being eaten, however, the body odor exuding from my pits, puts up a fair argument. Saray's warning about the General then comes to mind, as well as the whips the guards carry. Gods damn it.

I take another long look at the dark water before closing my eyes. "Fuck," I say and jump in. The water is shocking at first, and as my body continues to sink, I choke when I ascertain there is no bottom to the demon pool. A monster really could be hiding beneath! My legs kick hard until I break the surface coughing, and I swim to the side as fast as I can before getting out and perching myself on a rock. I breathe heavily, drawing my knees in. As my heart calms, I notice something's different but can't quite place what it is. I stare within the dark depths searching for an answer. Oh . . . "I don't feel like shit anymore."

My body is somewhat revived after being in the water. My limbs hum with newfound energy and the burning sensation across my face has dulled. I purposely reach for the wound and run my fingertips along the bridge of my nose only to draw back with a hiss of pain—it's still tender and raw, though nothing like before. Okay Saray, I can see the allure of the scary black water now.

As she mentioned, I find a bar of soap on the ledge and begin to lather my skin, having to put in some work on the worst parts and taking extra time to wash my hair. After I'm finished cleansing, I watch the black churning water and try to gather my courage to jump back into the pool whose bottom could be in fact, endless. I've no choice in the matter when the soap begins to drip into my eyes from my hair.

Let's try this again. Inhaling, I take the plunge. This time, I let myself sink beneath the surface without panicking. Instead, I concentrate, trying to summon my Gift—the gut feeling that tells me what should be unknown. To my amazement, I sense what I've been searching for:

Safety.

It's an odd feeling, like being wrapped in an invisible blanket, or the sure arms of a loved one. This sixth sense of knowing, I wonder, how far does it go?

//Can you hear me now?// I ask the girl inside me.

//*We always hear you. It's you that can't always hear us.*//

//Why is that?//

//*Think of Gareth and what it took for him to heal Zadok. It's the same when we speak. The drain will lessen as you become stronger.*//

Gareth. I shoved him from my mind, deeming myself unfit to even think of him after everything that's happened. //Is he safe?//

//*We don't know. But he wouldn't think ill of you, so you shouldn't either. You did nothing wrong.*//

I have no comment.

My lungs begin to burn from lack of air and I'm sad when I kick my way back to the surface. Afterward, I float on my back, my fear exchanged for grief as I contemplate all the could-have-beens. The desire for revenge swirls round and round as I study the cavern ceiling. I wish to become as cold and piercing as the stalactite above and strike anyone who tries to hurt me ever again. My eyes widen as the water begins to heat around me. It's like a warm embrace, as if the water is alive with a will of its own and trying to bring me a measure of comfort. It grows hotter, and more of my aches slip away.

I cup my hand and let the dark liquid slide between my fingers. //What's in this water?// I ask my sacred-self. There's a pause, as if *she,* is searching for an answer.

//*The essence of a god is here, but we cannot see which one. They're shrouded in darkness. No harm is meant for us.*//

For a moment, I'm chilled by the thought of yet another god lurking in the shadows. Steilos is right, nothing good can come from them. But as I continue to drift, the black water caressing my aches and healing my wounds like the gentle kiss of a lover, I come to a conclusion.

I no longer fear the dark.

CHAPTER XXI

10th Week of Summer

Eimear

By the time Saray returns, I'm rejuvenated and begrudgingly give thanks to the unknown god who healed me. I use the ledge to hoist myself out of the spring, and she nearly drops the bundle in her arms when I stand before her.

"What in the worlds happened to you? It's like you're not even sick anymore!" She sets her things down and then proceeds to wrap a towel around my body. Saray squints, studying my wound closely, puzzlement etched into the lines of her face. "By the gods, that burn is almost healed over." She traces a calloused finger over the scorched part of my skin. It doesn't sting.

Oh! There's also no pain—I glance down and see that my ankle is entirely healed from where the shackle rubbed my skin raw. Only a thin line of a scar remains, a permanent reminder of my time on the slave ship.

"Saray, you could have told me the water down here is special. I almost didn't get in at all. That color is . . . off-putting to say the least."

"Color? What color? What do you mean?"

I point at the spring. "It's black."

She peers behind me and shakes her head. "You must be seeing things. That water there is crystal clear. One of the only good things about this place. Though, I must say, I'm a bit jealous! I've been bathing here for over four years. Gods know I still feel my aches and pains every morn." She continues to assess me with awe-filled eyes. "You must've received a god's blessing[41], because there's nothing sacred at Notos, not here in this catacomb of misery."

I look back at the spring just in case, and sure enough, the water is still dark as shadows. It takes me a moment to digest that I've started *seeing* things, along with *hearing* things. If I were back home, I'd have Chrysanthe pray for my mind. "It must be for laughs," I say to Saray, "because how can I be blessed yet be a slave?"

Saray cringes at the word. She then surveys my hair—which must be as tangled as a rat's nest—with a tired expression. "Well, as much as I love a mystery, it can wait for the suns' rise." She leads me toward a wood bench that rests against a cavern wall and instructs me to

---

[41]To receive a god's blessing is to possess true luck. Unexplainable wonders are said to be blessings from a god. This is true of curses as well.

sit. "It's well past our sleeping hour, but we still need to get those knots out."

I wrap the towel tighter around myself before I do as I'm bid. The situation reminds me of how Mana used to style my hair. Saray pulls a comb from her apron, and when she runs its teeth through my hair, emotions crash down on me like a falling star, the memories so bright, they burn. Among these constellations of memory are Mana's stormy eyes reflected in her bedroom mirror as she put my unruly mane to straights. The last day she was alive. I've been numb up until now, and this small gesture of a comb through my hair ushers in a tidal wave of feeling that bursts the dam I've built over my heart.

She's gone. She's really gone . . .

My body may be healed, but my soul is very much battered and bruised. All the hurt I've been holding, gives way into a long heavy sob. It's as if I'm there again, dragging her through the trampled grass and placing a charred blanket over her cold frame. My shoulders shake as I drown in sorrow, the gulf now deep enough that I may never stop sinking.

Saray puts the comb down on the bench and gently places a hand on my back, rubbing me between the shoulders. She doesn't ask me what's wrong nor does she tell me to stop, or hurry, she simply lets me be. When my body trembles from the aftershocks of heartbreak, she gives my back a gentle pat.

After a few moments, I wipe the corners of my eyes and try to calm my chattering teeth.

Breaking the quiet, Saray says to me, "You know, there's a myth about this spring, now that I've thought on it."

"What's that?" The words are a struggle, but I manage.

"It's an old legend, but it's rumored the spring was a gift to Minthe[42], Hades' lover. These waters here are supposedly connected to the Underworld."

"Minthe? I thought Hades was married to the Goddess of Spring. I think her name's Persephone?" Saray resumes combing my hair and at first, I flinch again but soon relax into it.

"Not all gods are faithful to their spouses." She laughs. "Zeus is a prime example of that! Hades took the nymph as a lover, and they would meet in secret, right here at this spring."

I hiss as the comb catches and pulls at my scalp. Saray rubs my back again. "Sorry dear, try to bear with it for now." She works out the knot before continuing her story. "Their affair caused Persephone to become jealous, and in her rage, she tore out Minthe's heart before dismembering her. The goddess then ground the heart into dust and threw it to the winds. By doing this, the nymph could never be brought back to life as an immortal."

"That's horrible!" I turn too quickly toward Saray, almost causing her to lose the comb. "My Elder never told us such a story."

She tsks. "Eyes front."

I do as she says. "What happened afterward?"

---

[42]A water nymph who resided in Cocytus, a river in the Underworld.

"Hades was grief stricken. He went on a quest to find her heart, begged the God of Death for its safe return. Thanatos[43] denied him the whole heart, but for a boon, he gave Hades a vial of the organ's dust. The God of the Under cried over what was left of Minthe, and his tears caused the dust to blossom into a mint plant."

Mint . . . "Wait! I've been smelling that herb here, but I thought it was something that was added to the water."

Saray works hard on another knot and shakes her head. "Not by us, the General wouldn't waste his coin on something like that. According to legend, this spring holds the essence of Minthe. Hades eventually abandoned it when his anguish over losing his lover became too great. Because of the myth, the spring's water was highly sought-after and Castle Notos was built on top of the wonder, to preserve it. But General Charos believes it's cursed by Hades and has the servants use it in his stead."

I notice again how Saray says *servants* instead of *slaves*, as if she's in denial. "That's an awful story. Were you trying to make me feel better or worse?"

The kind woman is silent for a moment as she braids my hair. "The lesson, missy, is that even gods feel pain, there's equality for mortals in this fact. And no matter what you experience here, no one can

---

[43]God of Death, many mortals confuse him with Hades, God of the Underworld. Thanatos has no reign over the Under or Elysium, but he does serve as a guide to the recently deceased. He delivers the dead to their afterlife.

deem you worthless or undeserving, not a god, or even a man who pretends to be one."

After my hair is finished, Saray gives me a fresh change of clothes similar to hers. Rope sandals and a sage green dress that falls just below my knees; it's capped at my shoulders with a wide neckline. She studies me when I'm dressed and gives an approving nod. "Much better." She pauses, lost in thought, and I become nervous under her gaze. "It would be wise," she says, "not to mention your quick recovery to anyone else. Some people don't do well with the unknown, so keep it between us. Understand?"

"What about the guards who already saw me?"

"The castle is cast in all kinds of shadows at this hour. The guards don't know what they saw."

She leads me out of the bathing cavern with a lantern in hand, and we return to the room by the stairway. I dread making my way back up the long steps but to my relief she cuts left toward another passageway. Before we enter though, she stops abruptly, and I bump into her.

"This way is toward the women's quarters. The other hall, over there, leads to the men's. Copulation isn't allowed, so think twice before having any such adventures. The General doesn't like his servants to be slow with child and will punish you for it."

My skin heats with embarrassment at her insinuation. As if I'd ever . . .

If Saray notices my discomfort, she chooses to ignore it. We continue along the passageway until we enter another limestone cavern. The space is long and narrow, in the shape of a rectangle, with a low ceiling and lit by a single lantern in the corner. The stench of mold hangs heavy in the air. Rows of scuffed wooden bunk beds line the longer walls of the cavern with a miniature dresser between each bunk. There's nearly ten bunks per side, and the beds are mostly occupied with snoring women. The mattresses they lay on appear thin and their blankets threadbare. On the far end of the space sits a rusted basin under a small, clouded mirror.

Saray leans into me, her voice a dark whisper, "Welcome home."

Not if I can help it. Although, if I don't find the citrine quickly, it's going to be a long six months.

Saray walks ahead of me on silent feet toward the last set of bunks on the left side of the cavern. Both top and bottom beds are empty with their blankets meticulously tucked in and adorned with a single flat pillow.

"The lower bunk is yours, as well as the bottom dresser drawer. A change of clothes is in there for you; be sure to take care of them. I'll give a full sermon later on what's expected of you, but for now, sleep. Morning comes quickly and waits for no one."

I peer around the sunless cave and wonder how anyone can tell time down here in the dark.

Saray sees the question on my face. "Don't worry, I ring a bell before dawn, so no one oversleeps."

"Right," I sigh.

She turns to go, but I reach for her elbow and she stops.

"Thank you, for everything. I know you didn't have to be kind, but you were. I won't forget it."

Her dark eye shines in the lantern's glow, and she gives my hand a tight squeeze. "For my daughter. Out there in the world." Saray then leaves me for her own bunk, the bottom bed closest to the entrance.

Under the chorus of snores, I hear a steady, *tap, tap, tap*. My eyes adjust to the dim lighting and just on the other side of my bed, is a bucket nearly full of water from the ceiling's drip. Already, the sound grates on my nerves and, on cue, my belly growls with hunger. Wonderful. I check the bottom drawer of the dresser, and as Saray mentioned, there's a spare set of clothes similar to the ones I wear now, along with a comb and paste for my teeth.

Leaning on the edge of the dresser, I slip my sandals over the curve of my ankles and place my feet on the rough but cool stone. It gives me a chill, but I welcome it as I bend down to crawl onto the mattress that is now mine, careful not to bump the bunk above.

As I start to lay back, I catch the lantern light reflecting off the edge of the mirror at the end of the room. If I look, whose reflection will I see? I'm no longer the carefree girl I used to be. No—now I'm a stranger in my own skin, the intricacies of my face unknown to me.

I get up slowly, my steps hesitant. I cast my gaze downward as I come closer to the mirror, my curiosity and fear battling one another. I know I'm not yet ready for the girl reflected there. My thighs bump into the basin, and I grab hold of its edge, the metal coarse under my palms, rust burrowing beneath my nails as my fingers clench with fear.

I take a long, slow breath. Whatever I see doesn't matter. I count to three, but I never look up when I reach the last number. Time passes, and I grow upset with my cowardice. I bite the inside of my cheek. It's just a face. My face. I then let it go—the fear of the unknown, and raise my eyes toward the filthy mirror.

Gods & Beasts of Miracle

Persephone to Hades

If I acquired a thousand reasons for you to smile,

would your lips stretch skyward?

If I grew you a garden with vibrant colors,

would your eyes brighten like they used to?

If my voice dripped with honey,

would your thoughts sweeten for me?

Husband, if I changed my ways,

could you love me?

I'm sorry for ripping out your heart.

CHAPTER XXII

12th Week of Summer

Nikko

I hate everything about these services. It's another tedious afternoon at the Great Temple, and the bell atop its roof is the bane of my existence. When it rings, the pew I sit in vibrates with the clamor. And thus far, it has rung at least ten times.

My fingers glide to the stitch in my earlobe, the small wound just nearly healed. Damn Jada. It's going to scar. My nose wrinkles with disdain and I glare at the gaudy decor around me. Like all other things in Ellanios, our great temple is dedicated to Zeus, but it makes my eyes hurt. The rectangular room is lined with rows of wide gold columns that have intricate designs of the god and his symbols etched into them. The columns hold up a tall, domed ceiling painted a deepest purple, and between each pillar is a large window that's been stained lilac. Light that shines through the glass bathes an altar of Zeus in the lilac color.

A priest fans incense around the temple from a gold box. Another priest follows close behind him and writes invisible symbols into the air with his fingers while chanting in a language I don't understand. They both wear long purple robes that balloon out at the elbows. I try to seem interested when they pass my pew, but I can feel annoyance creeping into my face, turning my false smile ugly.

Once they've made their way around the temple, the priest with the gold box, places the box at Zeus' altar to let it burn until the next service later in the evening. History states that the Holy City is blessed by the God, which is why we've always had peace within our walls. Staring up at his gold-plated statue, his chest bare and robes billowing about his waist, I think about how I'm nearly bored to tears. The service should only last fifteen more minutes.

I'm no devout, but it's good for the citizens of Ellanios to see a royal family member at a service, especially with the rise of Heracles' supporters inside the city. During my nightly outings I've seen more of their propaganda painted on the walls, my worry for my family increases with each new sighting.

I lean my head back and groan. I'm not even supposed to be here. It's my punishment for losing to Jada this morning at the sparring ring. It was technically her turn to attend, and I send curses her way under my breath. It's a fool's errand taking her on in hand-to-hand combat. I never seem to learn.

Styx, I should've brought my novel.

Sadly, the worn leatherbound, *Eros' Philosophy*[44] was left in my bedroom. Thirteen more minutes. Can one die of dullness? I try to occupy my mind with anything but the service in front of me; like the woman I encountered the night before. My attention travels far into the gutter, the priest's words fading. If Zeus himself were to see, the god would blush, and for the remainder of the service I sit in the pew with a shit-eating grin.

Because I'm preoccupied with thoughts of silky thighs and dancing tongues, the Luminae's[45] song barely registers. I sit up a little straighter as their procession of ten passes, their pristine white robes swishing. Each carries a lantern, and their voices harmonize in a song that only Zeus can understand. It's said, that if their song ends, the Holy City will fall to ruin. As a child, I really thought the men sang day in and day out until they died. My younger self believed they possessed the powers of Zeus, enabling them to achieve such a feat. I felt silly when I learned that they rotate out every hour. After that, I stopped holding them in such high regard. Still though, their song is beautiful, and I close my eyes to enjoy it.

---

[44]Deliberations from the God of Sex and Love.

[45]High Priests vigorously train for the position of Luminae. Their songs praising Zeus must never end, for if they do, the city will be plunged into darkness, or so the story goes. At all times, there are ten singing at once. For Zeus said, "As long as you sing for me, I will shine my light on thee."

A priest rings a set of bells, one after another, their echoing chimes are melodious. When the last one is struck, signaling the end of service, I look up at Zeus' glowering form. "Thank the fucking gods."

As I stand to leave, I spy the boy Gareth in line for the exit. His head is now shaved, and he fills out his clothes a bit better than when I first encountered him. I'm reminded of my father's counsel to befriend our new guest, and my eyes roll skyward. "Duty beckons."

I follow Gareth outside, watching him stop and stare into the waters of the temple fountain. In its center is another ornate figure of Zeus where water pours from the spear in his hands. The kid's face is the epitome of gloom, and I find myself bothered by it. He's here now, a guest. What complaints could he have? I approach him. "Did you enjoy the service?" The boy blinks with surprise. I forget he doesn't know Ellanion, and switch to the common tongue, repeating my question.

His eyes narrow at the statue, "Not really, but it reminds me of a girl I used to know. Although, where I'm from, Metis is worshipped, not Zeus."

Maybe I should warn him to keep his beliefs to himself, considering my people believe his goddess was a witch who seduced Zeus into doing her bidding. They'll call him a heathen worshipper. But another look at his sad face, I think better of it. So grim this one is. I gesture to the fountain in an attempt to make conversation. "Legend has it, if you make a wish to the waters, it will come true at the next thunderstorm. Maybe you should make one for her?"

The boy deflates. "No, your highness. I don't think even Zeus can bring back the dead."

I'm caught off guard and pretend to cough into my fist. Fuck, I'm an idiot. His entire village was slaughtered. Of course, he's depressed. Now I wish I never followed him.

"You're from Paidia you said, right? If it's not too difficult, can you tell me what happened there with Heracles?"

He takes a shuddering breath and is silent for a moment, as if he's struggling to find the words. Meanwhile, a pair of children run past the outer temple gate, giggling as they play a game of chase. Gareth gazes after them with longing.

Shit. I think I've made him more upset. "Pay me no mind for the intrusiveness, you don't have to elaborate. I understand."

"No, it's all right," he finally says. "I didn't even know about this Heracles fellow until I was brought to Ellanios. No one did. The others and I were trying to make sense of it all on the ship."

How could they not know who Heracles is? The continents have been at war for years now.

Gareth sees my confusion. "Please don't look at me like that," he says. "We weren't idiots, just uninformed of all the political strife. We only had one vessel crafted to cross the Thyellodic and it wrecked several years ago. I scoured the maps in your palace library. Paidia wasn't on any of them. I think the raiders discovered us by accident after sailing too far Southeast."

"I see . . . it must be difficult, being somewhere so large and unfamiliar."

The boy scowls at me and raises his voice. "What was difficult was witnessing a hoard of barbarians burn my home, rape my people, and then watch the ones who were lucky enough to survive, die on the ship or be sold at a slave yard in Sklirós.[46]" Tears well up in his emerald eyes and as he stares at his trembling hands, he whispers, "I saved my mum from dying of disease aboard the ship, only to watch her be branded as a whore once we docked. I should've let her die; it would've been a kinder fate."

I'm at a loss for words. I don't know this kind of hurt. I can't fathom it or begin to understand what it's like to lose everything I've ever known. A prince I may be, but I'm still powerless to help this boy. I feel inadequate.

Gareth quickly wipes his face. "While we sailed, I tried to keep as many as I could alive. They would stretch as far as their chains would allow just to touch my hand. I almost died several times from the Return. But it wasn't enough, so many of the people I grew up with didn't survive." He chuckles but not happily. "Once we got to Sklirós, Elder Solon tried to save his own skin and told one of the raiders that I had a Gift. I was separated from the others at the slave yard after that, and then brought here." He looks skyward at the West Window and the

---

[46]A plot of dark earth home to the largest black market in Ehvara. The devilish city hosts anyone seeking refuge from the law, that is, if you can survive its harrowing streets full of thieves and cut-throats.

Lunetas Bridge. "I don't know what happened to my pa, or the girl I loved. I assume they've crossed over to Elysium by now." He smiles weakly. "But she would be happy with that at least."

As I watch Gareth mourn, I'm reminded of what's at stake and of the price millions of Ehvarians have already paid for Heracles' bloodlust. Of the sacrifice my sister is willing to make, how she is willing to renounce her freedom and befriend her enemies, all to keep the people of Ellanios safe. And what have I been doing all this time?

I clear my throat. "I'm sorry for all your loss, and your current circumstance. But know this: you have a home here if you wish it. If there's anything I can do for you, please just ask, and I'll grant it if it's within my ability."

"Thank you, Prince," he says in perfect Ellanion.

I raise my brows high. "I see you've been learning our language. Your accent is quite good for the short time you've been here."

The boy turns his back to me and stares at the fountain. "Eimear was much more proficient at languages than I. She'd probably poke fun at my pronunciation," he says switching back to the common tongue.

Eimear? That must be the girl he spoke of.

Gareth looks at me. "But there's no position for me here. All I have to fill my time is researching in your library. There's only so much I can read before I feel like tearing my eyes out. I've been entertaining myself with learning Ellanian for the most part, but if I'm being honest, I'm very bored."

He's a straightforward one. For some reason I think of Erebos, and I grit my teeth. Why does that prick come to mind?

Gareth's forehead wrinkles with worry. "Sorry, your highness. Please don't misunderstand; I'm very grateful to be here. The King has been very kind, I shouldn't have complained. I think I shouted at you too. Please forgive me." The kid mistakes my silence for anger and bows low.

I put my hand on his shoulder, hoping to be of comfort. "No apology needed. You spoke frankly and, considering what you've been through, you deserve some grace. My father doesn't want you working against your will. But, if you need a task to fill your time, I can talk to him about putting you in the infirmary. Maybe you can continue your training there and get more practical experience."

A spark ignites in Gareth's grieving eyes. "It wouldn't be too much would it? I think I might turn into paper if I open another book."

Hmmm, not all books are boring. I think back to the collection in my room. "Tell you what, I'll have an arrangement made with one of our healers. In the meantime, if you're desperate to escape the library, meet me at the sparring ring in the mornings. You can work up a sweat there."

He hesitates. "I've never trained with a sword before, Sir. I don't believe, with my background, I'd be good at it."

I wave him off. "You seem to be a fast learner, and I won't take no for an answer. I insist. Besides, I could use the distraction as well." I think he's going to decline again, so I cut him off, pointing at his chest.

"Sparring grounds. Morning. Be there." Judging by the way he nods his head with reluctance, I'm certain he regrets running into me. "I'll be seeing you later then," I say and make my way toward the temple gate. However, before I exit, I turn to observe him one last time. He stands forlorn, still, staring into the fountain waters.

The boy is in a strange country where he barely knows the language nor any of its people. He must be lonely. I close my eyes with a sigh. Gods' damn it all.

"Hey!" I call to him.

Gareth glances up in surprise.

"Want me to show you how wonderful the city is? Or do you have more insufferable books you'd rather read?"

He smiles nervously. "If it'll be no trouble, I think I'd like that."

I thought I was Prince of Ellanios, but it seems between him and Erebos, I've been demoted to tour guide.

I spend the next few hours pointing out historical markers within the Holy City and stopping at stalls for Gareth to try our cuisine. I adamantly avoid *Erotes' Delights* when he points to it, telling him that "the fruit is sour." By the time we arrive back at the palace, he appears a bit livelier, and his olive skin has regained some color after being in the Twin Suns all afternoon.

There's a comfortable silence between us as we walk down a corridor lined with artwork of Zeus. The god is depicted in his different forms that he's been known to take throughout history. Gareth suddenly turns to me, "Ellanios is truly amazing," he says. "It's unlike anything I've ever seen before. If only Eimear . . ."

And just like that, the boy shuts down. The excitement leaves his face, his green eyes dim, and his mouth sets in a firm line.

Ah, the girl again. I wrack my brain for some sage advice to give when I hear my sister's tinkling laughter before she appears around the corner. Jada is accompanied by Erebos and they walk arm in arm.

"Really, you are too funny," she says to him, although his expression is blank, as always.

"It's you!" Gareth yells with rage before launching himself ahead of me and tackling Erebos at the waist. My twin is quick on her feet and sidesteps the attack with ease before the two hit the floor.

Seeing Heracles' emissary get his arse kicked holds its own kind of satisfaction.

Gareth sits astride Erobos and is punching him in the face. "You watched as we were loaded onto that ship, writing in your book, making inventory of us like chattel! And then you had the gall to not even recognize me when you shackled me with those gold chains." He continues to strike the emissary relentlessly.

Jada goes to stop him, but I hold out a hand. "Let them settle this. The boy is owed a debt of blood for his losses. Let Heracles' lackey pay it."

"You can't be serious! He's protected under our roof by the king's order."

A throaty growl draws our attention and we stop bickering to stare. Gareth's breath is labored and Erebos has a firm grip on both the boy's wrists. But his fingernails have lengthened into claws, and his eyes have turned a deep shade of crimson.

What in the Under? I point and ask my sister, "Is it just me or are his teeth longer too?"

Erebos speaks with a deadly calm. "You mistake me for another. Though his sins are mine just the same."

"Liar! You let them destroy everything . . ." Gareth is weeping now, his tears land on Erebos' face.

The emissary releases his grip. "I'm unable to fully explain, but I did not attack your motherland, nor did I imprison you. If you wish to vent your fury though, you have my permission to do so." He retracts his claws, and his eyes revert to the darkest of black.

Gareth stammers, "What . . . ?"

"It doesn't matter how much you hurt me. I heal quickly."

My twin and I share a confused glance. What's going on? Does he possess a god's ichor like Gareth? I know Jada is wondering the same thing.

The boy who has lost everything, who watched his people die as victims of brutality, fire, and disease, who witnessed his mother be sold into slavery, makes a choice and lowers his fists.

He rises to his feet. "I must remember," Gareth says with conviction, "that of all things first, I am a healer. I'll not let the cruelty of men, nor the world for that matter, change the good inside me. I'll never raise arms against you again, even though it may feel as if a thousand blades cut my insides." He extends a hand to Erebos, who takes the olive branch with hesitancy.

For the first time, I witness an emotion flicker across the emissary's face as he stares at their clasped hands.

Hope.

CHAPTER XXIII

12th Week of Summer

Eimear

My heart sinks to my stomach as I face a terrifying monster, except it's not really a monster—it's my own reflection taunting me mercilessly through the glass. Unnaturally bright gold eyes are sunken into their sockets with hollowed-out cheeks to match. The face, once olive, is now pale and disrupted by a bright pink burn nearly an inch wide. The trajectory of my melted skin starts at the right side of my forehead, goes in between my eyes where it skips the sides of my nose and then continues down my left cheek. Only my rose-colored lips remain unmarred to remind me of the face I once had.

Inside the mirror, the disfigured girl laughs at me. Her canines then begin to grow until a chimera appears in her stead. Girl or monster? The new face and what lies underneath is a reality I'm not yet ready to confront, even in my dreams. I run from the mirror and it's just like that time when I stood before Metis, when the ground was an endless black and each footfall could be my last. Hot breath reaches the back of my neck as the monster closes in. I surge forward, faster than before. I think I've outrun it, but the beast catches up. I'm forced to turn around, only it's not myself I'm confronted with, it's the man I murdered. He bleeds from his gouged sockets, his skin bruised and rotting.

The man reaches for the collar of my white dress and I try to evade him, but my feet are frozen in place. He shoves me backward, and I fall through the dark void, my stomach rising to my throat as I plummet. Images of my mother flicker above me, but they're not kind ones. No, I only see death and a burning home. The air is knocked out of me when I land, and the back of my head cracks against the ground.

The landscape of illusion changes to an open field, I try to get up, but a boot presses into my chest and forces me back down. I know who it belongs to, and my body seizes up with fright. It's always Jud first and Armon second—this nightmare is no different. My mouth opens in a scream when suddenly my attackers disappear into tendrils of black smoke.

"*Enough* of this," an ageless voice demands, masculine and alluring.

Once the vapors fade, I'm left in an empty space full of color. It's as if a rainbow has been stretched in every which way to make a room. When I take a closer look, I notice the colors move, but at a speed my eyes can't keep up with. Shapes form, but then they disappear just as quickly. It makes me dizzy. I stand on shaking limbs and notice that my body is too solid for a dream, the tears on my cheeks are very much real. I search the area and see black tendrils of smoke hovering several yards ahead. The vapors move about much like a snake would, as if studying me. I'm transfixed by it.

I don't know how long we stare at each other for, time feels like it doesn't matter in this place. The trance is only broken when the smoke suddenly shoots forward in my direction. Frightened, I fall on my arse, and scramble backward, but it catches up to me quickly and cocoons itself around me. I'm surrounded by darkness but, oddly enough, it's a comfort. The scent of narcissus clings to the black layer and my body relaxes one muscle at a time.

"I've found you Eimear. From now on, in this realm at least, you'll be safe," the god says, his words dipped in honey and shadows.

Nightmare forgotten, my eyes close, and I drift into peaceful oblivion.

The clamor of a bell yanks me back to the world of mortal woes. It's been two weeks since I arrived at Castle Notos and I'm still not used to the waking bell. I'm groggy but left with the impression that I was just speaking with someone. I reach for the memory, but it's illusive, and I can only recall black smoke. I try to probe further but then it's gone completely. Why am I still in my bunk? I better hurry.

I sense the movement of others around me and Selene, a slave in the lower bunk next to mine, groans with complaint, "It's too gods damn early for this." Her bunkmate, however, is already climbing down.

As my eyes adjust to the dimly lit cavern, I set aside the thin blanket and swing my legs over the bed. I hiss when my feet touch the frigid stone floor. In front of me, Selene makes her bed with little regard to her open nakedness. She's even bonier unclothed, every ridge of her spine highlighted by malnutrition. I avert my eyes. Like some of the others, I keep my clothes on when I sleep, for extra warmth. I turn to my own bed, making sure to tuck in each corner and smooth out any wrinkles. If it's not perfect one of the guards will beat me.

The bunk above mine remains empty, which is for the best. I wouldn't damn another soul to live here. A handful of women are already fully clothed and have formed a line to use the basin and mirror at the back of the cavern. I almost join them but then think of my reflection and decide that I don't wish to gaze upon that image again anytime soon. I've avoided my face since my first night here.

Standing in line, Neyda, an older girl with jet black hair and a mole on her cheek catches me staring and spits, "ftou, ftou, ftou," in an attempt to ward off evil[47]. Neyda then taps the back of her friend's

---

[47]Spitting three times, or simply saying "ftou, ftou, ftou" is believed to protect against the cursed.

shoulder and leans forward to whisper something in Arete's ear. Arete is another brunette but with lighter tresses. She turns, annoyed, but then her eyes widen at the sight of me. The pair of them are only a few years older than myself and have made it very clear what they think of me with their backhanded taunting. Suddenly I'm homesick and miss the children of Paidia and the games we would play, even if I was too old for it.

Neyda giggles, and the two begin talking in hushed tones.

Their mockery pierces my heart with hurt, and my eyes begin to swell with tears. I had hoped to make friends in this horrible place, given that we all arrived against our will. One would expect some level of comradery, but no—cruelty only begets cruelty here. Pretending indifference, I turn away and quickly change into my spare clothing before re-braiding my hair.

They continue to snicker behind my back and my jaw becomes tight as my teeth grind together. They're both bitches. Despite the healing benefits of the spring, its waters did nothing for the scarring on my face. All optimism I had for the recovery of my skin died when I took one look in the clouded mirror. I've seen enough burns alongside Mana to know my face will never be the same.

"Ladies! Move it along! You're wasting daylight!" A familiar voice calls out, catching my attention. Saray stands near the entrance of the cavern, not a hair is out of place and her clothes are free of wrinkles. She radiates an energy that shouldn't be felt at this time of morn.

Someone groans amongst the throng of women. Saray doesn't seem amused. "Cecille, you sound like a dying sow."

A few of the women giggle at the exchange. We all form a line and make our way out of the cavern. I'm at the end, and there are thirty or so others ahead of me. Delta signs are branded onto the backs of their calves, the mark of a slave. A painful reminder of what we are. I've been spared the branding thus far, but I know my time must be coming soon. No one escapes the brand. Saray follows me out the door.

When our herd makes it to the stairs, I inwardly groan. This climb is awful. If I ever thought going down was terrible, going up is a thousand times worse. Several horrible minutes pass and I'm out of breath by the time I reach the top of the stairs. The muscles of my arse are afire.

Fuck all," I gasp.

"Language!" Saray snaps at me from behind.

"Yes, ma'am," I manage to mumble and continue to follow the line of women down the hall. Every morn, it's the same. I'm full of nervous energy, not knowing what to expect. There's been no word of General Charos, which both alleviates my stress and ails me at the same time. He could return any moment and then what? How could he possibly be worse than the guards left here to tend the castle?

As we make our way to the morning meal, our group passes room after room. The fortress is impressive with its high ceilings, and stairways that lead up to additional sections. There was no structure ever this large in my village. One could easily get lost in the maze. I've taken to running my fingertips against the stone walls, counting my steps in an attempt to memorize where I've been. And around every corner, there's a guard lurking with a bored or stern face. Some seem to have trouble keeping their eyes open today. I can sympathize, as it is ungodly early, but that's where my sympathy stops. They're all tyrants constructed from the same cloth. The whips they wear fastened to their belts are a constant reminder to tread cautiously.

Our procession slows and we stand in line outside the double doors of the kitchen. Women go through the left door and then out the right with food in hand. My stomach growls impatiently when it realizes that relief is just mere moments away. We're never given much for all the work we do. I haven't met him yet, but I know the General is a stingy bastard.

By the time it's my turn to enter, I peer around the person in front of me to see Angus, a large, dark-skinned man wearing a tunic and trousers the same sage green as my own uniform. He stands behind a long wood table at the kitchen's center. There isn't a single hair on his head, making it shine in the light, and his apron shows the evidence of his work over a hot cauldron.

Piles of browned apples, moldy cheese, and stale bread are laid out in a line on the table. The General doesn't waste fresh food on us. Those ahead of me pass the table, single file, and Angus distributes their share of the morning meal. Some give a quick thanks, the majority of the women speaking in the common tongue but with various accents, from countries I can't place. An indication that Heracles' grasp is far reaching; a fact that only deepens my resentment toward the demigod.

Surrounding the food-laden table are stone walls painted creme, and slate-tiled flooring the color of rust. A hearth is built into the wall at one end, and at the other is a large window with pink ivy sprawling the exterior of the glass. A slack-jawed guard by the name of Felton, sits on a stool with his back against the window, eyes closed. When Angus turns away for a second, Ruby, a young woman, just a few places ahead of me in line, takes an extra apple from the table and quickly shoves it into her dress pocket.

Fear settles in my belly when Felton shifts on his stool, one eye half open. He apparently was feigning sleep. "What do you think you're doing?" He jeers and moves to stand. The guard, with his curly mouse hair, pocked face, and oversized girth, would under normal circumstances, not strike terror into the heart of anyone, but the whip and long dagger at his side do.

Ruby freezes, her hand slowly coming from her pocket. Those nearest to her give a wide berth as if she's diseased. Ruby already has a suspicious dark bruise on her chin. I'm afraid for her. I move behind Saray and grab onto her skirts, as if the fabric will shield me.

Ruby sputters, "I missed the evening meal and—" Her voice is cut short when Felton surges forward and grabs her by the neck. The moldy contents within her arms fall to the floor.

"Don't think you can take extras because the General isn't around." He then shoves her face down onto the table and proceeds to saw off her ear with his dagger.

Oh gods! Oh gods! My breath hitches as the woman shrieks in pain, and I press myself further against Saray who rubs my back in turn. Angus, on the other hand, stares with an impassive face while Ruby's blood stains the wood. When the guard lets her go, she stands and presses the injured site with a trembling hand.

"You'll be expected to join the next Confessional," Felton barks at her.

Ruby's pale face blanches further, but she bows her head without argument before replacing the stolen apple. She then crouches down to pick up her spilled food, but the guard stomps on the bread with his foot.

"Leave it," he says. "A thief doesn't deserve to eat."

Her lip quakes and snot leaks from her nose before she rubs it away, smearing blood as she does.

The guard looks at her with disgust before spitting in her face and returning to his stool. Eyes on the rest of us, he plops down with an exaggerated sigh.

Everyone stays frozen, including Ruby; the air is thick with uncertainty. Shocked by the violence, a sickness stirs within me. I want to throw up but hold it in. I mustn't draw attention to myself.

"Did I tell you dumb cunts to stop?" Felton hisses.

The other ladies ahead of me resume getting their morning meal but do so more quickly than before. Ruby hurries from the kitchen, leaving droplets of blood in her wake.

Saray leans in close to me. "An obvious lesson for you: don't take more than what you're supposed to." She stands to her full height, and surveys the dwindling line. "Ruby never has been the brightest amongst us."

"What's Confessional?" I whisper to her back. It's the first time I've heard of it since I've been here.

"A near death sentence. Unless you like whips, do as you're told."

I swallow. Will I be able to survive six months of this?

When it's my turn for rations, the first thing I notice is the blood seeped into the wood grain of the table and the severed ear sitting on its ledge. As I stare at it, I'm reminded of the roughness of chains beneath my fingers and a screaming man. I glance at Angus, my face now green. He stands stoically with his dark arms crossed against his chest. I've not gotten to know many since my arrival, as there's no time for it. Slaves, for the most part, keep to themselves, but I'll never forget the medicine he brewed for me. It's a nice secret shared between two strangers.

Angus sees me glance at the ear again before handing me my food. Despite the repulsiveness of it all, I eat.

CHAPTER XXIV

12th Week of Summer

Eimear

The sea breeze tickles my neck, cooling my sweat-soaked skin just enough. I'm helping Saray with the laundry. There's an eternity's worth of clothes and after hours of scrubbing, we're hanging the wash up to dry on a rope line. My hands are chapped raw, and I try to focus instead on the scenery around. The castle grounds are actually quite beautiful, a stark contrast to the ugliness within.

Castle Notos was built on a rockface, its back is to the south, and overlooks the Aethiopia Sea. The entrance faces a downward slope of rolling hills where large stretches of lush cobalt grass host a number of red bushes. Beyond, toward the north, are mountains. The castle itself is impressive with its round twin towers and stained-glass windows. A mass of pink and red foliage has grown around the enormous double doors and colored windows giving the structure a romantic appearance even though Castle Notos is anything but.

Several yards ahead of me is a craggy path leading down to a bluff that hangs over the beach below. At its center, there's a life-sized statue of a bull, crafted of bronze. The figure is so intricately detailed that, even at this distance, I can make out the folds of the bull's neck and the latch at the bottom of its belly. A stone bench has been built in viewing distance of the bull. It makes me wonder what perverse fascination the General has with cattle. Up above, just a small spec now in the distance, is the ever-damning presence of the East Window.

What used to be my beacon of hope, is now a source for my rage. Every time I see the eye slit in the sky, I'm reminded of my loss and pain. So much pain, that I believe the fetid stench of it must be seeping out of my skin for others to detect my misery. I stare long and hard at the Lunetas Bridge and the Window. I wish it would all fucking collapse and burry the gods within.

I cling to my sanity by imagining that Zadok has been found by some happy couple who always wanted a child, and that he's far away, untouchable by all the turmoil Heracles has caused. My fingers graze the scar on my face. It's sensitive still, but no longer painful. So much has changed and in such a short time.

Next to me, Saray mutters something under her breath and I look in her direction. I notice how her palms shake as she tries to hang a pale green tunic. She's been acting odd since a guard came by earlier and pulled her into a conversation I couldn't hear.

"Is everything all right?" I ask.

"Yes, yes. Everything's fine," she rattles off without looking at me. An awkward silence hangs between us for a few seconds. "Actually, I need to go check on something right quick. Be a good girl and keep at it."

Perplexed, I watch her retreating back. I try not to let her strange behavior bother me, and instead, focus on the task at hand. I'm a bit at odds with myself. I no longer crave company, not wanting to become attached to anyone here. But when I'm alone like this, my thoughts seem to stray to the shadowy recesses of my mind where everything unpleasant is stowed. In my current solitude, horrible memories resurface, and I hum a melody to drown them out.

Stay back, I tell my specters and sing louder. I envision what I must appear to be, a happy girl singing while hanging laundry under the Sister Sun with a beautiful castle as a backdrop. The imagery is nauseating when I compare it to what's going on inside my mind. I'm miserable and pay no heed to the footsteps from behind, thinking Saray has returned. But soon I'm sputtering as the dirty water from the day's laundry is dumped over my head. Turning toward the shrieks of laughter I find Neyda and Arete guffawing at my expense. With them is a small bird of a girl who is silent, eyes downcast. I think her name is Lyra but can't be certain. She rarely speaks.

The wash bin falls from the laughing girls' hands and rolls to a stop at my feet. Neither of them could be considered great beauties with their shadowed eyes and gaunt frames, which remind me of a fish picked down to its bones.

Neyda sneers at me, "I was trying to help you out by washing the shit off your face, but it seems like shit stains don't come off so easy."

Her comment stings, but I say nothing and show nothing. Arete grabs Neyda's arm and leans in close, saying, "What if she's a mute like that old cook?"

"Poor thing," Neyda tuts. "Then she's dumb *and* looks like a whore's slit." The bitch's smile is cruel.

Arete snickers. The birdlike girl behind them finally dares to speak, her voice tired. "We should go. Leave her before we're missed."

I stare at the three of them, my insides cold. It's not the hateful remarks from the two slags that makes me snap. Nor is it the fact that I now smell like a street beggar's arsehole. The truth is, seeing that woman's severed ear this morn reminded me of the time I gouged out a man's eyes, and I've been spiraling downward since.

Neyda turns on the small girl. "Shut the fuck up, Lyra, just because you like sucking the guards off while the General is gone doesn't mean—"

Arete screams when I smash the empty water bin into the side of Neyda's face, catching both girls off-guard. The mean bitch falls to the ground, and I snuff out Arete's cries by shoving the bin over her head before kicking her in the groin and sending her sprawling. Lyra's blue eyes widen, highlighting the fresh bruise near her temple. The girl's hand darts to her belly, and I understand more than I want to.

Neyda's face is split open at the cheek, blood slowly sliding down to her chin as she stares at me in shock. I'm captivated by the red trickle, knowing I caused it.

"You—you—hit me!" she manages to sputter.

Arete removes the wash bin from her head and cups her privates with her hands, face pinched in a grimace. Women don't have a cock dangling between their legs, but a good kick to the cunny will still do the job it seems.

I smile at Neyda, my scar pulling. She tries to get away from me, but I bend down, grabbing the front of her uniform and bring her bleeding face close to mine. My hair is soaked from the laundry water and droplets fall onto her face, mixing with her bloody gash. "Bother me again, and I'll cut your throat when you're sleeping."

Her eyes widen and her mouth opens and closes, giving her the appearance of a fish drowning in air. Now that I'm closer, Neyda's breath is foul, the stench making my nose turn up. I shove her back into the grass. "And brush your fucking teeth for gods' sake."

She brings her hand to her mouth as if to check while Lyra steps closer and helps the two to their feet. I turn my back to them as if they're nothing and resume hanging the laundry. Only when their footsteps retreat, do I release a shaky breath and allow my hands to tremble on the clothesline.

I'm hanging another tunic when I see Saray out of the corner of my eye walking toward me. She wrings her hands. My stomach spasms with fear, did Neyda and her dimwitted friend snitch on me? I take a deep breath. I've survived to this point. I'll handle whatever comes next.

"Eimear, follow me."

I exhale. Here it comes. When I reach her side, she looks skyward.

"I tried to delay it for as long as I could, but . . . it's time now."

Oh. So, I'm not in trouble? "Delay what?" I ask.

Saray turns, and we walk in silence across the grounds; it's not long before she speaks again. "I'm not sure you know, but every *slave*," she stumbles over the word, "is marked with their master's brand."

A bark of laughter escapes me when I realize why she's been so cryptic. Saray whirls around, and stares incredulously. I point a finger to my face. "Do you think after *this*, a little brand would scare me?" My bravado is partially fake, but she doesn't need to know that.

She's taken aback by my response. "Well, it's certainly not a pleasant experience! One of the worst days of my life if you ask me." Saray glares and shakes her head like she wants to say something else but turns instead and resumes walking.

I play with the fabric of my uniform, rolling it between my fingers, and think about how she has avoided using the word *slave* and instead pointedly uses *servant*. Shame washes over me, and I almost want to apologize, but instead, I ask, "What were you before?"

Saray stops and doesn't speak for a moment, as if lost in some memory. "I was traded to Notos from another master's house. Before that, I was shipped to the Southern Region like an animal. I used to be a respectable nanny to a wealthy house in Kanthar. However, the Autokrator destroyed that and everything else with his army." Her face looks pained for a moment, and then she masks it. "That was some time ago, though, and matters no more."

"Did you lay eyes on him? Heracles, I mean."

Saray chews on her lip, when she speaks her delivery is malicious. "Oh yes, I saw him all right."

I grow excited. "What was he like?"

"They had so many of us penned up like sheep. I had myself pressed against the edge, hoping to catch a glimpse of my daughter or the other children, when I saw *him* pass by with his men. It had to be Heracles, no ordinary person could appear like he did." Saray crosses her arms against her chest. "I'll never forget those eyes, so dead, and carved within a body that just…glowed? Like you'd imagine a god would glow if you met one."

I don't tell her that I've seen a god, but her story confirms what I've feared. Heracles must be immortal.

She straightens and draws in a great breath. "My daughter, Maya . . . she was but a child when she was taken from my arms. She'd be a little older than you by now. I always hope that life turned out good for her, my little girl."

There's a quiver to Saray's voice and my heart aches for the daughter she'll most likely never see again. I'm quiet, respecting her grief as we walk toward the eastern grounds of the castle and take a path that leads downhill. A set of guards sit on crates by the castle wall, some hold playing cards in their hands while others cast dice to the ground. They look up as we pass, but then ignore us when they see we're headed towards a smithy at the bottom of the hill. The building is small, made from stone, with a chimney on the roof and an open doorway in the front. Saray goes through the entrance, and I follow.

It's unbearably hot, and I immediately begin to sweat. Tools hang from the walls, the amount of use evident by their dark color. A strong fire burns in the forge, along with some swords. The blades are bright and almost ready to be molded into something stronger. A branding iron rests amongst the weaponry in the flame, and I'm certain its warm end belongs to me. A boy on the cusp of manhood stands awkwardly behind a stone worktable, fidgeting with the leather gloves he wears. The uniform under his black apron is similar to my own, identifying him as a slave. The blacksmith must be hated by the other slaves for what he does to them.

Saray and I stand in the doorway. There's a guard who leans against the wall in the corner. His auburn hair is damp with sweat, and it sticks to his scalp. The man's pale skin is blotched red, his expression miserable. He holds a makeshift fan that he waves rapidly in the air around his face.

"Sir," Saray mutters to the guard. "I've brought the newest for her branding."

He peers up with tired blue eyes and lets out a grunt. When we don't move, he motions with his head toward the blacksmith but doesn't speak.

The boy sees the interaction and clears his throat. "Well, let's get to it then, shall we?" his voice cracks and pitches an octave, causing his neck to flush scarlet.

"Ah bloody fuck," The guard says abruptly, dropping his fan. He barrels past me, knocking Saray in the shoulder, which sends her sideways. I grab hold of her in time, though, preventing her fall. The guard retches outside, the smell of it makes my own stomach twist. Eventually, he returns and leans against the door frame with his elbow. A dribble of vomit remains at the corner of his mouth.

The guard addresses the blacksmith, "Egan, I'm stepping out for a moment, brand the little bitch quickly and then back to the General's order." He then gestures to Saray and I. "You bleeding cunts better be gone by the time I get back." He pauses before leaning in closer to me, his face scrunched with disgust. I can smell the bile from his mouth. "Fuck. Looking at you, I think I may be sick again." He shoves me, and I stumble backward into the smith's table. The guard then glances at the forge and mutters a curse before leaving.

Saray spares me a pitying glance as she reaches for my hand. I turn away from her, though, and stare at the iron dipped in flame. I don't want her sympathies.

"Ate something bad, did he?" she asks Egan.

The blacksmith shrugs his shoulders. "Nat gets like that sometimes, the heat from the forge is too much for him." Egan gestures to me. "You ready?"

I attempt to mentally prepare myself for the pain to come, but nothing is going to make this better. I sigh. "I think so." An apology is on the tip of the boy's tongue, and I hold up my hand to stop him. "Don't. I don't blame you; just make it quick."

He presses his lips together and nods before walking to the forge. I think Saray is more nervous than I am because she begins to pace.

"You may want to take a seat," Egan says. "This is going to burn." His eyes widen as he takes in my scarred face. "Well…it seems you've plenty experience with that."

I give him a wicked smile before taking a seat at the worktable. "It's all right; I know it's hideous."

He looks away from me quickly. The boy's distress makes my smile widen, and I decide that I like making people feel uncomfortable.

Saray comes up beside me and places a hand on my shoulder. "Eimear, it's very rare that we get to choose something for ourselves here, but for this, you can pick your poison—calf or arm. Most get the brand on the back of the calf."

She twists her leg toward me and raises her skirts to expose the delta sign that's been burned into her flesh. The triangular scar, now old, spans nearly three inches. My palms are sweating now, yet it's not from the forge's heat. I knew at some point this would come, but to be branded like an animal is still humiliating. Steilos must've known this would happen, and I curse him for it. Gnawing on my lip, I regret how I mocked Saray for trying to keep a semblance of dignity.

"We need to hurry before Nat comes back," Egan says, clearly rushed.

I glare at him, and he suddenly finds new interest in the ground. Saray touches my arm, her good eye watery, and I know she knows I'm scared. "I can hold your hand through it if you like."

The inside of my chest constricts; this woman just pierced the armor I've been trying so hard to build. My throat is too tight to respond, and I clench my jaw.

She doesn't smile when she takes my hand. "You don't have to be strong for this one."

Blood rushes to my face as I try to keep the tears from coming. I nod to her and squeeze her calloused hand tightly.

//Remember, I'm here for you too, every awful step of the way.//

//That's right, I'm not alone in this.//

//Never.//

Egan takes a few steps closer to the forge and clears his throat loudly. I imagine myself punching him in the face. He turns to me, all business.

"So, what will it be, calf or arm?"

Whatever may come, I know my journey doesn't end here as a slave. I won't allow it. I've too much spite built up in me now to die so low. "Fuck it. Let's go with the arm."

I lay my left arm on the stone table, palm upward. I'll make it serve as a memento to persevere no matter what happens.

Egan pauses at the forge, looking hesitant.

I meet his gaze, my eyes steady and fierce. "Do it."

Saray holds my hand tightly as the boy pulls the iron out of the forge, the brand glowing brightly. He comes to the table, giving me one last look, questioning my decision. I take a moment before consenting with a final nod.

Egan sucks in through his teeth and grabs my wrist to hold my arm steady, and with the other he places the hot iron against my inner forearm.

I don't scream, but oh does it fucking burn.

Later in the kitchen, I grit my teeth as I plunge my newly branded arm into a bucket of cold water; it stings at first but then fades to a dull throb. Saray sent me here to help Angus, but really, I think it's just a ploy to have him doctor my arm. Whatever he mixed with the water is working miracles, or it could be the mead he had me drink a little while ago. I would've preferred the mead before the branding. But I'm nothing more than a beggar at this point, so I don't complain.

I sit at a long table, there's a dark green bowl of flour nearby. I watch Angus at work over a large pot near the hearth, stirring the contents. It's the first time I've been alone with him, and I find him odd. He doesn't speak at all, only smiles, and points when he needs to give instruction. I note how the pots and pans, are clean and shining to perfection on the wall in front of me. Below them are rows of food and spices, all neatly organized by category. The kitchen itself is immaculate. The only things out of place are the ingredients currently laid out for tonight's meal.

It's just the two of us for now, as the women who usually help Angus in the kitchen are delivering the guards' afternoon meals. Shortly after the women left, so did Felton, the brute from this morning. He decided that watching only two slaves wasn't worth his time. I have the impression that the guards are lax without the General around. Finally, some useful information.

The smell of Angus' cooking makes my stomach rumble loud enough for him to hear, and the shoulders of his broad frame shake with silent mirth. A minute later, he pours a ladle of beef stew into a bowl and grins before setting it in front of me. My body freezes. I'm mesmerized by the contents of the bowl, especially as I recall Ruby's severed ear over a single apple. We're granted two rations of old bread and fruit per day, my second not to come until later this evening. This meal isn't fit for a slave like me.

"Are you sure?" I ask, managing to pry my eyes away from the stew.

Angus raises a silent finger to his lips and gives me a wink.

Why would another slave offer me food? There must be a guard listening at the door, waiting for me to make a mistake. It would give them an excuse to do their worst. I'd like to keep all my body parts attached, thank you very much. I shove the bowl away, and some of its contents spill onto the table. "No," I say and stare defiantly at the cook.

He looks perplexed, and reaches to take the bowl from me when my sacred-self decides to speak up.

//Eat. You need your strength. It's safe. This is not a trick, and there are no guards nearby right now to catch you. We can't feel them.//

My fingers quickly curl around Angus's wrist, and stop him from taking the bowl. "I'm sorry, I've changed my mind. Thank you, I'll gladly eat it."

He raises a dark brow and gives me a silent shrug of his shoulders before returning to the hearth.

I take the spoon from the bowl with my good hand and lift it to my lips, moaning loudly when the taste reaches my tongue. What bliss. I don't think I've had anything of substance since leaving Paidia. I rashly decide that if Felton returns and tries to take the stew from me, that he can have a fucking ear. I have an extra one anyway.

I wolf the contents down like a savage, and when it's empty, my tongue licks the bowl to get every last drop. When finished, I lean back from the table, with glazed eyes and a full belly. Angus takes the bowl from me with a knowing smirk, and I feel slightly embarrassed.

"Thank you," I mutter, my ruined face probably a deep shade of pink.

He takes a handful of flour from the green bowl and scatters it on the table. He then uses his finger to write in the powder and points to me. I lean forward to take a closer look. *Too skinny. Need food*, is written in the common language.

My fingers skirt my ribs. They protrude from beneath my dress, proving his case. I grin at him weakly. "It may take a while."

Angus nods his head before going to the shelf behind him. He comes back with an arm full of potatoes and a knife and starts to peel them. I glance at my arm still submerged in the bucket and realize the branded skin has numbed. He used Zechan.[48] It's better than when he prepared the gravinroot. At least I'm not passing out this time.

"Saray mentioned you were a healer."

Angus glances up from his potatoes to give a nod.

"My mother—" I tear up thinking about her and can't finish what I was going to say because it doesn't matter what she was. Not here, not

------

[48] A yellow flower used as a numbing agent when chewed or pressed against a wound.

in this place. Angus puts his knife down and writes in the flour again, then places his large hand over my own.

It better with time, I read.

My throat closes up, and I recall the feeling of Saray's warm hand when I stood trembling before the forge. And now, another unexpected kindness in a place filled with cruelty. My eyes narrow in distrust. "Why are you being so nice to me? This—" I gesture to my branded arm in the bucket, "the gravinroot, and the stew. Why?"

Angus goes to write in the flour again but then shakes his head and wipes it away. He speaks, but it's with great effort. He has to move his mouth wide and the words he's able to form are clipped and loud. The sound reminds me of a screaming goat. I'm shocked by it, in truth, till the jarring movements of his mouth reveal their secret—a large part of his tongue is missing. I can understand him, but just barely.

"LIFE…CAN…BE…MISS..ER..ABLE…SOME PEO…PLE…TAKE THEIR…PAIN…AND…HURT…OTH…ERS…SO…THEY…CAN… FEEL…SOME…THING…I'M… TI…RED… OF… BE…ING… ANG..RY…I…WANT… TO… FEEL… GOOD… DO…ING…A… LIT…TLE GOOD… PUTS… A… LIGHT…IN… ME… LET ME…BE…KIND…TO…YOU." Angus finishes and massages the sides of his jaw. Then he gives me a wink before resuming his potato peeling.

I watch him for a while in a stupefied silence, wondering about his severed tongue and mulling over his butchered words. It all makes me wonder if I can ever be light again.

CHAPTER XXV

3rd Week of Fall

Nikko

"No! No! No! You have to use a firmer grip," I say, exasperated. Gareth was right, the blade doesn't suit him. He's terrible at it. I watch him attempt to best his straw-filled enemy, but his wooden sword *misses* as he charges and runs past. Some nearby soldiers on break snicker at the poor boy. "How is that possible? The target can't move; a *child* could hit it blindfolded," I say.

Gareth turns to me, his tunic soaked through with sweat, and digs his practice sword into the ground before leaning on it out of breath. "You know, for a prince, you're quite the prick."

I grin. "You have it wrong. *Because* I'm a prince, I'm quite the prick."

He glances at the practice dummy over his shoulder with disdain. "I think I'm best left in the infirmary."

He really is hopeless. "I'll have to agree with you for once. After a month of drilling and little-to-no progress, you may just yet be the worst swordsman I've ever seen." There's a pause as we share a look before bursting out in simultaneous laughter. Becoming Gareth's friend isn't a ruse for Ellanios anymore; turns out I actually enjoy his company. His blunt honesty is refreshing amongst people who'd jump at the chance to wipe my arse if they could.

He lifts his sword from the ground. "I have to go now. I told the lead physician I'd be at the infirmary by midmorning."

I nod and wave him off. "Yeah, yeah. I have my own duties to attend to as well." Father has been allowing me to sit and observe his council meetings, and there is one being held today. I don't want to fuck it up. "Should we meet up for a drink later?"

Gareth points to himself like an imbecile. "With me? I don't think I'm old—"

I clasp him on the shoulder. "You're practically a grown man now. You're drinking with me. I won't take no for an answer." No need to mention that the tavern's home brews aren't as good as they used to be, and the hangovers are worse. He can find that out for himself the hard way.

Gareth sighs. "Why do I get the feeling you're leading me to trouble?"

"Not trouble. *Fun*," I say with a wink.

My father raises a brow when I enter the dome-shaped council chamber. "Nice of you to join us."

"My apologies," I say curtly and bow. I'm ten minutes early, which is late in his eyes. I take a seat and observe the three men who are my father's most respected advisors. Each of them has dark skin and bright gray eyes, indicating they are trueborn Ellanions. They were handpicked as babes by my grandfather to be his advisors and are nearly the same age as the King.

Brontes, Dareios, and Jakab, my own childhood playmates and future advisors, are currently on their seven-year sabbaticals. I miss the bastards dearly and pray they haven't met misfortune with the rise of Heracles.

My father only gave me permission to join the council on the condition I don't speak. I'm here to listen and learn, but mostly, I try to keep myself from falling asleep. Today is different though, because the King's best and brightest are currently in an uproar over my sister Jada's fate.

Hain is the first to express his concern: "This war has taken a turn for the worse! Surely by the end of this week General Charos will defeat the Avantians and our soldiers who fight alongside them." Out of the three, Hain usually seems to be the most cautious of my father's advisors in terms of tactics. He tends to fiddle with a timepiece he has on a long chain around his neck.

Idan, who wears his head shorn, shares his opinion: "We need to submit to Heracles. Tell King Ranvir, that because Avanta can no longer uphold their end of the treaty, neither can Ellanios. Let's bring our men home and spare further bloodshed."

"Our citizens have become restless. If we reason with the demigod, then everything will continue in the Holy City as it was before this mess," Hain adds slowly.

Bacchus, the Commander of Ellanios' army, mutters something under his breath, his fists clench against the armrest. "'Before this mess'? What you mean to say, Hain, is before the fall of Kanthar and Anyalay. Never forget, they were our allies for decades—that has to mean something. Too much blood has been spilled, slavery reintroduced. The Queen's own people now toil away under General Valdez's hard-pressed boot. We have a moral responsibility to free them, and Heracles refuses to relinquish their shackles as part of the treaty. It's pertinent to our honor that we continue the fight."

A military man through and through, Bacchus is clean shaven, hair cropped close to his scalp. He wears his integrity like a medal and has my deepest respect. Better than the King, he has acted as a father figure for Jada and I, even adopting the endearment 'uncle' from us as children.

The advisors look in unison to the King, who appears to have aged ten years overnight, his face is marked with exhaustion. "My brothers . . . I am torn and must speak truthfully. While it is imperative that our goal be to preserve lives, our people have grown soft through the long years of full bellies and peace. It troubles me they no longer have the fortitude to stand by the loyal neighbors we have fought alongside and have grown our economy with." My father's eyes flicker to Idan in particular. "We also must not forget our family members in Anyalay and Kanthar who Heracles binds in servitude still. Though of mixed blood, they are still Ellanion, and we are responsible for their safety."

A vein appears at Idan's temple. "My King and brother, respectfully, not a day goes by that I don't think of my nieces and nephews in Kanthar. The horrors they must be experiencing while I sit in the comforts of my home, it's deplorable. But they, like other Ellanions, chose to leave the safety of the Holy City's walls and Ellanios' borders to grow their families elsewhere. It pains me to say it, but we cannot save everyone and must do what is best for those who live on our soil. Sacrifices must be made."

The room goes deathly quiet and the tension builds. Heracles has backed us into a corner. Jada's hand only purchases us the safety of those living in Ellanios, leaving everyone else to fend for themselves. I study each of their grave faces, knowing the lives of many weighs heavy on each of them. The claws of panic begin to tear at my heart. I don't want this responsibility. I just want my sister and I to be happy.

My father breathes out a heavy sigh, then speaks. "Let us adjourn for today and give ourselves time to think. You're all dismissed."

I'm the last to leave the council chamber, and a sad weariness settles on me as I make my way through the palace halls. I don't want to be king. I won't be able to make the hard decisions. Such a feat is meant for greater men than I. For the first time, I begin to view my stoic father in a different light, and wonder if he's ever felt the same misgivings.

"That's an expression I've not seen on you before, Prince. Can't say it's to my liking."

Erebos leans against a wall, wearing a perfectly fitted attire of black cloth. He reminds me of a sculpture that was carefully carved to create the paradox of an angelic demon. I haven't seen him since Gareth's fists collided with those high cheek bones of his and he scurried off, tail between his legs. I won't be forgetting the flash of crimson eyes nor his long fangs any time soon. Erebos may very well be a demon beast from the Under, instead of gifted.

What would it be like to take such a creature to bed? To have his claws rake down my back as we— I immediately curse myself and stamp down the intrusive image. It bothers me to admit it, but the graceful slope of his neck adorned with that silver chain of his, has wandered into my thoughts unexpectedly a time or two. I'm not sure why the bastard takes up any space in my head, but he certainly doesn't belong there. We're enemies.

Erebos tilts his head sideways in a dog-like manner. I've taken too long to respond.

Flustered, I snap at him. "What do you want, interloper? Are you here to brag about Heracles' gaining ground at the trenches? If you are, please fuck off."

"It is not my intention to ever cause you or Jada distress," he says. "I am simply, as she put it, a messenger of sorts."

At the mention of my twin, I bristle. What exactly are they to each other? She wants to know her enemy, but could it be more than that? "You would do well to leave my sister alone and take your interests elsewhere. She has enough to worry about without the entanglements of yet another awestruck suiter."

Wishing to be rid of his company, I pick up my pace and briskly pass Erebos, not sparing him another glance. He truly grates on my every nerve.

"Jada is not the one I'm interested in, Prince," he says smoothly.

My stride falters only momentarily before I continue onward.

It's evening by the time Gareth and I are able to meet again. There's an unusual quiet as we stroll the streets of the Holy City. The normally bustling metropolis is subdued, making the structures that surround us more eerie than pleasant.

Gareth, not noticing the difference, stares up at the Lunetas Bridge. "It's never truly dark here, is it?"

I turn my head, surveying the buildings bathed in the bridge's bright light—so bright, there's no need for sconces or lanterns. I've never experienced a true dark night. Maybe one day.

"It reminds me of our Twin Moon festival . . . all this light," Gareth says.

"Do tell. We don't celebrate such a thing here."

His eyes crinkle with sadness. "During the winter, those who're of age in my village pair—or are paired—with their life-mate when the bridge changes color for one night under the twin full moons."

I've heard of phenomenon with the bridge, it happens rarely in other countries, but never in Ellanios. Still, I'm a bit surprised. "Life-mates? As in marriage? How old is 'of age'?"

"Fourteen, sometimes older," he says, while looking at the two crescent moons that shine above. "The West Window here is also magnificent, Eimear always wanted to see it. She'd love Olympus and the Holy City."

"You mean to tell me, that by the age of fourteen, it's decided who you have a toss with for the *rest of your life*?"

Gareth cocks his head, his expression serious. "I've never thought of it that way, but sure, yeah."

My brows shoot up. What a horrible custom. It's standard for royalty to suffer such a fate, but a commoner? Wait… isn't he sixteen? I point at him. "You're already *married*?"

Gareth glares at me. I haven't seen him this angry since his encounter with Erebos. He walks ahead quickly and says, "Not anymore. She's dead."

Fuck, I've gone and stepped in it again. I run after my new friend and drape my arm around his shoulder, pulling him close. "I didn't mean to bring her up like that. But your past is behind you and the only choice you have is to move forward,"

"Move forward?" he whispers.

I nod. "Yep. Now how about that drink?" I say and take him into the nearest tavern.

Time goes quickly when the drinks are plenty. It's two hours later, we're at Cerberus' Maw, and my fingers drum slowly against the wooden table. I'm marginally annoyed. "Styx," I mutter and take a swig from my mug which tastes of the worst kind of homebrew.

Gareth is a crier when he drinks.

Any woman slightly interested in us has run at the first sign of his blubbering.

"You don't understaannddd," Gareth slurs with his cheek pressed to the table, mug in hand, his tears like small rivers down his face. "I loveddddd her, and now she's goooonnne."

"No, I don't." I chug my drink until it's empty, then I slam down the tankard. "I've never been in love." When he doesn't respond, I glance across the table to see that his eyes are closed and his breathing steady. When I poke him, he moans but doesn't stir. "Well, fuck." I raise my hand and signal the barmaid for one last round. When she brings me a fresh draft, I notice the carved wooden pendant at her breast. It reads *Darja*.

I wink at the beauty and pay her in full, but she rolls her Ellanian eyes, not captivated by my charm. She saunters off, rolling my coin between her painted fingers. Darja disappears behind the bar, and I'm left alone with my thoughts. *Jada isn't the one who I am interested in, Prince*, comes the memory of Erebos' invasive voice. That fucker. What did he mean by that? An image surfaces of those depthless crimson pools of his. Why in the Under am I thinking of him at all? Stop it. I survey the room instead, trying to entertain myself.

Usually, Cerberus' Maw is filled with bawdy laughter and drunks who stagger about making a mess. But like the streets tonight, the drinkers in here are subdued. Most of their shoulders are hunched and they talk in low voices. This shitstorm with Heracles has formed a black cloud over the city. The people are torn between wanting to fight, believing that Zeus will protect us—thinking otherwise would be blasphemous—or signing a treaty with a tyrant.

After sitting in on the King's Council, I fear they plan to go through with selling Jada off like a whore in the name of peace. Head already buzzing, I finish the remainder of my draft and listen to the conversation at the next table, where two older men sit.

One has his head shaved and his beard trimmed close. "We should stand our ground and fight. Ellanios has prospered for hundreds of years. With Zeus on our side, the army can defeat that bastard," he says.

His friend, a dumb-looking fellow, takes a long swig from his drink before leaning forward on an elbow. "Cael, let's be honest. The King should just let the princess do her job and spread her legs for Heracles. No reason for anyone to die over a woman."

I don't think. I just act. And hit the dumb fucker in the back of the head with my empty tankard, knocking him unconscious. He slumps onto the table, spilling his draft.

Cael is up in a flash with a knife drawn. "You lookin' for a fight, eh?"

I crack my neck from side to side and roll my shoulders. "Seems so. Your friend should be careful of who he insults."

Cael points his knife at me. "You should be careful to mind your own."

Darja spies our quarrel and runs over. She gestures towards the door, "Leave, now. I won't have yuh fighting in my tavern and upsetting my other customers."

I glance around at the other patrons and, sure enough, my small scuffle sparked a heavy tension in the room. Those who were subdued before are now ready to have their fists flying.

"Ah, Styx!" The bar maid yells when a patron throws a chair at another guest. The fellow jumps aside in time before it smashes against the wall. Cael tries to take advantage of the distraction and lunges at me with his dagger. I'm better with a sword, but that doesn't mean I didn't learn a thing or two from the Queen. I dodge my attacker and grab his elbow with my left hand, his wrist with my right. When my feet pivot, I take his knife hand with me, sending Cael to his toes before shoving my left arm up and flipping him forward. Before he can stand, I kick him in the face and twirl my new knife in the air. "I'll be keeping this, thank you."

Cael moans from the floor.

I scan the room, searching for Gareth and see him sitting with his head still down on the table, his cheek plastered against the wood. He's oblivious to the maelstrom of curses, fighting men, and splintered chairs around us. I whistle, "By the gods, now that is impressive." When a tankard goes flying past my head, I decide that our welcome at Cerberus' Maw has run out. I walk over to Gareth, put his arm around my shoulder and lift him with my own weight "Time to go, buddy."

"We can't sleep here?" He slurs his words, breath sour.

Two men tumble to the ground in front of us, their fists a blur. A tooth slides near my foot. "No. No we cannot."

I'm able to get us out of the tavern, and we're halfway up the street when I finally breathe a sigh of relief. Glad that's all over with.

"There! That's the one!" I hear Darja and look back to see her pointing us out to three palace guards.

"Gods damnit," I curse and let Gareth go. He slides to the ground beside me in a heap.

The guards take us away, and I don't bother trying to explain that I'm the Prince of Ellanios. They would just think I'm a drunken agitator. Which isn't far from the truth.

Later, from a cell in the palace jail, the Sister Sun's rays shine between the bars onto Gareth's snoring face. He lays in piss-infested straw. My back is against the cell wall, where I sit and watch him. "I wonder if he'll consider this to have been fun?" I say to myself.

He burrows his face into the fetid hay, and I cringe. I'll just leave that detail out when I tell him later. I turn my head at the sound of distinct footsteps, and I'm surprised to see Jada peering at me through the cell door. Her night clothes are rumpled, as if she'd just been wakened. The jailer stands beside her.

"You've really gone and done it this time. An entire bar destroyed! Really?" she says without smiling as the jailor unlocks the door.

I can't help but grin as I exit the cell. "All in the name of your honor."

Jada snorts. "You can explain that one to father yourself."

My smirk fades. "Fuck. He's going to be livid with me."

My sister doesn't respond with her usual banter, and I know something other than my nightly antics is amiss.

"What's wrong?"

She sighs, "There's something you should know . . . It's been decided. Father is going to sign the treaty with Heracles. He sent a messenger with Erebos just an hour ago. They're on their way to the trenches as we speak. It's done, Nikko. The war is over." Jada reaches for me, her gaze reflecting all the fear and sadness she's been trying to keep at bay these past several months.

All my cockiness disappears in an instant. I pull her close, hanging onto her tightly. "It may be over, but the price is too steep. You shouldn't have to pay it," I murmur against her hair. It's then that my sister lets down her defenses and cries into my shoulder, her sobs fill the empty spaces of the surrounding cells.

Gods & Beasts of Miracle

Ares

To my father Zeus:

You disowned me,

because I am the most hateful of all your children.

But how can you turn your back on my heart,

when it was you who bred me for war?

To the others who stand proud on Olympus,

you scorn me because I am the most human among us.

Did you ever stop to ponder,

that the human aspects of my godliness

are my greatest strength,

not a weakness?

As for the sons and daughters who grace the worlds below,

I applaud your disgust,

for I know it's because I remind you of the worst parts of yourselves.

Take head my dearest loved ones,

for I am chaos,

and I am violence,

and I am coming,

for you all.

CHAPTER XXVI

5th Week of Fall

Eimear

I smell like shit. Literal shit. Piss and shit beneath my nails, splatters of it coating my skin. I want to fucking scream. Thank Hades and his adulterous ways, I'm sure I'd have an infection or worse by now if it weren't for the mysterious spring under the castle.

"Oy! Yuh busted face bitch, you missed a spot," Faas calls.

I bite my tongue and scrub the privy bucket harder; something splashes on my cheek and I cringe. Within the castle walls, there's running water, a wonderous feature my village lacked. However, the same can't be said for the guard barracks. Faas sits atop a crate that he's set up against the outside back wall of the smithy; he's the blond guard I first encountered when arriving at Castle Notos. Under normal circumstances, I'd consider him handsome with his blue eyes, straight nose, and full lips, but quite frankly he's an utter bastard. Regrettably, I'm his current object of affection. It must be due to my good looks.

My admirer assigns me the worst duties and stands watch as I suffer. This morning, he pulled me from the meal line and had me cleaning cobwebs around the castle by hand, spiders and all. Now, I'm to scrub all the guards' shit and piss buckets. I'm hoping that he'll soon find his jollies elsewhere because I can't simply smash him in the head with a bucket like Neyda. Although, that idea is becoming more appealing by the minute. *Just. Four. More. Months,* is becoming a mantra I say repeatedly in my head.

There's a water pump at the back of the smithy that I'm using to rinse the filthy buckets. I had to haul them all here from the barracks by myself and will have to take them back when I'm finished. Other than the sound of Egan pounding away at metal by the forge, and Faas's seemingly endless string of insults, it's been a quiet afternoon of scrub, pump, rinse, scrub, pump, rinse; over and over again. I try to keep my head down as I labor, I don't want to attract more attention from my tormenter, nor do I wish to see the Gods' Window hanging in the sky. A faint breeze gives very little relief to the endless heat; the skin on the back of my arms and neck feels tight from Sister Sun's burning rays. My nose tickles from the wind, and I have an agonizing itch to scratch it, but I must resist because I'm elbow deep in excrement. My jaw clenches hard enough to crack a tooth. Fuck Steilos and this stone fuckery quest! I made a fool's gamble by coming to this place. I'm never going to find that citrine.

Yesterday, before my evening ration, a group of guards beat a slave senseless. The crime I'm not sure of, but his face was unrecognizable when they were done. He never cried out despite all the kicks and punches, but when he was told that he'd be joining the next Confessional, he begged for mercy. It's as if I've been thrown into a den of hungry chimeras. I'm too much of a coward after all the atrocities I've witnessed to go sneaking around looking for the stone. I'll just bide my time instead. It's safer this way. Like Steilos, I too can be duplicitous.

"I never said you could stop washing!"

Too late I realize that my hands are still. Faas explodes with fury and rushes over to me. His boot slams into my stomach, knocking the breath from my lungs and making me spill the remaining shit-stained water from the bucket down the front of my dress. He kicks the other half-empty buckets over and they drain around me. I go to pick them up, but Faas puts his boot to my chest and shoves me to my back. His eyes are filled with a cold excitement as he looks down on me through a sneer.

"Thought you'd go and get all lazy on me, huh? Do you want to know what we do to dumb twats like you?"

The back of my head is soaked from the dirty muck, and the bastard's boot on my chest is a familiar sensation from the night my life took a turn for the worse. My mind wants to be strong, to fight the fear, but my body remembers and betrays me. I tremble and wet myself as the pressure from his boot intensifies, crushing my chest.

"That's right—that's the face I want to see. Now beg me not to beat—"

"Faas! You dumb shit! It's the General! He's back!" Nat, the other guard, comes around the corner of the smithy in a hurry, his pale face is flushed red. Saray follows soon after. Her eyes widen when she sees me on the ground.

"Did you hear me?" Nat demands. "Quit playing around with the help, fucker. We gotta go!"

Faas looks worried. He spits on me before he removes his boot. "Shit, I thought the bastard wasn't due back for at least a few weeks' time," he says and walks away.

Nat clasps him by the shoulder. "Play time's over. I hear he massacred the remaining resistance at the trenches. The former King of Avanta is now dangling by his balls over their gates as we speak."

I'm shocked by the last few moments, but this must mean Heracles now has dominion over the entire Southern Region.

When they round the corner of the smithy, Saray runs to me and helps me up from the muddied ground. Her dark eye is filled with worry and she strokes my dirty hair. "Oh, sweetie, I'm so sorry."

Tears sting my eyes as my body continues to shake. The large droplets spill down my cheeks and barely contained fury flares in my chest. I'm angry at myself for letting my fear consume me. "I'm fine," I lie.

She tsks and brings me closer to the waterspout while sidestepping all the buckets. "Let's try to get you cleaned up as best as we can. But we have to be quick about it; the General is coming." She holds out her hand to me. "Your dress if you please."

I'm numb inside and don't give a second thought as I bring my uniform over my head and stand naked in broad daylight.

She pumps water over it, rubbing the fabric between her hands like a makeshift washboard. "Come on; get yourself washed up and quick. There's no soap to get the stink off, but the water is better than nothing."

I thrust my arm under the spout as she pumps, and I try to get the muck off as best I can with my fingers. Once I've washed my entire body, I stick my head under and run my hands through my mess of hair. Saray rings out my dress before handing it back to me. The uniform clings to my small frame, and the odor from the buckets lingers. But at least the dampness will offer my back a reprieve from Sister Sun for a little while.

Saray gives me a once over, biting her lip. "You should try to hide yourself in the back of the line."

The air changes as a different kind of heaviness descends upon the grounds of Castle Notos. Everyone has assembled outside the castle entrance and stands at attention, expressions solemn. As we wait for

General Charos' arrival, the slaves stand in rows of two on either side of the walkway, separated by gender. The men are on one side of the walkway and the women directly opposite. With all of us gathered in one place, I see now that there are just as many male slaves as there are female.

I spy Angus toward the end of the lineup, closest to the castle and not far from Egan. Saray made sure to put herself in front of me, and a slave by the name of Cecille, to my right, stands sour faced with a hand covering her nose. I can't wait till I can bathe in the spring tonight.

The guards positioned behind us are in no better mood. Taut silence envelopes all but the wind tickling the trees, leaving me to stew over the humiliation of being shoved to the ground. I fantasize a slow agonizing death for Faas. But truly, I long for night and for my bed so I can fade into oblivion and not have to feel anything at all.

At the first rumble of horses galloping in the distance, there's a collective intake of breath. The sound raises the hair on my arms. When the small group becomes visible at the bottom of the hill, the tension reaches a new high. The first to reach the fortress are less than a dozen travel-worn mounted soldiers, their breast plates and helms caked with a fine layer of dirt. The group splits off, bringing their horses to a halt behind both lines of castle guards.

He must've left the remainder of the army in Avanta. I guess a general of his nightmarish accomplishments doesn't need thousands of men to keep him safe. A scary thought.

A carriage pulled by two black horses follows the soldiers. It comes to a stop, and a hunched man is pushed forward by a guard who barks, "Attend to the General!"

The slave peers around at the rest of us, frightened, before ambling towards the carriage on shaky legs. He fumbles with the curved handle of the door but manages to open it slowly. The slave then moves aside as a black boot emerges from the carriage followed by a tall muscular body clothed in dark breeches and a deep red tunic. He wears a bracer that encloses his entire right forearm, it gleams gold in the Sister Sun's light. General Charos isn't an old man just yet, his hair only speckled with the beginnings of gray. He has a handsome, but stern face with ice blue eyes. The General turns his head a fraction toward the slave who opened the door of the carriage.

"You made me wait," his baritone voice is barely a whisper.

Before the bent slave can run, his body is swallowed by hard soil that has sprung up from beneath his feet. In a span of two breaths, his screams become muffled beneath the casing. My eyes widen as the General reaches up and caresses the head of the clay figure before running a sword through its middle. When Charos retracts his sword, blood trickles out from the wound.

I cup my mouth to keep from screaming. My body quakes, and I recall Jud's exploding head at the dock. Gods' Gifts are nothing but curses for others.

//Careful, you're beginning to attract the attention of the guard behind you.//

I heed her warning and force my hands back to my sides, urging my shoulders to relax and, through sheer will, I return my breathing to normal.

The General stares at the dripping blood on his blade in disgust, and another slave is prodded forward by a guard's spear. The woman stumbles in front of him and keeps her head lowered and eyes closed. Her lips move silently, praying for her life while General Charos wipes his blade clean on the shoulder of her uniform. "Leave," he tells her, as he sheathes his blade. She bows deeply and resumes her place in line at a run.

Charos then turns back to the carriage and holds out his palm before a pale, trembling hand comes from the doorway. The girl is near my age and wears long sleeves despite the heat. Her long brown hair is streaked with premature gray, and her eyes, the same color as Charos', are full of tears. Plainly, she is frail. He helps her down but then leaves her and walks toward the castle.

"Saray! Escort Astera to her tower," the General orders without looking at her.

The girl begins to cry harder when Saray takes Astera's hand, ushering her towards the castle.

Who is she? Saray has never mentioned her before.

General Charos reaches the castle steps and turns swiftly to address the entire crowd. "Disperse," he says. The words ring like a hammer on an anvil even though his voice never raises in volume.

When Charos disappears behind the castle doors, I gasp for air as my heart batters against my ribcage. Blood still pours from the wound of the dead slave, he's been turned into a grotesque fountain. I realize I could die here. The General could take my life at any moment on a whim. There's no guarantee I'll survive four more months. I have to start searching for Steilos' citrine. I have to.

I thought my heart was closed to the gods, but as I watch the man's blood pool at his clay feet, I pray to Metis, begging for luck and speed.

//Good. Let us begin.//

It's the middle of the night, and I lie awake in Saray's bunk, terror keeping me from sleep. After washing off today's horrors, she let me crawl in bed with her where I cried. The day was too much. She stroked my hair until my tears subsided, and I found sleep. I'm small enough for both of us to fit on the thin mattress, and having a female body next to me reminds me of the comfort Mana used to give when I was sad or scared. I observe Saray's resting figure; her hair is unbound, the long tresses lay in waves against the worn sheets. She removed her eye patch, the eyelid droops over the empty socket in her sleep. It's dark in the cavern, but even in the light I've come to find the flawed face beautiful.

Rest eludes me. I'm still on edge from the slave's brutal death. A group of guards used his body as a practice dummy. They took turns hacking away at him with their swords until there were only chunks of the man left. I can still hear it in my head. *Thack. Thack. Thack.* A strangled sob comes from my throat. I cover my head with my hands and press my back more deeply into the mattress. I need to stop thinking about it.

Saray rolls the other way and moans, unsettled. I stare at her back and try to calm my breathing so I don't wake her with my struggles. When her body moves again with the rise and fall of peaceful sleep, I wonder how she's been able to endure Notos for all these years and still harbor kindness for others. I know I wouldn't be capable of the same if our roles were reversed.

My hands fist the threadbare sheet in anger at my own cowardice. Two months have come and gone, I should've been searching this entire time. I need to find Steilos' stone and get us out of here before it's too late.

Us.

I'm surprised by the word in my head. Despite barely knowing Saray, at some point I allowed a kernel of love for her inside my heart. Styx, it will make escape that much harder. Lifting my arm close to my face, I examine the ugly delta brand. A constant reminder of what I've become, I rally against it. Slave, but not for long.

I listen carefully to make sure everyone is asleep. But I'm uncertain because the water bucket that catches the annoying drip seems to echo throughout the cavern. There are thirty women down here; no telling how many lay awake thinking about how much they hate their lives, just as I do. Finding the citrine requires stealth.

//Did you forget about us? We're free to explore as we wish.//

I'm immediately seized by anger. //Why don't you tell me these things sooner instead of letting me struggle fruitlessly?//

//You didn't have the will to look for it before now. We told you, we can't make you do things you don't want to. As you search, you'll know when it's safe and when it isn't.//

I ponder the annoyance of this *Gift* for a moment and wonder again why Metis couldn't have blessed me with something more practical. For instance, something powerful like the General's or even Ker's Gift so I can smite whomever I wish.

//We are more powerful than you can imagine. Like any other Gift, practice is necessary.//

//Sure, I'll remember to find time to practice in between scrubbing shit from buckets.//

Silence is her response.

Fuming, I swing my legs over the mattress, careful to not wake Saray or anyone nearby. I try to calm my nervousness. My sacred-self is right, I've been so angry and scared that I haven't even attempted to use what the Goddess blessed me with. I need to at least try. I close my eyes and search—for what, I'm not entirely sure. After minutes of this, nothing happens, and I become aggravated again.

//You have to ground yourself.//

//I still don't know what you mean when you say that.// I can hear her sigh.

//Imagine merging yourself to the ground with your feet, sensing the life around, and pulling it to you with an intention in mind. Every person is unique and has their own specific essence. Look for that.//

//Sounds complicated.//

//It isn't. Your negative beliefs are what complicate things.//

I breathe out, it's worth a try. I attempt to do as she asks and imagine myself connecting to the ground, the soil below the cavern pushing up to meet my feet. Instantly, it's like a flame flickers into existence, and I can sense an iridescent version of Saray who sleeps behind me. She reminds me of warmth, like the kitchen hearth on a cold morning. I look over my shoulder at her, and I'm surprised to see a faint pulsing aura that surrounds Saray's body, the color is akin to a golden sunset.

//That's her life force you're seeing, you'll learn in time that a person's colors reveal a lot about them.//

//Aren't I invading her privacy by looking?//

//Do you think you'll be saying that when 'invading someone's privacy' saves your life? Now do it again but reach more deeply and set an intention of what you'd like to know.//

I'm hesitant at first but expand what I imagine as an invisible dome over the entire cavern and soon, I sense all the women around me. Their forms are in colors of various shades, but the onslaught of information is too much for me. Some of the women are warm like Saray, others cold and close to death. A few possess a hot anger that threatens to scourge me, while others are filled with sorrows so deep their emotions are ready to capsize everything I am. I feel all their pain as if it's mine and become instantly nauseated. I drop the dome in a hurry and gasp into the crook of my arm. //That was terrible!//

//*You didn't set an intention as we instructed. Your Gift is sensitive, more so because it doesn't have a physical form. Metis is the Goddess of Wisdom and you've been touched by her. Think on that. Knowledge is powerful but having it all at once can destroy you. Intent will be your key to mastery. Try again but set your intention this time.*//

My body shakes with effort, the complexities of the other women's emotions rolling off me still. When I'm ready, I close my eyes and cast my net once more. Is it safe to leave? A tightness pulls at my belly and the familiar fluttering sensation returns as the cavern comes into view within my mind's eye. I sense the other women, but not for everything they are. *Safe*, the response rings throughout my being like an instinct, the suddenness of it shocking.

//I did it!// Elated, I attempt to go even farther, reaching outside the women's quarters, but soon, I hit a boundary. //My Gift's range must be limited.//

My sacred-self laughs, *//You're just beginning. Have patience with yourself. Now go, while you still have the cover of night.//*

//Right!// I shove my feet into my sandals and back away from Saray. A benefit of going to sleep in her bunk is that it's the closest to the exit. I slip beneath the archway without a sound and, much later, after the dreaded climb out of the cavern, I'm at the top of the steps and out of breath. Staring at the cluttered storage space around me, I think of the massiveness of Castle Notos and all its rooms. Finding the citrine is going to take time.

Under the guise of night and weighted silence, every passageway and shadowed crook is menacing. I tiptoe down corridors and up staircases. Before rounding a corner, I ground myself and check for nearby guards. When it's clear, I move on. If a passage is guarded, I experience a tightness through my body, as if my muscles are bracing against a threat. My throat constricts and there's a heaviness to my thoracic cavity—it's unpleasant to say the least, but I backtrack into a different hallway when it occurs. After several successful attempts at evading the General's lookouts, my confidence grows and I imagine myself one with the night, moving unseen.

I've managed to search some unoccupied rooms, and I'm on my third when the euphoria starts to fade. After sensing for guards and my net coming up empty, I search the area from top to bottom, riffling through the contents of the chamber. The castle is too large, I'm not covering enough ground considering the amount of time I have.

With an annoyed sigh, I collapse into a chair near an ancient desk and stare at the shelves of books around me. I'm in a study of sorts that is illuminated by the Twin Moons through a large west-facing window. If only the books could speak. I feel weariness deep down within me and rest my head against my arm on the wood desk. All this exploring is hard after laboring most of the day. Lightly drumming my fingers, I begin to wonder if it's possible to sense a lifeless object such as the citrine. My hand brushes against a figurine of a man riding a horse. Well, what would the harm be?

I reach out with my Gift, testing once more. The figurine itself doesn't pulse with life, but there's a faint glow on its edge, like a residue. My eyes squint, studying the figure, when I realize the residual energy is my own and comes exactly from where I just grazed the marble. Interesting. Can I identify who last touched an object? I close my eyes for a moment and sink further into the chair; the skill has the potential to be useful but won't help me locate the stone.

As I stare out the window, I realize there are only a few hours left before I'm supposed to be up for the day. Fuck. I better stop searching for now. With a defeated spirit, I exit the study, which opens to the large ballroom I entered through before. The ceiling is high, and curtained archways surround the dance floor. I'm careful to step lightly so my footfalls don't echo as I head back the way I came. I'm about to head down a flight of stairs when I hear singing—the voice feminine and haunting. My curiosity piqued, I concentrate on it and try to follow the sound. It leads me back across the ballroom and to one of the archways.

Behind the curtain, there's a spiral staircase leading up. The voice continues to sing and I begin my ascent.

Sometimes I feel the world

crashing down over me,

I remember the good times,

the way it all used to be.

And it's like I'm in a nightmare

unable to wake up,

I run and run and run and run,

But all I feel is—

The singer stops by the time I reach the top of the stairs. Who else would be up at this dark hour? I walk toward the end of the long hallway to a single wooden door. Light shines from underneath, and I'm careful to be quiet as I lean against the wall of the passageway. There's a scratching of quill to paper beyond the door and then a "No, that isn't right," before the sound of crumpling parchment.

"—And now I'm screaming,

screaming out loud,

can anybody hear me?

The girl sings before she writes and then crumples up the parchment again. She does this over and over until there's a loud clatter, as if an object has been thrown. Then there's a scrape of a chair against the stone floor. I hear the footfalls of her steady pacing, and the girl begins to cry while muttering to herself—the sound makes my heart ache. Grounding myself, I reach out with my Gift. Who are you? My stomach flutters when I join with her energy, a color resembling a twilight sky, lavender, pink, and hues of blue. I discern it's Astera. Through our connection, her pain becomes my own, a loneliness so vast and overwhelming that it makes me want to carve out my insides and die where I stand. No, no, no. I don't want to feel this! I quickly pull back from her, and realize that I'm openly crying.

"Who's there?" Astera calls from the other side.

Spooked from the encounter, I take a few steps backwards before I turn at a dead run.

"Who's there!" She shrieks and pounds her fists against the door, the sound chasing me down the stairs. Astera must be locked inside, otherwise I'd imagine she'd come after me.

When I arrive at the women's quarters, I'm moving at a crawl and stumble into my bed, almost waking the person in the bottom bunk next to mine. I practiced too much and ended up draining myself. I wrap the thin blanket around my shoulders and tuck my knees to my chest. Astera's forlorn song is trapped in my head, the melody plays as my body relaxes and drifts to sleep.

My nightmare greets me in my dreams. It begins as it always does with me running in the woods. Armon is the one chasing me this time. I know what's coming when he catches up. I try to force myself awake, but then my dream fades away, turning to vapors. I'm in the colorful place again, but this time when the black smoke appears, I stride toward it and let it envelope me in a warm caress.

My friend smiles from within the haze, "Hello again."

CHAPTER XXVII

6th Week of Fall

Nikko

As punishment for my scrap at Cerberus' Maw, my father ordered me to personally help with repairs. I took the reprimand without complaint, not bothering to mention that the type of punishment is exactly what I excel at and what he and the Queen consider childish and beneath me. The irony has been a nice lift to my spirits as I've spent the past weeks engrossed in the depths of woodworking, enjoying the feel of a hammer and nail. I've built new chairs for the tavern and stained the old tables for good measure. It's a welcome change of pace going from designing plans to actual construction. The King wanted me to learn a lesson in responsibility but, unbeknownst to him, I've simply been having a merry time.

I moan with pleasure behind the bar and grab a fist full of Darja's hair—my cock spills itself inside her mouth. When I'm finished, she looks up at me and licks her lips, smiling.

Woodworking isn't the only activity I've been enjoying at the tavern.

I help the barmaid up and kiss her mouth, pushing her backward until her ass rests against one of the tables I recently mended. She laughs when I grab her by the waist and hoist her on top of the wood while my lips trail kisses down her throat. With quick fingers, Darja removes the brooch at her shoulder, and the fabric of her peplos falls away, revealing her breasts to me. I kiss those too.

She giggles. "I must say, now I'm not so upset that my bar was nearly destroyed."

I nip her breast with my teeth. "Neither am I."

She sighs when I disappear under the folds of her peplos and bring my mouth to her wet bud, sucking in and claiming her desire with my tongue. My head is firmly pressed between Darja's shapely thighs as she finishes against me, her voice giving way to a breathy moan. My cock stiffens again at the sound of her pleasure, and she complies when I bend her over the table and fuck her with slow, deep, strokes. I reach past her hip, towards her center, until my fingers find her swollen sweet spot. I begin to make circles there and she writhes against me as I play with her. When Darja's close to coming undone, I pound into her hard and fast, until her ass bucks with the intensity of another climax that I soon follow.

We're both panting hard, and I wince when I withdraw from her, my tip still sensitive. She fixes her peplos and turns toward me, face flushed. "You should be off soon. I need to open shop."

My smile widens as I adjust my chiton. A specific trait I admire in Darja is that she's all business—it's what keeps me coming back again and again. Well, that, and she lets me.

"Same time tomorrow?" I ask and give her a parting kiss before tucking a strand of hair behind her ear.

"Aye," her response is slightly breathy.

I'm caught by her sultry gaze but strangely feel dissatisfied, wishing instead that her eyes were the color of dark shadows.

Gareth is in a crouched position and ignores me as I stand near his right shoulder. What he's doing, is a most spectacular sight to behold. Even trumping the magnificent breasts of the dancer who let my curious, virgin fingers examine the great swells of her bosom when I was but thirteen. I was forever ruined after the encounter, as she is the one and only who inspired the collection of curious leatherbound books that I now read religiously in my chambers. Till the day I die, the woman will be immortalized as a goddess in my mind.

I wonder, where is she now? I shake my head, it doesn't matter. This here is astonishing.

The wounded soldier on the cot is barely conscious, though he moans and his eyelashes flutter. In truth he should be dead by now, if not from blood loss, then surely from infection or fever. His right arm is bent at an unnatural angle, as if the bone snapped in two, but gods, it's the left leg that has me squeamish. Below the knee, the man's tibia peeks through swollen, festered skin that leaks puss and other unidentifiable discharge.

Nausea rolls up my throat, and I swallow hard, willing it to cease. It's grotesque but I simply cannot look away as Gareth's deft hands touch the wound. His face is pinched in concentration, and the soldier's inflamed wound slowly begins to decrease in size until it's near back to normal.

Gareth studies the bone still peeking from the open wound. "I'll need to set it first," he mutters to himself and stands up. I back away to give him space. Gareth wears a smock and he fishes a stick of sorts, from its pocket. He then pats his patient's cheek. "Bite down on this so you don't bite your tongue off. It's going to hurt." The soldier, now more alert, does as he's asked and nods.

"Nikko, don't just stand there, hold him down."

I straighten in surprise and hurry to the head of the cot and press my hands against the injured man's shoulders. "Like this?"

Gareth shakes his head no. "At his thighs, so he doesn't knee me in the face."

I readjust until I'm in a better position.

He addresses the soldier, "On the count of three, I'm going to push your bone back in. Are you ready?"

His eyes go wide, and he gives a groaned "no" in the common tongue.

"Okay now, one…two…"

Gareth doesn't get to three before I hear the crunch of moving bone, and the soldier bucks under my grip until he passes out. My friend goes to work quickly, using his Gift, and I watch fascinated as the tibia is mended before the skin seems to repair itself under his hands.

"How do you do that?" I ask in wonder.

Gareth shrugs as he moves on to the soldier's bent arm. "It's hard to describe, but it's like . . . I ask his body to listen to me, and then it moves back together how I want it to."

"I'm lost, but I was never a good student."

He grins at that and sets the arm.

I wince at the sound it makes.

He gestures to the comatose soldier. "From the echoes I get from this one, he had a pretty big fall. He was running from something . . . or someone. He was terrified."

"You mean to say you feel all that when you use your Gift?"

"Not entirely. I call it an echo, because it's like a memory I guess, though faint." His face is grim as he stares at all the wounded. He sighs like a time-worn man instead of a boy of just sixteen. There are over a hundred cots in the makeshift infirmary that's held together by cracked doric columns. Other physicians flit about the space overwhelmed—they don't possess Gareth's skill. "I have a lot of work to do," he says.

I feel for him and the wounded. A fraction of our soldiers who were sent to make good on our treaty with Avanta, began to arrive home by ship just a few days ago. We sent thousands to Avanta's aid and barely half returned. It was reported that many were swallowed by the earth itself. The injured filled up our sanatorium quickly but more kept coming and had to be taken to this infirmary in the ancient sector. Others are recuperating in the homes of dutiful civilians.

I grit my teeth. This is all Heracles' doing and that General of his. I turn to Gareth. "Don't overexert yourself. I may not be Gifted, but I'm aware of the Decay that comes with the gods' ichor. Don't let it get to that point." He starts to speak but I continue, "We're friends, but I want to officially tell you, as the Prince, that Ellanios gives you our humble thanks for aiding our wounded. We're in your debt."

He smiles self-consciously. "No thanks needed. This is my home now."

I clasp him on the shoulder, grinning in return. "That it is, brother."

A shadow crosses his face. "I feel guilty you're the only one who got in trouble for the night at the tavern. It's not as if you destroyed it yourself. And you were only there because of me. I heard your father's rantings from the hall. He's terrifying when he's angry."

Ha! This kid. Like the King would punish one of his greatest assets amidst a war. "It's of no consequence, so don't worry yourself.

And I have to say, the tavern owner is quite—"A soldier nearby wails in pain and grabs Gareth's attention. "Go do your—" but my friend has already left and is bending over the next ailing soldier.

Right . . . he has truly important duties. Unlike myself. I feel massively inadequate standing between rows of my people who I can do nothing for. Meanwhile, there are others sacrificing all. It must be hard for Gareth to take in all those echoes, to consume their pain. And yet, as I watch him, he speaks gently to his patient while healing the stab wound in the man's belly, as if there's nothing amiss.

And Jada . . . gods, Jada! I don't know how she does it. Remaining calm and still her cheery self in the face of preparing for a betrothed who will undoubtedly make her miserable.

Even though Gareth and Jada are both incredibly busy, I still try to insert myself into their lives just to rid myself of my own loneliness, not because I'm actually needed. I miss the brothers of my cradle terribly. Their absence leaves a gaping hole in my life that I've tried to fill with Gareth's and Jada's attentions. And now they have their hands full, with no time to spare for an incompetent prince like myself. I'm alone.

I sigh, dejected, and wish I could be of more use.

Gareth moves on to his next patient, and this one also has a broken bone to reset before he can use his Gift. Observing all the groaning soldiers in need of medical assistance and the other physicians who appear overwhelmed, I can't help but think their methods are inefficient. There is something I can do, although it's not much.

Eyes searching, I locate the lead physician, an older man with a clean-shaven face. The red sash he wears designates him the most experienced.

"Excuse me, sir, may I have a word?" I ask.

The physician turns to me with a scowl. He was stitching a soldier's arm and is likely ready to chastise me for interrupting. But then he recognizes me and stands immediately.

"Of course, my Prince," he says, though his voice is a touch exhausted.

"The King put Gareth in the infirmary to study—is that correct?"

He glances over at my friend who is now aiding another patient. "Yes, but there's nothing I can teach him nor the others. Whoever oversaw his training knew what they were doing. He's been an outstanding addition with that Gift of his, and we need all the help we can muster."

"Were you able to observe how his Gift works?"

The lead physician nods his head. "Yes. Though only a time or two." He gestures to the soldiers around him. "My hands and eyes have been kept too busy to further entertain my curiosity."

"Might I make a suggestion?"

He raises a brow, clearly skeptical, as if to say: What would you know about healing the wounds of men? But he plasters a false smile on his face instead. "You are the Prince of Ellanios and will be my king one day. You may do as you like."

"Well then, I think you should delegate a few of your staff to giving sedatives and setting the broken bones of your patients. Gareth must pause each time to make sure a bone is in the correct place before he can use his ichor. It's inefficient and slows him down. If the bone is already set by the time he sees the patient, he'll have more time to spend on others."

Plainly, the physician is surprised. "That is a great observation. My upmost apologies for not thinking of it myself. I'll task two of my team with setting bones immediately."

I try to hide the relief from my face. He doesn't need to know I was unsure of myself.

I clear my throat, "Good then. Please see to it, and make sure Gareth is getting adequate rest. We don't need the Return to begin, and Decay slow him down."

The physician bows. "Yes, my Prince."

"Also, show me where the supplies are and put me to work. I may not be a healer, but I can make bandages."

His eyes widen. "Certainly, and it will boost the soldiers' morale to see their prince among them. Here, come this way."

The next few hours go by swiftly as I prepare bandages and speak with the wounded. When I finish for the day, their stories weigh on me, but my heart is lighter as I walk through the ancient sector. It feels good to finally do something for my people. To be of service. By the time I near the palace, my head is full of my own praising, and I barely have time to jump out of the way when a horse comes barreling past the large gates. Instinctively, I fall with a roll, but quickly regain my footing and dust myself off.

The rider pulls on the reins of his steed and the beast neighs with disagreement. The man calls out, not looking at me, "Watch where you're walkin' you worthless slag! I'm on important business for the King!"

I grit my teeth. "Now, why would *my father's* messenger try to trample the Prince of Ellanios to death and then proceed to call me a worthless slag?"

The rider quickly turns, his mouth in a giant "O" that takes up his face. He dismounts quickly and goes to his hands and knees. "My Prince! I did not see you! I swear it. Please forgive my blind stupidity."

I roll my eyes with attitude befitting my station. "You may rise. Be more careful in the future. You could've killed me, if not someone else."

He picks himself up, eyes downcast. "Yes, Your Highness. I'm deeply sorry. I have this letter, you see. And King Zephyr says I must get it to Vorna as quickly as possible. I'm not to stop for anything but to change horses. I'll be sleepin' in my saddle until the deed is done."

"Vorna? The country of the so-called dragon people? What could he possibly have to say to them other than to leave our borders and go back to their snow-filled mountains?"

The messenger rubs his face, clearly frustrated. "Sir, but an hour ago I was sworn not to speak a word of this to anyone, and I've already said too much and can say no more, lest the King have me in chains."

Interesting.

"In the future, keep that tongue of yours in your mouth. I'll not tell the King of your slip, as you've served him well for years, but don't have me mistake my faith in you nor earn my ire further."

As the messenger gallops away, I try to comprehend why my father would send a letter to an enemy Ellanios has been at odds with for centuries.

Gods & Beasts of Miracle

Drakaina & the Three Kings

She-dragon, witch, or minx? The half reptile, half-woman set her sights on Heracles and seduced him. With his seed, Drakaina bore three sons, Agathyrsos, Gelonos, and Skythes, each without wings for flight. A disappointment they turned out to be, simple men, fighting amongst one another. Drakaina cast them from the sky, each roaming the desolate land of Vorna, taking wives and crowning themselves jealous kings. Between the three, many children were had, though sons were cherished most of all.

Gelonos was the first to sire a dragon-daughter, dissatisfied by her sex until he saw the scales that kissed her face and decorated her arms. The girl, after her first bleed, took to the sky and became her father's most prized possession. Agathyrsos and Skythes coveted such a child and continued to sire children until they had dragon-daughters of their own. Even still, it was not enough. Blinded by their greed, the brothers and their growing tribes stole the dragon-daughters from one another before their wings could grow, dividing their people and the land further until they considered themselves brothers no more.

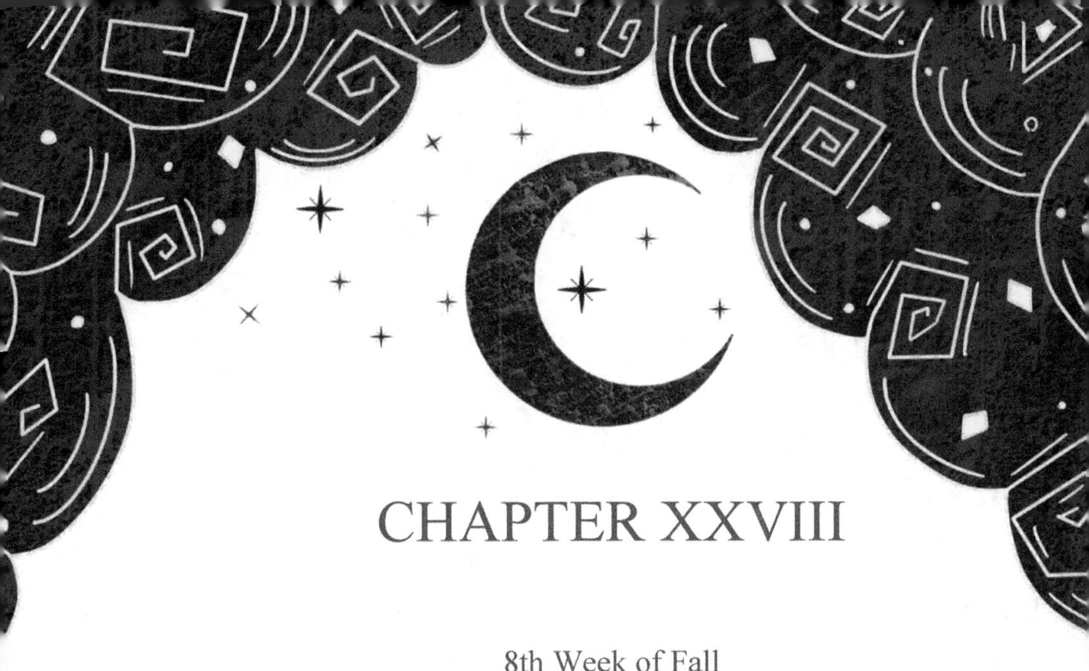

CHAPTER XXVIII

8th Week of Fall

Eimear

Since the General's arrival at Castle Notos, I've learned that he is a quiet man. He secludes himself in his chambers at the east end of the castle for the most part. It's better that way: for when he emerges, nightmares come to life.

I drape fresh wash on the line in front of me. The uniform I'm hanging is dripping wet. Big droplets land on the indigo grass below. The bronze bull on the bluff fills my gaze, and I almost throw up my rations from this morning. It's hard for me to believe that just two days ago a man was tortured to death in front of me. I was working alongside Saray, taking down the dried laundry, when Faas and another guard dragged a slave toward the bluff. The man was bound at his wrists and ankles, screaming so loud that I thought his lungs would burst.

"Gods no . . . not another one," Saray whispered.

I looked in her direction. "I'm afraid to ask."

"Don't. You'll see soon enough," she said with a grim face.

I stared at Saray expectantly, but she turned back toward the line, deciding to pay close attention to the tunic she was hanging. Faas and the other guard paid us no mind as they struggled to lift their squirming captive off the ground and carry him down the craggy path leading to the bluff. Out of breath, they dropped the man to the ground, where he landed with a hard thud and moaned before curling into himself. But when he opened a swollen eye and caught sight of the bull, he began to scream again.

Faas kicked him in the jaw three times. "Shut your trap! You knew the punishment for tryin' to run, so take it like a man."

I glanced at Saray for clarification, but she refused to stray from her duties. I turned back to watch the scene below and nearly leaped from my skin when the General himself walked past, merely a few feet away from me. One peek at his cold face, and I was quickly pretending to rummage through the basket at my feet.

After minutes of this, Saray sighed, "You can rise, he should be at the bottom of the path by now."

"Thanks."

Faas and the guard beside him stood at attention as the General took a seat on the carved stone bench in front of the bull. "Begin," he said. The word powerful and frightening all at the same time.

The slave looked between the three of them, "No, no, no, no, no, no!!!!" he begged as Faas opened the latch at the belly of the bull. The two guards then hoisted him up and proceeded to shove him inside before closing the latch once more. Cries for mercy resounded from the bull's open mouth.

With horror, I finally understood when Faas started a fire under the bull's stomach. The tunic I was holding dropped to my feet. "They're going to cook him," I said to no one.

Just like today, the Sister Sun was overly bright in the sky. Birds flew chirping overhead while small waves crashed against the beach below. I will never forget the man's cries of anguish as he was slowly roasted alive. The screams intertwined with the birdsong and waves, creating a cacophony in my ears. Meanwhile, General Charos sat at his stone seat with his legs crossed, and hands folded in his lap as if he were enjoying the sound of minstrels. Saray and I were forced to endure the man's shrieks as we worked. It took a long time for him to die.

Steilos did warn me that the General likes to inflict pain. My hands tremble at the memory and I barely manage to hang the garment on the line in front of me. Eyes closed, trying to calm myself, I will my body to behave. When I open them again, the Gods' Window looms in my vision just as it does over everything else. Always watching, but never protecting those who need it most—like the man in the bull, or me and my mother.

//Can the gods be killed?//

//*That's a dangerous thought you have there.*//

//But can they?//

She's silent for a while, but then finally says, //*Anyone with a physical state of being, has the ability to die.*//

I stare at the garment in front of me, puzzled. //So, that's a yes?//

She doesn't answer me.

Why did I do this to myself? The suds from the scrubbing brush bubble up around my cracked hands, making them sting. Where would I be if I didn't come here? Fueled by anger, I put weight into my elbow and scrub the stone floor with more vigor than necessary. Maybe a nice family would've taken me in. Maybe I'd have a full belly instead of the gnawing hunger. Maybe I wouldn't be constantly worried about being fed to that damned bronze bull or the threat of being beaten on a daily basis? It's three more months until this is all just an awful memory. I'm halfway through my agreement with Steilos, but will I survive the remaining time?

I blink wearily, it feels as if there are grains of sand under each eyelid. The constant routine of work and searching nightly for the citrine is taking its toll. The stone has to be either in the General's quarters or on his person—not that I've seen it. But if I'm right, it makes my nightly escapades futile. I don't have the courage to search his quarters, yet. If caught, the General would concoct some creative way of killing me slowly. I'm sure being cooked alive in the bull isn't the worst way to die, but my mind simply can't imagine another, and I don't want to tempt fate.

My consolation, or so I tell myself, is that my nightmares have completely stopped. Although, I've noticed that I'm not dreaming at all now, so there's no respite for me, waking and working has become my life. I plunge the brush back into the water with a sigh and continue scrubbing. This is all for Zadok. I shouldn't forget that. The stone will lead me back to him.

//Don't give up on yourself just yet.//

Scrubbing harder, I groan. *//I'll try not to.//*

Taking a much needed respite, I stand and arch my spine, stretching my aching back. I then survey the ballroom floor. I'm nearly finished with this area at least. Suddenly, heavy rapid footfalls come from the staircase behind me, and I turn, ready for the worst. But it's just Saray out of breath. She carries a silver tray of food and promptly shoves the platter into my empty hands.

"Take this to Astera. She's through that archway there, go up the stairs and then down the hall, you can't miss it," she says gasping.

"Is everything all right?" I ask, worried.

Saray pats her hands around her apron, searching. "Yes, yes, I just don't have time to feed her right now. I have to finish the General's personal wash before sundown today." She pulls a key from her apron and places it on the tray. "Give this back to me tonight, and don't speak to her. It's not allowed. General's orders."

I've been meaning to ask Saray about the girl but haven't had the opportunity before now. "Is there a reason she's confined? Is she dangerous?"

"No idea. When you're tasked with something around here, you learn not to ask questions." She looks at me pointedly with her one eye. "I have to be off now before it's me he decides to skin. She doesn't bite, so don't worry." She leaves me then. Confused, I turn towards the curtained archway, and think of the girl beyond.

I haven't laid eyes on her since the day she stepped out of the carriage. No one speaks of her; it's as if she doesn't exist at Castle Notos. I can't fathom what it must be like, having General Charos as a father. I'd hate to be on the receiving end of his love. Sometimes, when I pass by her room, she's silent. Other nights she fills the empty passageway with her haunted singing or wailing. We've never spoken, but I sense her loneliness through the barricade of the door.

I'm nervous as I stand outside Astera's room. What will she be like? Balancing the tray, I twist the key in the lock and rap my knuckles against the door, but there's no answer. "I'm coming in," I say so she won't be surprised.

When I enter, I see hundreds of pieces of paper fixed to the walls. There's writing on the parchment, some are entirely full but others feature just one word, "*Silence*" being one of them. Though what stands out the most are the various charcoal drawings depicting demons of the Under. Natural light seeps through a large window, but the bars against the glass cast odd shadows about the space. Opposite the window, a desk is piled high with loose sheets of parchment and quills; a large bookcase is beside it, stuffed with worn books. In the corner, there's a large four-poster bed with ripped pink curtains.

"Hello?" I call out, uncertain, and don't receive a response. I set the tray of food down on the desk, careful not to set it on the paper. Saray said that speaking to her isn't permitted, but there were no guards on my way here, and I don't sense any now. I'm about to take a gamble with my life. I'm not sure why I want to talk to her so badly. There's a nagging feeling that won't go away, prodding me toward her; the same reason I keep coming to her door at night.

"I know you hear me, and I know that you cry on the nights you aren't singing," I blurt out, heart racing. A pale hand emerges from the curtains and moves the cloth aside. Astera watches me from the bed, her appearance is disheveled. She wears a wrinkled gown covered in tiny pearls that remind me of stars. Her ice blue eyes are alert and wary.

"Who are you?" she asks with a voice as haunted as the songs she sings. The sound is eerie, and gazing into her dead eyes makes me want to run for the door. I swallow, thinking about Angus in the kitchen and the soup he gave me. How he chooses to be good, to make his days better. I want to find that light too. My next words are chosen carefully. "A friend if you like."

Emotion breaks across Astera's face. "Truly?"

I barely hear her but nod my head.

Anger flashes in the girl's eyes, and her small frame moves with surprising speed as she leaps from the bed to stand in front of me. She grabs a fist full of my hair and pulls me close until we're nose to nose. "Don't lie to me. I don't like liars."

She reminds me of a wild animal backed into a corner. My hand slowly moves to hers, covering it. When I speak to her, I mimic the soothing tone my mother used when I was scared. "I promise to find a way to help you, and to be your friend."

We're both silent for a few breaths, her face unreadable, before she releases me and returns to her bed. She crawls back into the sheets and forms a cocoon around herself, turning away from me. I'm disappointed. She must not want company after all. My hand is on the door when her muffled voice calls, "Don't get my hopes up."

A skeleton of a plan forms in my mind as I twist the key in the lock.

CHAPTER XXIX

8th Week of Fall

Nikko

"Make it tighter," I hear the Queen say as I enter Jada's chambers. A tall, triptych mirror made of gold has been brought to her room. She stands before it on a circular platform wearing the strangest garments I've ever seen. Spying a decanter of wine, honey cakes, and fresh fruits from Avanta that are arranged in the sitting area, I decide to make myself at home on a klinē amongst its woven blankets and feather pillows.

Two ladies pull on the ribbons of the contraption my sister wears, and her already small waist becomes nonexistent while the pale skirt reaching her calves flares wider. Jada presses a hand to her abdomen, which is encased in some sort of boning. "If it's laced any tighter, I think I may die."

I pop a grape in my mouth and take a swig of wine, closing my eyes at the explosion of flavor. Simply exquisite. I can't say I'm thrilled that Ellanios is allying with Heracles, but the shit I've been drinking these last few months has nearly destroyed my fine palate. I hurried to Jada's quarters immediately upon hearing the King had the first of the shipment brought to her room. The rest he's saving for tonight's festivities.

My mother circles my sister and speaks to her like a military commander would a soldier. "You will wear the customary gown of my motherland. I want that bastard to know we do not fear him, and that he may have taken much from Anyalay, but he cannot destroy our traditions. We'll show him that we're unbreakable."

Jada sighs. "Honestly, mother, I don't think a gaudy dress is going to make such a statement. I would be much more comfortable in an Ellanion—" She gasps when the two ladies pull on the ribbons for a second time. Her brows pinch in anger. "For Styx sake! I'll be unable to move with this damned thing on! I thought your people were warriors, how could they possibly—"

"The women of my time could move like the wind itself under any circumstance. I see I've been too lenient in your training." The Queen eyes the vice grip apparatus. "Maybe I should have another made and you can wear it while you go through your drills."

My twin guffaws. "You can't be serious—"

I interrupt and point, "That's a *wedding gown*?"

They both turn in my direction, surprised to see me. Intent on their bickering, the women of my family didn't notice my arrival.

Jada is first to comment. "What are you doing here?"

Then my mother. "No, you imbecile, these are the undergarments."

"It's called a corset," Jada says.

I nearly spit up the wine I just sipped. In all my dalliances I've never come across such a fortress to break through. "Ladies *wear that thing*? How in the Under does it come off?" I may need to know for future purposes.

"That's my wine, you rogue! Put it down." My sister raises a fist and teeters on her pedestal, almost falling. One of the attendants reaches up to balance her. Jada glares at me. "Just you wait, I'll scar your other ear when I get the chance."

"Really, Nikko, walking in during your sister's fitting is unbecoming." The Queen gives me a disapproving stare.

"I'll have you know the door was wide open!" I gesture dismissively toward Jada. "She's wearing more clothes than women do out and about during the winter months. If there are any more layers, she's going to melt during the ceremony . . ." I become somber when I remember the event will be in a month's time. Erebos returned a few days ago with news of Heracles' chosen wedding day. The usurper is to arrive the morning of. It's really happening.

My twin notices the shift in me and squares her shoulders, adopting a formal appearance. "It will be all right. You shouldn't worry," she says gently. We share a look that is made of a thousand unspoken words.

The Queen breaks the spell. "I heard that King Narcyz and his daughter will not be in attendance for tonight's symposium. Poor girl, it seems her father has fallen ill. Pretty soon it will be just Princess Andromyda to oversee Apotmos' prosperity. Granted, your father will ensure those reptiles of Vorna will not bother her doorstep. Nikko, for the time being, write to Andromyda. Let her know of your affections and offer your sincerest condolences for her situation."

The little witch is probably responsible for her father's imminent demise. Not that I'll inform the Queen that the girl is an adept in poisons.

Jada stares pointedly at our mother, her eyes lit with fire. "Why in the worlds would he do such a thing? He's not courting her."

I involuntarily cross my legs, thinking of Princess Andromyda's threat to remove my most prized possessions should I attempt anything of the sort. When she's of age, no one will be safe in her bed.

The Queen shrugs. "Because he should be. It would benefit Ellanios for Nikko to marry the princess. The alliance would expand our borders and make our nation stronger."

Jada's face clouds with fury. "So, you're telling me that you would subjugate your son to the same treatment you and I must endure?"

"The situation is not as bad on men as it is women. You know that." My mother says this with her head partially tilted and eyes narrowed.

My other half, incredulous, shakes her head. "This is ridiculous; it's his right as first born to marry whom he wishes. It's one of the ways, Ellanios is seen as being progressive. Neither our country, nor others, will ever evolve if we keep repeating the same old patterns of tradition." She whirls on me. "And you! Do we keep secrets from one another now? We are the closest of blood any could ever be, and you've not said a word about courting her."

I glance hesitantly between my mother and sister while holding up both hands. "Let us be calm for a moment." I then address the Queen. "For your knowledge, I've been in correspondence with Princess Andromyda for months now. Since we first were reacquainted. We've exchanged dozens of letters already."

My mother nods her head. "I'm very proud of you for taking the initiative, it's most surprising."

Jada opens her mouth, but I speak first. "*However*, the two of us will never marry." I see that my mother is about to take back her compliment, but I press forward before she can. "It's not the princess's wish to ever marry, and I will fully support her in her endeavor. As such, we've become good friends."

"That's preposterous. She can't do that. Her advisors won't allow it," the Queen says with certainty.

This time, it's my turn to shrug. "When she's queen and the sole ruler of Apotmos, I think she'll be able to do whatever she wants, and Ellanios will continue to support her in our current relationship. Should her advisors attempt a coup, our soldiers will slaughter them, and she can stand over their bodies in triumph for all I care." The mental image of a tiny Andromyda crushing a tower of lifeless bodies under her feet comes uncannily to mind.

Jada claps slowly, a smug smile coming to her face. "Good for her. Very good indeed. And Nikko, you say you will not make a respectable king, but I think you already are. Don't you see what you've done here? You brokered peace with a coming regime with only a quill, ink, and thoughtful understanding."

Or because I fear Andromyda chopping my balls and cock off otherwise, though I don't say that and take my victory in stride.

"Come on now, you've got to at least try it," I say as I shove the goblet of wine into Gareth's hands. The ballroom is alive again for father's symposium, and the nobles chatter excitedly, having been starved for palace entertainment these past few months.

I keep my back to the center of attention, the sculptor is—at Father's behest—creating a likeness of my sister and her newly betrothed. What an obsequious bastard my father is. Why even bother? Except for Erebos, none of Heracles' people have come to behold the embodiment of his embarrassing flattery.

"Do you remember what happened the last time I drank?" Gareth shoots me a look. "I woke up alone in a cell, face first in straw smelling of piss. The sourness was in my nostrils for days. *Days*! It was beyond terrible. I can't believe you left me there."

He tries to hand the goblet back to me, but I refuse. "I've already told you, something important came up, and I couldn't carry you back, so I let you sleep it off."

He scowls. "Then why was the cell locked? You could've left the door open."

But where would the fun be in that? "Hmmm . . . for your safety perhaps?"

"Safety from what?" Gareth's green eyes inspect the clear liquid in his goblet with disinterest. "And that stuff you had me drink at Cerberus' Maw was gods awful. I don't know how you could stomach it."

I wag my finger at him. "We all make do with what we must during hard times. I'll have no judgment from you. But this—" I raise my goblet to him, "this is the good stuff. From the fields of Avanta, the grape was raised near the Thyellodic." Bringing the glass to my nose, I inhale the aromas. "It's refreshing; you can smell the apple and hints of citrus and lemongrass."

"I don't like being pressured," Gareth says, although he takes small sips and then surprises me with a satisfied smile. "You're right. It *is* good."

I down my entire glass, not bothering to savor the wine. If I have to stomach political horseshit all night, I might as well be drunk.

Gareth glances around at all the guests and flashy décor. "I'm a bit nervous. I've never been to something so . . . elegant? What if I make a fool of myself?" He stumbles over his last words in Ellanion.

"It's dreadfully garish. No need to make niceties. My father has bad taste." I grab another goblet from a serving tray and notice that the nobles stare at the two of us intently. Actually, no . . . they're watching Gareth. I offer him a sly smile. "My friend, I must say, your Ellanion has improved considerably from when we first met."

"It helps working in the sanatorium. I converse with the wounded when I can, and they assist me when I don't know a word."

"Well, looks like you'll be practicing further because the masses eagerly await your attentions. Your Gift is such a rarity. They must be dying to meet you."

I clasp Gareth by the shoulders and turn him toward the nobles.

"Wait. What?" he sputters before I feed him to the wolves.

"Good luck!" I call merrily and he gives me the moutza as a few nobles begin their approach. Gods it's fun to mess with him.

For the next hour or two, I flit between the guests and flirt with their daughters for sport, though none of them hold my attention longer than a minute at best. Where did the fun go? Darja and I have been steadily keeping our arrangement, but that's all it is, an understanding to give one another a scratch when either of us itch. However, that too is starting to feel hollow. When did I get so boring?

I find myself alone on a rug, nestled amongst the pillows and drapery of one of the hideaways created for guests should they wish a respite from the festivities. My head is abuzz with wine, and I watch as an Ellanion girl laughs at something Gareth has said and he grins hesitantly in return. At least he's moving on.

With a sigh, I lean back into the pillows and the room spins. I rub my forehead. Is Jada as drunk as me yet? I saw my sister partake in several glasses after she stopped modeling for the sculptor—it was when he carved a smile onto her likeness that isn't at all hers. We must be twins, with how we each turn to alcohol for our heartaches.

"Something troubling you, Prince?"

My heartbeat quickens at the sound of Erebos' voice.

He's Heracles' emissary for Styx sake. My people have died under his sword, Jada is to be married to a life of misery, and yet, my heart quickens for the enemy? I've never hated myself more than in this moment. It must be the wine.

He misunderstands my silence. "I'll take my leave then."

"Don't. You may stay." The words come too fast for me to take them back. Why am I doing this? I should hate him, I tell myself as he takes a seat beside me. He wears a loosely fitted crimson chiton that exposes the rich brown skin of his chest. That silver chain of his glints in the light, and his dark hair is free for once. It lays in waves until it curls at the ends where it meets his shoulders. His expression is detached as he surveys the room.

"It doesn't look like her at all does it? The sculpture. Your sister is fiercer than that." His voice is low and smooth.

I sit up to view the sculptor's progress and snort. "She looks so stupid." Her eyes are opened too wide, her mouth parted in delighted surprise as she stares in wonder at the still blank face of her soon-to-be husband. I fall back in a fit of laughter until there are tears in my eyes. I really am drunk.

I finally say through gasps, "And what of Heracles? Is he an unsightly ogre, or will my sister at least have someone pleasant to gaze at?"

He slides slowly down until we are shoulder to shoulder, almost touching. "I'm not at liberty to say. I've been sworn not to." His voice is quiet.

I frown at that and turn to face him. My heart skips. We're so close. Mere inches separate us. "What do you mean by that? You know all about us, but Jada and I know very little about the man she's soon to wed. You can't further elaborate to ease our anxieties?"

Erebos opens his mouth, his brow furrowing momentarily, and then he says: "I cannot. I've been sworn."

I should be angry, should protest. I should say that his master is not here, and he can say and do whatever he pleases when he's with me. But I cannot, because my head is buzzing, and I'm transfixed on the fullness of his lips and his proximity to my face. Is that the scent of sandalwood at his neck? I lose my mind, and touch the chain he wears, lifting the thin piece from his chest. He stiffens with surprise, and I pull him closer, tugging on the silver. My mouth hovers just above his lips. My eyes find his, and I await his permission to continue as I gaze into his black fathomless pools. The color is what I imagine the night would be like in the Holy City without the bridge looming over us. But I'd also like to see them turn crimson again. When his stare lowers to my waiting mouth, I take the plunge and lean forward just as he escapes backward.

"Stop," he says firmly.

I sit up hurriedly as waves of humiliation crash down upon me. I've never met such rejection before.

Erebos turns his face away. "You should not be so trusting of me, Prince. I don't deserve it, nor will I ever."

I'm about to demand an explanation when Gareth stumbles in and falls to his knees at my feet.

"Nikko . . . I don't feel so good. I think I had… too much wine." The boy's eyes are rimmed red, and his face has turned a sallow color.

I keep forgetting how young he is. The experienced veteran that I am, I know what's about to happen. Thus, I try to wave him away. "We have vases set up just for that! Go to one of those quickly."

Gareth drunkenly shakes his head and lowers to all fours.

I slide away from him. "Can you not heal yourself? Make yourself, I don't know, unsick?"

"It doesn't . . ." He then spills his guts all over the makeshift tent.

Erebos got himself out of the way as soon as Gareth mentioned being unwell. I, however, was not as smart, and my chiton is now soiled with flecks of vomit.

The emissary dips his head at me. "It's best I go so you can attend to your friend. Remember my warning, for your own good. Don't share your trust so easily."

I watch his retreating back with a mixture of longing, regret, and confusion when Gareth heaves once more.

CHAPTER XXX

9th Week of Fall

Eimear

Every step is laced with dread as I follow Saray's lead. So far, I've kept my head down and done as I'm told by the guards, dodging any threat of Confessional. When they insult me for being hideous, I remain impassive. When they order me to continue cleaning because they see a speck of dust on the floor, I eagerly oblige. I naïvely thought that I could avoid Confessional by following orders, but I was wrong. Everyone's attendance is required.

Saray takes me to a closed-in courtyard on the west side of the castle with the other slaves. We stand near a wall in a semicircle. The courtyard is completely tiled and barren of ornaments but for a large fountain at its center and a post that has been hammered into the ground in front of it. I don't have to be told what it's for, and grow queasy. One of the General's soldiers, a thick-muscled man, approaches the post with a whip coiled in his hand and parchment in the other; a satchel is tied to his waist. The water trickling from the fountain is deafening when paired with everyone's silence.

Two male slaves enter the courtyard carrying a wooden throne with a catlike creature carved into each arm. Their faces are flushed and sweaty as they set the large chair down within viewing distance of the whipping post—it must be heavy. Following them, General Charos holds a sapphire jeweled leash tethered to a large chimera that walks leisurely at his side.

The size of the beast is at least double the one Steilos and I encountered. It would look like an oversized panther if it weren't for the sharp horn protruding from its skull and the giant bat wings at its shoulder blades. Styx, it can fly. "You couldn't have mentioned the chimera at some point?" I whisper to Saray.

She shrugs her shoulders. "Sweetheart, if I told you everything that goes on here you would never have a day of peace again."

I survey the chimera's hungry, sapphire eyes and think of the bronze bull—Saray knows me well. My throat goes dry. "I think you're right about that."

General Charos takes a seat on his throne and, wings twitching, the beast stretches and yawns, revealing its pointed fangs. Once finished, she lays at the General's feet with a satisfied growl, careful to tuck her membraned wings. Along with being roasted alive, I can add being eaten by a chimera to my ever-growing list of ways I don't wish to die.

The General gives his soldier the briefest of nods before saying, "What do you have for me?" His words sound like a death sentence.

The soldier reviews the parchment in hand and calls out, "Ruby," with a stoic voice.

She steps from the sideline of slaves and walks slowly toward the post at a shuffle. The skin around Ruby's missing ear is grotesque from not healing properly, and she's even thinner than before, her eyes sunken and lips cracked. Her face is tear-stained when she stops in front of the soldier and lowers her gaze. My heart aches for her and, at the same time, I'm relieved that I'm not the one at the whipping post.

He grabs Ruby by her wheat-blond hair, forcing her to look at the General, and bellows, "Confess!"

Her body shakes, and when she finds her voice, it's small and quivers. "I stole an extra apple at morning meal while the General was not there to see."

Charos stares at the woman, his face passive, and he taps a finger on the side of his clean-shaven cheek. "Twenty lashes."

Ruby lets out a sob before a piss stain blooms on her skirts and ends in a small puddle at her feet.

The General wrinkles his nose in disgust. "Thirty now."

The chimera's tail twitches, and she growls before closing her eyes.

Ruby is forced to her knees by the soldier as he takes a hammer and set of nails from his satchel. My mouth drops open, he wouldn't. But oh, he does.

Ruby's hands are splayed against the post above her head, the sound of her screams on beat with the fall of the hammer as the nails are driven through her hands. I grab Saray's skirts for comfort, knowing I'll hear Ruby's cries for many years to come.

The soldier backs away from Ruby and raises a thick arm to the sky, his fingers curled around the handle of the whip. He looks at General Charos for permission.

The General gives a slight flick of his hand, and his henchman brings the whip down hard. It lands with a pop on Ruby's back, splitting it open. Blood swells and trickles from the wound as she cries out and sags against the post. It happens quickly, but in my mind the whip cuts the air at a crawl before slicing Ruby's exposed skin like butter. When the soldier hits her for the tenth time, I choke on my own air. Saray grabs me by the elbow, giving me a hard shake.

"Missy," she whispers low into my ear, "keep yourself together or you'll be on the list next time." When I start to hyperventilate, she clutches my chin and forces me to look at her narrowed brown eye. "Do you want to die?" she hisses.

I can't speak, but manage to shake my head.

I screw my eyes shut, and Saray draws me close to her side. All the while Ruby continues her guttural screams.

"Is there a pattern to it?" I whisper against her. "I've been here for months and haven't seen such an event."

"Nay, Confessional occurs at the General's whim."

Great. Something else incredibly hard to avoid.

When the final lash is given, Ruby's back is a ruined mess resembling minced meat, and her blood is splattered across the ground. The chimera's tail twitches in the air, as if annoyed, and General Charos leans forward in his chair with a look of sickening satisfaction. The soldier takes his hammer and removes the nails from Ruby's hands. She moans all the while, and is soon dragged away by two other slaves who are ordered to take her.

By the time the soldier calls for the eighth victim, he's out of breath and sweating from his exertions. I'm sick to my stomach, bile barely holding its place in the back of my throat. The person called forth is a young man. He appears weaker than the rest of us as he walks to the bloodied post.

His face is gaunt, and his clothes swallow him like a child playing dress-up in a parent's clothes. The slave before him, another man, did not survive his sixty lashes. It's psychological warfare. Those on the list give up long before they even make it to the post. Maybe if they were in healthier condition they'd survive, but the whip has nothing to hit but bone and a thin layer of worn skin.

Similar to his henchman, General Charos has also worked up a sweat. He dabs at his forehead with a neatly folded cloth, his nose turned up in displeasure. The climate of the Southern Region is much warmer this time of year than it is in Paidia. It's midday now, a still, airless day. The mixture of blood, piss, and closely pressed bodies doused in their own fear, has made an unpleasant aroma to say the least.

The General himself addresses the slave directly with narrowed eyes, "Confess."

The young man, restrained by the solder, has been reduced to a husk of his former self, but a spark of defiance lights his eyes. With his jaw set, he lifts his chin and remains silent.

General Charos ignores the small attempt at bravery and speaks to the soldier instead, "Is this the last one?"

"Yes, sir!"

Charos nods. "Release him then."

At the order, the young man falls to his knees, fire gone. He begs to the General, "Please, I didn't mean it! I'll confess! "I'll confess!"

"Start running," is his clipped reply.

I can see where this is going and more than anything, I wish I could hide.

The slave shakes his head. "No, no! Please! Whip me instead."

General Charos again ignores the man's pleas and reaches down to pet his chimera, scratching her under the chin while she purrs. The soldier slowly backs away from the crying slave and soon blends in with the others standing near the wall. Charos unclips the sapphire leash from her matching collar and the chimera bounds away from him, her muscled legs pumping. She tackles the slave.

The beast doesn't bite her victim but wraps her claws around his midriff before unfurling her giant wings and launching into the air, I'm caught between feelings of wonderment and terror. She lands on the roof of a nearby tower, crushing the tiles beneath, and proceeds to eat the young man, starting with his thigh. From their new height, his shrieks are amplified. My self-restraint is gone along with the contents of my stomach, and the person in front of me shifts out of the way to avoid my mess.

Saray rubs my back gently, but her voice is urgent, "Eimear, you have to stop."

I glance up and stare at the General's face as he watches his pet devour her meal. His smugness only deepens my anger, and I can't mask it. The bastard turns his head in my direction and our eyes lock. His gaze is like ice but I don't lower my eyes. Charos gives me a handsome smile before turning his attention back to his chimera. From the small interaction, I'm certain of my doom. When the man on the roof is at last silent, a guard instructs us to "clean up this mess," and we're supplied with scrub brushes and buckets of water.

The courtyard tiles are stained with blood, bits of skin, and other bodily excrements, making my stomach lurch again. Instead of puking, I do what I couldn't before and make myself go hollow inside. It's not me on my hands and knees scrubbing gore from the tile, it's someone else. There isn't a chimera on the roof playing with a dead body like a cat with a mouse. Even when the corpse falls and lands with a bone crunching smack, I tell myself, no that's not real either.

//Don't let the General crush your spirit. You—//

I don't hear the rest because her voice fades away, and I'm too numb to care why. I'm doing so well at pretending to not be me that I don't recognize my own name when it's called.

"Hey, you better go over there."

My eyes finally register the slave cleaning next to me, and he motions with his head. I turn to see Saray waving as she stands next to General Charos. I get to my feet, the violence mixed with water, has stained my dress. I walk numbly toward them and tell myself that it's not me taking the steps. The General's gaze doesn't leave my face as I draw closer, and I barely wonder why someone would gaze at me with such loathing.

When I reach him, his reflexes are quick, and he grabs me roughly by the chin. The Sister Sun shines her light on his gold bracer, creating a glare that blinds me. For a moment, I detect a whisper, but it slips away in my daze. Charos lets out an amused laugh as he moves my head to the side to better inspect the scar on my face. Still, I feel nothing.

"What pit did Steilos pull you out of?" he asks smiling.

I remain silent, but the General doesn't seem to mind.

"Saray, remind me to dock his pay for bringing me something so foul."

"Yes, sir," she says quietly and bows her head.

The General's mouth suddenly turns into a snarl. "Gods, I can't stand the sight of you."

I wake from my stupor when his fist collides with the side of my face. My body flies sideways, hitting the ground. Did I honestly think I could wish it all away? General Charos addresses me again and this time, I focus on his voice.

"You disgust me. I want your face covered at all times." He turns to Saray. "Make sure it's handled."

"Of course, sir," she says.

I prop myself up on my forearms, making sure to keep my head lowered. Rage bubbles up beyond the self-pity, and I remember the man I killed—the light leaving his eyes, how it felt to hold such power. If I could only do that again.

The General claps his hands together twice, and his chimera roars, making me flinch. She flies from her perch to his side. The beast rubs against him as he fastens her leash.

"Such a good girl," he tells her, and they leave together, followed by his entourage, throne in tow.

When he's out of sight, Saray runs to me, "I'm so sorry!" Tears flow down her cheek, I reach up and wipe them away with my thumb.

"Not your fault."

She helps me to my feet and envelops me in a gentle hug. In her arms, there's a blanket of safety that surrounds me, reminding me of Mana. I'm aware it's an illusion, nothing can truly keep me safe here, but I can wish.

"Get back to work!" A guard screams, and we jump apart.

With slow steps, I walk back over to my bucket and resume washing blood from the tiles, my face has already begun to swell. I scrub harder, and let the exertion take my mind elsewhere, a fantasy land where I'm back home with my family and not at this godless place. I convince myself that I'm tough. I've survived this far; I can continue surviving. I work myself up until I actually believe the idea. It isn't until Saray comes to me, and places a burlap sack with two eyehole cutouts over my head, that I feel something entirely else: Shame. I try to look on the bright side as I cry underneath. At least now, no one can see my tears.

Gods & Beasts of Miracle

Cerberus

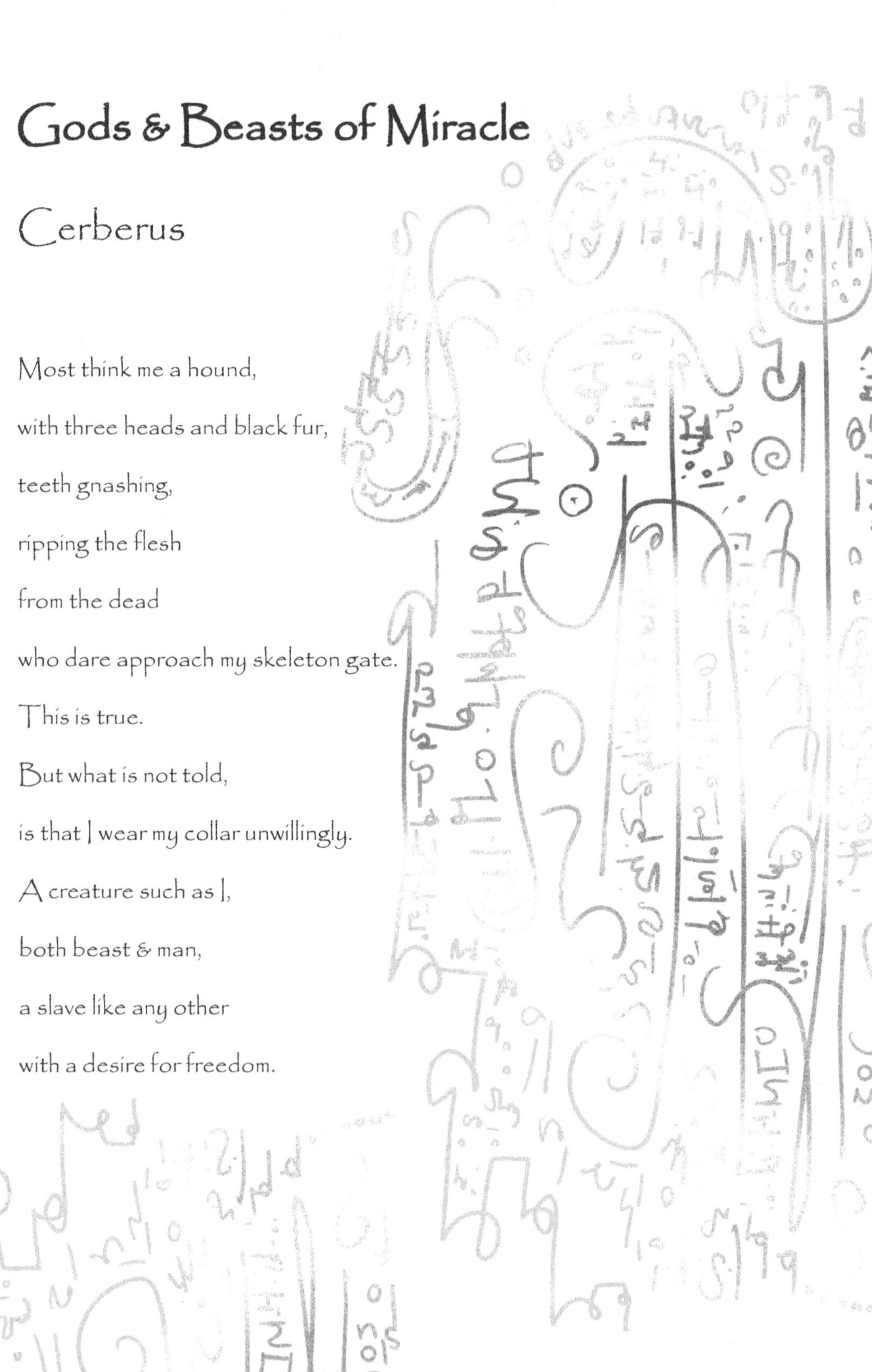

Most think me a hound,

with three heads and black fur,

teeth gnashing,

ripping the flesh

from the dead

who dare approach my skeleton gate.

This is true.

But what is not told,

is that I wear my collar unwillingly.

A creature such as I,

both beast & man,

a slave like any other

with a desire for freedom.

CHAPTER XXXI

9th Week of Fall

Eimear

I lay brooding in my bunk and pick at the material of my burlap sack; I wrap a loose piece around my finger. It's hot and scratchy within the bag, but I'm almost used to it now. I only take it off to bathe. Fury has been my constant companion, ready for a chance to be unleashed. A part of me holds Saray responsible for the hooding, even though it was on the General's order. The other half of me knows she's sad when she catches a glimpse of my covered face.

I'm sick of it.

I'm angry with Zadok and Mana as well. Why should I be the one to survive and then be trapped in a castle of nightmares as a slave? Why should I have to suffer alone without them? Death would be easier than this business, I should've died in Paidia when I had the chance.

Fuck Steilos too. I haven't been able to find the citrine at all, and it may not even be here. His informant could've been wrong, and now I'm the one paying the price. Many times, I've thought about calling off the search and lighting the lantern, but then I gamble Steilos leaving me here to rot when I don't have the information he needs. We made a deal after all. But then again, he could double cross me just as easily.

I'll bide my time until this contract is over and if the bastard doesn't come for me, then I'll find the highest staircase and jump from it! I won't wait for a death of General Charos' choosing—that at least I can steal from him. Elysium be damned. I'm sure the Under is a better place than this living hell.

//You're sulking. Free will is such a funny thing.//

//You jest, surely? After everything I've seen and been through? Of course I am!//

//You're more than welcome to wallow in self-pity, it is an experience after all. Makes no difference to us.//

//Kindly fuck off and mind your own business. I don't want to talk to you.//

Silence follows for a long time afterward. My insides are hollow as I lay in bed listless. I let out a long, irritated sigh, not caring about Selene in the next bunk. She moans in her sleep and turns to face the other way. Like tonight and every other since my hooding, I've been so angry that I can't rest. I toss and turn, thinking about how everything has gone so wrong, twisting the threadbare sheet until it's time to rise and face a new day of horrors. Even if I chanced the mirror, I know utter shit would be reflected back at me. With my dark circles, burnt skin, and haunted gold eyes, I've become quite the ghoul. I should be grateful for this fucking sack.

I flip onto my belly and shove my face into the pillow. "And I'm screaming, screaming out loud. Can anybody hear me?" I whisper Astera's song. It's been stuck in my head for some time. I think about how I told her I would be her friend and help her. That was weeks ago, I've done nothing but feel sorry for myself and never went back again. I bet she's been waiting all this time. I'm worse than shit, I'm fucking scum at this point.

"Screw this," I growl into my pillow and punch it. Selene grunts again, and I wait until she's settled back into a rhythmic slumber before I reach out with my sixth sense. My instincts react and I'm assured it's safe to leave. I walk to the front of the cavern and stop beside Saray's bed. When I returned the key to her last time, she put it in her dresser drawer.

With careful fingers, I quietly open it and begin rummaging. Her face is cast in sleep, the eye patch removed and her socket drooping. I feel guilty for taking it from her. But it'll be fine, I'll put it back before she notices anything's amiss. The metal slides beneath my fingers, and I take the key, close the drawer, and slip into the dark.

When I'm outside Astera's door, I stare at the ceiling above and hope that she forgives me for taking so long. Our friendship isn't off to a good start. She's singing, her voice lonely as ever. I raise my fist and lightly knock. Her song abruptly stops, and silence hangs between us for a moment. "Astera, it's Eimear, can I come in?"

"What? How?" she rasps, barely audible.

When I enter the room, it's bathed in moonlight, not a candle is lit, making her artwork on the walls all the more unnerving. She stands at the center in a long nightgown, her hair is a tangled mess. I shiver. By the Under! She looks like a demon.

"Do you honestly stand around all night singing in the damn dark? Do you know how odd that is? Do you have any idea what you look like?"

Astera's eyes widen with fright, and she steps away from me until she's against the wall, she hunches down and curls into herself like a wounded animal.

I stare confused until I realize that I'm the one who looks like a monster with the burlap sack and muffled voice. I put my hands up, "It's me, it's me Eimear! I'm sorry, I didn't mean to startle you."

Astera looks up, her voice is small when she speaks, "You came back?" followed by a confused, "Why *are* you wearing that?"

My fingers reach up and touch the burlap, I should remove it but can't bring myself to. "Courtesy of your father. Now, we can stand around here all night or could we go somewhere else?" I gesture around her prison. "I'm sure you're tired of this place?" I don't have to tell Astera twice because she's already walking past me out the door. She doesn't bother to change or even put on sandals.

"I have a place," she says, so focused on her freedom that she doesn't bother to ask how I'm able to move about undetected.

She directs me to an unkempt garden on the western side of the grounds. I've never seen it before, didn't know it existed. We're surrounded by dilapidated stone walls covered in red ivy; the night sky is open to us, and Castle Notos can be seen through the broken spaces in the stone. In times past, the garden may have been beautiful, but now all the plants are dead, and the space appears forgotten. Astera lays on a patch of overgrown indigo grass and runs her hands over it as if she's savoring the experience. I observe her from a cracked bench that's about ready to crumble from my added weight. Why did I think this was a good idea? She is the General's daughter for gods' sakes.

"I used to come here with my mother before she died. She loved to take care of her flowers and would let me help her even though I'd make a mess of everything." Astera doesn't sound sad, she speaks plainly, as if stating an inconsequential fact.

"How long has she been gone?" I ask.

Astera closes her eyes and spreads her arms and legs out in the grass, her long hair tangled around her. Under the twin light of the moons, the scars on her limbs become visible, a multitude of tiny, healed zig zags. "Seven years, I think."

I'm not sure what to say to her or if I should ask about the scars. I didn't plan for conversation.

"I haven't been outside since she died, not without *him* around." She turns over and plants her face into the earth and inhales.

She's strange to me. But I guess I would be too if I spent most of my time locked in a tower. "Why do you have to stay in your room all the time?"

Astera sits up and fixes her eyes on me—eyes that are so like her father's. Their iciness reminds me of Confessional, making me uneasy.

"He doesn't allow me outside unless we're moving with the army, and even then, I'm kept in a tent at all times. It's for my protection," she says with a bit of sarcasm. "It's been this way since mother passed."

I perk up at the mention of an army. "How often do you go with them?"

Astera picks at the grass with her bare feet, "Anytime my father gets a summons from the Autokrator."

My body freezes as I put it together: Astera is with the army anytime a city is conquered. "Have you met him then? Heracles?"

She sounds defensive when she answers. "No. I never see anything outside the tent, but I hear it. Even far away from the fighting, I can hear the screams."

She's just as much a victim as the rest of us. Standing, I walk over to her. When I touch her shoulder, she flinches as if afraid I'm going to strike her. I suck in, imagining what violence Astera has endured. "I won't hurt you, I promise."

She eyes me warily like a dog trying to decide whether to bite or not.

Her hair is beyond knotted. "Do you ever brush your hair?" She stares at the ground silently which is answer enough.

I let out a sigh. I'm not sure myself why I'm drawn to her, but maybe I can learn more about the General and Heracles if I show her some kindness. I take her hair in my hands; she cringes at my touch, but when I start to run my fingers through it, working at the knots, she relaxes. "My mother used to do this for me," I say, my smile sad.

We sit for a while in silence, but eventually, this simple human contact breaks the dam inside of her, and from Astera's lips pours a horrifying tale. I listen and, when she cries, she holds on to me. I hold her too, realizing, as her tears wet the shoulder of my uniform, why I couldn't leave her alone in the tower. For like calls to like.

After returning Astera to her room I hurry down to the cavern and collapse in my bunk. The suns are soon to rise, but still, sleep eludes me. Tonight, it's not only anger that keeps me from closing my eyes but shock. I recall memories of Papa and his tenderness toward me. Astera never had such a father. How can a man be so cruel? And to his own daughter?

General Charos began torturing Astera soon after her mother died giving birth to a stillborn son. He locked her in the tower and for years, cut her daily. She had many many scars from what my eyes could make out in the moons' light. Gods know, they don't stop at her exposed skin. Last summer, Saray became Astera's only attendant when it was found that her guards had been abusing her night after night. The General must have some heart, because he had the men drawn and quartered.

I cry into my pillow, my heart hurting for her and the torment she's had to endure. My fingers shook as I combed Astera's hair, taking in her pain. Her aura—from what I could discern—is that of a gentle nature with shades of blue and lilac, reminding me of twilight. However, there were points of black and gray twisted within her field, which tells me that Astera is ill. Her mind is sick. Can something like that be repaired?

I close my eyes, cringing at the remembered sound of whatever object Astera threw at the tower door as I locked her inside once more. Her devastated face clear in my mind when I took her back to her chamber. Saray would be punished if I had let her roam free. I take the pillow from my bed and press it close to my chest, squeezing as hard as I can for comfort. It helps, but just barely. I settle onto my back and stare at the bunk above me, my resolve building. There's just a few more months left. I'll continue waiting for Steilos and when he comes, I'll demand that he take both Saray and Astera with us. I won't take no for an answer. Steilos will just have to amend our agreement and deal with it.

Sleep finally claims me an hour before a new day begins. Black smoke pushes my nightmares aside, and I find myself in the colorful space again. The scent of narcissus fills up my senses, and I become giddy because I know who's coming. The outer world drops completely away. My friend smiles and I eagerly take his hand, cursing myself for not going to sleep sooner.

CHAPTER XXXII

11th Week of Fall

Nikko

The King and his advisors drone on and on about city matters. My attentions should be focused on the council meeting, but my mind keeps drifting back to the humiliation I experienced at the symposium. It's been three weeks. Even still, I incessantly pick at the memory like a scab, keeping the wound open: Erebos turning his face away at the last second, my failed attempt at a kiss. A first for me. Ever since, he's avoided me all together.

Why did I do that? I can't believe I got so drunk that I would make such advances on him. I try to think of why I'm attracted to him in the first place. His personality is terrible. He's not funny, he's dry as the

Colossus Desert.[49] In fact, I don't think I've ever seen him smile. Do I have a new fetish? Is that it? Maybe I simply want to know what it's like to fuck someone with real claws and teeth. Not that I've seen them since Erebos' scuffle with Gareth. But still, I've thought about it in bed, pleasured myself to it. This sudden infatuation must be with the mystery of him and not the man himself. It will pass.

Still, I wonder, why did he reject me? I nibble on the tip of my thumb. Maybe he has no interest in men? I don't know where he's from. Some places find the pairing dumbly offensive. But he didn't seem disgusted by me, I saw the way he looked at my mouth. We did just become allies. It'd be wise of him not to reciprocate; a relationship could get messy. Styx, it already *is* messy with how I've treated him and who he serves. I'd be happy if the treaty fell through with Heracles. Even so, the crimson chiton he wore that night and the exposed planes of his brown skin come to mind, along with the scent of sandalwood. My cock instantly stiffens.

"Fuck!" I blurt with anger. Will my turmoil ever cease?

King Zephyr and the entire council immediately halt their conversation and stare at me pointedly.

My father raises a brow, "I thought you of all people would be delighted?"

---

[49]A desert where it's rumored giants roam as well as other dangerous beasts.

"I beg your pardon?" I can't tell the King that I've been fantasizing about my body pressed up against a certain ambassador's, instead of focusing on matters of state. I wonder, does Erebos cry out when he comes? I'd like to see the expression on his—

Bacchus, my adoptive uncle, is a godsend. "Prince, Jada will no longer wed Heracles. We've managed to gather enough supplies to withstand a siege since trade has resumed. When the tyrant arrives for the wedding in a week's time, he'll find his invitation rescinded. He won't set foot in our city."

My head turns sharply toward my father. Jada will no longer wed the usurper? She's free? "You're turning down peace for war? Whatever changed your mind?" I ask.

Idan slaps his hand against the table in outrage. "Exactly," he says to Father. "We'll be back to war. Shedding more blood. Innocent lives will be lost all because you let your affection for your daughter get the better of you."

"I suggest you watch your tongue," the King says. "Though we may be brothers of the crib, I am still your king, and you will show respect."

Idan glowers.

"If I may, my King . . ." Hain fiddles with the timepiece around his neck, voice quiet. "I don't think this choice is wise. We'll earn more of Heracles' ire by going back on our word. I fear the civil unrest it may cause. There are those who still believe that he's a true son of Zeus. The faction supporting him may revolt, and we'll have to fend off enemies inside and out."

"If the citizens turn on their own king, won't they be expelled from the city gates because of the protection Zeus grants us?" I ask. My father and his advisors turn their attention to me, although by their unamused stares I see I've got it wrong.

Bacchus clears his throat, then says, "Zeus' ancient protection is rather… complicated. It's a matter of perception. Should the citizens who rally against your father wholeheartedly believe their actions to be for the good of Ellanios, then they are free to do as they please. However, if it's not for the benefit of Ellanios and for their own greed, they will be struck by an obsession to leave the city until they are driven from the gates. Still, our enemies outside the gates may not enter at all."

I recall the graffiti I happened upon in the alleyway a few months back. The poor drawing depicted my father and I hanged at the gallows. Did they think it for the benefit of Ellanios? Or were they struck by Zeus' power and left the city immediately?

Idan turns to the King. "My dear friend, I beg of you. Put your heart aside in this matter. The people may not turn against you because of your diluted lineage to Zeus, but they will under the threat of starvation."

"You're a coward!" Bacchus says to Idan, interrupting before my father can respond. "Where is your backbone, my man? Heracles has made slaves of your own relatives, and you would simply open our gates to him? Have our city genuflect to him? I'm ashamed to call you a Crib-Brother."

Idan appears miffed. "And you're a war-hungry prick who can think of nothing besides the tip of his sword."

Hain drops his timepiece nervously, eyes on his fellow advisors. "Maybe we should all calm ourselves for a moment—"

Both Bacchus and Idan yell at once, "Quiet Hain!" and then all three trade insults, their shouts filling the room.

I watch my father's demeanor grow colder and colder as his Crib-Brothers turn on one another. He raises his voice and they quiet down. "My friends, do you think I want Ellanion blood spilled? I've lost countless nights of sleep before making this decision. You must ask yourselves if you really want our people to be under the rule of a tyrant. Heracles promises freedom, but all I've seen are the shackles on those he's conquered or bartered with. You don't think the pretender will do the same to you after I give him my daughter? I've been stringing his emissary along all these seasons to buy time. I'm prepared to exchange Jada for his goodwill should it come to it, but we must at least attempt the opposite. Ellanios has been a peaceful nation for nearly three centuries, any bloodshed before then was due to our own greed. We are the beloved people of Zeus; he has always protected us, and he will continue to do so. The Holy City will not bow to this imposter who claims he's a son of Zeus. No; we will fight and teach this usurper a lesson."

"And how do you propose we battle him beyond the walls?" Idan counters. "Our troops are spread thin with the losses we took in Kanthar, Anyalay, and now the entire Southern Region. Even if we call our soldiers home from Apotmos, it still would not be enough. Heracles' Maketae warriors and supporters now vastly outnumber our own men."

Hain speaks up, "And let's not forget about the Gifted who fight with him. Per the reports, our soldiers were useless against General Charos."

"Do not fear, my brothers. We'll defeat Heracles with the help of the Voranians." My father throws an envelope on the table, its Voranian seal broken. "Their leaders recognize that once our borders fall, Vorna will be next. Three of the larger tribes have agreed to come together and fight with us, making our numbers nearly even with the imposter. Their Drake-Women are sure to tip the scales in our favor and be of equal match to those Gifted generals of his. This entire time, I've been keeping up the pretense of a ridiculous treaty with Heracles to secure an alliance with Vorna."

The room erupts once more.

Idan slams his fists on the table. "Voranians? Those barbarians? We've been battling them off our borders for years. We can't trust them to fight with us!"

"Their nature is that of a serpent," Hain says while shaking his head. "Their Drake-Women will surely devour our soldiers when our backs are turned and our eyes on Heracles' men. This alliance is too risky."

Bacchus interjects, his baritone louder than the rest: "I agree with the King. We can't just open our gates to the enemy because a delusional pretender demands it. Zeus has granted Ellanios good fortune since he claimed the Holy City as his crown jewel. There's no reason why his protection wouldn't aid us now. And although we've never had good relations with Vorna, should we be victorious against Heracles, it would create an alliance between our two countries."

Seemingly grateful, the King nods at my uncle, then turns his gaze to the others. "Don't you think what Heracles has done to our fellow countrymen is barbaric? Would you rather sit idle and let the man put a collar on us like dogs? We should not be so proud that we spit on the good will offered from Vorna. As your king, I'm not asking for your permission. My mind is decided on the matter."

Idan and Hain share a defeated look. "This will be our undoing," Hain says, picking at his timepiece.

"But you are our king and our brother. You'll always have our support." Idan dips his head toward my father.

Awkward silence fills the council chamber, each of us knowing that history is about to be made.

Bacchus peers around the room and clears his throat, "Well, if we're all done squabbling, I'd like to discuss strategy. We have a war to win."

Hours have passed since the King's decision, and the twin suns have begun to set. A headache throbs at my temple. My eyes have become gritty as we all stand over a replica of Ellanios with pieces that symbolize the three armies. A multitude of tactical maneuvers have been discussed at length, each rejected when they fail within the model. It's been decided that the Holy City will withstand siege, and when Heracles' armies have waited long enough to grow lax, the Voranians will split in formation and attack from the rear and western side, while our soldiers attack from the front and the east, decimating them.

"The Drake-Women will be our biggest asset," Bacchus says.

Although Hain has been mostly quiet, he offers: "They won't be expecting it, Ellanios allying with one of our oldest enemies."

My father nods in agreement and meets the eyes of everyone around the table. "The Voranians are unexpected allies, I know, but we'll show them our gratitude once we've crushed the greater threat."

Idan considers the pieces, his mouth slightly downturned. "We may pull this off after all." He then smiles at my father, "It will be a grand day indeed when I can welcome my nieces and nephews home."

After the tactician board is put away, we all resume our designated seats, and my father orders the guards to escort Erebos to the council chambers. My heart coils with dread as I wait for his summons.

It seems my budding attraction to him is as futile as I thought. It's something that can never be. While I'm grateful my sister will not have to sacrifice herself to a lunatic, I'm also saddened that Erebos and I will be enemies once more. A knock finally comes at the door and I close my eyes. I wish we didn't have to do this to him.

"You may enter," my father calls.

The arched doors open, and Erebos arrives with palace guards on either side of him. The emissary bows. "King Zephyr, this is unexpected. How may I be of service to you?" His gaze drifts over to me momentarily, and I sit up straighter.

"I'm calling off this farce of a betrothal. Princess Jada will not wed an imposter who claims to be a son of Zeus. Ellanios will not bow to him. I hereby revoke your status as a protected guest and declare you a prisoner of war."

Erebos' face remains blank, unsurprised. Instead of trying to sway my father toward peace, he bewilders me and the entire room by saying, "I would suggest instead, that you kill me."

He wishes to die? As I stare at his proud form, at the face I've never seen smile, I have regrets that I did not get to know him better. I'm about to plead on his behalf when he speaks again.

"I'm sworn to Heracles and him alone. Not one truth of his character or plans will fall past my lips under torture."

Torture? My father is soft, surely, he wouldn't—

"With the right amount of prodding, every man breaks. I'm certain a few truths will spill from that tongue of yours." The King signals to the guards. "See that he's escorted to a cell." My father then addresses Erebos again, "Though I wholeheartedly agree about killing you, if I did, it would be dishonorable of me. Emissaries are protected in war; I will not take your life as you request. Think of it this way—the quicker you speak, the less pain you will suffer."

Heart in my throat, I turn to my father, "Surely, you're posturing? You wouldn't really torture this man? It's a barbaric practice. And . . . Jada holds affection for him now, they've become friends. She won't stand for this."

My father fixes me with a stern gaze. "Nikko, this is war. Jada will be happy enough not to wed a monster. Her anger will pass. As for me, I won't be the one torturing him. An experienced soldier will do the deed."

Horrified, I don't recognize the man I call Father.

As the guards grip Erebos' shoulders, he doesn't struggle. I've seen his prowess in the sparring ring and the hints of an extraordinary Gift. He's a warrior and could take their lives in a matter of moments, but he's making the choice not to. Before he's pulled through the chamber doors, his eyes find mine, and what I find reflected there is an unspeakable sadness.

What are you not telling us?

The King sighs deeply. "This meeting is adjourned for now. Everyone rest up, we'll meet again when the suns rise."

I stand with the others, and we bow to the King. Logically, it makes sense to torture an enemy to gain information, but my heart disagrees. I can't help but be bitter. I start to leave with the rest, but my father calls out, "Nikko, Bacchus, stay."

What now? I clench my fists and bite the inside of my cheek. I don't think I can maintain my show of calm much longer.

The King appears tired as he rubs his temples; the meeting must've worn him down. "Bacchus, I want you to work on an exit strategy to evacuate our citizens in the event not all goes as planned."

My uncle sputters, "Your highness, if you don't mind me saying, that's a fool's request. There are over 400,000 people within the city. It's impossible to evacuate them all without detection."

My father's face is grim. "I'm very much aware most would have to be left behind. But regardless, I want an escape route that can save as many lives as possible. Make sure to set aside supplies as well. And be discreet, the fewer who know, the better our chances of success."

"I'll do my best your highness."

"I don't want your best. I want it done. See that it is. You're dismissed."

"Yes, sir." My uncle stands erect, beats a fist to his chest, and exits the chamber.

Despite my interest in the King's secret plan, I'm still angry. "Why an escape route if we have assurances the Voranians will fight with us, and we'll torture the right information out of Erebos to end Heracles?" I ask snidely.

The King is slow to answer but he does. "I'm selfish. I need to know that you, your mother, and sister will survive this. No matter what happens. Promise me that. Not as your king, but as your father. Promise me that if Zeus abandons the Holy City, that you'll live on."

His tone cools my fury. I've never seen my father so desperate or so human. The rare display of affection sets true fear in my bones. What if we fail?

Gods & Beasts of Miracle

Harpies

Spirits of the wind and the oldest ministers of Zeus, harpies are rarely seen by the human eye. They soar high above the clouds, their domain neighbors Olympus and is unreachable by mortals. Should one be graced by a harpy's presence, it is wise to bow in respect, for they are delivering the God of Gods' word.

CHAPTER XXXIII

1st Week of Winter

Eimear

I jolt awake just in time to keep from falling forward. I'm sitting in the grass and just dozed off. How long can I keep this up? But as I look at Astera planting the squash seeds I dug out of the kitchen scraps, my weariness becomes less important. They won't sprout pretty flowers for her, but squash blossoms are something. I caught a glimpse of a smile from her when I pressed the seeds into her hand. Maybe one day I'll hear her laugh, but I think we have a long way to go. Styx, now that I think about it, I don't even know if I'll ever laugh again.

For the past month, we've come to the garden every night. The fresh air has done Astera some good and a sense of sanity has returned to her eyes. She hums to herself as she digs, her hands dirty from the soil. The melody is soothing and I make a bed for myself in the indigo grass. Lack of sleep is beginning to take a toll that not even a bath in the spring can fix, but I've come to look forward to these meetings. It's nice to have someone to talk to at the end of my long days. We've actually become friends in a strange way. The thought makes me smile.

My eyes fly open when I become aware that Astera is crouching beside me. I have the sensation I was just talking to someone but can't remember who or what we spoke about. A thread of longing remains for another heartbeat and then, it too, disappears. I'm left instead to look at the girl next to me.

"Did I wake you?" She asks. "I can't tell with that bag over your head." Astera chews on her lower lip. "It's unsettling; you should just take it off when you're with me. I don't understand it."

I yawn, something she can't see but can hear.

"I *knew* you were sleeping," she says and pokes the burlap. Astera now keeps her hair brushed, and it falls perfectly around her face in waves. A pang of jealousy hits me. She's lovely, her face unmarred. I used to be that way. When she tries to lift my hood, I grab her hand to stop her. Under my fingers, I feel the puckered skin of a scar and become ashamed of my envy. We're the same, I remind myself.

"I prefer it this way," I say and let her hand fall.

"I don't mind it, you know, the burn. You shouldn't either. There's nothing wrong with your face. I think it's beautiful," Astera says and looks away.

It annoys me how she won't let it go. It's not as if I really want to wear this damn thing. But every night, I can't bring myself to remove it. I don't want anyone to see *me* anymore, what I've become. I'm irritable from lack of sleep, and snap at her, "That's funny coming from someone who hides their scars with sleeves." As soon as the barb leaves my mouth, I regret it.

She grabs me by the collar of my dress and pulls me toward her. There's a wildness in her eyes, reminding me that she's still not well. Something I forget from time to time. "That's not by choice and you know it. The General chooses what I wear, all my dresses have sleeves—" She looks me up and down. "But when I'm the only one with you, what's your excuse for wearing that thing?"

I place my hand once again over hers and try to remain calm. "I'm sorry, I wasn't thinking when I said it," I tell her and mean it. I grapple for words, not knowing how to express myself anymore, after pushing everything down for so long. "And this—" I reach for the burlap, "I can't explain it, but I can't bear to take it off right now. It's like my own little armor."

Astera's eyes widen when she sees a wad of my dress bunched in her fist. She quickly lets go. The wisp of a girl pulls at her hair and stammers, "I'm just like *him*. I deserve to be in that tower. He's right, I'm too dangerous to be around others." Confused by her ramblings, I reach to comfort her, but she jerks away. "Don't touch me!" she cries.

Through my Gift, I sense how scared she is, the black spots scattered in her starlike aura are pulsating, and I worry that she'll injure herself somehow. I hold out my hand, giving her the option this time. "It's fine, you didn't hurt me. I promise. We're both being awful, that's it, let's just forget about it." I recall past arguments with Gareth and grimace at the pain that comes with the memories. "This happens with friends."

"But I could kill you." She sobs, and tears spill down her face.

My eyes narrow, sensing . . . something. "What do you mean by that?"

Astera shakes her head, refusing to answer. She hugs her knees to her chest and hides her face in her arms. As I stare at the frail girl in front of me, I think of the nameless man I killed on the ship. All the blood, and how his life slipped between my fingers. How I want to kill General Charos, Faas, and many others. I have murderous thoughts on a daily basis. My lips curl into a dark smile she can't see. I kneel beside her and extend my hand once more. "Don't worry, I could kill you too."

Astera raises her head, and peers at me with puffy eyes. "Truly?" She sounds relieved.

I find her to be a strange person. But I guess we both are. I sigh, exasperated, "Gods damn it all. Yes, you crazy girl. I could. Now take my bloody hand already."

She wipes her eyes, then her fingers find mine and we rise together. "I want to go back to my room," she whispers. "I don't feel like being outside anymore."

I give her hand a squeeze and lead her from the garden. "That's fine, but I'm coming for you again tomorrow. I won't let you rot alone in that tower anymore."

"Even after all that? Even though we may kill each other?"

By the Under, this one. I shake my head and say gruffly, "I told you, we're friends. I meant it." Her hand trembles in mine, and I turn in time to see her holding back laughter, her shoulders shaking. When she finally laughs out loud, I'm caught off guard. I don't think I've ever heard anything more lovely.

When she's done, she looks at me and deadpans, "I think we're an odd pair, the two of us."

I picture us then, two girls bathed in moonlight, attempting to navigate a semblance of friendship. One half-mad from isolation and torture, the other wearing a dirty bag over her head, whose bloodlust has become almost second nature. My snort turns into a burst of laughter, I get a stitch in my side from it. "Oh gods, yes, we are a very odd pair. Do you think we'll ever be normal?"

We pause for a second, staring at each other, and then say at the same time:

"It's unlikely—"

"Not a chance—"

And then we're both doubled over, gasping for air, laughing uproariously. Hand clutched to my chest, lungs heaving, and my friend—as broken as I—beside me, I come to a conclusion: even in the darkest of circumstances, there's always a little light somewhere. As long as you're willing to search for it.

CHAPTER XXXIV

1st Week of Winter

Eimear

When I sense someone coming toward the area where I'm sweeping—an empty hallway not far from the kitchen—I grip the broom handle tighter and go still. I only relax when I detect Saray's sunburst energy, but when her face appears around the corner, her grave expression makes my hackles raise.

She fixes me with her eye before quickly glancing away. "Eimear, we've been ordered by the guards to assemble at the courtyard."

My mouth goes dry. Whose death am I about to witness next? I follow her in awkward silence. There isn't ill will between us, but a wall has gone up that we haven't been able to breach since my hooding.

The two of us aren't the last to arrive, but many have already gathered. I have to stand on the tips of my toes to see over the people in front of me. Both male and female slaves have been summoned. There's tension in the air, no one knows why we've been assembled.

Isn't it too soon for another Confessional? I witnessed my second one mere days ago when Charos himself whipped a man to death. He did it with a sick smile. By the time he was finished, the slave's face was unrecognizable. My stomach turns just thinking about it. Surely there can't have been that many infractions since then?

Three guards are stationed in front of us near the fountain, their agitation apparent. When I get a better look, I see that Faas is among them.

He calls out, "Is this everyone?"

Silence follows.

Faas rolls his eyes and proceeds to pace leisurely. "I've been asked by the General to find someone out of the lot of you who can read and write in Voranian."

Those around me shift and glance at each other in confusion, myself included. Vorna is made up of a barbaric populace at the northern border of Ellanios. It's not common for outsiders to interact with them. For all my father's traveling, he rarely conducted business there because he found the dragon people to be difficult. I can't imagine why the General would need someone to read and write in their language.

Not a soul steps forward.

Faas unfastens the whip from his side and proceeds to play with its end. "You can't tell me, out of all you useless shits, that not a one knows Voranian?" He turns suddenly, the whip unfurling in a grand arc. When he flicks his wrist, the tip lashes out and hits a man at the front of the crowd. The slave cries out, and from what I can see, he falls to his knees. A fresh wave of fear rolls off the masses around me. Faas continues walking, this time, dragging the whip behind him. "Listen well you cunts. If the General's demand goes unfulfilled and it's discovered later that one of you withheld information, then that person will pay a visit to the bull—" He stops, his blue eyes piercing as he surveys the crowd, "and I'll stuff you in there myself."

//This is an opportunity.//

My jaw clenches, and I scowl beneath the burlap. *//It's been a while. I thought you left me for good.//*

//We're always with you, through everything. Your pain is our pain. We are one; we couldn't leave even if we wanted to.//

I snort, *//Well that's comforting.//*

//Volunteering will put you close to the General.//

//I don't want to be near him! It's a death sentence.//

Faas raises his voice. "All right pissants, I know there are Voranians among you! Don't make me wait a moment longer."

Out of the corner of my eye, I see an older man who coughs and begins to make his way through the crowd toward the front. He's thin and bent with age, but his large build pegs him as Voranian.

//This is it, now or never. Your choice.//

Steilos did say I only had to locate the damn thing. I observe Saray beside me and think of Astera in her tower. We all need to get the hell out of here, and the sooner the better. "Fuck all," I say under my breath and shoot my hand to the sky before I lose confidence. "I know it, Sir!" I'm surprised my voice doesn't waver.

 The old Voranian suddenly stops, plainly relieved.

"What are you doing?" Saray hisses, stunned.

The other slaves move away from me as if I'm diseased. Faas sees me through the divide. "Gods, it would be fuckin' you out of all of em." He crinkles his nose with distaste. "The rest of you are dismissed."

Everyone makes their way back toward the castle. My legs shake as I walk towards him. What have I gotten myself into? I clench and unclench my hands, knuckles popping as I crack each one.

Faas reaches up and pinches the fabric of my hood. "Looks good on you," he says before slapping me upside the face. My head moves from the force, but I don't stumble. He turns on his heel and walks away, and I follow, my cheek stinging.

I'm taken to a wing of the castle I've yet to explore, due to the fact that it's where the General spends most of his time. Like a rat, I can sniff out danger and know where not to stick my nose. Until now that is.

Faas stops in front of a set of large double doors before knocking. "General, I found someone."

"Enter," Charos sounds from beyond.

I'm sweating profusely as the door opens. The General peers up from a massive oak desk, spectacles on his face and sheets of parchment in his hands. Two bookcases filled with leather bounds are behind him. He almost seems to be a normal man, a scholar even, but I know better. His pet chimera is curled lazily beside the desk, like a loyal dog. The beast cracks an eye open at our arrival before closing it again. General Charos removes his spectacles and leans back in his chair. "Ah, you're the unpleasant thing from before."

I flinch.

He nods to himself. "I like it. Saray always seems to know what will please me. She's the only one with any real worth."

I lower my eyes and dare not speak.

"Now let's see if what Steilos brought me has any value, because so far I'm not impressed." He snarls at Faas, "You're dismissed!" He then settles his specs back onto his face and motions for me to come closer. The guard takes his leave.

I approach, gripping the cloth of my dress and rolling its fabric between my fingers to help calm my nerves, but it doesn't work. My eyes dart to the slumbering chimera. I saw her feed on someone just days ago.

The General takes a sheet of paper from a drawer and begins to write, the feather pen scratching as he ignores me. I don't know what to do with myself. Then I sense something, almost like a hum. It takes me a moment to realize that the barely audible sound is not being spoken out loud but in my mind, like the presence of a shadow.

//It's here, in this room. The stone.//

//I've felt this before.//

//Yes, with Zadok.//

I try to recall our last moments together, when I said goodbye to my brother. The azurite in his pocket and my warning him of it. But when I push the memory for more detail it's like it never happened. My brow furrows beneath my hood.

//The Goddess took the knowledge back, it wasn't ours to keep.//

//Of course, she did,// I tell her sarcastically. //The stones aren't like normal objects; they must possess a power of some kind. If I can hear it, do you think I can locate it with my Gift?//

//It's worth a try.//

I ground myself and try to search for the gem, feeling for its energy. But I only detect the aura of one monster in front of me, the chimera's, instead of two. I can't sense the General at all. //Styx! I know it must be here, but I can't sense it. I can't see the General's energy either. What's going on?//

My sacred-self is silent for a few moments before answering. *//He must be wearing it. Our sight can't see our possibilities with the General. It's dark. The stone must interfere somehow.//*

As Charos continues to write, I allow my eyes to wander over his intimidating frame. His neck and chest are unadorned. He wears a silk tunic of the deepest green with no embroidery and no pockets in sight. The loose sleeves end at his elbows, his left arm bare. My eyes go to his writing hand, to the gold bracer he always wears. I'm close enough to him now to note its intricacies; the cuff is the length of his forearm and seems to fit tightly against his skin. I skim over the hammered etchings, and nearly miss the thumbnail-sized gem embedded in the plating. The golden stone almost blends with the metal. //It's been there all this time!// It takes every ounce of my willpower not to ogle the citrine and draw attention to myself.

//What do we do now?// In response, there's a sniffle and what sounds like an overexaggerated sigh in my mind. //Is something wrong?//

//*You just called us 'we' for the first time. We should take a moment to rejoice.*//

//I swear to the Under, if I could choke you, I would.//

//*Don't be such a sourpuss. Survive the next several minutes and then light the lantern tonight. Try not to die on us,*// she says and goes quiet.

Why is my Gift, so infuriating? I really wish I could make people's heads explode. Now *that*, would be helpful.

Despite being in front of the most terrifying man I've ever encountered and a creature that could devour me in seconds, my heart beats with happy excitement. I've finally completed my goal and can leave with Astera and Saray. I'm not sure how Steilos plans to swipe the gem, but that's not really my problem. He asked me to locate it. I've done my part.

As the General remains silent and continuously scratches his pen against the parchment on his desk, my lower back beings to ache. I know he's making me wait on purpose, trying to scare me, the bastard. I survey the room, trying to learn what I can about him. His study is large, practical, includes a sitting area with a simple table and chairs. A decanter full of golden liquid sits on top of the table. There's no artwork to brighten the room like the rest of the castle. The General doesn't have need for useless things, I guess.

A deadly flail hangs on the wall above the table, reminding me how dangerous Charos is. The weapon appears to be well taken care of, the striking head is round with spikes, and its long, coiled chain reflects the light. Only the worn handle indicates any prior use. How many people have died under that spike's razor edge?

"The flail is still my favorite, even though it's been some time since I've wielded it on the field."

I nearly jump at the sound of the General's even voice, and my eyes go back to him at the desk. The chimera yawns, her maw wide and displaying killer's teeth.

Charos continues, "Something about the way the bone breaks under each swing is satisfying."

He expects a response from the way he speaks. "I wouldn't know, Sir," I manage to stutter.

The General studies me and leans back in his chair, "No, I don't think you would. Your build is small, not like a Voranian warrior, which tells me you aren't from Vorna. I pray you aren't wasting my time."

"I'm not, Sir . . . Not Voranian, and not wasting your time," I quickly say. "My father used to trade for my village and was well versed in languages. He taught me a few, and I studied more of them after his passing."

"Good. Steilos isn't a complete imbecile then, for purchasing you." He opens a desk drawer and pulls out a dirty, crinkled envelope. "Read this to me," he says and slides it across slowly with a pointed finger.

I pick up the envelope and turn it over, noticing blood stains and a broken, purple seal. I flip the top open and pull out the rumpled letter. But when the crude symbols don't immediately make sense, I begin to panic. I can't read it. Voranian is such a duplicitous language, and it's been months since I've studied.

General Charos grows impatient and slams his fist onto the desk. I flinch. "I'll not ask you again," he says.

My insides become all jumbled up. I stare hard at the paper, but still, nothing makes sense. I've just sentenced myself to certain death.

//Remember to ground yourself and breathe. You can do this.//

She's right. I shove my panic down and slow my breathing. I root myself in place and search for the knowledge within me. "The Lion will devour the Hatchlings. The Eagle soars with the Drake. Let the fire burn now," I finally say and glance hesitantly at the General before folding the letter, returning it to him.

Afterward, he drums his fingers, and seems to be deep in thought. Charos has intercepted military correspondence, but I don't understand the meaning behind the message. I continue to wait until he takes blank parchment and an ink quill from another drawer, he hands them to me.

"Write, the Lion sleeps. The Eagle soars with the Drake. Hold fire."

I consider the man before me, his eyes like a storm on the brink of destruction. I wet my lips, "In Voranian?"

The General nods his head. "And if you decide to be creative and write something other than what I've exactly told you to write, I'll find out, and you will suffer beyond your worst imaginings. For I will stuff you full of food, strip you naked, and then lock you inside a pillory. The guards will coat your body in honey and milk, and they'll hang a wasp nest from your neck. If the wasps don't kill you after a month, I'll have you disemboweled. Your organs will then be fed to Nova," Charos gestures to his pet chimera.

I thought the bull was the worst way to go. But I've been proven wrong. I swallow, "I won't be creative, Sir."

"Good. Now write."

My hand pauses when I place the quill to paper, but the words come naturally. I'm not as rusty as I thought. Or maybe, fear is just a great motivator.

The General makes me write the message over and over, until I've made my handwriting nearly identical to the original letter. As I watch him seal the envelope with purple wax and a stamp, I struggle with the fact that someone's life, maybe many, are about to be destroyed. I know I shouldn't have volunteered for this. It was a mistake. But, like I do with many other feelings, I bury the guilt. I remain silent as the General takes out another sheet of paper and begins writing in Ellanion.

CHAPTER XXXV

2nd Week of Winter

Nikko

What the Holy City's ancient scripts fail to note about being under siege, is that sieges are incredibly dull. My fantasy of Ellanions up in arms, and taverns filled to the brim with drunk soldiers singing ballads of our enemy's demise, has not been brought to life. A siege, I've learned, is quiet and angry, which is the worst kind of anger. It lashes out unseen, and it's hard to pinpoint the source when it seems to be everywhere.

Even the King's reneging on the treaty was quiet and dull. When Heracles' army arrived by ship nearly a month ago, sporting their gold lion banners, there was no audience. No fanfare or theatrics. Father simply sent a letter beyond the wall, calling off the treaty. It was delivered by Ivor, who wrapped the letter around an arrow and shot it toward an enemy soldier's feet while the gate was still open. The soldier picked it up and that was that. We didn't even lay eyes on Heracles. And still haven't. But in laying siege, the tyrant has done exactly what my father predicted he would do.

Gripping the terrace railing, I look past the Holy City and stare at the colossal 400-meter wall. Zeus' protection is the only thing keeping our soft citizens alive. Beyond it, I was informed by Father's council, is an encampment of Heracles' soldiers, and a fleet of ships anchored in the Havmand Bay. The ships' sails are reported to be oddly translucent, and the wood painted the color of the water, making them barely visible to the eye. They can't be ordinary ships.

Feeling tense, I continue to stare at the wall. We're safe, but I think it's worse not seeing the enemy, knowing they're just beyond, waiting for us to succumb to our fear.

"Sister, there are so many of them," I say, my voice forlorn.

She replies from the parlor room, "Didn't father's advisors say otherwise? That Heracles' eight thousand men is of no concern compared to our numbers and reinforcements? You said they actually laughed about it in the most recent meeting."

But those reinforcements haven't arrived yet. It's supposed to be this way, lulling Heracles' men into a sense of complacency and then striking them when their guard is down. Even still, having them outside the wall, so close by, makes me nervous.

I turn, leaving the view of the city behind me. Jada rests on a klinē and holds a feather pillow close to her chest. I tell her, "You and I have never been this close to war. I'm surprised you don't find it worrisome that eight thousand enemy soldiers are right outside the gates.

She tosses the pillow at me, and I catch it. "I never said I didn't. And I know it's wrong, but the smallest part of me doesn't mind the soldiers being here. I enjoy watching the incompetent ones try to storm the city gate, oh-so-much. The satisfaction I take from it is paramount. Zeus' protection is truly a sight to behold."

I have to smile at that. She's right. it *is* fun to watch.

She groans. "I'm sad I only got to see it when they first arrived. I know it's for our own safety, but I despise that Father has confined us to the palace. It's tedious being cooped up."

My nose wrinkles. "You mean you've actually been staying put this entire time?"

Her mouth drops. "Don't tell me you're *still* sneaking out? Even when he's forbidden us from attending our temple duties, of all things? He says the citizens have already begun to panic and could attack us. If he catches you, he really will make good on his threat to throw you in a cell."

If that happened, at least I'd be near Erebos. He's still a prisoner of war and well-guarded. I can't even visit him. Which is why I keep going outside the palace when I'm not supposed to. Pounding myself into Darja gives a brief respite from the persistent want I harbor for Heracles' emissary. I don't know the details of his torture, the specifics aren't discussed in council meetings, something I'm grateful for. But so far, Erebos is loyal to his master through and through. He's not given any information, which irritates Father to no end, and something I have mixed feelings about.

But I don't share any of this with my sister. She's under the impression that Erebos was let go and is now somewhere beyond the wall. A lie Father told her that I wish were true.

I clear my throat. "The citizens are . . . a bit agitated." The number of skirmishes and knife fights I've had to avoid on my way to the ancient sector has been troublesome. "But I've had no issues with being detected. It's relatively safe."

Jada is quiet for a moment as if considering something, then she says, "I want you to show me how to leave the palace." Her gaze is playful. "Let us go to the gates, even if it's only for a little while. It's not every day we get to witness Zeus' protection in action. I want to see it again."

I can't help myself: I clap slowly. "Finally! The righteous Princess Jada is ready to lower herself from the high horse she rides and get her feet dirty. I've waited long for this day."

"I swear, you are insufferable," my sister says as she searches for another object to throw at me. I beat her to it and pitch the same pillow she used against me. It catches her upside the face, and her eyes narrow briefly.

My smile is cocky. "You aren't the only one with a good throwing arm. Now, go get your cloak. We don't want anyone to recognize us."

As the suns set due west, the mixture of blood orange and indigo, along with the glare of the Lunetas Bridge, covers our descent down the palace walls. If I didn't know any better, judging by my sister's adeptness with the ropes, it wouldn't surprise me if she's been using them all along.

"Put your hood up," I whisper to her when we reach the ground.

She nods and does as asked, and I follow suit. We both wear long cloaks of deepest purple, standard attire in the winter months. We'll blend in with the other citizens perfectly, although our current weather is only mildly chilly.

We make our way past the boulders and rocks towards the city's agora when Jada tugs on my elbow, and I stop mid-step to look at her.

She leans in close to me. "Has it been this quiet in your other outings? Its eerie."

I glance around at the deserted street. Normally, vendors are out at this time. Tavern doors would be open to welcome customers, and nearby residents would watch from their balconies, but now, everything is shuttered. The citizens here are holed up in their homes. But in the ancient sector people sit idle and stare angrily, looking for a brawl.

"I'll admit, it's gotten worse since father mandated the food rationing five days ago. But, Sister, trust me when I say it's better that it's quiet." In this sector, at least, the citizens aren't fighting.

We make it to the edge of the Holy City, toward the northernmost wall, which shines like a pearl under the glow of the

Lunetas Bridge. We crouch, hiding behind a large tree as we watch a handful of soldiers who man the main entrance gate, several yards away.

"Styx! They'll catch us if we go any closer. We won't get to see anything at all." Jada sounds disappointed.

I snort. "Did you think we were going to waltz right up to them?" I pitch my voice higher to imitate her. "Hello Sir Guard, don't mind me, but I'd like to take a gander at the enemy lines, even though the King has expressly forbid it. It's all good, I'm an exception."

She smacks me on the shoulder. "Oh, will you shut up! What's your plan then?"

"Well, it's good we're both in shape, because we have a lot of work to do." I gesture to the obviously bored soldiers who must've committed an offense of some sort. Only the daft get charged with guarding an impenetrable gate. "Keep an eye they aren't looking this way while I count."

"What?"

"Just do it *please*."

Jada huffs. "*Fine*."

While my twin is busy being a lookout, I run my fingers against the wall while pressing firmly. I don't stop until I've counted to sixty and come across a stone that is slightly more indented than the others.

"Found you." When it gives way, the outline of a door appears in the wall. I have to shove against it with my shoulder before it opens to a narrow passageway. I go inside and find the old lantern hanging on the right. I quickly light it, using a flint I brought with me, and my knife. Once I'm finished, I peer around the doorway.

"Jada!" I hiss, "quit playing around and come on."

She whips her head in my direction. "I am *not* playing aroun—" She gasps when she sees me. "How did you—"

I beckon with my hand. "Quickly, before they see."

She darts from the safety of her tree and joins me in the cramped space inside the wall. We close the heavy stone door together. I hold the lantern high, and she looks around, "How in the worlds did you know this was here?"

I wipe my gritty hands on my cloak. "When father gave me the task of rebuilding Ellanios, I had access to some of the original blueprints in the library. I found the one for this wall while I was studying. I'm sure some in our military are aware of it, but really, they haven't needed it. There are other entrances along the wall, as well as hideaways across the city, although I've yet to explore them all."

"Do you come here often?"

I chuckle. "By the Under no. But I promise it's worth it."

I hear the confusion in her voice. "Why not?"

"You'll find out shortly. Follow me."

We walk for several yards down the dusty passageway until it opens to a small room. At its center, is a large wooden platform rigged with a pully system. I walk over to it and hang the lantern on the platform's middle post.

I tell my sister, "It's a bitch to pull yourself up. So, I'm glad there's two of us. But try not to fall off, because you will die."

She looks up to the cutout in the ceiling. "The wall is 400-meters high. You don't mean . . . ?"

"Yes, I do. Now, do you want to see Heracles' men bounce off the wall or would you rather go back to your room?"

Jada answers decisively, "challenge accepted."

I hand her some gloves.

$$\lightning$$

"Gods! This is brutal." Jada groans as we pull on the rope together. We've been at it for over an hour, and I understand her frustration because my arms are killing me, and I'm sweating everywhere. But I see that we're close to the opening above and I'm filled with new vigor at the thought of getting off the platform.

"We're almost there," I say out of breath.

In fifty pulls or so, we finally reach a short steel ladder attached to the wall. Above us is open sky, the cool air feels wonderful on my skin.

"Finally," Jada sighs.

I climb up the ladder and roll onto the top of the stone wall. Panting, I crawl back to the opening and help my sister up. The wind whips at our cloaks, and Jada's hair is a tangle of flying braids when she collapses beside me and heaves, "never . . . again."

"Don't be so sure," I barely manage to say. "Look."

A grin spreads wide on my face at her sudden intake of breath. "It's beautiful," she says.

I sit up and stare at the scenery beyond. Though night has fallen over the surrounding areas, the Lunetas Bridge makes the view possible to see. It's difficult to decide which side of the wall to admire first, the Holy City within it or the land and waters beyond. Roughly fifteen meters of stone separates the two. Facing north is a lush red and indigo forest, beyond the trees are mountains. On the East side, is the Havmand Bay, its waters crash along a beach made of light pink sand. Heracles' peculiar ships mar the view, but only slightly. In the Western sky is the Gods' Window, its night sky twinkles with bright stars.

My sister shivers against the wind and pulls her cloak snug around her shoulders. "How often do you come up here?"

I shrug. "This might be my fifth time? Its lovely but getting up here isn't."

She makes a face at the hole we just came out of.

Getting to my feet, I extend a hand and help her up. Jada holds out her other arm for balance and keeps her knees bent uncertainly as if she may fall at any minute. "What?" she snaps when she catches me staring at her odd stance. "It's really high up! This is as close to the sky as I'll ever be."

I wiggle my brows. "I was going to suggest we sit on the edge to watch the show."

Her mouth drops open, "Surely you jest." She glances at the edge of the wall and back to me, a tinge of fear in her eyes.

I give her a smug smile. "Are you afraid of heights?"

Her answer is a silent but deadly stare.

"You are!" I hoot. "Who would've thought that my grand sister is terrorized by a mere few feet?"

She points toward the city below. "You call that a few feet? I have every right to be scared. And you can take me off whatever pedestal you've decided to put me on. I'm no better than you, Nikko." She pulls her cloak about her more tightly and stares at the Havmand Bay filled with ships. "I never have been. That's always been your silly way of thinking."

I'm caught off guard by the serious turn of the conversation. I feel like a chastised child. Something awkward passes between us, and I choose to ignore it. "Well, if we want to get a look at Heracles' soldiers, we'll need to sit close to the edge."

She sighs. "I didn't come all this way to turn back now." She points at me. "But you're gonna hold my hand the entire time! If I fall, I'm taking you to the Under with me."

I pretend to be insulted. "The Under? This chiseled jaw belongs only in Elysium." I step closer to her and take her hand. "You, however, will need to work something out with Hades so he doesn't feed your soul to that demon dog of his. But I'll put in a good word for you up above."

My sister rolls her eyes, but she smiles too, and I know all is right between us.

As we move closer to the edge, her legs wobble, and she clings to my arm. All the while the wind continues to blow south. "If you keep shaking like a leaf, we may actually fall," I say.

"I'm trying not to."

When we are as close as we may dare, I help her to a seated position. We then scoot the remainder of the way to the edge. I'm the first to let my cothurnus hang over, and I kick my feet back and forth against the wall. "See? It's not so bad, now is it?"

With her free hand, Jada clutches her chest, and her breathing is labored. "Easy for you to say—"

"Look, there's a camp."

She follows where I point. At the base of the wall are hundreds of white tents, with gold flags depicting a lion waving in the breeze. Every twenty tents or so, there's a lit fire surrounded by Heracles' men.

Jada scowls. "We're too far up to hear what they're saying."

"No matter, we just have to wait until one gets a bright idea to touch the wall."

And wait we do. The minutes pass into hours, the wind biting, but Jada and I remain in good spirits as we chat away.

The topic of Erebos finally approaches when Jada asks, "Do you think he's down there somewhere? Heracles' emissary?"

No, he's been imprisoned and tortured. I chew on my bottom lip. I hate lying to her. But then I recall an impossible report the council received a few weeks ago. Half-truths are better than a blatant lie, I guess. "There was a report from the scouts that Erebos was on one of the ships." I gesture to the bay with my chin.

"But what if that wasn't him?"

My eyes narrow. "What do you mean?" Does she know Father and I lied to her?

"Remember when Gareth and the emissary fought? He said that Gareth mistook him for another. Maybe he has a twin, just like you and I, but maybe they look alike?"

I feel my shoulders relax, but then I pause for a moment. There could be something to this. The council didn't think our scout was lying, just incorrect. But maybe he wasn't? Maybe he just saw someone else? "You're the one who knows him best. He could have a twin. Did he not mention a brother on any of your walks together?" I can't keep the hint of jealousy out of my voice.

Jada raises a brow as if she knows my secret. She probably guessed but avoids saying so. "He was mostly quiet with me; I was the one who did all the talking. He never mentioned any family, but every now and then he would ask . . . questions."

"What kind of questions?"

She laughs and touches a finger to her chin as she remembers. "He was so silly, he asked about human emotions, and the faces humans make and why, as if he isn't human himself. Very bizarre. But I still found him good company. It was entertaining to say the least." Her smile fades as she studies the white tents below. "It's too bad we have to be enemies in the end."

The guilt I try so hard to keep at bay returns, punching me in the gut. I'd like someone else to feel just as shitty as I do about this mess. If she only knew where Erebos really was and what's happening to him. "Don't tell me you would rather wed Heracles to spare him? We both know you must've been thrilled when Father called the engagement off."

"Nikko . . . do you think it horrible of me?" She gestures to the army. "All of this is because of me. Our people are suffering, but I'm so relieved that I don't have to marry Heracles. It isn't right."

I'm shocked at her admission. Jada has always put others before herself. I never expected her to admit otherwise. "I don't give a damn," I tell her firmly.

She appears stunned.

"Don't look at me like that. I'm a selfish prick. I've never been gallant. It's why I won't make a good king. I don't care enough about the people. I wouldn't sacrifice you for the entire city *ever,* and I won't spare a moment feeling remorseful about it. My offer still stands you know." I glance at her. "The day the crown falls on my head, I'll pass it to you. There's nothing standing in your way. If Andromyda can be a queen of her own making, so can you."

"We already talked about—" Jada's eyes go wide as she focuses on a movement down below. She squeezes my hand tightly. "Do you see him there? I think he's going to do it!"

I follow the direction of her gaze and my face breaks into a wide grin. "He is."

A bearded soldier leaves his group by the fire and makes his way closer to the main gates. The comrades he left behind are laughing and pointing while clapping one another on the back.

"They must be starving for entertainment as well," Jada says in anticipation.

The man stands only a few feet away from the Holy City's entrance and brandishes the sword at his side. He raises it chin level and takes off at a run for the gate. As soon as his weapon makes contact, the stone beneath Jada and I thrums with energy, and we both inhale in nervous excitement. The entirety of the iridescent pearl wall flares to life, lighting up in a magnificent hue of purple that nearly blinds me. Before I know it, Heracles' soldier is flying through the air as if a giant struck him. The man collides with a tent and sends it sprawling until it knocks down another. The soldiers nearby disperse in the sudden frenzy.

"Oh, my gods!" Jada shrieks. "That was *extraordinary!* I swear I never tire of seeing it!

"I don't either. When we're allowed to attend temple again, I may actually pray and give my thanks to the God of Gods for the entertainment," I manage to say in between bouts of laughter.

Jada's gaze goes to the West Window and, after a few moments, her happy expression turns to one of puzzlement. "Brother, tell me . . . How did you know the wall wouldn't repel us as well? We *are* sitting on it."

My body stills and my laughter slowly dies. I stare into my twin's face and deadpan, "Styx. I didn't know. I honestly didn't even consider it. We could've *died* just now."

A strangled sound comes from Jada's throat before she manages to say between clenched teeth, "So help me, Zeus, I am going to *murder* you."

Arachne

O' what a tragic tale is spun for the Queen of Spiders. Long ago, she was once mortal and the daughter of a poor shepherd in Apotmos. Arachne was skilled in the art of weaving. Her deft fingers spun wonderous tapestries that earned boasts so great, that it was said her work was grander than the goddess Athena's. Even Zeus could hear songs of the girl's praises all the way from Olympus, and he became enraged by her prowess. For what mortal could be better than the great daughter of he and Metis?

With one tap of Zeus' mighty scepter against the castle tile, the God of Gods summoned Arachne to Olympus and demanded a contest between the mortal girl and Athena. It was decreed that whoever lost would swear an oath to never weave on a spindle or loom again. Much to the mortal's anguish, her skilled fingers were no match for a goddess'. Zeus declared Athena the winner and maimed Arachne's hands before casting her back down to the mortal. Athena, who was just as clever as her mother, took pity on her rival. She transformed Arachne into a spider, so that she may weave to her heart's desire without ever breaking her oath.

CHAPTER XXXVI

3rd Week of Winter

Eimear

Peering over the banister to the glossy marble tile that is two floors below, I imagine leaping—the air whipping through me just before my body lands with a solid thud, bones fracturing and head spilling everywhere. Would it be quick if I fell from this height? Or would I survive and feel every agony?

Every night, I've been lighting the lantern in the highest north window of the castle, and not a visit or word from Steilos. It's been two weeks since I found that damn stone. My fear increases with each silent day that passes. What if he's not coming? What if he never does, and I'm just imprisoned here until I meet some gruesome end? I think about wasps daily now.

//He'll come,// my sacred-self says.

//You really think so?//

//If you'd train and focus yourself more, you'd know the answer.//

Easy to say but hard to do when anxiety claws at me, waiting to be fed. I try to push the macabre thoughts away and instead give my attention to the task at hand. My arms ache after carrying a bucket of soapy water up the stairs, just a bit farther, and I'll make it to the ballroom. At the end of the week, General Charos will be hosting a gathering of sorts, and he wants the castle to be in pristine condition.

Entering the ballroom, I'm about to set the bucket down when someone shoves me from behind. I fall forward and my chin hits the marble floor. My burlap hood useless, does nothing to soften the blow and water I labored to get up the stairs, spills across the tile.

My jaw hurts terribly and when I try to get up, I'm pushed back down. My assailant pulls the sack from my head and then grabs a wad of my tangled hair before shoving my face into the water. The soap burns my eyes.

"You think you're better than the rest of us, don't you? What's it like being the General's whore?"

I recognize Ruby's voice and note that offering my language skills to Charos must've put a new target on my back. I regret ever pitying the bitch as she presses down harder, nearly breaking my nose.

"Saray is only nice to you because you're an eyesore. Don't mistake her mercy for kindness."

Ruby's knee is in my back, and I don't have the strength to throw her off despite my roiling anger. I only manage to turn my head sideways and yell out at as I claw at her hands with my nails.

She smirks at my feeble attempt to fight her. "There's nothing special about you so don't get comfortable. You're going to die here like the rest of us."

I scream louder hoping that someone will come, maybe Saray. My plan works, because soon heavy footsteps approach from the stairs.

"You're a stupid cunt, you know that?" Ruby says before spitting in my hair. When she eases her knee from my back, I quickly roll so that I'm facing upward and kick my foot out, catching her in the chest. Her face gives a surprised "O" before she collapses on top of me and starts sending hurried punches to the sides of my stomach. I make myself into a ball to ward off her attacks. She stands, panting and gives a final kick to my back before disappearing from view. I lay in pain with my eyes burning, and my breath comes in shallowed gasps when new footsteps enter the ballroom.

"What in the Under is going on in here?" A guard growls.

His voice travels across the room and I nearly start to cry. No one is coming to my rescue. I should've kept my mouth shut and taken the beating from Ruby.

"Look at the mess you've made," the guard walks toward me and reaches down for my discarded hood.

I recognize Anders from around the castle. He's slightly older than me, but still possesses a boyish face. His black boot takes up the field of my vision as he crouches down and examines the burlap sack. Reaching for me, he squeezes my cheeks firmly between his fingers.

"Ah you're the one with the burn. I've been wondering what you look like under that hood of yours."

I can't control my hate and jerk my face from his grasp.

Anders' smirk is lopsided. "You shouldn't have done that," he says before standing. He wipes the hand he touched me with on his leg as if cleaning himself. "Get up."

I wince as I do, and Anders shoves the hood into my hands.

"The General's order was for you to wear this at all times, and you were caught dallying from your duties. On top of it all, you made a mess. That's a long list of infractions."

I stay frozen, not sure how to respond to the threat in front of me, my emotions running rampant. What's going to happen to me now?

Anders' voice is calm, "Put that back on and go to the wall."

I do as he says.

"Turn around and put your hands out. Keep em' there. Move a muscle and I'll make this worse for you."

I follow his orders and face the wall; the stability of the stone does nothing to stop the tremors of my arms.

"I'm in a forgiving mood today, so I'll go easy on you." He says this lightly as if we're old friends.

I hear the whip whistle through the air before it lands on my back. My nails dig into the stone, bracing myself. I grit my teeth as the pain feeds my rage. I don't cry out.

"You're a tough one." Anders sounds surprised. He paces behind me methodically, taking his time. The waiting is almost worse than the fall of the whip, but when he hits me again, it's with more force than the first. My legs wobble beneath me. I remain impassive through the third lashing, even though the skin of my back has opened up. By the time the whip comes down for a fifth time, I break with an agonized scream.

"Finally! My arm was starting to tire."

I bite back a retort as tears stream down my face. The humiliation is unbearable.

Anders places a hand on my shoulder and leans in close. "If you think this is bad, wait until the next Confessional. I'm adding you to the list."

I watch Astera in the garden as my insides churn with hatred. Ruby . . . the resentful bitch. She shouldn't have been able to sneak up on me like that. My sacred-self is right, I need to be more diligent at practicing my Gift. But it's difficult to do when I all can focus on is how afraid I am every waking moment. It's been hours since the whipping, my back is nearly healed after a dip in the spring. I should be practicing right now, I'm physically well. But instead, I sit quietly, reliving the past afternoon and Anders' threat. I'm terrified of Confessional.

I wring the burlap hood in my hands. It's rare for me not to be wearing it, but it's the only act of defiance I can muster to keep my spirit up. Even still, I'm uncomfortable with my face exposed. I've grown used to hiding it.

I'm going to die here if I don't leave soon. The General could order a Confessional at any moment. I could be Nova's next meal. I tremble at the thought of the chimera feasting on me, chewing on what little meat my bones possess. I've done my part, Steilos should've come for me by now. It's not fair.

The idea of leaving without any help from him becomes more and more alluring. I could bypass the guards easily. I'm not sure if Saray would believe me, but maybe I could convince her to run away with me, if I showed her what I can do with my Gift. But then—where would we go? Two runaway slaves? People would know what we are, we're branded. And what about the wild chimeras? Steilos had mentioned they were migrating more this way since the war started. I couldn't possibly fight them as I am now. Feeling hopeless, I rip a handful of grass from the ground. I wish I was stronger.

I watch Astera tuck a strand of premature gray hair behind her ear as she goes to pull a weed from her flowerless garden. I wonder how she fits into all this. Would Astera even come with me? Would she want to?

She notices me staring. Her hand hovers over another weed. "Something upset you today, you've barely spoken a word. What happened?" When I let silence hang between us, her brow furrows with hurt. "I've told you everything there is to know about me, but you don't do the same. You keep things from me, and it isn't fair. That's not how friends act."

I bristle at the accusation but then relax just as quickly because she's right. I've told her a very condensed version of how I came to be at Notos, and I don't speak about my day-to-day for obvious reasons. Who wants to hear details about the dull life of a slave? I've spoken of my village, and the happier times with my family and Gareth. Astera seems to enjoy the stories I spin from my lessons with Elder Marcus the most.

I sigh, defeated. "That's because there's very little good that happens to me here, and the best thing about my days are coming to see you. I don't want to plague you with tales of cruel guards and unhappy slaves."

Astera turns to face me, the light from the Sister and Brother moons makes her eyes more beautiful. "Friendships aren't one sided. They mean telling each other everything. If you're hurting, I want to hear of it," she says.

Crickets chirp and the sound of a nightbird trills across the darkened sky. I don't know if it's because the string that's keeping me together is beyond frayed, but Astera's sincerity cuts through and something inside me gives way as I tell her my story.

All of it.

The things I haven't been able to speak of: Jud and Armon, the man I murdered, burning my face, the horrors I've witnessed since coming to Castle Notos—all is finally spoken until I'm left sobbing. At some point, Astera sat beside me; now she wraps her frail arms around my shoulders and hugs me.

When my breathing steadies, and my tears slow enough to see her face, she pulls back and looks at me. "When my father used to come to my room, with his knife . . . after a while I began to welcome the visits because the cutting was better than being alone. And when he stopped, a part of me missed it—" She lets out a frustrated sigh. "I don't know how to phrase it, nothing will fix anything you went through. I'm a complete mess because of him, *but* meeting you has made me better, and I want to live again." Astera gives my shoulder another squeeze. "I want to be that for you too, is what I'm trying to say."

Mixed emotions swell within me, and I battle with the question that I've been longing to ask for weeks now. At the heart of it all, she's still the General's daughter, but I can no more blame her for her parentage than I can blame the suns for rising each day. I give up and press my palms to my wet eyes. "If I had a way of leaving this place, would you come with me?" My hands drop slowly when I don't hear an immediate answer, and I glance at Astera hesitantly.

Her eyes are wide and brimming with tears. When she catches sight of my face, she laughs. It's only the second time I've ever heard laughter from her.

"Did you honestly think I'd say no?"

I bite my lip. "I wasn't sure, with your father—"

"You know how I hate him."

"The plan isn't fully worked out yet but—"

"I don't care. At your word, I'll be ready. Even if we die trying, I'll be satisfied. I won't spend the rest of my life here."

I breathe out, "Good, I was hoping you'd say that because we might. You know. Die."

Astera nods slowly. "I don't remember what freedom feels like. But I'd risk death to find out."

I close my eyes and conjure an image of rose-colored foliage on a bright sunny day. I remember the feeling of running through the woods with Gareth, Zadok was at our heels, trying to keep up. The way the wind whipped through my hair and the lightness in my heart as if it was years ago and not a span of months. And then it happens, that spark I've been missing, it comes backs to life, like fuel to a dying fire. It continues to spread throughout my breast, down to my toes, out to my fingertips until I feel the certainty in my bones. Steilos will come.

CHAPTER XXXVII

3rd Week of Winter

Eimear

Days later, I'm laboring in the kitchen. It's too hot inside with the flames from the hearth and the space is overpacked with bodies at work. The smell of roasted venison hangs in the air, making my mouth water—I haven't tasted meat for months, not since Angus snuck me that bowl of stew. My stomach rumbles loudly, and I try to recall the feeling of a full belly but find that I can't. I'm grateful to be rarely assigned to the kitchen; being surrounded by food when you're starving is its own kind of torture.

The room is a frenzy of activity. All of Heracles' generals are gathering for dinner tonight, and Charos is to play host. Only the finest food can be served to his honored guests, and everything must be perfect. Fatigue is set deep in the eyes of the five women who stand with me at the kitchen's center table. We each work on separate tasks for the meal preparation. Arete in particular, seems troubled; she frantically stirs the batter in front of her. We both remember the retaliatory kick to the cunny I gave her, but for now, we have mutual reason to be anxious and are acting civil.

The kitchen needed extra hands, and she was one of the unfortunate victims to draw a short reed from Saray's clenched fist this morning. Me, however, I was *singled* out. I don't know how much more fright I can take. It's one thing to labor in the kitchen, that I can manage, but we're also to serve the meal itself—to a roomful of killers. And the General specifically asked for *me*. I pray I'm not the entertainment.

Even Angus is in a harried state, running from person to person to check the quality of everyone's work and shaking his head when he isn't pleased. I swear quietly as more sweat gathers around my neckline underneath the burlap sack. I ache to take it off. I'm currently rolling dough and covered in flour up to my elbows. I take my frustration out on the thick paste, pounding it harder than necessary, which earns me a cocked brow from Angus. He rushes over and inspects the dough with his finger and frowns before reaching inside the canister beside me for more flour. However, his hand comes up empty. We both look at the crumpled flour sack left in the corner of the kitchen, Arete poured the last of it into the canister earlier.

Angus taps the container and struggles with his severed tongue, "…MORE," he manages to say.

I nod, happy for any excuse to leave the inferno and the stress, even if it's only for a short time. I glance at Felton, the current, sweaty kitchen guard, for permission and he motions his thumb towards the exit. I feel the change in temperature as soon as I step into the hall. I pull at my dress collar to let the air flow in, and sigh with relief. As my head clears, a thought occurs. Tonight, all of Heracles' generals will arrive at Castle Notos, and I'll be *serving* them. If I don't die, it'll be a good opportunity to observe them, and possibly get information. I bite my lip. But, what does it matter? What could someone like me do with the information anyway?

//You never know what you can use in the future. The possibilities are endless. Never doubt yourself.//

Despite my hunger pains and exhaustion, I grin. //Do you see the irony in that? The 'future,' couldn't you just give me a prophecy or something. Tell me my outcome?//

//Very funny. It doesn't work that way. And all the fun of living comes from not knowing what happens next.//

With my smirk intact, I make my way to the storeroom and try to imagine what the other generals will be like. Are they similar to Charos? Or different monsters entirely? I'm passing the castle foyer, when I catch sight of a guard arguing with a large man whose back is turned to me. He holds a sack of grain slung over his shoulder.

"I'm sorry, I'm not permitted to leave my post. General's orders." The guard doesn't sound at all apologetic.

The other man adjusts the grain that has begun to slip down his arm. "I understand, but I have a delivery for General Charos, and there isn't anyone out front to help unload my wagon. The cases of wine will sour under the suns if it sits too long. Where's Saray? She's the one who usually handles my cargo."

It's Steilos! He's here! I halt my steps.

The guard is annoyed but knows better than to upset the General. "Just move it to the shade for now and be gone. One of the slaves will unload the wagon later."

"Excuse me, Sirs, I may be able to help," I say.

Both the guard and Steilos turn in my direction. "I'm going to the storeroom to fetch flour for the kitchen," I say to the guard. "I can show him where it is and help move the perishables if you like."

The guard's eyes narrow at my apron and sweat stained uniform. "Are you trying to get out of your scullery duty?"

"Nnn...oo—" I stammer. "I just thought—"

The guard reaches for the whip at his side.

"Stop! Stop," Steilos swears at the guard and takes a step closer, his frame towering over the man. "I need the General's wine unloaded. Now. If it's sour when he's trying to enjoy himself, I'll be sure to tell him why that is. Understand? Let the girl show me to the storeroom, and I'll handle everything else."

The sentry deflates. "Fine," he says with a sniff.

Steilos turns his attention back to me. "Shall we?"

"Yes, Sir," I tell him and bow slightly to the guard before turning on my heel, heart racing. He's really here. I'm far down the vacant corridor when Steilos' footsteps catch up to me.

"What the fuck are you wearing? I didn't even recognize you," he hisses.

"Not here," I whisper back. "Sound has a way of traveling across these walls."

Steilos grunts and shifts the grain over his shoulder. He follows me the rest of the way in silence.

When we arrive, I open the storage room door for him. "After you," I tell him sweetly. There's a lit sconce beside the door's frame, giving just enough light. He eyes me as he walks across the threshold into the dim room lined with shelves of supplies. Not able to contain my anger any longer, I shove his backside with my right foot. He stumbles forward and drops the sack of grain. I shut the entrance behind me, my eyes never leaving him. "Look who finally decided to show up? I lit the lantern over two weeks ago! I thought you abandoned me!"

Steilos rights himself, his mouth set in a grim line. "Did you think it was that simple? I need a reason to come to Notos. The General must grant me an invitation first, otherwise, it would raise alarm."

I scowl under my hood. My anger isn't sated by truth. I notice his bright eyes without shadows, his glossy hair and muscular body. A perfectly healthy man. He hasn't suffered like I've suffered. Standing this close to him now, I can smell the leftover clove from his pipe. A storm of emotion brews within me at the sight of him. I think I hate him, and yet, he's my salvation.

"It's been hard," my voice cracks, chin quivering with imminent tears. The shock of seeing Steilos in the flesh, ready to keep his promise, is nearly too much for me. It's almost over. I'll walk away from here soon. Free.

Steilos' face contorts, his guilt palpable. He reaches for my hood and attempts to remove it, but I slap his hand away. "Don't." He's about to ask the question, but I answer him before he does. "I want to wear it, so just leave it be."

He raises a brow but doesn't question my choice. I know he wants to talk about the stone, but it's plain that he's uncomfortable. Steilos must be too ashamed to ask. I, however, want to get the fuck out of here. I'm not in the mood to mince words. "You don't have to dance around it, we both know why you're here. I found the citrine, the General wears it at all times. It's embedded in that gold bracer of his. It would be suicide to try and steal it though. You'll need an army to get it." I'm surprised when I don't see disappointment in his eyes, but excitement.

Steilos grins, "I don't need an army, just the right people."

"He's won the entire Southern Region. Don't you think you're being a bit presump—" I'm surprised again when he pulls me into a tight embrace with his giant arms and lifts me from the ground. He twirls me in a circle.

"You've found it, kid. Thank you," he says, voice filled with emotion. Carefully, he puts me back down. "I've been searching for a long time. Thank you for everything you did to find it."

"Spare me the gratitude, it doesn't make a damn thing better." I push him away. "Whatever this stone is to you and Ares, whatever game you're playing at, it wasn't worth my suffering." I give him a pointed look. "Now what do we need to do to get me out of here?"

Steilos straightens up and puts space between us. "You stay here while I unload the cargo, when I bring the last crate, you'll sneak out with me. I'll put you in the false bottom of the wagon. It's perfect timing."

A sinking feeling hits the pit of my stomach, because it isn't *perfect timing* as he says. There's no way I'll be able to convince Saray to come with us and retrieve Astera from her tower in time and unseen. No matter the ability of my Gift, it's too risky.

"What's wrong? Steilos asks. "You don't seem like someone who's about to make a break for it."

I'm fighting the overwhelming urge to say fuck-all and leave with him now. I want to scream, but I don't. "I need more time," I manage. "I have to stay."

"Are you fucking kidding me?"

I don't respond.

"Gods, you're serious. Kid, why in the Under, would you want to stay? Did someone knock your sense out of you?"

I recall my various beatings and wonder about my state of mind. When I tell him my reasons, tell him about Saray and Astera, Steilos puts a hand on his hip and stares at me. "You want me to get *three* of you out? What you're asking is unreasonable and stupid."

I don't bother telling him Astera's parentage, I don't want to give him another reason to be dissuaded. I make myself grow taller, squaring my shoulders, and press my finger into his chest. "Steilos. You owe me. You knew what I'd be facing here when you asked me to find the citrine. You know that Charos is a monster, and still you took me to the den of the beast. I've seen things that I'll never unsee. I've been starved, beaten, and whipped. You're indebted to me at least one hundred-fold if not a thousand."

He looks miserable—perhaps engulfed by guilt—and looks heavenward, as if to plea with the gods. He should know better; that they, of all beings, don't fucking listen. He seems lost in thought, hopefully taking my demands seriously. When Steilos curses, I know I've won.

He rubs a hand over his face, tired. "I've been putting a crew together of some of my . . . associates. We want to ambush the General, but we're not ready yet. I don't know how long it will be until I'm back. You're risking too much by not coming with me now. You understand that right?"

//Another choice. Another splitting branch in the great tree of life. What way will you choose to grow?//

I know better than to ask her what choice I should make. For a moment, I think about my encounter with Anders, and how I'm on the next Confessional list. What if Steilos doesn't come back before then? But I also know, that if I go with him now, Saray and Astera's chances of being rescued are slim. My gut is telling me to stay, I have to trust in that. My instincts wouldn't lead me to death, would they?

"I comprehend all too well unfortunately." I cross my arms. "But before you leave me again, I think it's time you told me the truth about this stone. You're not a dumb arse. You would've searched every text and legend after Ares tasked you to find it. I've suffered and gambled too much on this mad treasure hunt. I deserve answers."

Steilos sighs and removes his pipe from his shirt pocket but then glances around the storeroom and decides against smoking. "Gods damnit," he swears before putting it back.

My temper flares. "For Styx sake. Answers. Now. I'm expected back any minute, where's your sense of urgency?"

He gives me a look. "Kid, has anyone ever told you that you're more like a crabby hag than a fourteen-year-old girl?"

I roll my eyes, but he can't see. I let my silence be answer enough. But I'm not really an old hag . . . Am I?

Steilos shakes his head, but finally answers: "The stone grants abilities similar to those who are Gifted with a god's ichor. The particulars, I'm not sure of. But I've a hunch that if it can be taken away, the General will be nothing but a man and easy to kill."

I recall having an odd sensation when I was around both the citrine and my brother's azurite. I wonder at the weapon left in the hands of a seven-year-boy and how he'll wield it. "So, you're telling me that General Charos isn't Gifted, that this stone is giving him the ability to manipulate the earth. He's nothing but a fraud?" It's hard to believe the power he used to kill that man on the day of his arrival wasn't his. I need to ask Astera to verify this, I'll speak with her tonight.

"I think so."

"Wait, so you don't know for sure? What do you plan on doing if you're wrong? The General could easily kill you and anyone you bring to Notos. I've seen it."

Steilos shrugs. "The risk is worth the reward. Imagine ridding Ehvara of one of Heracles' most powerful generals. And a brutal one at that."

The smoky crimson energy around him pulsates just slightly, and I shake my head at his dishonesty. I've become more adept at using my own Gift. "Being a nuisance to Heracles isn't what you're after. Don't lie to me. Why do you want the citrine so badly? I know a god told you to find it, but I've a feeling there's more to it than that."

"What if I told you, it's because I want more power of my own? Isn't that reason enough?" Steilos cocks his head to the side.

His aura pulsates again. Why lie about this? What's he hiding? I decide it doesn't matter and that I'm out of time. I'm due a beating at this point for taking too long. The kitchen guard is going to ask questions. "I know you're not being honest and that you're hiding something—" Steilos is about to interrupt but I push on, "Whatever it is, fine. I don't care as long as Charos dies. Just make sure you hold up your end of the bargain and come back for us. But remember my previous warning, your lies will be your undoing."

Steilos' eyes narrow. "I honor all of my agreements."

A hint of a smile plays across my lips, finally, some truth. I uncross my arms and head towards the door. "I'll light the lantern again when I'm ready for you. Try to make it here faster next time," I say over my shoulder then blow out the candle. For once, I leave Steilos in the dark.

My swollen eye makes it difficult to see as I work. The time with Steilos earned me a punch to the face from the kitchen guard. I was expecting worse, so this is good. I'm almost gleeful, feeling like I got away with something. I'll be free soon. Steilos restored my faith in him. He's a man of his word, he came back for me, and he'll come again. Whatever happens next, the dinner, Confessional, I'll be damn sure to survive it.

The afternoon passes in a blur of kitchen work. Every so often, I take note of everyone else, especially Angus, and guilt strikes. Is it right to leave without them? There are some that are cruel like Arete, Neyda, and Ruby, but the others have never wronged me. What could they become if they weren't here? They deserve freedom just as much as I do. Then again, if Steilos can have the General killed, then couldn't we all be free?

But as Heracles' generals begin to arrive one by one, I worry more about myself and pray I survive the evening ahead. From the kitchen, I can't see the generals when they enter the castle, but their presence is noted as their men make camp outside. By nightfall, hundreds of tents can be spotted through the rose-colored ivy of the kitchen window. There's a chorus of birdlike screeching from beyond the castle gates, a sound that has everyone in the kitchen, including Felton, spooked. This isn't a normal dinner party.

Nerves frayed, my fingers shake as I garnish the last plate in front of me. I try to calm my breathing just as Saray enters the kitchen. She claps her hands.

"Everyone, our guests are about settled. General Charos has requested the meal to begin, get ready."

I remove my food-stained apron, and hang it on the wall behind me, as do the five other women who've been working with me all day. Angus lines up the first course of plates, and places domed silver covers over them. He loads them onto a cart. Saray leads us out of the kitchen, pushing the cart in front of her, and the six of us walk toward the dining hall. Angus stays behind, already busying himself with the second course.

When we enter, the atmosphere is thick with tension and loud banter. Usually, a long barren table occupies the space, but it's been replaced by a triclinium arrangement. The klinai with their large cushions, have been arranged in a U formation. Small, personalized tables are in front of each kline and colorful rugs cover the floor. The lackluster room has been turned into one of overindulgence for merely five people.

To my surprise, Astera shares a klinē with her father, who sits at the right end of the U, facing the door. She wears a black silk chiton, and her hair is delicately coiled atop her head, making her almost stunning. Saray worked wonders to prepare her, but no amount of powder can hide the shadows under her eyes or her sunken cheeks. I'm worried for her. We lock eyes briefly before she averts her gaze. No one can know that we're friends.

Quickly, I glance around at the other generals, and on the left end of the U, opposite to Charos, sits a man with his back to me. He's so massive that I've never seen the like. His skin is a deep brown and he has a booming voice. I pick up from the conversation that his name is Lysias. Next to him, is a young man cut from very different cloth. Fine-boned and skin the color of cream, he sits quietly, eyeing the giant as if he would like nothing more than to see him drop dead. But truly, it's the woman at the bend of the triclinium who draws my attention.

While the others sit upright, she lays like a queen against her pillows with an air about her that isn't human. In fact, she glows. Her face is angelic, with eyes of crystal blue, like the clearest spring. Her skin is a cool dark, reminding me of rich soil buried deep underground. The woman's black crown is multicolored, long bright blue and magenta braids cascade down past her shoulders. She wears a white dress that hugs every curve, the soft fabric drops dangerously low to put her voluptuousness on display. Power radiates from her perfect body, making every hair on my arm raise. She is ageless, breathtaking, and terrifying all at once. I'm certain I'm in the presence of a god.

//If Persephone sees your eyes, she'll know you've been marked by Metis. Like the stone and Charos, we cannot foresee your probabilities with her.//

//The Goddess of Spring? Why does she serve Heracles? I thought Persephone was one of the kinder gods?/

//A kind god can also be ruthless. Thus is the nature of duality. We recommend keeping your identity concealed from her.//

I recall the story Saray told me when I first arrived, how Persephone murdered Minthe for lying with Hades, and know this to be true. The goddess laughs, the sound is gentle, like springtime rain, and a part of my heart twists in jealousy. A need overwhelms me, like that of an animal seeking dominance. It feels like Persephone has touched something that is *mine* and should be punished for it. My nostrils flare angrily under my hood. Just as quickly, the spell is broken, and I wake from my sudden possessiveness in a haze.

What is wrong with me?

I don't have time to contemplate my irrational behavior as Saray rolls the cart toward the triclinium, and I follow behind with the others.

When she stops in front of General Charos, he gives a nod of his head for permission to serve. Saray gestures to the five of us, and we each take a silver plate from the cart. A woman at the front of our line serves Lysias first. I count the women ahead of me and I'm relieved to know that I'll be serving Astera. To Arete's misfortune, General Charos is her charge. I sense the girl's overwhelming fear behind my back. When it's my turn, I keep my head down and shuffle forward; I'm careful not to look at Persephone or the other generals.

"What's wrong with that one?" The man beside Lysias asks before taking a sip of wine.

My body is taut, muscles screaming to flee as I place Astera's platter in front of her. This is it. Charos must've wanted me here as a form of ill entertainment, and it's my time to perform. Astera and I lock eyes, I know she's holding her breath just like me.

"You don't approve of my servants, Valdez?" Charos almost purrs.

"Not at all, I just find it mysterious. Why the hood?"

"Because she's terribly revolting, and I don't like looking at unpleasant things."

Valdez's eyes glitter. "And yet she's here. Why keep her at all?"

My heart flutters with fear. Shit. Shit. Shit.

"She can speak and write in Voranian," Charos boasts.

Lysias' explosive laugh is a spell that breaks the tension, the giant leans back, his legs splaying wide. In the process, his knee knocks against General Valdez's table, nearly spilling his wine. Valdez purses his lips. Lysias stares pointedly at General Charos. "Your scheme only worked because of a mere slave? You're quite the lucky slag, worming your way into Heracles' good graces despite being *Gifted* so late in life. And you just so happened to acquire a Voranian when they aren't so easily found beyond their borders."

Charos leans forward in his seat. "I never said she was of Voranian lineage, although I do have an older one in my collection. I didn't see you complaining when I delivered what was needed. So, shapeshifter, what are you trying to imply? And under my own roof as I host you?"

I swallow. This has to do with the letter I wrote. The two men stare at each other in silence while I'm caught in between. I'm not sure if I'm excused to move on with my duties, and begin to sweat profusely.

Persephone sits up from her pillows. "I'm famished, can you both continue your pissing match at another time and let the slave finish?" Enough power radiates from the goddess to make both men comply, and Charos eases slowly back into his cushion.

The fact that Persephone can so easily reprimand two formidable men without batting an eye doesn't escape me, and my hands shake as I arrange Astera's utensils for her. She looks up at me, her expression frightened, but she reaches for her fork, lightly brushing my thumb in the process. I think she's trying to comfort me. The gesture goes unnoticed by the others, and I'm reminded of why I'm here, and why I stayed behind today. Astera deserves to be free just as much as I do. I bump her hand in return, a brief show of solidarity, and go to join the other slaves against the far side of the wall.

Saray rolls the now-empty cart in front of us and speaks in a lowered voice. "I'm returning to the kitchen for the next course, make sure to keep their wine glasses filled."

We nod and as Saray leaves, I turn my attention to the generals feeling lucky for the moment. From this vantage point by the wall, I'm of little significance and can ogle the four of them freely without being noticed.

As the dinner commences, Persephone traces her graceful finger around the rim of her goblet. The goddess' plate of food remains untouched. She seems bored and slightly dissatisfied.

General Charos notices. "Is the meal not to your liking?"

She fixes the General with a gaze that would make any man's thoughts turn to lust; he visibly blushes.

"Please excuse me, Charos, but I don't have fond memories of this place and seem to have lost my appetite. Though the passing of time has changed much." Her eyes scan the room.

The General appears as if he doesn't understand the goddess' comment, but I do. Below the castle is where Hades and Minthe used to meet in secret. I turn the story over in my head, I don't understand how the God of the Underworld could be unfaithful to Persephone. She's so beautiful.

Charos clears his throat. I've never seen the almighty General caught off-guard, and I relish the moment; even Astera hides a brief smile with her hand. The two of us will have much to talk about later. It's interesting to watch Charos pander to other generals, especially Persephone. And there's that barb Lysias made. Apparently, Charos was Gifted later in life, which *is* an enigma. Gifts usually manifest quite some time before adulthood. Steilos' hunch may be correct. The citrine could be fueling Charos' power.

I speculate from Persephone, Lysias, and Valdez's interactions with one another, that the three have known each other a long time. Whereas Charos seems to be new to commanding Heracles' armies. It appears he's trying to win favor. But aren't there five generals? I remember Steilos saying five, but only four are here.

As the third and fourth courses are served, there's still no mention of Heracles, no slip of extravagant plans despite their wine's being topped up numerous times. The only change is that Lysias' laughter has become increasingly louder. With a sigh, I lean against the wall, and begin to worry about what trouble my letter may have caused. I tell myself that a piece of paper can't have much of an impact on anyone. But the lie to myself is little comfort as the raucous dinner continues into the darkest hours of the morning.

Saray brings the cart in for a final time, and I serve Astera some honey cake. Her wine glass is empty, her cheeks have taken on a rosy sheen, and her eyes are glassy. She lifts her chin toward me and whispers, "I don't want to go."

I pause briefly, but then remember myself as she shouldn't know me well enough to speak so boldly, and back away from the center of the triclinium. What did she mean by—the sound of a goblet hitting the floor interrupts my thoughts as well as the Generals' conversation.

Valdez turns angrily toward Lysias. "For once in your life, can you not be a brute? Look what you've done, spilling my wine because you want to act like this is some sort of bacchanalia and not the eve of battle."

I back away quickly to join the others against the wall as ice begins to creep from Valdez's fingers. It spreads quickly and encases both their tables, freezing Lysias' dessert entirely and making the room drop in temperature.

"You're a bastard! I was going to eat that!" Lysias picks up the plate that is now a block of ice and throws it at Valdez's head. Astera gasps and Valdez leans back with unnatural speed as the plate just barely misses his nose and shatters against the wall. Persephone falls back onto her cushions in a fit of laughter.

Charos rubs his temples. "Do I need to remind you two that this is my home and that you're merely guests? Do you need to be restrained?"

The ground begins to quiver, and the silver plateware rattles, I steady myself against the wall. In the span of a breath, Valdez and Lysias are encased in stone up to their shoulders, the floor around them is broken and turned to rubble. The General grips Astera by the arm, and she looks as if she's about to faint.

The room is briefly silent like a tomb before Lysias throws his head back and laughs deeply. He struggles for breath as he speaks, "I'll behave, although I can't say the same for him." The giant juts his chin toward Valdez, who stares daggers in return. Stupefied, I watch as Lysias' skin starts to bubble and collapse in on itself before he completely disappears. All that remains of the man is the stone that previously encased him, it stands by itself like a hollowed-out sculpture. But then, a large black fly emerges from the shell. The insect flits about Valdez's head before landing on his nose, it twitches its wings.

"Get off me Lysias before I turn you into stalactite," Valdez hisses at the bug before blowing it upward. The fly then morphs into a crow and beats its wings while cawing, as if to say, *fuck you.*

"Same to you, asshole," says Valdez and the stone that encases him freezes over before exploding into icy shards that fly in all directions.

I throw myself to the floor, dodging ice that immediately smashes into the wall behind me. Astera cries out and I look up to see that her face is cut and bleeding. Her cowardly father erected a barrier of stone and earth to shield himself, but not her. Cautiously, I turn my head, and find that most of the other slaves ducked out of the way, just as I did. They're eyes are wide with fear, but no injuries. Saray, however, crouches low beside a brunette slave who bleeds from the neck. A frozen piece of stone must have nicked her artery.

I'm shaking as I get to my feet and note the wreckage of the room. Fragments of stone are scattered everywhere, the small tables have toppled over, and food goes to waste on the floor. The earthen wall General Charos created suddenly crumbles to dust, revealing him to be uninjured. Valdez crosses his arms over his chest and leans back in his chair, eyes never leaving Charos. "Try to contain me again, and I'll kill you, old man."

I don't think Heracles would sanction that," Charos counters, voice clipped.

Persephone gets to her feet, not a hair out of place, the ice looks to have flown directly around her. She walks slowly over to General Charos, her hips sashaying from side to side. When she comes up behind him, the goddess leans forward until her breasts slightly graze his shoulders; Charos visibly straightens and Astera presses herself against the far edge of the kline, putting distance between herself and the two.

Persephone grabs Charos by the hair and jerks his head sideways, "Never presume what my brother would sanction, you despicable man." She then arches a perfect brow at Valdez, "Prepare the troops. We're leaving."

A cruel smile spreads across his pale lips.

I feel so much sorrow as I contemplate the last few moments of chaos. They're monsters, Heracles, and his generals. Any gallant thoughts I had to avenge my village and mother are put into a new perspective. I'll never stand a chance against them. Styx, all of Ehvara won't. My heart breaks all over again.

Persephone plants a kiss that promises death on Charos' cheek before she gives a flip of her hair and leaves the room. Valdez follows close behind but, before he exits, he turns and addresses the General: "Don't keep us waiting, Charos. It's time."

Charos stands and rolls his shoulders, his hair mussed. He catches sight of me and the other women staring at him and scowls. "Out with you now!"

We practically run from the dining hall, leaving the dead woman behind. Astera is crying as we depart, a sound that makes my stomach twist.

Once we're back in the kitchen, the other slaves and I watch awestruck through the window as the generals exit the castle in a parade of torch-bearing soldiers that light up the dark night. Thousands of them stomp their feet to the generals' procession, making the windowpane rattle. Persephone leads the front of the line dressed in a white cloak, followed by Valdez, Lysias, and Charos, who are outfitted for war. Astera follows reluctantly behind her father, chained at the wrist. *I don't want to go,* she had said. Now I know with horror what my friend meant.

The goddess stops at the edge of the of the castle fields. She raises an arm, and her army yells a cry of war; the unidentified screeching outside the gates reaches a crescendo. Persephone gives a wave of her hand, and above her fingers, a faint emerald and crimson light begins to grow. The colors swirl counterclockwise and the light expands until it reaches a very large size, within the light, a long tunnel of stars appears.

"I've never seen such a thing," Saray gasps beside me.

I watch open-mouthed as Persephone walks through the tunnel and disappears. "It must be a portal, an actual portal," I whisper back, amazed. All the myths and legends Elder Marcus spoke of become reality right before my eyes.

The other generals begin to follow suit and enter the tunnel. Astera shakes her head and screams words I can't hear at her father before trying to run. Charos pulls on her chain hard enough to make her fall. He gives Astera a look of disgust before he walks into the portal, dragging her behind him. She kicks and screams, but soon disappears inside. I cup my mouth with my hand, fighting back tears. *My friend.*

The troops yell a cry of war and begin their march into the portal. Those who arrive from behind the castle gates pull bulky cages on wheels with them. Feathers stick out from behind the bars, the source of the screeching makes me draw in my breath.

When the portal swallows up the last of the soldiers and disappears entirely, I sag against the window. A sinking feeling begins to well in the pit of my stomach, and my shoulders become heavy as the weight of the truth settles there. With an army that size, Heracles doesn't seek to conquer a mere city, but to annihilate an entire kingdom. The letter I forged will aid in their destruction.

//Why…did you suggest I volunteer that day?// I ask my sacred-self.

//*It was a way to create more opportunities for ourselves.*//

//What? So, you *knew* this would happen? Thousands if not millions of people will be enslaved or even killed!// The treachery hits deep.

//Not precisely, it was simply one of the many probabilities that could occur. You now have more options for play in the Great Game. Congratulations.//

//Game! What game?// I shake my head, tears finally falling. //It doesn't matter anymore…I don't want to know. You're a vile creature, and I want nothing more to do with you.//

Enraged, I throw a wall up and shut her out completely.

Part IV

When Light Fails

"Forever heavy are the burdens on our shoulders,

but brother, know this: my back will not bend,

nor will my knees buckle."

— Jada

CHAPTER XXXVIII

3rd Week of Winter

Nikko

For once, I'm in my own bed, but I'm awakened by the sound of high-pitched shrieking. What in the Under? Are those birds? The racket seems to come from outside.

With a yawn, I slip the covers off and pad naked toward the terrace, moving the curtains that block my view. I open the door just a sliver and the noise intensifies—I've never heard such a terrifying sound. For a moment, I feel like prey. Danger is near.

As I stare out from my balcony, I'm not entirely sure of what I'm looking at. The citizens who have gathered in the streets seem just as confused as I. Large stalks wrapped in leafy indigo vines and nearly twice the size of a person, have burst from the ground. The streets are infested with them like an invasive weed as far as I can see. The source of the bird-like shrieks is nowhere in sight. Could it be coming from beyond the wall? It's almost impossible to comprehend a sound carrying this far into the city.

Down below, a brave citizen approaches one of the stalks with a broom stick and, with its handle, pokes a vine. To my amazement, a bright yellow flower blooms. The man turns to the crowd as if to say, it's safe, when the blossom starts to emit a gold powder that shimmers in the air. It takes only seconds for him to crumple to the ground. He lays there, still as stone, as if dead.

It must be poisonous. My eyes widen at the realization just as the citizens begin to panic and scramble to get away from the fallen man. Someone is pushed in the mayhem and barrels into another stalk. More flowers bloom along the vine, and they burst with pollen, dispersing a cloud of gold. Some of the citizens drop like flies while others continue to run, trampling the fallen underfoot. Soon cries from all around the Holy City blend with the screeching from beyond the wall.

We're under attack.

I immediately slam the terrace door shut, dress quickly and belt a sword to my hip. Not long after, I'm in the council chamber with my father and his advisors. They're on high alert, stress carved into their weary faces.

"Bacchus, what's the report?" The King asks.

My uncle's mouth moves, but it seems he has trouble finding words, his expression a mix of shock and grief.

"Out with it, brother! We must act quickly."

Bacchus closes his eyes, takes a breath, and then straightens, becoming the dignified commander we all know. He addresses my father. "Our scouts report that a flash of emerald appeared outside the wall and tore a hole in the air. It seems to be portal of sorts. An army of men came through it, at least one hundred thousand soldiers. They've joined Heracles' other men at the wall. There are also hundreds of covered cages. We assume it's where that wretched noise is coming from."

Even now, the devilish shrieks can be heard from inside the palace.

Hain speaks up, "A portal? Does that mean a god is among them? A god hasn't graced this land in centuries."

"Goddess," Bacchus corrects his Crib-Brother. He turns his attentions back to my father. "The scouts reported a woman of great beauty that glows like a sun. She closed the portal once all the soldiers were through. It's my belief that the stalks are her doing. They respond to touch. Otherwise, the poisonous flowers lay dormant. Their pollen seems to affect some but not others. We don't know why. Generals Charos, Lazarus, and Valdez have also been sighted. My King . . . war is officially at our doorstep."

My father's face is stoic as he digests the information.

Idan taps the table with a finger and looks at each of his brothers. "How were those damned plants able to grow inside the city? It's a direct attack. Has Zeus' protection failed us?"

"Vegetation doesn't have a working brain like we do." Hain offers.

The rest of us stare at him in stupefied silence.

Hain clears his throat and fiddles nervously with the timepiece hanging from his neck. "Think about it, a plant can't feel or think. It just is. There's no intent from its being. Zeus' protection functions on a person's intent, their thoughts that are for or against the Holy City. Now, this goddess may have the power to make them grow, but she isn't forcing nature to attack us. It sounds like if left alone, the stalks themselves would pose no danger. There's also the matter of where they came from. They're plants, and grew from the ground, easily bypassing the wall. Who knows when those seeds were planted, or how long they've been there."

Idan rubs his temples. "Fuck. Centuries of safety and we're brought to our knees by some gods' damned flowers?" He looks at Bacchus. "And what of the poison? What's it's progression?"

"The victims appear alive but unconscious. Our healers are unable to rouse them. The poison is eventually lethal, we have fifteen dead so far. The lead physician is researching a remedy as we speak. But it may be futile, it seems that only those with gods' blood can cure it. The boy with the Gift, from Paidia, he's been successful in waking a few."

Gareth. My hands clench to fists with worry. He better not overdo it. If the Return starts, it will put his life at risk.

The King appears grim. "We'll issue a warning to the citizens to stay clear of the stalks. Hopefully this will buy some time until we find a way to be rid of them."

"The solution, my dear Crib-Brothers, is to surrender," says Hain who twists the long chain of his necklace around a finger.

Bacchus glares. "You'd give up so easily, then? The army just arrived."

Hain looks to my father and pleads, "Can't you see it? The gods are against us. A goddess has allied with Heracles. He *must* be a legitimate son of Zeus. Please don't take offense, but if he desires the Holy City, he has more claim to it than you."

It's true then . . . he isn't an imposter. Our enemy is the legendary Heracles of all people. My mind struggles to process the revelation. How can we defeat him?

"You treacherous bastard!" Bacchus erupts from his seat, chair toppling. "How can you speak such an insult to the King!"

"Please don't look at me like that. My love for our King is true." Hain meets the eyes of every man in the room before continuing "You are my brothers, but we're in an impossible situation. The people will see Heracles as the rightful king, not Zephyr."

My uncle Bacchus is about to argue when Idan interrupts. "May I say something before we continue down this path?" When he has our attention, he sighs. "I've been pondering it, and must ask: Does Heracles even exist? I see the confusion on your faces but think on it. None of our soldiers have ever witnessed him in the trenches, we have no conclusive reports from when "he" attacked Kanthar and Anyalay. And what about now? Did our soldiers happen see him outside our walls?"

"No. There are no reports of Heracles in the flesh," Bacchus confirms. "There is word though, that he never leaves his stronghold in the Blood Isles."

"And what do we know of the Blood Isles? The land is unhabitable and nearly impossible to sail to. A very convenient place, in my opinion, for a false son of Zeus to say is his home. What if the previous treaty for Jada's hand was merely a ploy to have us open our gates to this heathen goddess so she can desecrate Zeus' holy place? What if she's the mastermind behind all this? In times past, the gods had their own wars between themselves." Idan shakes his head. "Before we raise our white flags, I suggest we wait and see what transpires. We still have supplies. This could very well be the largest ruse in Ehvarian history."

Hain crosses his arms, considering Idan's words, then directly asks the King, "What of Vorna? Are the Voranians still on schedule to arrive?"

"They'll be ready to attack by the time the twin suns rise tomorrow. We only need to last until then."

Hain's shoulders relax with the knowledge, and he eases into his chair. My father continues on, his hands clasped in front of him. "Have no fear, my brothers. I'll always do what's best for Ellanios. I don't wish to see our people in chains, which is what I fear if we surrender. But whoever this goddess is, she's made an egregious error in targeting what is sacred to Zeus and threatening his beloved people." With a steel gaze he turns to Bacchus. "Burn their ships."

My nose and mouth are covered by a cloth I've wrapped firmly around my face to protect myself from any lingering pollen. I watch as a soldier tosses a barrel of lamp oil into the canal and it disappears out of sight, under an archway. The canal eventually feeds into the Havmand Bay. A second soldier takes the rope attached to the barrel's end and connects it to another barrel before they repeat the process.

"You really shouldn't be here, Nikko, the King will have my head." Bacchus' voice is muffled beneath his own makeshift mask.

It's the middle of the night but there was no way I could simply *go back to bed*, as Father suggested, after the council meeting finished. "Uncle, I think your head is quite safe; he loves you too much. Now, tell me how this plan is going to work. Their sails are made of Arachne's silk, if my memory serves. Isn't her work inflammable?" How Heracles managed to acquire a vast amount of Arachne's thread is a mystery for a less exciting evening.

"The arachnid sails might be, but that doesn't mean the hull has the same protections."

"Commander, I think this is the last of it." A young soldier huffs, rolls the final barrel into the canal, and ties the end of a rope to an anchor at his feet.

I stare at the floating barrel warily. Fifty barrels were thrown into this canal alone. There are ten groups of soldiers around the Holy City completing the same task at other waterways. This will use all our stores of oil for the winter . . . although it's worth the loss if Heracles' fleet is destroyed in the process.

"How are we to get the barrels to the ships and then set them afire?" I ask my uncle. "The ships are too far away to be shot at from atop the wall with flaming arrows—and Hercules' army is camped right outside. They'll ambush any archers we send to the beach." I turn to peer down the canal's dark tunnel. "Once the barrels have made it to the sea, what then? We're not Poseidon. We've no control over the tides. They won't simply float to the ships because we want them to."

Bacchus glances at me sideways. "We need just one excellent archer to hit a single barrel with a fire-tipped arrow. They're all tethered. A chain reaction should occur, and the ships will be caught up in the blast. We'll have a diversion in place at the wall, so the army's attention won't be on the sea."

He's being evasive. "But how does the archer get close enough to do this?"

My uncle doesn't respond.

A group of five men approach us. They're naked despite the chill in the air, and have lidded cylinders that have been rolled in tar strapped to their backs. A bearded man with a build larger than the rest, has a hefty line of rope coiled around his left shoulder. I spot Ivor, my sister's overly handsome archery instructor among them, his bow is slung across his back. I'm appalled when I put together their dress (or lack thereof), the barrels, and my uncle's caginess.

"You're going to have them swim out to the ships with the barrels in tow," I say quietly. In my head, I quickly do a rough count of the other canals and the men delegated for the task. "That's nearly fifty of our own who would be on a suicide mission. They could be in the crosshairs when the barrels catch fire, drown, or even captured by Heracles' men aboard the ships."

Bacchus's expression is somber. "Such is war."

"And do they know that?" I look at the men who are soon to become sacrificial pawns and then back to my uncle. "Does Father?"

"The answer is yes to both. We've been planning to destroy the ships since they arrived," he says coolly.

"Prince . . . if I may speak," Ivor interjects. "I volunteered," he gestures to the men around him. "We all did."

The other four meet my gaze and dip their heads in acknowledgement.

"But Ivor, why? You're not a soldier."

"I'm not . . . but my sister was in Kanthar when it fell. I've not received a letter from her since, and I can only imagine the worst," he says. "Son of Zeus or no, that bastard is going to pay." He shrugs and motions with his thumb to the others. "Also, I'm the best shot with a bow in all of Ellanios, unlike these fellows who only seem to know their way around the pointy tip of a blade. They need me."

The man with a solid build and braided beard growls, "I'll have you know my *pointy tip* is going to save your arse, pretty boy, if we're discovered."

There's bravado in their voices, but the tremble in Ivor's right hand doesn't escape my notice, nor does the way the smallest soldier shifts uneasily from side to side. He appears barely older than me. They know they're risking death, yet they still put up a brave front.

This whole scheme makes me uneasy. I told my sister I would sacrifice the entire city just to keep her safe. And I still would. But seeing these men, ready to lay down their lives, stirs something in my selfish heart.

I pull my uncle closer and whisper in his ear, "We should wait until tomorrow, for the Voranians to get here. There's no reason to throw these lives away when help is so soon to arrive."

"Nikko, you must learn, in war, breaking your opponent's spirit is just as important as pushing a blade between his ribs. Maybe even more so because, when they fall, they stay down. If we burn their ships tonight, we deal the enemy not just a physical wound but a mental one. It relays the message that we're strong and, despite this poison plaguing our people, we don't fear them. And tomorrow, when the Voranians arrive, we'll crush Heracles' army so thoroughly they'll repent to Zeus for daring to set foot on Ellanion soil."

Suddenly, small flames appear above the wall, flickering to life one by one. Their illumination outlines hundreds of archers with their strings pulled taut. In seconds, they release their burning arrows all at once and the cries of soldiers on the other side soon follow when they find their mark.

Bacchus quickly addresses the men. "That was the signal! Go now, while Heracles' army is distracted. Stick to the plan, trust that your fellow squadrons will be in place. Godspeed!"

The five men beat their fists against their chests. "Yes, sir!" they yell in unison. I watch them wince as they ease themselves into the cold water of the canal, each with their own floating barrel to cling to.

As the last of them disappears under the archway and into the tunnel, my uncle says under his breath, "May your souls find rest in the Elysian Fields."

"You don't expect them to come back at all, then, do you? The King has sent fifty of our men to their deaths." My brain begins to work quickly in search for a solution. Fuck. Why am I doing this?

"Don't think him cruel, this is for—"

I hit Bacchus with a carotid strike, my hand like a knife against his neck. My uncle's eyes roll back, and he slumps against me. I lay him gently on the ground. I'll always prefer the blade, but I have to admit, training with Jada and the Queen has its perks. I stare at my father's unconscious advisor and dismiss any remaining indecision. I've only got seconds before he wakes; I must hurry.

Tossing my chiton to the side, I jump into the canal and gasp. Ellanios' winters are mild, it's not cold enough to harm, but fuck—it's uncomfortable. The water flow helps, but still, I swim as fast as my limbs will allow down the algae infested tunnel and think about how idiotic I am.

I'm no hero, so why?

All those nights policing the streets were to inflate my sore ego and better my chances of landing in another's bed. It wasn't because I actually *cared*. I'm not like these men who volunteered and had weeks to talk themselves out of this suicide mission but then didn't. I recall Ivor's earnest face and grin. Preventing Jada's pretty boy archery instructor from showing me up is reason enough. Plus, she'll cry if he dies, and that simply will not do.

The smirk on my face disappears when dim light begins to fill up the tunnel. The end swiftly approaches with the pushing current. I assess the water flow. Fuck all. Just. Fuck. I can't help but yell out as I attempt to swim backward.

I'm quickly swept under, my eyes burn, and saltwater goes up my nose as I lose my sense of direction. I'm held under by the rushing water, my lungs tight and soon to burst. This was a bad idea. One of my worst. I'm such a dumb slag. Just when I think I may drown, the current slows, and I begin to sink. Getting my bearings, I remember to kick my legs. I struggle at first but soon I'm breaking the surface and gasping for air.

"Is that the Prince?" Comes a voice over the water.

My eyes are on fire as I try to wipe the salt from them and swim forward at the same time. Four of the men bob up and down with the waves, clinging to the ropes tied to their barrel while Ivor sits astride his own barrel with his bow and arrow raised and pointed directly at me.

He lowers the weapon and grimaces. "Seems like it, Pip."

"This wasn't part of the plan," comes the quick reply from the young soldier.

The man with the braided beard is next to Pip and stares daggers into me. "No, it isn't, and his girlish screams probably notified Heracles' entire army that we're taking a fucking swim."

Closest to me, there are two other soldiers floating. One must be a descendent of Anyalay as the elderly man shares features similar to my mother. The other is in his mid-thirties, his wet hair at his shoulders and in tangles from the seawater.

"Sorry about that." I'm out of breath and reach for a free-hanging rope on the older man's barrel. "Don't mind if I hang out for a bit, do you? I think I'm about to drown if I swim any longer."

He shrugs his shoulders and looks to Ivor who, to my amazement, still manages to sit atop his barrel with perfect balance.

Ivor slings his bow across his shoulders and then stashes the arrow back inside the tar cylinder. "Due to the circumstances, I'm going to drop any pretense of royal pleasantries. So, tell me, what the fuck are you doing here, Prince? And don't say it's because you decided it's a nice eve for a swim."

I lean against the barrel, which gives my already tired muscles a rest. "Much as it might surprise you all, I don't like the idea of you dying on a suicide mission. I figured if I came along, you aren't allowed to let me die because I'm next in line for the throne. Thus, none of you can die. It's simple really."

I hear Pip swear, and Ivor stares at me without comment.

The soldier with the tangled hair, who's adjacent to my barrel, speaks up. "If we take him back now, we'll miss the window for lighting the barrels. You're important Ivor. The archers in the other groups aren't as skilled as you," he says and pulls a timepiece from the cylinder he wears around his neck. "We're already behind schedule."

Ivor swears. "Sandros I'm afraid you're right." He then addresses the man, Natsuo, whose barrel I share. "Uncle, what if you leave our company and escort the Prince to the palace?"

"While I appreciate you trying to spare an old man some hard work, my dear nephew, your mother will kill me if I let her only son die on a fool's errand." Natsuo then eyes the barrel we share. "Also, you need a minimum of five. It will slow the group's progress being down a man. You'd still miss the window if I leave."

Ivor punches his barrel. "Fuck!"

The only sound to be heard is the slosh of the lamp oil in its barrel as it moves with the small swells of the tide. Ivor sits up straight and says evenly, "since we're all about to die, I just want you to know what a dumb cunt I think you are, Nikko. You're selfish and entitled and a right fucking prick who takes his life for granted. If by the grace of the gods we get out of this alive, I'm going to punch you."

The slightest bit of shame runs its course, but still, I reply arrogantly, "Are you going to moan and bitch all night, or do you want to burn some ships?"

Ivor glares and slips back down into the water, hanging onto his barrel. He calls, "Get to swimming, everyone. Prince, keep up or drown trying."

CHAPTER XXXIX

3rd Week of Winter

Nikko

My limbs are heavy as we swim through the bay's cold waters. I try not to think about all the monsters that could've migrated here from the Thyellodic. The light from the Lunetas Bridge is considerably dimmer outside the Holy City and offers some visibility but doesn't completely expose us. The army ashore hasn't fired any arrows at us yet—a good sign. In the distance, I can barely make out the large hulls of Heracles' painted ships, their spider silk sails completely invisible as they blend in with the night.

"We need to hurry; it's almost time," Sandros says as he places the timepiece back in his tar cylinder. My throat tightens and my heart jumps a few beats. The danger is starting to feel real. Yiannis, the bearded soldier who is now in front of me, kicks his legs harder and propels himself and his barrel farther ahead. Natsuo and I share a barrel still, and follow suit. I'm nearly out of breath, we've been at it for an hour already. Or has it been longer? Time passes slowly when you're miserable.

Earlier, Sandros told me that Hain and Idan have been observing the tides and the turn of the ships for the last few weeks. The advisors have a decent idea of how long it will take for the barrels and their prospective soldiers to reach the vessels, and the best time to attack. Ivor is to fire arrows when the hand on Sandros' timepiece reaches the fourth hour. The archers in the other squadrons will do the same.

"How much time do we have?" Ivor asks while breathing heavily.

"Twenty-seven minutes, archer," comes Sandros' quick reply.

"Styx! We're cutting it close; that barely gives enough time to get out of the fire's range."

Natsuo speaks up, and I startle at the sudden sound of his voice, he's been mostly quiet. "Time to swim for our lives. Prince, join my nephew."

I swim over to Ivor's barrel as he hoists himself up and settles on it like he would a horse. Yiannis follows close behind me and attaches one end of the rope he's been carrying to the front of Ivor's barrel and fastens the other end around Pip's chest. Yiannis tests his handiwork with a firm tug and drops the rest of the line into the water before he turns to me. "So we can find our way back to you. Be of some use,

Prince, and keep pretty boy here steady for us. Don't let our group drag him too far forward."

"Aye!" I say seriously.

Sandros tosses his cylinder through the air, and Ivor catches it. "Try not to blow us up, friend."

Ivor shares a long look with his uncle, Natsuo. We then watch as the four tug their barrels closer towards Heracles' sleeping fleet and then disappear from sight. The line of rope attached to our barrel pulls every now and then, signaling that Pip is still on the other end. Whenever it happens, I do my best to kick in the opposite direction, so we aren't dragged with them.

Ivor looks down at me. "Now do you see how useless it was for you to come along? You can't shoot for shit, I've seen you practice. And we can't risk having you transport the barrels within range. All you managed to do was cost us precious time with your stunt. Are you proud of yourself?"

The archer's words feel like a punch. It's true. I've not been much more than a nuisance. "I'm sorry," I manage to say and mean it. But I follow it up with, "I'm not *that bad* with a bow. Also, I *am* keeping us from being pulled along with the others."

"Something I could easily have done without you." He casts a sideways glance at me and sighs as he peers out across the dark sea. "I am grateful not to be alone out here. I'll give you that much."

He sits with perfect balance atop the barrel despite my hanging onto it, and despite the choppiness of the water. I don't imagine he'll have any trouble firing his arrows.

"How do you do it?" I ask gesturing toward the barrel with my chin.

"What, this? Oh, it's been rigged with weights underneath to keep it steady. It would take a god's miracle for me to sit on it otherwise." He laughs. "You actually thought I was that grand? You're funny, Prince."

I knock my knuckles against the barrel and note how there's no lantern oil inside. Thank the gods.

Ivor notices and sneers. "Did you really think I'd shoot a flaming arrow while atop an explosive drum?"

I let my silence be answer enough for me. I already appear a halfwit, it isn't necessary to add to the growing list of my faults.

The minutes tick by. Ivor taps his thigh nervously.

"We should all be able to float our way back to the city with this one barrel, right?" I ask.

"That's the plan." He swears to himself when he checks Sandros' timepiece. "They have five more minutes."

Despite the heavy mood, I foolishly decide to ask another question. "How do you light the barrels if they've been sitting in sea water all this—?"

"Could you just shut your royal mouth?"

Properly chastised, I keep my remaining questions to myself.

Ivor shakes his head and looks at the West Window. "The tar cylinders on their backs are filled with oil. Once they're close enough to Heracles' ships, they're to douse each barrel with oil and swim back. Which will hopefully be—"

"There they are!" I whisper excitedly.

Natsuo and Sandros appear in the near dark. Supported between them is a nearly unconscious Yiannis. Pip follows up in the rear and doesn't seem to be fairing much better. I leave the safety of the barrel to relieve Natsuo, which garners me a wordless thank you.

"Fuck, you're a heavy brute," I mutter as I attempt to shoulder Yiannis's weight while kicking my legs to keep afloat.

"I…heard…that…" he moans.

Sandros is breathing heavily, gasping for air. "Don't you dare," he says to Yiannis, "pass out again." He pauses, takes a deep breath. "Or I'll let your sorry arse drown for real."

"What happened?" I ask.

Pip says from behind me, "Cramp."

The drum Ivor sits astride rocks dangerously when we all attempt to grab hold of the rope handles fastened to its sides. Once the barrel settles, Ivor checks his timepiece a final time and then removes the cylinder from his back. He opens it and pulls out four pitch-tipped arrows—balancing them on his thigh—a wax candle, and a flint. Ivor tosses the cylinder into the water and advises the other three to do the same with theirs. "Tar makes them waterproof, but it's also highly flammable, not to mention the residual oil inside. We don't want to go catching ourselves on fire," he says and spears the candle onto a notch hammered into the edge of the barrel.

The others quickly do as Ivor says, and he proceeds to light the wick.

Not long after, seven other small flames flicker to life across the sea. Ivor dips his arrow into the candle's fire and the tip burns bright blue and orange. "Two squadrons didn't make it," he says quietly and nocks the arrow, pointing it high in the sky.

"May their souls find rest in Elysium," the soldiers around me whisper, I along with them.

With eight arrows burning in the night, shouts of alarm soon carry across the water from Heracles' fleet. They know we're here.

Ivor pulls his arrow back. "This is for Kanthar, you cunts. I hope Hades strips you of your flesh and returns it at the end of each day for the rest of—"

"For the love of all fucks!" Yiannis snaps. "Shoot the arrow already you damned pretty boy!" And he does, and we all cheer as Ivor's arrow, along with seven others, hit their mark across the sea and the casks light up in a blaze. When none of them immediately explode, however, I'm a bit disappointed and concerned.

"Well. That was anticlimactic," I say.

The archer glances down at me from the drum and nods his head, "Yeah, it was, I thought…you know," and he purses his lips while making a gesture with his free hand and bow.

Yiannis, fully revived from his near-death experience, grabs Ivor by the ankle and gives him a good shake. "Fire another you damn idiot!"

And then I fully understand why Ivor has been titled the best archer in all of Ellanios. In quick succession, he lights one arrow after another and sends them flying through the sky, not one fiery shaft misses its target. The archers in the other squadrons are shooting as well and soon Heracles' armada is surrounded by a sea of burning barrels. There are hundreds of them floating in the bay. The men aboard the ships are oddly quiet however and busy themselves with lowering smaller crafts into the water.

"It's too late for you bastards!" Ivor yells. "Any second now—

The first barrel explodes, and then it's a chain across the bay. I'm deafened by the noise and taste salt as a wave of water crashes into us and sends our barrel sideways. I'm hanging on for dear life and cough up sea water when the barrel rights itself. Both salt and smoke burn my eyes, and I don't know what to do but curse.

"Is everyone all right?" Sandros is the first to ask.

We each confirm in different ways that we're alive and conscious.

"We did it!" Ivor hoots. He raises his bow skyward in triumph when a stray arrow whizzes through the smoke with a zing and catches him in the shoulder. He falls backward and topples into Sandros, taking the man with him into the rolling water.

"Ivor!" Natsuo cries as another arrow flies directly at us and anchors itself into the barrel.

"Keep your voices down." Pip warns quietly.

I search every direction, but only see Yiannis's surprised face and smoke. "How are they able to attack?" I ask. "They should be charred fish food by now." I hear screams of men in the distance. "We need to find Sandros and Ivor and get out of here while we still have the cover of smoke."

Yiannis nods in agreement, "Natsuo, on your order."

Ivor's uncle, peers around the other side of the barrel. "We won't find them in this madness. We'll have to pray to Zeus they find something to grab onto and are spared."

From the grief in his expression, I know it pains him to say it.

Pip asks, "Which way do we swim? I can't see nothing."

"The opposite direction of where the arrows come from," Yiannis says dryly as another finds its home in our barrel.

I kick with everything I have, and so do the others, but after hours of exertion, we're slow at it. Soon, our exhausted bodies fail us and we become still. Clinging to the barrel, we rely on the waves to push us. Fragments of debris from the explosion float along with us and the screams of dying men echo across the bay. I have plenty of time to reflect on how I inserted myself into this mayhem and decide that if I live to see another day, I'll take the coward's way out for all future circumstances that involve danger. The Holy City's walls, which offer Zeus' divine protection, become more appealing with each passing minute that I am cold, wet, and miserable.

Something bumps against my shoulder and my eyes jolt open. I'll drown if this keeps up, I was falling asleep. When I spy the bow that begins to drift away, I reach for it and pull it closer. It's not Ivor's. I don't want to think about what may have happened to the owner. Yiannis' body sags in front of me, and he slips down into the water.

"Hey! Stay awake!" I rasp and whack him in the head with the bow.

He hisses and touches the back of his head. "That fucking hurt, Prince!"

"Better than the alternative. You were falling asleep."

"I know," he grumbles.

"How's everyone else?" I call to the other two.

Natsuo's voice is a dry rattle, "Still here."

"I'd give my left nut for a good smoke and a warm bed," says Pip.

There's a second of silence, and I have to say it: "No one wants your left nut, Pip." I make a gagging noise for good measure and ease the bow I found around my shoulder.

"Why not the right?" Yiannis muses out loud.

"To the Under with you both."

I don't know how long we drift for, but through patches of smoke and fog, the sky begins to change as dawn approaches, a mix of blue, lilac, and hints of yellow. I wonder if the Voranians have arrived, if the battle on land has begun. I turn to look over my shoulder and go still. Through the plumes, I detect a portion of Heracles' fleet bobbing in the distance, the painted ships unmarred.

We failed.

The others see what I see, and there is an agonized silence around the barrel. How many men died? Did we lose Ivor and Sandros for nothing? Was all this for nothing?

"But any normal vessel . . ." Pip stammers.

Yiannis bangs his fist against the barrel. "Don't you get it? They aren't normal ships! The fucking sails are made of spider silk for gods' sakes. We were all fools to think Heracles didn't strike a bargain with the spider witch for the hulls too."

I ask: "But what kind of paint, or wood for that matter, is fire repel—"

"It's no use. The mission was a failure, and my nephew is probably at the bottom of the bay," Natsuo says.

The rest of us go quiet.

The additional soldiers from Vorna may very well be Ellanios' last hope. The thought doesn't sit well with me.

"Help! Please help me!" Comes the faint cry from behind us.

An Ellanion soldier clings to a piece of barrel yards from our group, his gray eyes are wide with fear. He casts wary glances over his shoulder as he kicks with urgency. There are two others that swim behind him.

One of them screams, "He's comin—" but he doesn't finish before his skin swells like a bloated corpse right before our eyes. The man explodes entirely with a loud pop, his blood and flesh flying. For a moment, the water is stained crimson before the tide disperses it, as if it was never there.

"Zeus help me!" screams the soldier nearest to the carnage.

Yiannis' voice is shrill for such a large man. "What in the Under was that?"

I gasp. Through the smoke and fog, Erebos stands on the bow of a small skiff. Two men work the oars, and Heracles' emissary has his arm thrust in front of him with his long fingers outstretched.

"Not what, but who," I finally answer.

CHAPTER XL

3rd Week of Winter

Nikko

Erebos is dressed in black, his face expressionless. The emissary's long hair is tied back, and whips in the wind. If I didn't know any better, I'd mistake him for Hades' ferryman on the River Styx. I stare at him, my exhausted brain trying to make sense of how he's here and not sitting in a cell under the palace.

Erebos' vessel cuts through the water, aiming for the two soldiers who still swim frantically in our direction. One kicks the other in the face, and he disappears for a moment before resurfacing, gasping for air. The gap between the two soldiers widens, and when the pursuing craft closes the distance on the man left behind, he explodes. Pieces of his body shower the air and return to the water like cast fish food.

How could I ever have fallen for such a monster?

"Keep swimming!" Natsuo commands from the other side of the barrel.

We all kick with newfound energy, leaving the remaining Ellanion to scream in protest behind us. If I had the time to feel guilty I would, but right now, I'm just fucking scared out of my mind. Nothing registers but the pounding of my racing heart and the sensation that my lungs are going to burst.

Seconds later, I think I hear his last cry, but it could be my idea of what I'll sound like when it's my turn.

Pip yells between ragged breaths, "I think that fucker . . . has a limited range." He pauses as he takes in air. "Fifteen, twenty feet."

Yiannis briefly turns his head to look at me, and then past, towards Erebos. I've been too afraid to do anything else but keep my eyes forward.

"The prick is gaining on us!" he yells to Natsuo.

There's a lull and not one of us speaks. Only the sounds of our labored breathing can be heard and the slosh of the sea.

"Men. You know what we must do. Are you ready?" Natsuo asks firmly.

What could we possibly do right now?

All of a sudden, Yiannis lets go of the barrel, as do the other two, and I'm left alone as they float away.

"What are you doing!" I scream.

"It was nice knowing you, Prince! Make lots of heirs for Ellanios," Pip calls out and kisses his hand in farewell.

Natsuo yells, "This is our final duty."

Yiannis stares at me as he treads water, silently glum.

They're buying me time so I can get away. "No!" I yell to them. But the men turn their backs on me and face their impending doom head on.

Fuck this and fuck their gallantry. My rage gives me the strength I need to hoist myself up and onto the barrel and straddle its girth. The barrel sways from side to side knocking me off balance, and I think back to Ivor who made shooting from it look so easy. That fucking cunt bastard lied.

I pull out an arrow imbedded in the barrel and attempt to nock it into the orphan bow I still have. It's morning and much of the smoke has cleared, but even so, my fingers are shaking, and the barrel is rocking with the waves. There is no way, even with the holiest of miracles, that I could ever shoot under these circumstances and hit Erebos. Fucking Styx!

I glance up and see the emissary's cold face as his vessel looms closer to the men who are trying to protect me. Heart in my throat, I don't think, I just do, and use the bow as an oar and row toward my certain death. Soon I pass Pip, Yiannis, and Natsuo.

Yiannis yells, "You damn slag for a prince! He's gonna kill yuh!"

I ignore him and instead call to Erebos across the water, "Hey! Hey you!"

He stares at me like I'm an insect and damn my traitorous heart for being a touch hurt by it. He raises his hand, and despite everything that's transpired, I'm shocked he hates me enough to wish for my death. I close my eyes and ready myself to explode, but nothing happens. I must still be out of his range.

"You bastard! Did you really just try to fucking kill me? You're supposed to be an emissary! But truly, what kind of man isn't smart enough to use their enemy's prince as leverage in war?"

Erebos cocks his head like a hound and lowers his hand just slightly. Then his mouth parts in surprise before curling into the semblance of a smile.

Something in my weary brain finally clicks. This isn't Erebos. I recall what he said to Gareth: "You mistake me for another." And there's the scout's report, and the conversation I had with Jada. He must be Erebos' twin.

I raise my voice. "Can we reach an agreement? I board your vessel and come with you willingly in exchange for my men's safety?"

Erebos' evil half stares at me for a moment then gestures with his chin toward the skiff. "On my word, your men will be spared."

Natsuo yells, "Don't do this!" But I ignore him.

When my barrel bumps against his vessel, the demon grabs hold of my left bicep and pulls me aboard. My legs want to collapse out from under me as soon as I touch the deck, but I use the bow to keep myself steady. This close to his face, I'm amazed. I know twins can be identical, but he's an exact replica, he even wears a silver chain around his neck.

"I'm not Erebos," he says flatly. "I'm Ker."

A small tinge of hope flares to life in my heart at the confirmation of Ker's identity, but this is neither the time nor place to be thinking of Erebos. Instead, I scrutinize the two panting soldiers who man the oars to my left. They're clearly exhausted from chasing us down and are of a solid build, but they don't wear the infamous vulture masks the Makatae are known for. Blessed Lady Fortune must be with me, they're a threat, but not as threatening as Ares' warriors would be.

"Did I say for you to stop?" Ker says to them.

I cringe as I'm reminded of his brother. Even their voices sound the same.

"No, sir!" the two soldiers say at once and resume rowing.

Ker's dark depthless eyes, that are so like Erebos', find mine. "You must be an unintelligent human. If you were intelligent, you'd have stayed clear of me."

Everything about Ker is predatory, and this close, he could murder me in an instant. My fingers tighten around the bow. I don't trust him to keep his word about my comrades.

Plainly, I'm no threat to him, because he turns his back to me and heads toward the stern. An arrogant mistake, because he's right, I'm mildly unintelligent and also desperate. I do something that would move the great Ivor to tears and use the bow as a club and swing with all my might. Ker grunts as the wood splinters against his left temple, breaking in half with a loud crack. The two men at the oars shout in surprise and I quickly shove Ker overboard. He disappears with the waves, and I hope to the Under, the demon drowns.

I turn just as Heracles' men spring forward to grab me. Kicking out, I catch one in his nethers, but the other soldier punches me in the jaw and I feel something break as I'm knocked on my arse. The man hovers over me and grabs a handful of my wet hair, I'm forced to look up into his fist. There's a crunch followed by blinding pain when his knuckles break my nose. Blood pours from my nostrils as my hand searches the deck for anything that could be used as a weapon. My fingers curl around one of the halves of the bow and I thrust it upward. The broken, sharp ridge impales his thigh.

My assailant flinches, giving me an opening, and I spring upward to elbow him in the side of his neck. Before I can push him overboard, the other soldier attacks, kicking my ribs. Then they're both on me with their fists. I'm so gods damn tired, and after a moment of attempting to fight, my body gives out. I feel something rupture inside my abdomen. My eyes focus on the sky through a haze of agony, the dawn now a bright blood orange. The colors are mirrored in the West Window. Who knew I would die by being beaten to death? I think I'd much prefer something quick. I regret sending Ker to the sea so soon, but at least the others should live.

Suddenly, someone cries out, followed by a thud. The blows stop and I hear Yiannis cursing. Then Pip's worried face is in mine, saltwater drips from his curly hair into my eyes. "Pardon my manners, Prince, but you're not looking so pretty anymore."

CHAPTER XLI

3rd Week of Winter

Eimear

Guilt is a new steady companion that sits right next to my fear. The emotion smothers me as I thread a needle and begin to mend a guard's old uniform. How many innocent lives did I destroy with that letter?

I glance at the slave brand on my arm. How many will receive the same mark? Experience the same suffering as I? The same...hopelessness? I suck on the inside of my cheek when my shame threatens to spill out into tears.

An image of Astera screaming as she was pulled into the portal suddenly comes to mind. I wonder how she's fairing. I miss her fiercely, but if I'm being honest with myself, I also fear her return—the story she's bound to tell me. I don't want to know what I've done.

And what will happen when I light the lantern again? When Steilos comes to rescue us? Am I worthy of rescue, worthy of survival? The thought gives me pause. Now that I've played a part in the death of a nation, will I be allowed to join my mother and father in Elysium when I die? Is my soul even redeemable at this point?

I hiss as the needle pricks my finger and draws blood. I bring my finger under the burlap hood to suck on it. Saray peers up from her own sewing and her look softens. We're alone in the room where we first met.

"Are you all right?" She asks.

No, but I don't tell her that. "Fine as I'm able to be, I guess."

She hesitates, as if mulling something over, and grimaces when she finally speaks. "I want you to know I'm sorry."

I'm surprised. "What for?"

"Well . . . I'm the reason you have to wear *that*," Saray gestures to my hood with her chin.

I instinctively reach for it and rub the burlap between my fingers. "What do you mean?"

Saray puts the uniform she's been stitching aside. "When he ordered your face covered, that damn sack was the only thing I could find. I knew that he wouldn't let you replace it, that's his nature, afterall. If I was smart, I would've found something else. Something a little more comfortable at least. I'm sorry that you have to always wear it now, and that I had to be the one to put it on you. I feel terrible about it. I really do."

The resentment I've been harboring toward Saray begins to thaw. It isn't her fault, not really. I shouldn't have blamed her. I've been treating her coldly just because she's the only person in this horrible place I can be outwardly angry with. In this way, I'm no better than Neyda or Ruby. "Don't worry yourself about it," I tell her. "Now the guards can't see when I make faces at them. I've mouthed all kinds of things under this hood."

Saray puts her hand to her chest and laughs, and I smile in return. She wipes away a tear and reaches for the uniform again. "Oh gods, I needed that. Thank you."

It's time. "Saray, pretend for a moment that you didn't have to be a slave. That you could leave Notos without worrying about being caught or dying, and we could go together. If that could happen, would you live with me afterward?"

She pauses over her work. "This is pretend right?"

I nod and Saray leans back in her chair with a sigh. "I would go with you, but we couldn't live together. I'd like to find my daughter, maybe after that I would live with her, wherever she is."

Another grin appears on my face that she can't see. "Of course. After you find her, I would come and visit then. I'd like to meet her."

Saray stares at me. "This scenario isn't real, though. It can't actually happen."

"Uh huh," I say and busy myself with the mending in hand. "But it's nice to imagine, isn't it?"

She nods, the corners of her mouth raising slightly. "It is."

A sudden knock comes at the door, and we both jump. Cecille enters, her face grave. Saray looks at her expectantly. "What now?"

Cecille is on the verge of tears and doesn't answer.

The hesitation seems to annoy Saray. "Well out with it."

She stutters and tries a few times without luck. Finally, she says, "We've all been ordered to go to the c- c- courtyard, for Confessional."

A heavy silence follows. Saray and I share a terrified look before I find my voice again. "But the General hasn't returned? There shouldn't be another Confessional just yet?"

Saray throws the uniform into the basket at her feet and stands. "Ornery slags these guards are. Acting up when the General is out. They probably just want to scare us. We should hurry though, or it'll be our hides."

Saray and I enter the courtyard together. Cecille who was nearly hysterical, ran ahead of us. We congregate with the other slaves who have formed a large semi-circle around the center of the courtyard. Everyone fidgets with nervous energy. Out of the group, I catch Egan's eye, the blacksmith. He runs over to me and asks, "Do you know what's happening? Nat, my guard, told me to come here."

I shake my head. "I'm not sure. Cecille mentioned a Confessional, but the General hasn't returned—" Suddenly, I'm hit with a wave of apprehension. Fear crawls over my skin, like a thousand skittering bugs. I grab hold of Saray's hand so that I don't fall to my knees. Something is about to happen. *This feeling*, it's similar to the night when Zadok and I entered the ceremony grounds, *before* I met Metis. But what does it all mean?

"A great change is coming," I say out of nowhere. There's a certainty in my bones, something that simply, *is*. No more, no less. I even feel different, calm. Strangely enough, I also feel like I'm really *here*. Whatever that means. I find the experience perplexing and marvelous at the same time.

Both Saray and Egan give me a puzzled look. Saray finally speaks up, "Your eyes Eimear… they're…glowing. They're very gold right now."

I snap out of the trance and my fear returns in full force along with confusion. It's like I'm an entirely different person than I was just a few seconds ago. "What…What just happened?"

Egan glances at Saray anxiously. The blacksmith opens his mouth to say something, but he's cut off by Faas. "Listen up, pissants! It's time to trim the fat and make room for the new, stronger stock." A line of guards quickly arrives at our backs, herding us closer in so that running isn't an option. I don't have time to think about what I just prophesized, because all I can feel is the rising panic from those around me, as well as my own fear of what's to come.

Faas stands in the middle of the courtyard and the chair where Charos usually sits has been brought forward but remains empty. In front of the whipping post, three guards toss a painted seashell between them. One side of the shell is white, and the other black—a longstanding tradition when an outcome is to be decided by fate. Anders tosses the shell, and it lands on the side painted white. The memory of his whip tearing into my skin becomes all too fresh.

Could I fight them when they call my name from the list? The thrum in my veins promises the Under that I'll die trying. My heart flutters frantically, and I wrap my arms around Saray, who has become my surrogate mother over these past long months.

She peers down at me, unafraid of what she saw in my eyes earlier. Her mouth is set in a grim line. "Don't fear, it should be over soon. You don't have to watch. Just keep your focus on me."

I won't get to light that lantern after all. There will be no freedom. No new life. I bury my head against her before raising my chin once more. "That's not it," I whisper.

Saray cocks her head not understanding.

"I'm on the list this time."

"That can't be," Saray says, voice shaking.

I give her a final squeeze before stepping away. I try to mentally prepare myself for what's to come. "Ruby and I were fighting, but I was the one caught and got in trouble. Anders put me on the list then."

She grabs my shoulder roughly. "You'll be fine. You're a strong one, I know it. You'll survive."

I pat her hand and lie, "Of course."

Faas goes to sit in the General's chair. He yells at the two guards at the post who still toss the seashell between them, "Can you fuckers decide already!"

Anders swears as the guard opposite him calls the dark side of the shell for a second time. "Lucky bastard. You always win, Maarav," he spits before joining the third guard who lost during the last round.

Maarav wears an arrogant smile as Nat strides forward and places a scroll in his hands. The guard unrolls it with a flourish and calls out the name, "Hagen," from the list.

A bent, older man takes small steps forward and glances around at the rest of us, confused. When Hagen arrives at the post, Maarav grabs him roughly by his uniform before forcing the slave to his knees.

"Confess," Faas demands from the General's chair.

The slave looks between the guard holding him and Faas, "But I haven't done anything. I've been following orders. I've worked very hard."

Faas leans forward, blue eyes gleaming. "Your crime is that you've lived past your prime. Fifty lashes."

"You can't do this," Hagen sputters angrily, "not without the General's permission! I'm his property not yours!"

Faas' smile is wicked, enjoying the moment. "Oh, but he has given permission. Fresh slaves will arrive any day now, someone will need your bed and rations."

A hush runs through the crowd around me. Faas just confirmed that this isn't a lesson for us, but an execution of the weak. Hollow, I ignore Saray as she begins to cry.

Hagen whimpers as his wrists are bound against the post with twine. A cold calm settles over me and a morbid thought crosses my mind: At least they aren't nailing our hands this time.

Anders comes forward and places, not a whip but a scourge in Maarav's outreached hand. The tails of the weapon are long and end in barbed hooks. Maarav circles Hagen slowly, letting the barbs drag ominously on the ground behind him. The slave frantically struggles against his bindings, crying as he does. A futile act.

At each strike of the scourge, Hagen screams. I watch the spectacle with a vacant expression, understanding that my death will be gruesome. Someone retches nearby, the sourness adds a stink to the crisp winter air. Hagen's body gives out well before fifty lashes. There's a ringing in my ears as other names are announced from the list, each petty offense not worthy of the punishment. Eventually, the courtyard turns bloody from all the death. The bodies are piled off to the side. When Maraav is tired, he switches out with another guard. The General must've pulled these fuckers from the deepest depths of the Under. They're all the same demon with a different face.

As my time of death draws closer, my mask of calm shatters. I have to do *something*. Anything. I glance around hurriedly; the slaves outnumber the guards; there are at least two of us for every one of them.

If we just fought back, maybe we could win? A sense of wild determination emerges from the depths of me. I don't think, I just do.

Heart pumping, I throw my hood aside, and run forward with a scream. The guard with the scourge turns away from his prey, his mouth forming an 'O' as I tackle him at the hips. We tumble to the ground and I don't wait for him to recover from the shock before I rain blows down onto his face with my small fists. In seconds, someone grabs me by the hair, yanking, but I hold onto the guard and bite down on his neck, tasting blood. He howls under me. I close my eyes and pray that the other slaves find their spine and fight back as well.

When my hair is pulled so hard that I think my scalp may come away, I take a chunk of the guard I bite with me. Maraav curses and hoists me up by my armpits to face him. I spit the lump of skin into his face. I look past him toward the cowering slaves and see that no one else has stepped forward. Saray stands in the crowd, an expression of horror on her face.

Not one of them is brave enough to fight back. My confidence falters.

Maraav slams me to the ground, knocking the air from my lungs. Anders and Nat subdue me as I lay belly flat, but I'm not yet ready to admit defeat. I scream to the crowd, "Gods damn you! Fight! There are more of us!"

The guard I attacked gets up and walks toward me. His face is a wreck and his neck is bleeding. "Stupid cunt!" He yells and sends a hard kick to my ribs. "If you wanted to die so badly you should've just asked."

Nat grabs me roughly by my hair and forces me to look at the post, to have a full view of Lyra. She's currently tied there and bleeding, her whipping paused by my assault. The bird-like girl is incredibly thin, but her pregnancy shows, earning her place on the Confessional list. Anders picks up the scourge, his eyes moving between the two of us. He then focuses on me and says, "I'm going to make it worse for her because of what you did, and then you're next. So, think on that as she dies."

Since leaving my small isle, I've witnessed mankind's great capacity for cruelty. I watch Lyra scream and scream for mercy and wonder how such brutality is taught. Or are we simply born with violence in our veins? If that's the case, why would any god go through the trouble of making us to begin with? But maybe life is about the choices we make, what we do with this evil we're born of. Maybe that's where true freedom exists.

Lyra's death isn't a good death, she dies slowly. As her corpse is tossed onto a pile with the others, I come to understand that a god couldn't have shaped mankind, or given us the power of choice, because if they did, surely it would've been taken away by now.

I buck my body as Nat drags me toward the blood-soaked post. I imagine the hooks of the scourge imbedding themselves into my flesh and ripping it away. I don't want the same fate as the rest. I'm suddenly terrified at the prospect of death and urine trails down my legs. I search for help around me, but there's none. If all these people wouldn't help themselves, then there is no salvation for me.

The post looms ever closer, and in a final act of desperation, I quit struggling to instead become dead weight. It's enough to catch Nat off guard and I kick him in the groin. He drops me with a grunt, but I'm quickly up, ready to run for it. I don't make it very far though before I'm tackled. I swing my arms wildly, refusing to give up. I didn't suffer all this just to die here.

Anders comes forward to help my assailant. "Quit being so fucking difficult," he yells and punches the back of my head. I'm blinded by pain and my vision spots black for a moment. I slip in and out of consciousness as I'm dragged the rest of the way. Out of nowhere, a voice who isn't my sacred-self, whispers to me, "*I love you.*"

I must be hallucinating.

My wrists are tied to the whipping post when Faas' voice interjects amongst the chattering guards around me, "Let me do it, I hate this burnt-faced bitch."

Anders hands him the scourge.

At least I won't be eaten by Charos' chimera, the only saving grace. I close my eyes as the world spins in front of me.

"*Eimear!*" The voice is louder, desperate even.

I can't make sense of anything. A whirring splits the air and pain explodes down my back. I slowly look to my right to see that a bit of metal sticks out of my shoulder. Faas gives the scourge a yank and suddenly the metal is ripped away, taking my skin and part of my uniform with it.

I scream.

Rage and hate consume my entire being. I recall the events of the last few months, all the suffering I've endured. My vision blurs from the pain. I'm not yet ready to die. I would give anything in this moment to be stronger so I can live—live and take revenge on those who made me feel worthless, who made me afraid. I want to return the fear I've been delt by a thousandfold. I would give up my place in Elysium gladly and serve Hades himself if I could receive the justice I'm owed.

Hot tears burn their way down my cheeks as the scourge's hooks tear into my back for a second time.

CHAPTER XLII

3rd Week of Winter

Nikko

I open my eyes. I'm sore all over. What the Under? A few seconds pass and then I recall getting the ever-loving shit beat out of me. But what happened after? I sit up with a wince. The bedsheet pools around my hips and I see that my abdomen is covered in bruises. I'm in my room, but how did I get here? Suddenly, I remember bloody flesh—the water turning red. I quickly cover my mouth, and fight an intense wave of nausea. I saw men die.

"You're going to ache for the next few days, but have recovered well otherwise. There was some serious damage to your large intestine," Gareth says in near perfect Ellanion. He sits on the klinē with his fingers laced in his lap. His expression is grave, skin pale, with dark circles around his eyes. "I would've taken away the bruising, but the Queen asked that I leave it to serve as a lesson."

My hand comes away somewhat shakily from my mouth. I have a multitude of questions to ask, like how I made it back to the palace, but I start with, "Gareth, are you well? You appear ill." The boy seems to have aged beyond his years. He rubs his face with his palms and messes up his hair. I note how his pinky and ring finger are oddly bandaged on his left hand.

He sighs. "I'll recover. It's been nonstop in the sanatorium since the pollen spread last night. And then, midmorning, I was pulled from my patients to come here, only to find you nearly dead. Don't do that *ever again* by the way," he says sternly. "If I had arrived a minute or two later, you would've died."

I'm about to ask him another question when there's a knock at the door. I glance at it but Gareth answers. "He's awake now, you can see him."

"Ivor! I feared you had drowned," I exclaim as he peers through the door. He enters, then closes it behind him. My smile fades when I register the grim set of his mouth. The archer strides over toward me with purpose and places a careful hand on my shoulder.

"Prince."

"Yes?" I say with hesitation, expecting that punch he promised me.

Instead, Ivor wraps his arms around me and squeezes. "You're a prick, but thanks for saving my uncle and the others." He pulls back to get a good look at me. "I would've surely drowned if they hadn't plucked me from the sea on the skiff you managed to commandeer. They were able to rescue six others as well, all thanks to you."

My eyes go to his shoulder. "But I saw you hit with an arrow."

"I found a piece of barrel to cling to in the madness before I was rescued." He gestures toward Gareth. "Your friend healed me afterward."

"And what of Sandros?"

He grimaces. "We never found him."

"Oh," I say, and we share a knowing look. "He seemed like a good man."

Ivor nods. "He was."

"Prince," Gareth says appearing guilty, "I hate to interrupt, but the Queen was adamant that I tell you to dress for the wedding."

Wedding?

I stammer. "What?"

The archer and healer glance at one another before Gareth speaks again. "A lot has transpired since the suns rose this morn."

"It might be best for you to look out the window," Ivor says. "News spread about our failed attack on Heracles' fleet. It's not pretty."

I make my way to the terrace door, and slowly turn its golden handle, the chilling shrieks of Hercules' beasts still echo from beyond the walls. My heart drops, and I grip the railing of the balcony as I stare out at what was once the greatest kingdom of Ehvara. Hundreds of citizens lay unmoving in the streets near the poisonous vines that now sprawl over every building. It seems in the attempt to burn them, some of the structures themselves have caught fire. But the sight that sets my skin crawling is the wall. Hordes of Ellanions scramble over one another to crack their heads against Zeus' holy stone. What was once pearl is now blood-smeared.

"Gods what has happened?" I whisper. I don't recognize my own home. A civilization that flourished for centuries, has turned on its head in just a day. I jump when Gareth touches my shoulder.

"I don't understand it, not being a Native of Ellanios," he says. "But some of the citizens turned against the city and are now under a compulsion to leave. But they aren't able to do so because the gates are closed."

"It started once word spread that Heracles' ships are immune to fire," Ivor says. "They began to riot and demanded that King Zephyr surrender to the true son of Zeus. Not long after, the god's protection was invoked."

I note that it's late afternoon and I think of the men from Vorna who should've arrived at dawn. "And what of our reinforcements from Vorna? Where are the Voranians? What happened after the battle?"

"No battle has occurred," Gareth says confused.

Ivor crosses his arms. "Why would the Voranians come to our aid?"

Right, they wouldn't know. Only the King and his advisors were aware of the arrangement. Why didn't the Voranians show as promised?

Where are their drake women who could char Heracles' men in seconds? But then my breath catches.

"Wait . . . A wedding?" I turn and stare at Ivor, whose jaw is clenched. The temple bell rings loudly, signaling that a ceremony is soon to begin. The clamor drowns out the noise of Hercules' army, and the shouts and screams of the Ellanions who have been struck by madness. My heart stills a beat before outrage hits. Father surrendered.

My emotions can't keep up. How did it come to this? Not even an hour after waking from my injuries, I stand in a foyer outside the temple doors with Jada. My arm is linked with hers as we wait for the ceremony to begin. I can't believe she's to wed a monster.

Despite the circumstances, my twin makes an elegant bride. Her dark skin is stunning against the deep purple gown she wears. It's cut in the style of my mother's people. Patterns of lilac flowers are woven into the fabric and the collar that ends in a deep vee is lined with gold lace. Her hair is unbraided and half up, coiled at the top of her head with rings of gold throughout. I've never seen her more beautiful—yet, the barbarity of the situation threatens my sanity.

"That was quite a stunt you pulled, going along with the soldiers to burn the ships," she says quietly at my side. "I've never seen mother so furious. Her rageful screams echoed throughout the palace halls all night." A slight smile plays at her lips. She then examines my bruised face. "I'm happy you're safe. I didn't see when you were rushed to your rooms, but I was told it was bad. I wanted to come to your side, but mother wouldn't allow it as we were pressed for time."

She's worried for my sake when she's about to . . . "You don't have to do this. We can run away," I blurt without thinking.

Jada shakes her head. "It wasn't just talk when I said I would do anything for Ellanios. If this marriage can save us all, I won't run from it."

I deflate in the face of her resilience. I'm reminded that I'll never be as good as her. She says I shouldn't place her on a pedestal, but the elevation is well deserved. Will she be whisked away to the Blood Isles afterward? How does one even live in such a land? What will become of her there?

She envelopes me in a tight hug, and the emotions I've been trying to stifle come to the surface. My eyes become wet. Jada is attempting to comfort me when she's the one who's been sold off like a prized mare.

Unable to accept it, I push her away. "Stop it! I know you can't be satisfied with this."

When Jada touches my cheek it's like a mother to a son, and not like the siblings we are. The shame of it stings deep.

"This is my burden to bear. And yes, I'm petrified, but I'll survive it, just like you will." Her voice becomes firmer. "Nikko, Ellanios needs you to become a great king. I fear the lasting affects this war will have."

I turn bitter. "We both know that's impossible. I'm a royal fuck up. Ellanios would be better off if we could trade places."

She opens her mouth to argue, but then the first bell chimes, signaling the ceremony to begin. I swallow hard as my panic rises. My fingers lock around Jada's forearm, and I pull her toward the exit. "You're not doing this. We're leaving."

She resists me, "Nikko. You have to grow up. This isn't a sordid plot line in one of your silly books. This is life. This is real." She jerks her arm from my grasp. "Ellanios is on the verge of ruin. Our citizens' lives are at stake, and your attitude is making this harder for me. From birth, we've known that our future does not belong to us. We were born into our roles, and duty has come calling. It's time to accept it, because I have." Her voice is soft, but she is unmistakably angry.

I stare at Jada, shocked. Though her expression is fierce I can see her fighting to keep the situation from destroying her. Unshed tears glisten in her eyes, and I know she is barely hanging on to her grace. I straighten my shoulders and hold my head high. I've dishonored my sister's courage by trying to run. The seventh bell chimes, signaling us to enter the temple. "I'm sorry."

She stands on her toes to kiss my cheek. "You'll always be my brother. And you aren't a royal fuck up, well not completely at least."

I swallow hard. "You'll write to me should anything happen?"

Jada gives my arm a final squeeze. "Of course."

As we enter the temple, my eyes go immediately to the man who started it all—and fuck, were we all wrong to refute his claim. Seeing him in the flesh, there's no denying that Heracles is a true son of Zeus.

The demi-god stands to the right of his father's altar with a waiting priest. The air around him glows in shades of gold. It actually fucking glows. He has tanned skin and thick, honey-colored hair that frames a face any artist would give their life to sculpt. Ageless though he is, Heracles appears as if he's in his mid-thirties. His perfect body is adorned with a gold breast plate, fustanella, and greaves. A garnet cloak made of finely woven linen is fastened to the armored plates on his shoulders. Heracles takes in my sister with unreadable amber eyes.

My lips pull back in a snarl, fuck this prick.

A handful of soldiers from each party are positioned on either side of the temple. Their gazes are alert, set on each other to kill. The men are ready to draw their swords at the command. Ivor is among them. His arms are crossed, and a bow is slung across his back with a full set of quills. I'm slightly comforted by his presence, although he's obviously stricken upon seeing my sister. The King's advisors sit in a middle pew to the left; Bacchus shakes his head when our eyes meet. He's most likely sore at me for knocking him unconscious. Hain bites the nail of his thumb and next to him, Idan scowls.

The Queen sits erect in the front pew, and her face hardens at the sight of us. Her only daughter to be given to the man who destroyed her homeland. Opposite to Heracles at the alter stands the King; my mother turns her heated gaze on him. "Husband, you bring great shame upon our house by agreeing to this farce. My right to blood has been dishonored."

I'm taken back by her boldness; Jada's grip tightens on my arm.

Father nervously glances at Heracles while the demi-god studies my mother. A moment passes before recognition is reflected in his stare. "Ah, yes. I remember now," he says in a voice that could coax flowers to grow and lightning to rip the sky. "Your father was a King of Anyalay am I correct?"

The Queen seethes, "Yes."

Heracles pauses as if searching, then finally says, "You also had a younger sister. My mercenaries were unkind to her. I'm sorry for that. Collectively, your family and people were very brave when they fought for your motherland. They were of strong stock; you should be proud."

Both my sister and I falter as the air evaporates. A series of emotions play out on my mother's face, but the fight seems to go out her, and she sags against the pew in defeat. I've never seen her so low. Her people are slaves now, so much blood has been spilled. I wonder how we can continue with this arrangement, how peace can be made with this barbarian.

The King clears his throat and turns toward the priest who stands uncomfortably between him and Heracles. "Let us begin."

I lean in closely to Jada and say in a rush, "It's not too late to put a stop to this." My eyes go to Heracles and then to his men in the room.

I don't care if any of them overheard, I'm prepared to fight to the death if it means her safety.

Jada reaches for my face with both hands, and says firmly, "Forever heavy are the burdens on our shoulders, but brother, know this: my back will not bend, nor will my knees buckle. My head is held high in this matter and so it will remain. You must let me go."

A canyon-sized gulf opens between us as she steps away and leaves me alone in the aisle. My final duty to my twin goes unfulfilled as she meets Heracles on her own and stands before him like a goddess at the altar. It takes everything I have not to crumble where I stand, but I force myself to join my mother in her pew.

Before sitting, I note the hint of something putrid nearby. The sour stench isn't strong, but it's close enough that it's bothersome. I scan the temple one more time. Behind us, Bacchus appears green in the face; either he isn't taking our relinquishment of Ellanios well or he smells it too. Across the aisle, the benches are empty except in the back where a man and a small girl sit. Her hair has a touch of gray in it, and her face is blotchy and red from crying. I find their attendance strange, but don't think the stench is coming from that direction.

"For the love of gods, Nikko, sit," my mother says softly with her eyes downcast.

Letting it go, I take a seat just as the door of the temple opens quietly. Both Ker and Erebos enter and slip into a nearby pew. The afternoon light spilling from a stained-glass window, bathes both men in a motley of color. Father must've released Erebos and his demon brother survived the bay somehow. If I'm honest, I cannot tell the two apart. One of them returns my stare impassively and, in case it's Ker, I extend my five fingers toward the bastard, giving him the moutza.

The priest begins to chant, and I promptly return my attention to the ceremony. The priest raises his arms overhead and I glare at Zeus' statue behind him. Why did his cock have to spit out a beast of a son? My deity's flesh and blood is here to lay claim to Ellanios and my sister—the mockery sits ill in my stomach. As the priest's chanting becomes increasingly louder, Heracles takes Jada's hands in his, and his right arm, which had been hidden by his cloak, is suddenly visible. The limb is stained black, the discoloration just reaching past his elbow. I cup my nose and mouth and try not to gag. That's where the putrid stench is coming from. My mother shifts uncomfortably in her seat and covers her nose as well.

I'm perplexed as I stare at Heracles' rotting flesh. It looks as if Decay has set in, as if—the Return has started. But how can that be? He's a demi-god, can his kind even lose their godly essence? I note two gold rings clamped tightly against the bicep of his decaying arm. Each bangle hosts a jewel at its center, one of amethyst and the other carnelian. Why wear jewelry on an arm that's slowly dying?

When the priest finishes, and the seventh bell has rung, Heracles reaches out and cradles Jada's face gently with his hands. She flinches, but he moves in closer, and kisses her slowly. My sister stands straight-backed with her arms at her sides, eyes closed and fists clenched. I see regret in my father's face as he watches. Heracles deepens the kiss. I can't bear the sight any longer and turn my face away. A few uneasy breaths pass and then the Queen stands and screams, "Get away from my daughter!"

I reach for her hand, but she slaps mine away. "Mother, it is done, let us—" But sudden shouts from the councilmen behind us drown me out. I look to the newlywed couple and watch, horrified, as Jada's beautiful face withers, and her skin seems to fold into itself. Her arms, once supple, now droop and sway as she swipes helplessly at Heracles' handsome face with a wrinkled hand. The golden air around him pulsates, and relief is plainly visible in his open eyes.

What's happening to Jada? In my shock, I'm unable to make myself move to help her. My sister's body drops to the floor with a thump. The priest backs away frightened, takes off at a run, and disappears behind a door at the back of the temple. My father grabs Heracles by the shoulders, "What have you done to my daughter?" The grief in his voice is absolute.

Heracles looks at the statue of Zeus, then at his own blackened arm. "My father condemned me, and now I must consume the lives of others to sustain my own, lest I fall dead in three days' time." The demi-god shrugs. "It's a punishment, but also a rule of the current game we play, just a minor detail in the long story of it all, an irksome handicap. I had nothing against her specifically, but my brothers, sisters, and I earn additional marks for killing royalty. I'm sorry for your loss, but it's the way of things, the way of the game. If not me, one of my kin would have executed her eventually to gain favor."

My father appears confused and heartbroken. His mouth trembles as he looks down at Jada's remains. "You speak of riddles while my only daughter lays dead? Have you no heart? She was my child."

Heracles' eyes fill with sorrow. "It has been many years since my heart was butchered along with my children. But their deaths are still fresh for me. Thus is the curse of love and immortality. I share in your pain, although yours will be over soon."

My father backs away but the demi-god closes the space between them. "The time is nigh for this part of the game to end Zephyr. I waited four centuries to sack my father's favorite treasure. When Zeus sees me annihilate the Holy City, I hope his heart learns a thing or two about agony. But soon, I will take his eyes and then he will know real pain."

Heracles then inserts his fingers into my father's side, puncturing the flesh with his godly strength. The King screams as his ribs are pulled from his body. "You have played well, made things difficult for me, and for that I am grateful, but you still lose. I couldn't enter Zeus' blessed city without its King's explicit permission. A rule I had to abide by, this game is tedious indeed. I had to wait for your daughter to become of marrying age to create an opportunity for you to invite me in." His eyes flicker to Jada's corpse. "She seemed like a lovely woman."

The gurgling sound my father makes penetrates my shock, and I reach for the hilt of my sword. My mother screams as I rush forward with my weapon raised. Heracles easily catches my sword with his left hand, the blade shudders, and I stare at him in terror. With a flick of his wrist, I'm flung sideways with great force and my head hits the side of a golden pillar before my body slams into the far wall.

There's a racket of metal against metal around me as my vision pulses with black. A girl cries out, and the floor of the temple begins to shake. I look up as Hain is pierced through his middle by a spear made of earth and stone. Idan backs away from his Crib-Brother and makes for the temple exit, but his body bursts before he can escape, his skin, blood, and bone are flung in all directions. The twin that I presume is Ker, stands by the door with a hand raised. Erebos is at his side. He takes a step in my direction, face unreadable.

I try to get my bearings as my visions spins. My mother rushes over to me, grabs me by the arm, and attempts to force me up. "Quick, we must follow Bacchus to sanctuary while Heracles and his men are distracted by our guards."

I stare past her to Jada's shriveled body and my father's open-eyed corpse, his blood soaks the floor. "We're all going to die," I say through clenched teeth. "It's pointless."

The Queen glares and slaps my cheek hard. "Quit wasting time. Get up."

I'm numb as she pulls me along behind her to the back of the temple where the singing Luminae and priests exit after services. Bacchus waits for us, his sword is drawn, and he holds the door open with a foot. As my mother and I run through the opening, I turn my head for another glimpse. Heracles' face is void of emotion as he mouths the word, "Run." Then, with a bloody hand, he rips the jaw from a palace guard.

Gods & Beasts of Miracle

Curse of a God

Elysium is a prize for souls,

but would a soul fear the Underworld

if it knew there are worse ways to journey?

It is better to taste torment

than to experience it endlessly.

O' the poorest of souls

whose lips swear

an oath to a God,

hold fast and take pleasure

in your last days with the living,

even when your flesh sours black,

and falls from your bones,

enjoy your last breaths O' cursed one.

For when the lungs petrify,

the heart stills,

and the blood runs cold,

your soul will journey no more.

CHAPTER XLIII

3rd Week of Winter

Eimear

My eyes flutter open to reveal a black cloud that hovers three inches above my face. I breathe in the strange but familiar scent of narcissus. For some odd reason, I have the impression that the cloud has a playful personality. Entirely too close for my liking, it reminds me of an eager puppy that wants to lick my face. "Shoo," I say in a low voice as I sit up and wave it off. The fluff darts away quickly, and beyond its dark haze, is an endless, iridescent color that spans in all directions. Stars of all shapes and sizes are speckled throughout the colorful abyss. I stand slowly in astonishment, it's very beautiful here, like nothing I've ever seen. I'm further surprised when I find that I'm barefoot and in a silk dress of all things. It's as if the fine material was cut from the same matter as the color and stars that surround me. I feel like I'm in a liminal space, like waking from a dream. I touch my forehead gently. I'm entirely confused as my memories fight to resurface—I'm not in pain but know I should be.

"Did I… die?" I say to myself.

"Not yet you haven't, but you will."

I turn towards the direction of the voice and feel my heart stop. There's a male figure in the distance. He's bathed in an almost blinding light, a white glow that makes my eyes water if I stare for too long. Slowly, like a torn seam being restitched, a steady joy builds inside my chest before I'm fully claimed by the emotion. With it, a shifting of the mind occurs. I regain all the conversations I've had with Hades since he began visiting me in my dreams, banishing my night terrors with his godly presence. During my waking hours, I don't remember these meetings, though a fragment of me longs for him, unaware that a close friend is missing.

The god moves in my direction, and I stare in awe. Nervous excitement dances in my stomach with each powerful step he takes. After the worlds were created, and Rhea[50] bore her first son, I wonder if the great goddess cloaked him in shadows because she knew all her children afterward would not compare to his splendor. It's as if Hades was spun from the stars themselves, his skin possessing a brilliant luster, and the planes of his face fashioned from heaven's first snowfall. His easygoing nature makes him even more enchanting. One would think

---

[50]Daughter of Gaia, Titaness, and the Great Mother of the Gods.

him to be arrogant, as most gods are, but Hades has only ever treated me with reverence and given kindness.

The God of the Under stops just a stone's throw away, his intense gaze holds every color, like a rainbow after a storm. But there's something amiss, his disarming smile is nowhere to be seen. My brow furrows. "Is something wrong?"

Hades drops his prism-like eyes and runs long fingers through thick white hair that curls around his ears and at the nape of his neck—a nervous gesture, unusual for a god. A silken black toga sits low on his hips, and the himation he wears across his torso leaves a part of his chest exposed. I stare a fraction too long and think about how soft his skin appears. I grow warm at the thought but then become insecure. I reach for my burn, suddenly embarrassed by my deformity. I realize my hood is missing. What happened to it?

Hades notices the movement. "Your scar adds a certain charm in my eyes," he says with sincerity, instead of answering my question.

My heart jumps, but I mask my feelings. "As if you'd know what it's like to appear as I do. You were created perfectly and I… well, I was made into a ghoul."

"I've seen enough monsters to know you aren't one. I've told you this many times now. When will you take it to heart?"

I can't fathom the kindness within his stare. I try to look anywhere but at him, though there's nothing else in this place but his dark clouds, which glide and twist playfully as if they have minds of their own. It's ironic how I hate the gods, and yet I long for the one in front of me. It's utter nonsense to feel this way about him. I'm a child in his eyes and a human to boot.

Hades' expression turns serious again, something I'm still not accustomed to seeing. He has a cheerful personality, nothing at all like the terrifying stories sung about him.

"You have to return soon," he says. "We're almost out of time. I can't hold you here much longer in your current physical state."

My physical state? What's happened now? Regardless, I become frustrated at the thought of leaving this sanctuary. "I'd rather stay here with you."

The god's bow-shaped lips quirk up slightly. For whatever reason, Hades finds nearly everything I say amusing. I'll never understand it; I'm not a funny person. His smile fades quickly though and he says, "Even if your situation wasn't dire, you know you can't stay here. Eventually you must wake up and *live*."

I ignore him, and instead, take another look around the empty dream. In this place, I can create anything, make it appear as anything, *do anything*. When I sleep, I become a painter and my dream a canvas. The god tells me it's like this for everyone when we close our eyes, we just forget when we wake up. I stare at my hands that seem just as real here as my physical body in Ehvara. But for half a heartbeat, their image flickers in and out.

Styx. Something *is* wrong.

I jump at the sound of Hades' voice: "Did you mean it? You would give *anything* for power?"

I suffer another moment of confusion before my memory of the waking world fully clashes with my dream. I recall the scourge slicing through the flesh of my back. Rage rekindled, my reply is sharp as broken bone. "Anything."

Hades steps closer to me, his shoulders hold a certain sternness about them. All business and no play, the lighthearted god I've come to know has vanished entirely. My mouth parts slightly in surprise as his beautiful eyes narrow. "It's within my ability to grant your desire. However, should you accept this boon, there's no going back. What I have to offer is cruel. The power I'll share with you is even worse. You'll be tainted—forever banned from Elysium. You'll never have the chance to see your mother again nor anyone else who passes through those fields. Your soul will become stagnant."

He tells the truth. There is a wrongness here, I *know* it. I can taste it on my tongue, like spoiled fruit. But all the hurt I've experienced comes to surface in full force. The loss of everyone, the pain I've endured. As if on cue, my body flickers out briefly before reappearing again.

My flesh is *dying* because of *them.*

"I want—" A cry for blood is on my lips, but then I think of the song of Mana's voice and the mischief in Zadok's smile, all the stories my father told me at his knee. I remember lying in a field with Gareth, our hands clasped tightly together. The way he smelled of his father's leather shop, and how he would tease me. How could I possibly give up seeing them again, even if it's only when I'm dead? What's power truly worth? If I die now, I'll shortly be reunited with Papa and Mana anyway. But…am I truly ready to die?

Suddenly, I'm gone from the dream and barely conscious at the whipping post. There's a cacophony of voices as I try to hang onto my life. Faas' laughter in particular, is harsh to my ears. No…I want to…*live*—I reappear in front of Hades, gasping, lungs fighting for air. My back is slick and bloody, dripping all over my dream. Pain has returned to me, though it's dull in this place.

"You're hurting Eimear," Hades closes the gap between us, he takes me by the shoulders. There's a sense of urgency in his grip. I barely manage to regain my composure. My eyes drop and my fists clench tightly at my sides. How could I let them debase me and get away with it? Lust for vengeance competes with the love I have for those I may never see again. Out of the two, the need for revenge triumphs. It seems a part of me is corrupted beyond repair. Hate overshadows love today. I beg my mother to forgive me.

With fire in my heart, I meet Hades' colorful stare. "I'll give whatever it takes. I just want them all to suffer."

The God of the Under slowly takes my hand, his touch gentle, like moonlight on a hazy evening. "I must admit, I would be sad to part ways, you've been… a pleasant friend. But Eimear, I truly caution against doing this. It was selfish of me to offer it, I know better. Death is not such a bad experience. For my kind, it's a rare luxury. I envy humans for it."

I feel broken as I hold onto Hades' hand. His soothing voice has quelled the anger in me, and I'm left with a deep sadness instead. Truth be told, I'm afraid to die. I simply want to live a little longer and do so happily. I am, after all, human.

"I want this. Please," I tell him.

Hades shakes his head. "Fine then," he says in a frustrated tone. "Do you, Eimear of Rhone, chosen champion of Metis, recognize that you come to me willfully seeking power, and that you're willing to offer your soul, as payment?"

I stare into the depths of his opalescent gaze, I still have my doubts, but I cast them aside. "I do." A painful silence opens up between us, as if we're farther apart now, instead of closer. I shift nervously. "Did I say something wrong?"

Hades speaks softly, "You will never get to *live* again once your body dies. It is done."

My heart begins to sink and my hand slips from his. "I don't… understand?"

"A soul you see, is a most precious thing. It never dies but merely changes shape. And you dear, just gave up your ability to transform."

"But you said—"

"I said that your soul would become stagnant, that you would be banned from Elysium. And you are. You can never visit or pass through the Fields to become something else, to live *again*. You will be stuck once you die. Never to be less... or more." Guilt seems to hollow out his eyes.

I try to digest this concept, a person living again after they die. It's hard for me to comprehend. All my life, I thought—life—this one, was it and that Elysium was an end to suffering. But it seems the Elysian Fields are merely a passageway to another life. My mother and father aren't dead, they're simply somewhere else, *living*. I feel myself slip into self-hatred; I've made a foolish choice. "This life is all I get? I'll never be born again?"

Hades' voice becomes flat. "I'm sorry, but no."

I look down at our feet. "I've made… more mistakes than I can count now. For someone whose namesake is wisdom, all I've come to learn, is that I am, wholeheartedly, a stupid girl." Hades takes a step closer and I, a step back. "Don't," I tell him.

"I'm sorry," he says again, this time, with emotion.

What hurts is that he really means it. I look at him then, really look at him. Not at just his beauty, but the ugly parts too, because there *is* something ugly there. I grow angry at Hades. "I'm the fool for not asking more questions, for not heeding your warning, but you know that I'm young and human. You knew that I had no knowledge of what truly happens when we die. So, tell me this, could you have elaborated on the stakes when offering your boon?"

The god appears ashamed. "Yes."

I nod my head. "A true friend wouldn't do what you did. I'm responsible for my own foolishness, for not asking the right questions.

But you… you've done this before and used my humanity against me. You should've told me every detail. Know this Hades, you are as flawed as any mortal. You gods are flawed just like the rest of us and are no better."

For a moment, anger flickers across his face, a sight I find truly terrifying, enough that I take another step back. He notices my fear and it's as if the fire goes out of him. "I already know this about myself," he says softly and looks away.

I cross my arms to hold myself together. I feel as if I may fall apart soon. "Well, you said that you consider me a friend. Now's your chance to be wholly honest. Why didn't you tell me everything when you could have?"

As if to avoid my gaze, the god continues to stare off into the distance. His expression appears darkly somber as he studies a patch of stars. After a long pause he finally says, "I am… lonely here. I don't consider what I do as living. That is something humans do. I simply exist. I enjoyed having someone to talk to these past months and wanted to speak with you again in the future at length. I have a selfish core. I am a god after all—this is how I was made."

I can't help but look upon him with complete bewilderment. His answer infuriates me, my existence has been whittled down to merely one life for some conversation. "Look me in the eye Hades," I command scathingly.

He does, and for a moment when I look into his colorful spectrum, for less than a heartbeat, everything shifts and then changes.

It's as if I'm me, but not me. I've become a version of me that *knows*. Like I've been here before, done this all before. My heart is big and wide open, and I just know that everything will be turn out and that everything is just right as it is. I look onward and see a lifeline in front of me that stretches on forever, something so very endless and painful— and at its center, I see a bright, lovely child with their hands outstretched, as if asking for help. And for all the hate that lives in my heart, I cannot help but reach out and let that child know I found them.

"You are safe, and welcome to return home," I whisper in a daze, not knowing that at some point, I moved closer to Hades and took his hand in mine again. I blink and find that the god has happy tears streaming down his face, like a crying angel. I feel confused, "what just happened?"

The god stares at me awe, "I'm not sure myself. But I felt something, a great joy I've long forgotten. Something has changed or will be changing soon. You truly are special Eimear, a Game Changer."

I sigh and rub my face as the magic of the moment dissipates as well as the memory of it. My anger swiftly returns. "Styx," I swear and note how my pain has slowly started to intensify in the dream space. "This is all truly exhausting, and I'm weary to the bone already. But I take it, I get to live in some form or fashion as you do when I die? I've bargained my soul, now, where's all the power you promised?"

The glow that returned to Hades' face quickly fades and he shifts to put space between us. "As is customary for most dreams, you won't remember any of this once you wake. Not even our bargain. After fulfilling my end, I won't be able to assist you for a time, your nightmares may even return. I'm sorry, but I can do nothing for that. You must slay them on your own for now."

We stare at each other for a moment. I may be a foolish girl, but I am learning. The god didn't answer my first question, but he didn't lie either. I'll need to be careful of him in the future, that is, if I remember to. "I don't think I'll be wanting any more assistance from you, *friend*," I say with contempt.

Hades has the audacity to look wounded but ignores my barb. "It's time for you to go, you're bleeding everywhere," he says gruffly and snaps his fingers.

CHAPTER XLIV

3rd Week of Winter

Eimear

I'm jerked awake to guttural screams. There's a searing pain on the inside of my thigh. I try to make sense of it all but can't.

Where am I?

Heavy exhaustion clings to me as if a dose of adrenaline has run its course. It takes all my strength just to turn my head to the side. Anders and the guard I attacked are on their knees shrieking in agony. Deep gashes have been carved into their faces by their own fingernails, leaving dripping trails of blood. They continue to claw at themselves as if a devil lives inside them, a nightmare they can't wake from.

Nat, the smithy guard approaches the two, yelling for them to stop. But Maarav comes up from behind him, knife in hand, and slides the blade across his comrade's throat. Nat falls to his knees with wide, confused eyes, as blood spurts from the fatal wound. Maarav then turns the knife towards his own belly and begins to stab himself repeatedly until he falls to the ground.

I'm unable to comprehend the madness I'm witnessing and search for reason. Faas stands at a distance, and we lock eyes. His face is ghostly white. The scourge falls from his hands. He mutters something under his breath and takes a fearful step back. It's as if Faas is seeing a monster that isn't there. His throat opens in a terrified scream before he drops to all fours and proceeds to bash his skull against the cobble stone until his head breaks. His body twitches before going still.

Silence envelops the courtyard, and my eyes take in the bodies and gore around me. They all just… killed themselves?

A guard with disheveled black hair, standing nearest to the crowd of slaves, glances around wildly, and yells, "What the bloody fuck just happened!"

But there's no logical explanation for the suicidal massacre.

He turns and shouts to the slaves, "Get the fuck back inside and return to your duties!"

No one moves for several moments and he draws his blade. "Are you all dumb slags or what? There's a demon in our midst! Do you want to die? Get a move on it!"

The slaves must believe him because they quickly begin to clear from the courtyard, talking amongst themselves in hushed tones. Once most of them have gone, the disheveled guard fearfully walks over to me with his sword still drawn. At first, he hesitates, but eventually he sheaths his blade and begins to loosen my bindings. His hands shake with the task. Once I'm free, I fall to the ground in a heap.

The guard backs away, his eyes never leaving my crumpled figure. "I don't know what kind of demon you are, or what ungodly power you have, but I want no part of it, and I don't want to go killing myself like those others. I'm doing you a favor by letting you go, see, so as payment, don't go seeking revenge on me." He then takes off into a dead run.

Demon? Power? What did he mean by that? My mind feels as if it's in a fog, but I make myself get up and take woozy steps toward the courtyard exit. Delirious, I start to worry about my shoes. They must've fallen off. Blood seeps between my toes, whose exactly, I'm unsure of. I slip, falling forward into a red puddle. I stay there a moment, unsure of what I should do, but look up when I hear someone approaching. It's Saray. She stayed back despite the guard's orders.

She tries to help me up, but I shrug her off. "You're a coward. You and all the others. You didn't fight back. You all just stood there. We could've won." I start to cry.

Saray looks stricken. "You're right. I'm a coward and make no excuses for it. But for now, you're on the brink of death and need help. So please let me do this for you."

I take stock of my condition and pause. I'm covered in blood, but don't feel a thing, only deep exhaustion. Are my nerves damaged? Still, I can barely move on my own. Begrudgingly, I accept her aid. Saray almost has to carry me down the long stone steps that lead to the caverns. On the way, those we pass give us a wide birth, as if they're afraid of me. I don't understand it.

"There, there. You've almost got it," Saray says as she helps me out of my uniform. Once the bloody dress is over my head, she drops the soiled garment with a gasp. "Eimear, your…your back. It's healed."

"What?"

"You don't have a scratch, not even a scar! I swear by the gods, I saw those men rip the skin from your back."

I tremble as I stand naked and bloody in front of her, my legs ready to give out. I've never been this tired. Not even in all the days I've labored. Finally, recognition flares, and I recall the feeling after Metis claimed me as her champion. The exhaustion is similar to then, worse even.

I can't think about this right now. It's too much.

Saray helps me into the spring's cool water. "I'll keep a firm hold until you can swim on your own," she says.

I suck in at the sight of the blood that begins to wash off my worn body, leaving eddies of red. Isn't this water usually black? Other than the blood, it's clear, like normal water. Several moments pass and nothing changes, I'm still exhausted. Why don't I feel any better? What changed? The healing properties of the spring have disappeared. Only the fresh scent of mint remains. I must've fallen out of favor with the god who aided me all this time. But then . . . who healed my back and ribs? Was it Metis? There's a nagging feeling in me, that something horrible has happened. Not just the whipping but something else. Something *other*.

When I can't swim on my own, Saray hoists me up to sit on the ledge. She takes a large shell, dips it into the spring, and pours the water over my head, washing my hair.

"What happened?" I whisper, interrupting the quiet between us.

She pauses, sitting the shell down before answering. "Sweetheart, there's no sense to it, none that I can make. You were brought to the post and those men . . . they started hurting you." Saray is hesitant at first, but then she begins to rub my back. "You took the whip at least twenty times. This is a miracle. *You* are a miracle."

My eyes close under her touch. "But what happened afterward?"

Her hand stills. "Those guards started killing themselves. For no reason. It was the strangest thing, but I'm glad they're dead."

I look at her then. "But . . . you aren't scared of me? The others seem to be."

Saray gives me a weak smile. "You're like a daughter to me," she says and resumes washing my hair.

I've no response, overcome with a mixture of emotions ranging between love and anger at the woman who has never faltered in helping me. But isn't that what family does? We become angry with one another and then forgive?

"Oh dear," she says and gives the hair near my temple a tug. "It's turned white."

"All of it?"

Saray cocks her head studying me, "The entire lock, but just in this one section. I didn't notice before. It was all covered in blood."

"It wasn't like that this morn."

She shrugs then replies, "Miracles seem to happen to you child. Maybe you've been touched by a god after all. You're lucky."

Not an hour later, I lay naked in my bunk. My body may not be battered and bruised from today, but my soul is. With effort, I sit up and observe the new mark on the inside of my thigh. My fingers trace the black lines of the narcissus flower, the etching similar to the gold owl on my chest. Saray was right, though she can't see it, I've been touched by a god. But which one? I purse my lips. Just what I need, more godly mischief.

The lock of white hair falls into my face. Yet more oddities for me to contend with. I roll the strand between my forefinger and thumb. Between the carnage from Confessional, mysterious changes to my body, and the fresh feeling of loss, I become overwhelmed and sink belly first into my bed. I exhale a ragged breath into my pillow and my fists twist the sheets. I'm consumed by a strange feeling where my heart is—as if something has gone, no, been *exchanged* with something else. But what? And why do I feel so lonely? Maybe I've gone mad after all.

Suddenly, I have the sensation of my head being split open. I cry out in the dimly lit cavern as a voice whispers in the back of my mind. The sound digs its way to the surface until it finally breaks through the wall I built.

//You'll be safe . . . Remember, we love you. We love us.//

I groan at the return of my sacred-self and roll to my side to try and gain a semblance of rest. When I finally drift off, Jud and Armon are there to greet me. They grab hold of my arms and push me down.

CHAPTER XLV

3rd Week of Winter

Nikko

"Stay close to me. I've ordered Ivor ahead to gather others," Bacchus says over his shoulder. Mother and I follow him down the temple's long deserted hallway. I don't feel scared as we run for our lives, just numb.

How can Jada be gone? What is a world without my better half? She was so full of life before Heracles took it from her. My memory then becomes a cascade of red as I recall my father's spilled blood. He'll never scold me again. I would welcome it now, if given the chance.

We reach an exit and Bacchus turns towards us. "No matter what you see out there," he says, "keep your eyes forward and your feet moving. Stop to help no one."

Without a second glance, he opens the door and takes off at a run. The Queen and I follow closely behind, and my numbness quickly turns to overwhelm. The Holy City is afire and encased in poisonous vines. Citizens run about panicked, bumping into the toxic yellow blooms. Heracles' men easily slaughter the ones who manage to avoid the flowers. I stumble and the stink of death fills my nostrils as my hands meet the pavement. There are bodies everywhere.

The Queen curses, and I hear cloth tear as my uncle makes quick work of a nearby dead man's shirt. He tosses me a lengthy scrap of it and orders, "On your feet and wrap this around your face. We don't want to inhale the poison."

I do as he asks with trembling hands.

The three of us resume our escape with our mouths and noses protected. But we're out in the open and the afternoon suns make us easy targets. Bacchus is a warrior through and through and navigates us through the mayhem. He thrusts his sword into anyone who tries to intervene without tiring. After pulling his blade out of another enemy soldier, my uncle leads us down an alleyway.

There are no adversaries to block our path, and for a moment, I think we may be out of the worst, but then a devilish shriek comes from above. I look up and my eyes go wide at the sight of myth and legend. A large beast—a harpy—drops from the sky. Her enormous gray wings scrape against the buildings as she lands. She cannot fly in the narrow space, but the talons at her hands and feet appear sharp as knives. The harpy's yellow eyes are blind with insanity, and old wounds cover her naked flesh where her feathers have been removed. A dark collar encases her throat, puss seeps from under the metal. She screams at the three of us with a jagged toothed mouth.

During the initial attack, there was a report of cages outside the wall. This is what must've been screaming inside them this entire time. My voice shakes, "why is a minister of Zeus attacking us? She should be our ally!"

The harpy completely folds her wings and takes a clawed step towards us with a screech.

Mother hitches her dress and pulls a dagger from her thigh sheath. "Bacchus, get my son to safety while I distract it."

I snap at her, "You can't be serious!" My mother may have assisted in my training but the threat this time is no straw dummy or clumsy soldier.

Bacchus nods and raises his sword. "I'll protect him with my life."

I'm about to protest again, but Mother runs at the harpy while Bacchus grabs me by the collar and follows close behind her, dragging me with him. As the Queen leaps forward and digs her blade into the creature's shoulder, Bacchus and I skirt around them. I dig my heels in, trying to stop him. "We can't leave her!"

My uncle turns on me and growls. "The Queen isn't the kind of woman to need help. She'll be fine, now come on!"

Almost immediately, we're met by a soldier, and Bacchus runs him through with his blade. The soldier's body hits the cobblestone with a thump, and I see Jada diminish and fall all over again. All I can do is stare at the blood while the harpy screeches from behind. Something strikes me hard against the cheek and my head snaps sideways before I register that Bacchus is screaming.

"—got to pull yourself together, boy!" He puts the dead soldier's sword in my hand and shakes me by the arm.

My mother yells from somewhere behind: "Get out of here!"

I want to cry then, like a child. I'm scared. Everything hurts, not just my body from the pummeling the night before, but my heart as well. Regardless, I grip the sword.

Bacchus claps me on the back. "There you are. Now let's go."

We weave through the streets and alleyways of Ellanios for nearly two hours, cutting down human enemies and dodging the mythical and poisonous ones. In my heightened state it feels like seconds. The deaths of Jada and Father are so fresh that I don't find my first kill difficult, nor the one after. My body becomes a repeat of run and parry before sliding my blade into the next enemy who dares to cross my path. I'm strained with exhaustion by the time we make it to a familiar part of the ancient sector, but still, we run.

"Nikko!" The agonized cry to my left forces me to slow down.

I stop altogether and nearly drop my sword when I meet the wide terrified eyes of Darja from Cerberus' Maw.

"Help me," she cries. Darja lays in the street, blood dribbles from her lips. A harpy is feasting on her back.

I throw up.

The monster hears my retching and screeches, as if I'm a threat to her precious meal.

A solid hand wraps around my arm, and Bacchus pulls me roughly in between two dwellings. "You can't help her, keep moving. We're almost there."

I'm sobbing. I know there's no saving Darja. "Can we at least put her out of her misery?" I ask.

"No. She'll be dead soon enough. We can't risk confronting the winged bitch."

I know his assessment is pragmatic, and that he's trying to keep us both alive, but it feels heartless.

Minutes later, I'm weeping quietly as I crouch low in a flower bed below a cobbled road, near a dried-up canal. We're surrounded by the ancient sector's dilapidated historic buildings. Bacchus scans the area. and after a few tense moments, he elbows me and points. "You see that large bridge over there? Walk out to it, go under its center passage, and wait for me to do the same."

I rub my face and study the lengthy canal and the cracked stone bridge that's roughly fifty yards away. It's a viaduct and has three arches—two reasonably intact but the third is partially caved in. "Have you gone mad? I'll be exposed to the harpies and gods know what else. I don't particularly want to be eaten today."

"Just means you'll have to be quick, now, won't you? Go on then, I'll keep watch."

I stare long and hard at him, my father's closest confidant. His quick reflexes and knowledge of battle have kept me alive so far. With a parting glance, I step out from our hiding place and lower myself into the dried-up canal. My breath hitches when the temperature suddenly increases by several degrees. What in the Under? Why is it so unseasonably warm? I give Bacchus a look but then he wordlessly mouths, 'Keep going.'

Feeling exposed, I quickly move into a fighting stance with my sword, eyes darting back and forth keeping an eye on the buildings and the streets and all around me. I'm sweating from the heat as I make my way down the canal.

I'm at the halfway point when a woman runs across the top of the bridge in a panic. I stop and watch as her body turns to ice, starting at the feet and working its way up. Her mouth is frozen open in a silent scream. A slender man with long pale hair, dressed in a powder blue tunic, walks up to her immobile form and speaks, but from this distance I cannot hear what is said. He must be one of Heracles' Gifted generals. My eyes search frantically for a place to hide and find there is none that I could possibly reach in time.

The general kicks his victim's frozen form off the bridge, and she shatters onto the bedrock in bloody pieces that quickly start to melt. He looks straight at me. Fear steals the breath from my lungs as I stand paralyzed. With his ichor, he could easily freeze the entire canal, killing me instantly. I'm left dumbfounded though when the general sticks both hands in his pockets and walks the remainder of the bridge, before disappearing from sight on the other side.

He clearly saw me! Why am I not dead? I whisper a prayer of thanks to Zeus, grateful that I may live to breathe and fuck another day. I move at a faster pace, arriving at the bridge's center, when suddenly, a disembodied hand appears out of thin air. It grabs hold of my sweat sodden chiton. I yell as I'm pulled underneath the archway.

"Be quiet!" A young man hisses. "My illusion mainly tricks the eye. It gets a bit dicey with the ear. No one can see us under the bridge, but they may still hear us."

I struggle against him until I break free.

For a moment, I stand bewildered in front of my childhood friend, Jakab. I'm utterly speechless. But then I'm grinning from ear to ear, and I wrap my arms around him in a tight embrace. His seafoam colored dreads press against my cheek. Pulling back, I stare at him and speak with my voice lowered. "You were on sabbatical. How did you make it back?" I frown. "Wait, how did you get into Ellanios?" I think of my other two Crib-Brothers, Brontes and Dareios, and wonder if they are safe as well.

Jakab shrugs. "It became obvious to me I was needed here when the first few cities I traveled to were sacked. I've been in the Holy City for over a month, but your father had me conceal myself in case someone betrayed my whereabouts. Heracles has been hunting my kind apparently. The King needed my Gift for this plan to succeed." His eyes search behind me. "Where's the rest of your family? You're the first to arrive."

I open my mouth and close it, before I grasp him by the elbow. "It's just me and the Queen now." If she survived.

I watch as the stages of shock and disbelief register in his gray Ellanion eyes. He and Jada were friends, and I know he secretly loved her. Jakab drops to his knee and pounds his right fist against his heart before looking up at me, eyes misty. "Long live the King."

I shake my head in denial while pulling him to his feet. "None of that now my friend. I'm no king. I'm unworthy."

Jakab is on the verge of arguing when Bacchus joins us under the bridge. My father's advisor looks at me pointedly. "Then become worthy."

Become worthy . . . It's what Jada would want for me. I step away from the two of them and try to hide my pain by observing the surroundings. A dozen or so injured lie on the ground as Gareth works tirelessly on them. The boy on the verge of manhood appears worse than he did when I saw him this morning. I rush over to my friend. His hands rove over a sword wound in the thigh of a man lying before him. I note how the bandage I saw earlier is missing from his pinky and ring finger, the digits are entirely black. The Return has started, and Decay has set in. "Gareth, don't be foolish! Take a break. You'll lose your entire had if you keep this up!"

He glances at me, then says wearily, "I'm glad to see you're still alive and uninjured—" His eyes roll back in his head, and his body spasms then collapses. I catch him just as his patient moans and goes to sleep, the man's thigh is fully healed. As I lower Gareth onto his back, Jakab rushes over and examines him.

"He's really something, this kid," he says. "The boy has healed nearly fifty people already. We've been sending those who've recovered to join Ivor, as well as the citizens who've been advised to come here."

"What do you mean?"

Jakab gestures toward an open sewer grate in the floor. "The sewage tunnels run beneath the entire city and beyond. Bacchus has been marking an escape path since the siege started." His eyes move to Gareth. "Don't worry about him, he'll be all right. I'm speaking from my own experience, when I've taken my abilities to their limits and the Return begins. He'll recover well enough to walk after some rest, but he shouldn't heal anyone for a few days, otherwise he will lose his hand or worse, die."

My uncle joins us and addresses Jakab. "How soon until you reach your limit and you're like him? Once the illusion falls, we're exposed and can't provide safe passage across the canal."

My friend sighs, "About two hours, maybe three at most."

Bacchus clasps him on the shoulder, "If it weren't for you there'd be no escape for anyone. Remember that." He then looks at me. "If you haven't realized it already, your Crib-Brother is quite the talented man. He put an illusion on the canal so powerful, that anyone passing through cannot be seen."

"It's a double illusion really, two spaces are at work." Jakab corrects him. "You couldn't see all of us under the bridge, right? In the event an enemy wanders into the canal, we'll still remain unseen here.

However, we can still see everything from our vantage point. I've been practicing the trick for months."

I marvel at my friend. "Jakab, you're amazing." Still entirely too warm, I wipe the sweat that slides down my face. It's unusually hot for the season.

Jakab notices. "That's part of it." He grimaces. "It gives the illusion away, the temperature change of where the illusion resides. I don't know how to remedy it, but unless someone is familiar with how my Gift works, they won't know any better. We should still be safe."

Ah, that explains why I was so warm in the canal.

Bacchus looks at both of us. "I've no doubt the Queen survived the harpy. She'll be spreading word of the canal to the citizens as we speak. I'm going to do the same. If she isn't back within two hours, both of you leave with the rest."

I scowl at him. "How could I abandon my own mother? What kind of man do you take me for?"

My uncle's eyes are cold. "One that needs to stay alive at all costs. Unless the bloodline of our people continues, this is all meaningless." He speaks to Jakab, "I don't care if you must knock King Nikko over the head and drag his unconscious body through the flowing shit below. You are to get him out of the Holy City alive."

With a tiny sheepish smile, Jakab says, "Yes, Sir."

My uncle turns on his heel and walks out toward the canal, he climbs up the wall, and disappears from sight.

"You wouldn't dare hit me," I say to Jakab.

"I've always wanted to. So, you never know, today my dream may come true."

"I'm glad you're back." I laugh, although the joy doesn't last. "After joining Ivor, where do we go?"

Jakab looks troubled, "We didn't get that far into our planning. But with the number of injured and shortage of supplies, we can't travel far."

We'll need to think of something. The brutal little princess of Apotmos who murders her kin, comes fresh to mind. Distance wise, Apotmos is literally our closest ally, and Andromyda *did* say we were friends. Maybe she'll extend us safe passage, if we can make it through the Colossus Desert, that is. A moan comes from an injured citizen trying to make it down the sewage grate by himself.

Right, one problem at a time. I should focus on what's in front of me for now. I move to help what's left of my people to safety.

CHAPTER XLVI

3rd Week of Winter

Nikko

Despite Bacchus' warning, we continue to wait for my mother and other citizens beyond the two hours. Jakab and I are not willing to leave the city after hundreds of people safely make the crossing. There could be more we can save if we last just a little longer. My Crib-Brother is on his knees, panting heavily, and he braces himself against the bridge with his right hand. Beads of sweat slide down his face and his clothes are soaked with perspiration. Jakab's other hand is raised in an effort to make his illusion hold. The Queen and Bacchus did well to warn our people to move in silence, as it takes everyone's cooperation and stealth to save as many lives as possible. Although they themselves have yet to arrive.

Gareth is still out cold. I propped him up against the wall next to Jakab so he wouldn't block the egress to the sewer. I worry if he'll wake soon and have enough energy to travel. Jakab too. His eyes now flutter with threat of the Return. After another group of people arrive under the bridge and climb down into the tunnels, I make a decision and touch his shoulder. "Enough. You've done enough. We must go. We can't wait any longer." He shakes his head no, his weary eyes defiant. I'm about to argue when I hear footsteps approach from behind.

"It took me some time to track your scent through the city," says a familiar voice, soft as silk. "I had hoped I wouldn't find you, but I wasn't lucky and neither—it seems—are you, Prince."

Tracked my scent? I shut my eyes slowly before opening them again, unsure of who I'm about to face. "Are you Ker or Erebos?" I say as I turn around.

"Does it matter?"

My sister, who I loved with all my being, the person I idolized and adored, now wastes away like rotten fruit, and I again visualize her final moments as she crumpled to the temple floor. Her death is a turning point I can't come back from, and, whether he's Ker or Erebos, the man before me played a part in her death. Does it matter? I grit my teeth and harden my heart. "It doesn't," I tell him.

I didn't know it was possible for his eyes to go a shade darker, but they do.

"I can't bring her back to life," he says. "But if I could trade places with her, please know that I would. I prayed to Thanatos, asking that her journey through her after-life be safe and that if she is ever to arrive in Hades' domain, that he look the other way and let her pass to Elysium."

Erebos then. I palm the hilt of my sword. "So, you fucking knew this entire time what Heracles was planning. *And you didn't say anything?*"

His voice drops to a low whisper. "I could not. I was sworn."

"You were sworn? And that kept you from saving the lives of thousands of people including the person who was kindest to you? People are dead now, the Holy City is in ruins, and all you can say is that you were sworn not to?"

There is a heartbeat of silence between us and then Erebos says with a blank face, "You don't understand."

"Who's that?" Jakab asks from behind, his voice winded.

"An enemy of the vilest sort."

"Kick his arse then and be done with it. You've always been best with a blade."

Jakab won't last much longer. I need to do this quickly.

Erebos removes his shirt and tosses it to the side, putting his toned body and the chain he wears around his neck on complete display. "Prepare yourself, Prince, I can only manage to hold off for so much longer."

I take a step backward in confusion, and when he unfastens his pants, my brain quits working altogether. "What the fuck are you—?" The words die on my lips as Erebos' face begins to stretch, his jaw lengthening with an audible crack. He drops to his knees and moans in pain while his spine curves upward. His bones snap and black fur begins to grow from his naked skin until it covers him completely.

The man I knew is gone. Before me now, is a large black hound with a wolf-like appearance, bright red eyes, and fangs dripping. The only item that remains of Erebos is the silver chain around his neck.

"What kind of Gift is that?" Jakab asks bewildered.

The beast growls menacingly, a sound that gives me gooseflesh. I have the odd notion that I've see this creature somewhere before. I stare at it with narrowed eyes. "Jakab, do you remember those books about the Under our tutors would make us read? Didn't one picture a hound of some sort? Does he not have a likeness to the great Cerberus, the gatekeeper to the Underworld? Granted, he's missing a head or two."

At the mention of the name, the hound snaps at me, drool dripping from its maw. I draw my sword. "Use the rest of your strength to get to the tunnels, Jakab. You're in no shape to keep up your illusion or to fight."

"Fuck you. I'm staying."

The hound lunges for me then, and I swing my sword in a wide arc, but the beast dodges. Erebos… or wait . . . Cerberus? Why did he hide Heracles' plans from us? I don't have time to think more on it as he leans back on his haunches for another attack. I run to the far side of the underpass, drawing him away from Gareth and Jakab.

"Now I'm glad Father tortured you for all these weeks!" I taunt over my shoulder.

The hound growls.

I pivot on my foot and raise my blade in front of me. "Go back to your master like the dog you are."

He lunges at me again, aiming for my chest, and I bring my blade down toward his neck. I'm really going to kill him. A part of me knew that I would, but another part wished that I didn't have to. My blade strikes the chain and rather than cutting deep, the sword shakes in my hand upon impact, jarring me up to my elbows. What in the Under? How did it not cut through?

Erebos collides into my chest with his front paws and my sword is flung from my grip. We go down to the ground hard, and I punch against the hound's soft fur. He snaps his teeth next to my ear.

"Nikko!" Jakab yells.

Erebos' saliva drips onto my face while I push against his sternum to keep his teeth from tearing me apart. He gives another snap of his maw and nearly takes off my nose. All those times I had fantasized us together, this was not how I imagined I'd taste his spit for the first time. I begin to lose strength and my grip slips, my fingers are forced deeper into his black fur and under the silver chain he wears. The metal slips easily over my knuckles. How could my sword be repelled and yet my hand is not?

I shout when he bites into my left shoulder, his teeth sinking deep. Before he can take another, I grab hold of the chain he wears and pull with all my might. It slides free from his head, but I've yanked with such force that my right elbow slams into the ground, I yell as the bone splinters.

Erebos gives a high-pitched yip and immediately bounds off me. I lay in pain while there's a pop and another snap of bone, followed by silence. Then Erebos says, "It's done. You've freed me of Heracles' authority. I will not fight you again."

I wince as I manage to sit up using my left arm and cradling my right close to my chest. Erebos stands before me naked and human. I clutch the silver chain tightly. "What do you mean, beast? Are you going to kill me, or no?"

He kneels and stares at my bleeding shoulder. He reaches for the wound with his long fingers, but I kick out at him. "Don't touch me."

He retracts his hand and whispers, "There is much you don't know."

"I would say that is a fucking understatement." I peer over my shoulder, "Jakab? Gareth? How are you two holding up?"

My Crib-Brother's skin is slick with sweat, his back against the wall, he supports one arm up with the other, Decay reaches well past his left elbow. When Jakab answers, I know it's a struggle for him to speak. "The kid is still asleep, and my illusion will fall any minute now." He eyes Erebos with reproach. "If he's cooperating, best get what information you can before we leave."

He's right. I turn my attention back to Erebos, who is still on his knees. "You heard him. Start talking. If you're not going to attack me, then tell me something useful." I'm surprised when he follows my order.

"I am…not human… but the offspring of monsters, Typhon and Echidna." Erebos clears his throat. "I was captured by Zeus as a child and then given to Hades to serve and protect the Underworld. The God of Shadows treated me as a son and raised me. When Heracles tricked my father and overpowered us, he parted the Underworld, dividing me in the process and chained my other selves. He has used me ever since for his bidding. I've known very little of free will. The same can be said of Ker, and the one who still guards the Under's gates."

There's a lot to process—things that I can't fathom in this moment, although I pick up on something vital and show him the length of metal dangling between my fingers. "Why didn't you just remove it then? You had plenty of time away from your master."

His eyes narrow and flicker a shade of red at the sight of the very thing that imprisoned him. "Only a blood relative of Zeus may lift the chain and bind me. To all else, it is too heavy to bear. I was sworn by Heracles not to ask for any aid in its removal."

Well, that explains a lot. I experience an array of emotions, but mainly a bone-aching fatigue and grief. My sister and father are dead, my kingdom destroyed, and I've a crown to wear that I never wanted.

"Prince, I don't have much experience being human, but please know that this agony in my heart is for you and Princess Jada alone. My first wish after being freed is to be relieved of it."

"That feeling is called guilt," I say flatly. All those times we were close enough to touch, the interest he held for me was because I could free him from servitude. Not because he had a care for me personally. He probably doesn't even know how to care for another human. Something about that stings.

Erebos touches his chest and says, "guilt" with a sense of wonder, as if putting a name to his experience gives him a measure of peace.

"If you're done discovering one of the worst parts of being human, I could use a hand getting up."

"But you said not to touch you."

I roll my eyes at that. He's always so literal. "Things change." I hold out my hand to him.

His fingers meet mine, and I pull him close so that our lips nearly touch. A cruel act, for the proximity of my face catches the legendary beast off guard—I slip the chain over his head, binding him to me. The silver flares bright and Erebos cries out just as a tightness wraps around my left wrist as if I'm wearing a bracelet.

I can't believe I'm taking a slave, which makes me more like Heracles than I'd wish to admit.

"What have you done?" Erebos pushes me away, his mouth quivering.

Can I ever become worthy of the crown? With this, I don't think so. In this moment, I become the worst version of myself. A person Jada would be ashamed of, one I'm ashamed of as well. The weight of duty is crushing.

I get to my feet and force myself to become cold. "You are an invaluable source of information. You know Heracles, you know of the other gods, and maybe even how Ehvara came to be the mess it now is. I cannot simply let you go."

Erebos' lips pull back in a snarl, and then I see a real emotion on his pinched face. I return his glare. "The burning inside, that you're feeling right now? It's called hate. Now go get dressed."

The chain around his neck glows faintly and then as if pulled by invisible strings—like a puppet—he goes to his clothes. I check my wrist, because a thin weight continues to press there, but visually there's nothing of note, just my own flesh. A peculiarity.

I can't stomach Erebos following my command, instead, I turn my attention to Jakab who is on the verge of passing out. He lays belly flat with his Decaying arm outstretched toward the opening of the arch. Gareth who is now awake reaches for him with his own blackened fingers.

"Jakab!" I run over to my Crib-Brother and help him to a seated position. Then I turn to Gareth. "Don't even think about healing him," I say. "You're in bad shape yourself."

The boy eyes my bleeding shoulder and the way I nurse my right arm. He then looks at Erebos, who stands as far away from us as possible. "It seems, a lot happened while I was out."

"Gods, you don't know the half of—"

A thunderous clap cracks the sky, the clamor so powerful, even the ground shakes. I leave Jakab and Gareth to peak my head out from under the bridge, eyes going to the source. I gaze in astonishment as the Gods' Window shatters and the sky swallows up Olympus. The Lunetas Bridge disappears with it, leaving Ellanios in true night. It's the first time I've witnessed a sky full of stars.

Gareth whispers from behind me, "As long as you sing for me, I will shine my light on thee."

I turn to him, not understanding, his emerald eyes are distraught. "What do you mean?" I ask.

"All my life, I thought Elder Marcus was a crazy old man making up stories, but they weren't just stories . . . they were true all along. Heracles must've executed the Luminaie, silencing their voices. The ethereal song is what connected the Gods' Window and the Lunetas Bridge to Ehvara. We've been cut off from the gods."

I think of the priests in the temple, their constant singing, an act I always thought to be a mere show of pageantry. All this time, they were the bridge to the gods. Their angelic voices will now forever be a haunting echo in my mind.

I study the complete night that has enveloped my city, the only time I've ever seen such darkness. The world seems colder without all the light.

There's a gagging sound from behind, and I turn just in time to see Jakab vomit all over himself. The air shimmers and the temperature drops significantly as the illusion falls. The four of us are left wide open for our enemies to see. We can't wait any longer for mother or Bacchus.

"Erebos! Help me get him to the tunnel," I command.

He answers my call, chain flaring to life, and my wrist becomes heavy again. We lift Jakab between us, Erebos' face is an unreadable mask. I push away the guilt. We can never come back from this. I can't.

Gareth sees the exchange, and asks, "Why is he here again?"

"I don't have time to sing you wild tales, the enemy will surely be here soon."

When we get to the sewer opening, both Gareth and Jakab look at me and in unison say, "You first."

I shake my head with annoyance but do as I'm bid. I leave Jakab to Erebos and begin my descent down the ladder, cradling my bad arm. Overwhelmed by the stench of shit and piss, my eyes begin to tear. At the bottom, I find myself ankle-deep in sewage, but it means little to me because I hear a familiar snide voice call from above.

"What are you still doing here?" My mother demands.

Bacchus growls, "I thought I told you to leave after two hours. And why is Heracles' man here?"

I call up to him. "Uncle, let it rest. I'll explain later, but he's our man now."

"He can't come with us. He's a risk, he's—

I pitch my voice with authority. "I *said*. Let it rest."

Bacchus stares down at me for a long moment but concedes.

Shortly after, I'm face to face with my mother. A combination of soot and blood covers her from head to toe. But still, she stands tall like the queen she is. The slap of her hand stings my cheek before she pulls me into a rare hug that surprises me. "You never were one for listening. Now we must go and join the others."

I rub my stinging face as she steps away. "Do you have a plan?" I ask her. "Where do we go from here?"

Tiredness shows in her eyes. "I don't know. There's nowhere safe now."

"I was thinking maybe we should try out chances in Apotmos. We still have allies there, but I worry many won't survive crossing the desert."

"Then let the weak and spoiled ones die," she says and walks past me.

Bacchus, Erebos, Jakab, and Gareth join us. My uncle takes the lead and we follow the path he marked earlier. A small lightning bolt is painted on each viable tunnel. We wade through the sewage in silence, the past few hours pressing heavily on all of us. The Holy City has fallen, the future uncertain, and I hold power over someone in a way no one ever should. Unable to help myself, my gaze frequently drifts over to Erebos who meets it with promised defiance. I deserve all the hate he's bound to feel.

I think of Heracles' wickedness, the deaths of Jada and my father. How Mother and Bacchus risked their lives to lead my people to refuge, and how Gareth and Jakab spent themselves to aid in their escape. I was useless to help anyone. Some king I am, I'm entirely pathetic.

"I wish I was truly powerful," I whisper to myself. If I were, I would make the world right again.

Without warning, the tunnel begins to tremble, and a flash of blinding light brings us to a halt. The scent of a fresh storm cleanses the air and the muddy water at my feet evaporates. I hear my mother gasp as I struggle to open my eyes against the glare.

A voice full of thunder bellows, "Blood of my flesh, is it true that you wish for power? Be quick with your answer, or I will choose another."

I lower my arms at the sight of the almighty Zeus. His face so bright, my eyes can hardly tolerate it. If I wasn't a true believer before, I am now. With the others, I drop to my knees in reverence, my insides twisting with fear. The power that pulsates from the God of Thunder is immense and causes debris from the tunnel to fall around us. I manage to find my voice in the fear. "Yes, God of gods. For my people, I wish to be powerful."

"And so, it shall be my Champion," he says, violet eyes flashing. I cry out as a searing pain consumes the flesh of my back, and my palms pulse with heat. I then stare in wonder, at the lightning that crackles from my outstretched fingers.

CHAPTER XLVII

4th Week of Winter

Eimear

Ehvara is darker today, and I don't refer to my considerably bleak outlook on life. The world is literally dimmer. At some point after sundown, the Lunetas Bridge fell. Evarah's bright link to the gods disappeared from existence and took the West and East Windows with it. There is now only one sun, one moon. The Brothers have left us, leaving their mournful Sisters behind.

I can't believe I missed it! The greatest event to ever occur in Ehvara's history, and I slept through it. I stare up at the windowless sky and wonder if the gods can really be gone from this world. Rumors have already spread around the castle. Some believe the gods have forsaken us, that we're somehow unworthy of their presence. I scoff at the bullshit. Why does anyone need a god to make them worthy? In my experience, gods are cunts. Everyone is better off without them.

It's afternoon, and under the lonely sun, I sit against a now-baren tree. The red needles are dead, scattered across the ground. The rest of the trees are the same, that must've happened in the night too. I pick at the indigo grass aimlessly, pulling up handfuls only to toss it aside. But something catches my eye and I squint at a handful. At the base of the blades, near the root, it's green—a color I've never seen before on grass. How peculiar. I remember a time when I would have been excited over such a thing, but now I realize there's nothing special about it at all. It's just grass.

I sigh. "So much has changed about me." I'm lucky to be alive after being whipped, I should be happy, should be grateful to have my life, but instead, I'm depressed. I feel as if I've fallen into a hole so deep that I may never climb out. There's something gone from me, and it's been replaced by a hungry thing sitting below the surface, growing angry with need. I don't know how to feed it.

The wind picks up and a strand of white hair is blown onto my face. I tuck it behind my ear, and my fingers graze the new mask I wear. My burlap hood was ruined by yesterday's blood. Upon waking, I constructed a replacement out of black cloth. There isn't anyone at Castle Notos who would force me to cover my face now, force me to do anything really, as scared as they are of me. But I stole a look in the mirror this morn, and couldn't stand the sight of my face. Self-loathing is a twisted heavy burden.

Without warning, a loud noise cuts across the castle grounds. It's strange, it sounds as if fabric is being torn. Confused, I stand and look for the source. Near the gates, an emerald light begins to grow until it's the size of a large door. Another portal. Soon, a boot emerges followed by the rest of General Charos. He walks with confidence toward the castle steps.

His plans must have been successful. I think about the Voranian letter and my belly turns with guilt for the deaths. When Astera emerges from the light, I know something's amiss. The shadows have deepened under her eyes. She looks as if she'll fade away completely. My heart hurts for my friend, and I resolve to light the lantern when night falls. For both our sakes, I hope Steilos can come quickly. I'm not sure what will happen once the guards brief Charos about yesterday's Confessional. I should find a place to hide just in case they spout the nonsense about me being a demon.

The portal disappears and, mercifully, Persephone has stayed on its other side. I take another look at the windowless sky. If she's still here… then not all gods are gone from Ehvara just yet. Some must've been left behind or chosen to stay. Heracles could still be here too. But what does that mean for Ehvara? Probably nothing good. The thought is disturbing enough that I set it aside for later.

Saray comes running down the castle steps and bows to the General. He waves her away, as if she's insignificant, and walks past. Saray takes Astera by the hand and leads her toward the entrance, presumably back to her rooms where she'll be locked away again.

Astera must sense my stare from the tree because she turns, and her eyes find mine. It's as if I'm looking at a stranger. The girl who enjoys gardening and long stories is gone.

She shakes her head at me, and I'm overcome by a sudden chill. I don't understand what she's trying to say. The two disappear inside. Perplexed, I lean against the tree and brew over what must've happened to her. I imagine the worst. When Steilos arrives, he better run her bastard of a father through with his blades. Suddenly, I feel a tugging sensation in my lower abdomen, followed by an unexpected urgency to follow Astera. What the Under? I can't go to her now. It's safer to wait until nightfall.

The feeling persists, becoming more insistent. I'm like a puppet on strings because my feet seem to carry me forward on their own accord. The pulling sensation becomes more intense with each step, urging me to hurry. I curse and break into a run. Something's wrong.

When I enter the castle, both guards immediately jump away from me. They let me pass without comment. I'd like to bask in their fear, just to torment them, but now isn't the time. I rush up the stairs and when I reach the top, my eyes go wide. Styx! On the ballroom floor, Saray lays unconscious, bleeding from her temple.

I quickly kneel beside her and am relieved to discover that she's still breathing. Her eyes flutter open when I touch her face. She moans.

"What happened to you? Where's Astera?" I begin to panic. The pulling sensation in my abdomen has become stronger, urging me to find my friend, but I can't leave Saray.

She goes to sit up, and I assist her. Saray appears confused, her eyes are dazed. She probably has a concussion. My fingers smooth the dark hair away from her face. "Are you okay?"

Saray blinks and looks at me. "That girl pulled a rock out of nowhere and hit me in the head with it."

"Wait . . . Astera did?"

She nods and touches her temple. "That child is about to do something reckless."

The tugging in my belly intensifies as I help Saray up then walk her to the stairs where she can sit. Everything must happen now, there's no more time. I observe the woman who has been like a mother to me. "Saray, what I was asking you about in the sewing room was real. I'm leaving Notos with Astera soon. I want you to come with us. I have a plan."

She stares at me like I've lost my mind and shakes her head. "My brains must be addled, but did you just say that you're *leaving*? I know you're a miracle, but the General . . . he's something else. He'll kill you both!"

My hand finds hers. "I can't explain it all now, but yes, I'm going. It'll be safe, you have to trust me. Believe in me *please*."

Saray is about to speak, but I must go to Astera *now*. I give her a quick kiss on the cheek, silencing her questions. My feet know where to go on their own, guiding me back down the stairs and through the castle. I run past both slaves and guards, all of them watch opened-mouthed but none step forward to stop me. When I realize where Astera must have gone, I increase my speed. The floor trembles under my feet as I draw closer to General Charos' wing. I'm barely a foot away from his hall when a shriek, followed by the sound of a crashing object, gives me pause.

I round the corner and see that one of the doors to his study has been completely ripped off its hinges. Cracks run through the stone floor like an earthquake has run its course. I pass a guard crouched at the base of the stairs, his arms shielding his head. Another guard runs toward me, then past, with a look of terror on his face. I'm not able to assess the scene because the ground shakes and a massive block of stone punches through the study wall heading right for me.

I throw myself to the side and hit the floor with a grunt. I lift my head to see rubble all around, this section of the castle is completely ruined. The General's unsettled laughter comes from the study and Astera lets out a frustrated scream. The ground shakes again. Afterward, a fresh cloud of debris wafts from a new hole in the wall.

The dust makes me cough and I go to stand. Breathing into the crook of my arm, I approach the punctured wall and peer through it. The study is in an upheaval, furniture is wrecked, books scattered all around, shards of glass from a broken mirror is among them. The flail that was previously mounted on the wall has fallen, with its handle now split.

The General's back is to me, and Astera pants with exhaustion, her face strained. My friend's eyes are wild as if her mind has wholly broken. Everything clicks into place. I wasn't the only one of us keeping secrets. Astera is Gifted with ichor like her father.

"You're going to have to do better than that, Astera. I won't die so easily," Charos says.

She yells with rage, her voice raw, "No, I just have to live long enough for what you stole from me to wear off." The ground quakes, and a spear made of stone rises from the floor. With a wave of her hand, Astera launches the weapon at her father, but he blocks the attack with a shield of his own making. Both spear and shield immediately crumble to dust.

"I'll need to break you again," he sneers. "It seems you forgot how to obey. I'll remind you."

Astera hurls more stone at Charos, but he dodges it with ease. Her breathing is labored, and I worry she won't be able to fight for much longer. If the Return begins, Charos will have the advantage. I step over the rubble, entering the study. I press my back against the wall and seem to go unnoticed.

Astera's teeth are barred at her father. "Without me, you'd just be an ordinary man. A weakling to be tossed aside. Heracles would have no use for you."

"Enough!" He snarls, and the ground beneath Astera's feet rumbles. Her legs become encased by stone, but she's stuck only for a moment before she breaks the restraints. The General however, is quick and leaps in front of her in an instant. He grabs his daughter by the throat with his braced arm that holds the citrine. She gasps for air, the color draining from her face. As Astera's strength is taken from her, she stares at the General with pure hatred.

He smiles in return, "You should feel proud of yourself." Charos surveys the destruction around them. "You could kill me if you were better trained."

"No thanks… to you," Astera manages to say.

"About that, it seems I've been too soft on you lately. I thought I taught you to fear your own power. We'll resume our daily lessons." Charos caresses her cheek, and Astera's ice blue eyes widen in fear.

My heart pumps with rage. I won't let him cut her ever again. I'm careful as I pick up the flail and coil the long chain around my hand, avoiding the spikes at the head. Neither one of them notices me as I make my way closer.

Astera struggles against the General. "All the deaths you've caused… stain my hands as well. But... no more."

I sprint forward with everything I have before releasing the chain of the flail. It swings in a wide arc behind me before I cast the weapon forward with all my might. The momentum brings the striking head down onto the General's arm, pulverizing the bone at the elbow. His severed appendage with the bracer hits the ground with a thud and I yank the chain of the flail, bringing the striking head back toward me.

Charos stares at his bleeding stump in shock, and I savor his expression with a grin when he finally howls in pain.

"This bastard will never use you again. Everything will be—" I turn towards Astera, and time slows as I register the blood blooming at the front of her chest. A stone spear went through her back and pierced her heart, it drips red at the tip. She gives me one last smile before her eyes close.

Astera killed herself. The pounding in my ears grows louder at the sight of her lifeless body hanging from the spear, her feet barely skim the floor. No… this can't be. We were going to be free together.

Charos' screams have transitioned to a dull moan. He drops to the ground and holds his bleeding stump to his chest. I watch as he struggles to remove his belt to make a tourniquet.

"She's dead," I whisper.

The General snarls. "I'm going to enjoy killing you." He raises his good arm at me, but nothing happens. The sheer surprise on his face is comical. I would laugh if my heart wasn't already broken to pieces. I bend down and pick up the severed arm, the citrine is still intact within the bracer.

"You were stealing from her all along, weren't you? All those years, locking Astera in the tower and only letting her out so you could take the ichor from her." My voice sounds detached even to my own ears. The General doesn't reply, his nose pinched into a scowl and mouth set in a flat line. I know he isn't sorry, doesn't even care that his own daughter has died.

I turn back to my friend, her face is slack and without color. I think about how she experienced little joy in her life. I don't know if she ever felt true happiness. I wanted to give her that and now I can't. It's not fair. A cold rage washes over me. I want the General to suffer as

Astera suffered all this time. A monster inside me rears its head, begging to be unleashed. It snaps its teeth, hungry for blood.

//Take heed. You have no control over this new strength you've acquired.//

But her voice is small, and in this moment, I just want someone to hurt.

The air around me pulsates, and changes. Every surface and object, even the General, are blanketed in a dull shade of gold. A black shadow that lingers just around the edges of it all, expands as far as I can see. I watch in fascination as the whites of the General's eyes turn black, and his head whips backward at an unnatural angle, his mouth open wide. Soon, the screaming begins, but it's not just his voice I hear. No, the sound of a hundred screams or more fill my ears. The shock of it brings me to my knees, and I catch my reflection in the shattered glass on the floor. My golden eyes glow behind my makeshift mask, and a dark silhouette in the shape of wings protrudes from my back.

The reflection reminds me of a beast, and I know for certain, I don't want to be this way. My fist smashes the mirror fragment, fracturing it further, but it doesn't drown out the shrieks of the dying. Charos' body begins to twist at grotesque angles, his legs and good arm snapping. Something no human can survive. He screams through it all and I'm horrified. I just want everything to stop. But it doesn't. It isn't until I feel the edges of my own life begin to fade, and I slip into unconsciousness, that everything falls quiet.

CHAPTER XLVIII

4th Week of Winter

Eimear

My head pounds and my body is stiff when I start to wake. There's a wheezing sound, and I want to know the source. The light is dim, and it takes time for my eyes to adjust. Once they do, I see that the General's severed arm is amidst the rubble. I must have dropped it. I take a deep breath and wince. My body really hurts. Every inch of my skin is hypersensitive, to move is an agonizing feat. I force myself to stand and turn my head toward the sound that woke me.

"Astera!" I yell, and do my best to hobble over to her, dodging the broken layers of floor around me. The girl's glassy eyes find mine, her hands are around the spear point, her breathing wet. I reach for her, "How are you alive? I can't believe it."

"Life must have different plans for me," she says, voice weak.

I wrap my arms around her waist. "This is going to hurt, bear with me."

Astera gives a slight nod.

I lift with my legs while pulling her backwards. She groans and passes out. When her body is freed, she collapses on top of me, and we both fall to the floor. With effort, I carefully roll her over and then gently touch her face. "Astera stay with me. Please don't die."

Her hand reaches for mine. "Turns out the General was right, I need more practice. I've a poor aim and missed my own heart." She chuckles slightly and then grimaces in pain.

I smile because I'm just happy for her to be alive, but then my eyes take stock of her bloody chest. She won't stay with the living much longer if she doesn't see a healer. I struggle to get up but manage to do so.

"I need to go get help. You're still bleeding."

Astera looks up at me. "Where's the General?"

I glance over at the husk of a body, bent at all angles like a dead spider. She hasn't seen him yet. I'm unsure of how to tell Astera that I killed her father. "He won't be bothering you anymore," is all I say on the subject.

"Good," she whispers before closing her eyes.

I step out of what remains of the study to search for help. The guards must have fled. Castle Notos is deathly quiet. Night has fallen, but it's still too early for anyone to retire, and how could they with the all the recent mayhem?

I need to find Saray. As I make my way to the opposite wing of the castle, I discover the reason for the silence. There are dead bodies everywhere, carcasses similar to the General's—dried up husks, bent, with their mouths gaping open in a noiseless scream. Their eyes replaced with an inky black substance. I keep walking toward the direction of the kitchen, fighting my rising panic. Where's Saray?

Soon, I find her at the bottom of a staircase, her body the same as the others, all twisted inward, with black tears. I choke on a scream. I killed her.

I walk toward Saray's broken form and my foot bumps into something. Peering down, I find a satchel on the floor with provisions that have spilled out. She was going to run with me. Tears stream down my face as I touch her cheek. What was once soft has turned brittle, and Saray begins to crumble. I watch stupidly as she turns to dust, only her uniform and eye patch remaining. I pick up the eye patch and cradle it to my chest. My sobs fill the empty spaces of Castle Notos.

I come to discover that everyone who was inside the castle is dead, even poor Angus. I found his remains in the kitchen along with other slaves who were preparing the evening meal. I go outside in hopes that whatever I unleashed didn't make it past the fortress walls, but it did. The guards stationed there received the same fate. I don't bother going to the smithy to check on Egan, knowing what I'll find there. All the people I've labored and sweat with these past months are gone, reduced to dried up husks, and it's all my fault. My sacred-self warned me that I had no control of what lies beneath my skin, but I didn't listen and everyone else paid the price for my rage.

My soul is forever stained. I'll never be permitted to enter the gates of Elysium. I'll never see my mother or father again. I don't deserve to. I let myself swim a few moments longer in my self-hatred, but then think of how Astera is still alive and waiting for help. I cling to the task of saving her life as if it were my own salvation. My fingers shake as I light the lantern in the top east window of the castle. Steilos is mine and Astera's only hope at this point, she'll die if she doesn't get medical attention soon.

Each time I pass a dried husk of a body, I wonder about the origins of this new power. It must be from the new god that marked me. My sacred-self is silent on the matter and doesn't confirm. After what I did, she may never speak to me again. I know now that I'm the one who killed those guards at the whipping post, their deaths were different but my doing all the same. The monster sleeps under my skin, waiting. It's satisfied with what it did, and I'm disgusted with myself because a part of me is satisfied too. But the more I think about it, the more puzzled I am that Astera was spared. The only explanation I can find, is that she was unconscious, while the others were awake.

I go back to the kitchen and gather an assortment of herbs that slow bleeding and infection. Angus kept his cabinet well stocked. He must've helped more people than just me. I slip the vials into my pocket and glance at his body on the floor. Thank you.

When I return to the study with an armful of clean towels, Astera is passed out. As I reposition her and doctor the wound, she moves in and out of consciousness, groaning. I clean up all the blood and, although my work is nothing like Mana's or Gareth's, it may keep her alive long enough until help comes. When I finish, I curl up beside her and wait for Steilos.

After a few hours, Astera's hand bumps against mine, and my eyes widen in surprise. "You're awake?" I whisper.

She interlaces her fingers with mine, her voice is soft when she speaks. "I've helped kill so many people. They took me to Ellanios this time, but before that, there were others. Wherever I went with the General, death soon followed. He used me to kill over and over again. I was never there to see it, but I could always hear the dying. I've had to live all this time knowing that because of me, people are dead. I've helped destroy so many." Her tears come fast.

At least now I know who I've hurt. The letter I wrote aided Heracles in the fall of Ellanios, aided in their destruction. I wrap my arms around her, trying to bring us both some comfort. "Shhh . . . it's fine, you were forced to do it, you had no choice," I tell her. She stills within my embrace.

"What happened to the General, Eimear? I saw him."

I wonder for a moment if I should lie, if I should tell her I don't know. Astera will probably be disgusted with me, the monster I've become. But if I lose her too, I deserve the punishment. So, I tell her everything. My throat becomes dry from speaking, and even though I hold her close against me, it feels like there's a canyon between us as I wait for her response.

To my astonishment, she squeezes me, even tighter. "I want to go wherever you go. If it's with this Steilos person, I'll follow you. Eimear, that man on the ship deserved it, and you didn't kill everyone in the castle on purpose. I know you, and your heart is good. The gods will understand, they'll let you into Elysium, I'm sure of it."

I don't need anyone to condone my actions, nor do I seek forgiveness for them. But I'm happy that Astera doesn't hate me. At least I won't be alone on my journey with Steilos. I don't think the gods will forgive me as easily as she has, but I don't tell her that.

"I believe we should both try to live in order to atone for what we've done," Astera says, "At least we can do that together. We'll find your brother in the process. I'd love to meet him." She sounds hopeful.

"I like the sound of that."

It's the early hours of the morning when she falls asleep. We're waiting for Steilos to come for us, but I'm not certain when that will be. I can't sleep though, not with the guilt of what I've done weighing on me. There's death everywhere I look.

My thoughts turn to the General's severed arm. I get up to retrieve it, careful not to disturb Astera. I remove the bracer and throw the appendage to the floor, kicking it aside. I then turn the bracer vertical, and peer down into its hollow. The stone embedded within isn't covered by metal but actually sticks out on either side. It must have been rubbing against the General's arm the whole time, touching his skin.

A soundless hum emits from the citrine, I hear the buzz in my head. The stone shines despite the low light, and I've a sudden urge to put the bracer on. Steilos said not to touch it, but fuck him, he isn't here. My fingers fumble for the stone and a tremor of power immediately travels up my hand. I drop the bracer in shock and it strikes the floor with a loud clatter. I glance at Astera, who remains undisturbed. Styx, what was that?

//Greed.//

//Ah, so we're still on speaking terms. This stone, it has a name?//

//More a purpose than a name. It's a powerful little thing, that's for sure.//

I bend down for the bracer. This time when I pull the citrine free, I'm prepared. Or so I think.

It's not just the sensation of power that courses through me, I'm hit with an overwhelming and shameless want. All my hopes and dreams, ripe for the taking. Everything should be *mine*. Everything *can* be mine.

The room is empty but for Astera and myself, however the touch of phantom hands feels solid as they caress my shoulders. My head turns towards her sleeping form.

Her power could be mine. I just have to take it.

My sacred-self is indifferent. *//If that's your will, there's no one to stop you from reaching for more.//*

I slip into a daze and move toward Astera. I could crush anyone if I had her Gift. Everything would be easier. But as I look at my friend, I know what I truly want.

I make a fist around the stone, its rough edges press against my skin. //You would've let me hurt her? Was the destruction of Ellanios not enough?//

//We experience through you. Your love. Your hate. The everything in between. But we hold no dominion over you. If you want to scorch the world, we'll support you in the burning. Want to do something different? Be the catalyst for change? We'll guide the way. So yes, we would have let you hurt her, solely because a part of you desires it.//

The citrine hums quietly in my palm, and I get the itch to take from Astera again. I turn the stone over in my fingers. I realize it doesn't *make* you do anything, only shows you what you want and how to get it. Just like this voice inside me. I chew my lip, eyes burning. It would be better if I had someone to blame for all my hateful thoughts and actions, but I'm simply the sum of all that is me, and I should claim every bit of myself.

I rip a scrap of fabric from the bottom of my dress and carefully wrap the citrine in it. When I feel nothing, I'm reassured that Greed needs skin to skin contact to dig its claws into anyone. I tuck the stone into my pocket, deciding to give it to Steilos as promised. I don't want to tempt the monster I've become.

I am wholly a dark thing now. I must learn to live with that.

CHAPTER XLIX

4th Week of Winter

Eimear

A full day has passed and Steilos still hasn't arrived. Astera is burning up with fever, her face flushed red and hair sticky with sweat. If it weren't for my limited knowledge of medicine, she'd be dead by now, but still, I'm not my mother or Gareth. She needs help and soon, or she won't make it. I checked the stables for a horse to possibly transport her, but like the people within the castle, the horses were all dead. Desperate, I went to the healing spring below, just in case it could help her like it did me. I brought the water to her, but it did no good.

I'm sick with worry as I watch over her frail body. I was able to find blankets and a few pillows to make her more comfortable. "I don't know what to do for you, I don't know why Steilos hasn't come yet. I'm so sorry."

"Stop that," she says while staring out at the broken window. "I didn't survive all this time just to die. I'm going to do so much. When I'm better, I want to go dancing and swim in the sea. Afterward, I'll lay in the grass and enjoy the sunlight drying my skin."

"All of those things, we'll definitely do," I squeeze her hand.

Astera frowns for a moment and turns toward me. "There's one more thing."

"What's that?"

"We have to stop him, Heracles. My father was merely a pawn. Heracles is the one controlling the board. Ehvara can't stand as it is. People shouldn't be slaves. Little girls shouldn't be locked in towers, and kingdoms shouldn't have to fall because of a demigod's whim. Heracles has to die so we can all be free."

Astera's glassy eyes are fierce, and I'm ashamed because I've wanted his death only for my own revenge, but she wants it for everyone. "He'll suffer for everything he's done. We'll find a way," I promise.

"Why don't you search Father's rooms? Maybe there's something useful hidden."

Between all the dead bodies and worrying about keeping Astera alive, the thought hadn't crossed my mind. "Will you be all right if I go?"

She nods her head and closes her eyes. "Yes, I'm just going to rest for a bit."

As I open the door to the General's private rooms, I wonder what I'll see. What does a cruel, yet weak-willed man want around him? At first glance there's nothing but rubble and the remains of luxury. A large four-poster bed stands at the center with its midnight blue curtains askew. Plush rugs are crumpled up on the cracked stone floor and the armoires and dressers that used to line the walls, have all toppled over. I begin my search only to find clothes and items of little interest. There really was nothing special about him. Frustrated, I walk over to the bed and rip back the curtains to discover the large, twisted body of Charos' chimera.

"Styx!" I put my hand to my chest and feel my heart race.

I survey the dead beast and can't say I feel remorse over its fate. A few months ago, I would have, but after watching men be eaten alive by the General's pet, my view of chimeras has changed. I hope never to see another again. I turn to leave but something doesn't sit right with me, as if I missed something. I ground myself, reaching out with my sixth sense, and from the center of the bed, a small heart beats. I sigh loudly and stare at the chimera's dried corpse. When the universe tells a joke, I wonder if there's any who actually laugh.

I touch the chimera and she disintegrates, just like Saray. The reminder makes my eyes sting. Left behind amongst the ashes is a large black egg, speckled with bright sapphire. The beast must've been curled up with her brood when it happened. I sigh again as I hoist the heavy egg into my arms. I can't just leave it here to die. But I'm not keeping a chimera, that's for damn sure.

As I make my way back to Astera, I sense Steilos' presence along with three others inside the study with her. Gently, I sit the egg down on the floor, and peer beyond the doorway. The four stand around my friend, peering down at her. Astera's eyes are closed, chest barely moving. I rush toward her, shoving a young man out of my way. "Astera, are you okay?"

She doesn't wake.

"Is that the General's daughter?" Steilos says flatly.

I glare at him, ignoring the other three. "Yes. And we're friends. Is that a problem?"

"As a matter of fact, it could be."

I rise, bringing myself a hand span away from him, the smell of cloves clings to his white shirt. I gesture to the room around us and point to the General's husk of a corpse. "I killed Charos. So, I would suggest you make sure there isn't a problem."

Steilos' expression is stern. "It appears that our skills aren't needed. We saw the bodies and almost turned back. I wondered what could've done such a thing, and now I know. Great work taking care of Charos, but did you have to slaughter everyone else?"

I flinch, and he cocks his head, amber eyes searching.

"You don't need to come with me," he finally says, "now that you can protect yourself. But the offer stands if you still want to join me." He juts his chin toward Astera. "She can come too."

I observe my friend. Everything she and I have ever known has been destroyed. We could survive on our own, but I'd like to do more than that. I want a home.

I look at the others who remain silent. They must be the associates Steilos spoke of before. A dark-skinned woman with a scar along the edge of her cheek—the jagged line gives her a fierce appearance. There's a man on either side of her. One carries an axe, his long beard is braided, and the sides of his head are shaved. The other is tall, with a young face, not much older than me. His messy dark hair falls into kind eyes, though the assortment of blades strapped at his hip say he's dangerous.

They seem like a capable group. I tuck a white strand behind my ear and speak only to Steilos "When do we leave?"

Castle Notos is behind me, and I stand at the beach below the cliff. I've fastened the chimera egg to my back, and in my right hand, I hold Charos' coiled flail. We all have our mementos, and this is one of mine. I plan on learning its ways intimately.

The smoke from Steilos' pipe wafts through the air as waves crash against the shore. His three companions load Astera into a small boat. I stare past them at the black ship that waits for us in the

Aethiopian Sea, its dark wood and translucent sails blend with the night, making it difficult to see.

I grit my teeth. Unpleasant memories of the last time I was on such a vessel resurface. I whirl on Steilos, "If you're a mercenary for Heracles, I swear to the gods I will murder you here and now."

He glances at me sideways with a shit-eating grin. "No. I'm not. But I won the ship in a bet against a very wealthy mercenary. I named her the *Wet Pearl*, on account of how much I love a good juicy clam." He winks.

I make a face. Gross. "You, *won* it?"

"Kid, I told you from the beginning. I'm a man of many ventures. One of which is gambling, and I'm a great gambler. I took a chance on a scrap such as yourself and now, Charos is dead. I always win a bet." He pats me on the shoulder before hoisting himself into the small boat. Steilos then holds his hand out to me, and I take it.

We row out to the *Wet Pearl* and, after we board, the next hour goes by in a blur. I'm given food and a change of clothes. Astera still hasn't awakened and is taken to a cabin where a healer changes her bandage and gives proper medical treatment. I leave the egg at her bedside; something tells me it wants to be with her. Odd as that is, better her than me.

The upper deck is a bustle of activity as we prepare to set sail. Steilos has an entire crew, and I can't help but be concerned. Where did he find all these people? Are they for hire, or do they follow him? Just who have I allied myself with?

//He's a decent enough man. We'll get where we're supposed to be with his help.//

//And where's that exactly?//

My sacred-self doesn't answer. Guide my ass, she's absolutely worthless.

I lean against the railing and take in the night sky that holds only one moon and no godly bridge or windows. It's so much darker now. My tongue tastes the salt in the air, and waves splash against the ship as we set sail. I'm on edge, recollections of the slave ship linger.

"Enjoying the view?" I startle at the sound of Steilos' voice behind me, and turn to find that he wears a mocking smile. "Really now, all this time at Notos, and you still haven't learned to not let someone sneak up on you? I have my work cut out for me."

I scowl, and he laughs.

He joins me against the railing and runs a hand through his wind-whipped hair. "Honestly, you outdid yourself. I'm curious to know how you did it, but I'm sure you have your secrets." He waits expectantly for my reply, but I remain silent. I'm not ready to tell others about the monster inside me. Not just yet.

Instead, I say, "Let's cut the bullshit. This is what you were after right?" I dig my hand into the pocket of my new oversized tunic and pull out Greed who is still wrapped in the cloth of my old uniform. I move it aside, so the stone is exposed to the night air.

Steilos stares transfixed, "Yep, that's it all right. Did you touch it?" I nod my head, and he swears. "I told you not to touch it, the stones are dangerous."

"How could I *not* after you told me I shouldn't? I was curious. But please take it, I don't want the thing anywhere near me." I hand Greed over to him.

Steilos takes the citrine from the cloth and closes his eyes. When he opens them, he peers around in search of something. I back away quickly not knowing what the consequences would be if he touched me. I'm not completely sure what lies beneath my own skin, but I'm certain it's not safe to duplicate.

Steilos finds what he's looking for and walks over to a discarded cord of rope. He picks it up before staring intently at Greed. When he drops the rope to the floor, an exact replica forms in his hand. He shows it to me. "Ha! It works!"

I examine both sets of rope unamused. "And?"

His eyes shine when he holds the gem out to me. "This is how we become the greatest thieves in all of Ehvara. Anything we want in the world is ours for the taking."

"I don't quite follow."

"With this, we can reproduce any substance, be it gold, jewels—

"Or other people's Gifts," I say harshly.

"Ah, so I was right. The bastard General was never Gifted after all. The problem with his strategy is that he always had to have a source nearby."

"Astera," I whisper.

Steilos nods. "If she was his source, there's a time limit for how long the stone can imitate another, whether it be an inanimate object or a person's Gift. In battle, you'd have to act fast or find yourself dead when the effects wore off." Transfixed, he stares at Greed and then shakes his head before wrapping it back up and placing the stone in the satchel he wears across his shoulders. "I was right to warn you, this is dangerous. It can bring out the worst in a person."

I squint my eyes in suspicion, "Will it bring out the worst in *you*? And while we're on the subject, how do you know so much?"

He taps his temple. "Kid, I've got an iron will. Only I can bring out the worst in me." Steilos gives me a wink. "Also, Ares himself told me about the stone."

I scoff. "I think it's high time you told me a little more about yourself and the God of War. I've earned that much."

Steilos stares out into the water, his eyes the slightest bit troubled. "When I was younger, the God appeared before me and offered a deal. He'd grant me power, and in exchange I'd gather the stones before my death. The seven sisters are scattered across Ehvara."

Seven Sisters? So that's what they're called. "What's the catch? What if you don't find them?"

He grins. "Then I'll spend an additional lifetime as a slave in his service. I don't know the specifics of how that'll work—being dead and all."

I stiffen. "Metis never made me promise anything in return. Why did Ares bargain with you?"

"She may not have when she marked you, but that doesn't mean she won't ask for a boon later."

"Styx!" I hiss. Owing a debt, especially to a goddess, never bodes well. My eyes go up to where the Windows should be and hope she won't be able to collect now that they're gone.

"Steilos, do you even know where the other six stones are? Or why Ares wants all of them? He's a god, what would he need with more power?"

"No clue. But I have a hunch where another is—though it's not been confirmed just yet. I was hoping you'd help me search for the rest as part of your employment with me."

A half-truth. "I can do that," is all I say, deciding to keep the knowledge of Zadok's stone to myself. If he's going to keep lying to me, then there's no reason for me to tell him what I know.

Steilos holds up a finger. "Ah! Before I forget, I see that you're still hiding that burn of yours."

Suddenly insecure by his comment, my fingers automatically go to the cloth tied around my face.

"Now, don't be upset with me," he says and reaches into his satchel, "but I saw this in a blacksmith's shop and thought of you. It's better than that damn sack you had or what you wear now. I don't think you should cover yourself at all, but if you're going to, you can at least look damn good while you're at it." He pulls out a mask made of dark metal from the satchel. It won't fully cover my face, but judging by the shape, the parts where my skin have melted will be mostly hidden.

Despite him being a two-faced liar, gratitude seeps into my heart as I take the gift. When I examine it further, the mask is surprisingly light with a flowery design that starts from the eyes and ends at the edges. A leather strap with a buckle runs along the back. I turn the metal over, run my fingers along the inside and find that it's smooth to the touch. The work of a master craftsman. I bring the mask close to my chest and look to Steilos. "I don't know what to say, but I think it's beautiful. Thank you."

He glances sideways. "Again, I don't think it's necessary for you to wear—"

I don't listen to him as I turn my back and remove the black cloth. I replace it with his gift. After I secure the mask, I face him again, my confidence already returning with the feel of the metal against my skin.

Steilos shakes his head at me, his smile sad. "Your choice, kid," he says and walks in the direction of his cabin.

When I return to the railing, my fingers hold on tight, and the wind whips my hair back, catching onto the corner of my new face. The mask is a part of me now and serves as a reminder that I'm a monster in hiding; the loss of Saray, Angus, and so many others are a testament to that.

My eyes go to the slave brand on my arm. I think about Metis' mark, as well as the narcissus flower on my thigh. So many scars, but the biggest is the one that can't be seen. There's a gaping hole inside of me, and I don't know how to fill it. It's been less than a year since I was forced from my home, and it's uncanny how a few months can make a chasm so deep that it'll last a lifetime. A goddess fulfilled my grandest wish for adventure in a way I never expected. If I could, I would go back to the moments in Paidia where I yearned for such a thing and tell myself to cherish what I have.

Inhaling deeply, I take in the new taste of freedom and stare out at the water. The sea seems to stretch on forever, making me feel small in my unrelenting world. Zadok is still out there somewhere, waiting for me to find him. I smile as I imagine his raven hair and azurite-colored eyes, so like Mana's. Someday, I'll see that deep blue again.

End

Acknowledgements

I would first like to thank my readers, from the bottom of my heart, thank you for reading my words. It took a long time for *Giving Up Elysium* to make it to your hands. I began writing it in early 2019 and it has been a saga of many ups and downs to have it printed in 2025. So, thank you for helping me make my dreams come true. All I've ever wanted is for someone else to read my words. Special thank you to all the people in my life who would message or call at random telling me not to give up. There were many times I almost did. Thank you, Vicky, Ali, and Krystine, for reading my earliest completed draft and Megan and Abraham for reading my very first chapters after they were written. These versions were terrible, and you were all kind. And Vicky—thank you for listening to 6 years' worth of bitching about the publishing industry. Diana, thank you for my first sketchbook. Kimberly, thank you for being so magical. Please never stop. States away and you always have thoughtful words for me. Thank you, Phoenix, at Writer's Rebirth for your labor in the early stages, *Giving Up Elysium* would not be what it is today without you. Editing a new writer is a courageous and hard undertaking. Thank you, MLC, for all your efforts, every single one of them, seen and unseen. I know this book was a hard one to sculpt. I am a better writer because of you, and I take that with me as I move forward. Mom and Dad, you were the first people to ever treat me as a professional artist and writer. Thank you for that honor. And lastly, I'd like to thank myself. I did it! Whoo-hoo!!!

About the Author

W.B. Clark is from small-town Oklahoma, mostly raised on a farm full of chickens and then partially on a commercial fishing boat in Alaska. She graduated from the University of Oklahoma in 2015, then moved to some big cities, where life happened. At some point she finally got a job that paid her bills but then quit that job to write books, illustrate, and paint pretty pictures. She now lives in Alaska full-time writing stories that have no end. W.B. Clark swears often, plays random instruments poorly, sings, and often finds adventure in the mundane. She likes to go on long walks, camp, scuba dive, and start complex projects, she knows little to nothing about. She loves breakfast, conversations that spark joy, and hearing other people's stories.

Visit **www.wbclarkbooks.com** for more books & art by W.B. Clark

* 9 7 9 8 9 8 6 5 6 4 9 4 4 *